Praise for S

"Wow! *Sisters of the Resistanc...
right up until its breathtaki...
tance, and love—Christine...
hits of 2021."

—Kelly Rimmer, *New York Times* bestselling
author of *The Things We Cannot Say*

"As dazzling as a Dior gown! *Sisters of the Resistance* tells the fascinating story of two sisters working with Catherine Dior and the French Resistance during World War II. With a gorgeous blend of fashion, heartbreak, heroism, and love, this book will transport you to France as the sisters navigate their way through the secrets and mysteries of wartime, and as they uncover some stunning revelations in postwar Paris."

—Natasha Lester, *New York Times*
bestselling author of *The Paris Secret*

"A beautiful homage to the strength and resilience of women spies during the Second World War, Christine Wells's *Sisters of the Resistance* is that rare jewel of a World War II novel that surprises as much as it delights."

—Bryn Turnbull, author of
The Woman Before Wallis

"Full of spies and harrowing near misses, Christine Wells's *Sisters of the Resistance* shifts effortlessly between the desperation of the final months of World War II and the glamor of Dior's postwar collection in this page-turner of a tale. Based on Catherine Dior's real-life resistance movement, this is a powerful story of the impact women have had on history."

—Stephanie Marie Thornton, *USA Today*
bestselling author of *And They Called It Camelot*

"Brimming with danger, adventure, and Dior, *Sisters of the Resistance* kept me guessing to the end. This story of two sisters working for the French Resistance beautifully explores the vast gray area between right and wrong, love and hate—no one gets off easily, and no triumph is without cost. A deeply affecting read."

—Kerri Maher, author of *The Girl in White Gloves*

"*Sisters of the Resistance* has it all! A richly researched historical novel filled with the glamor of the 1940s fashion world and page-turning suspense and romance, all wrapped around a cast of courageous and unforgettable women. The sisters at the heart of this novel, Gabby and Yvette, could not be more different, and yet they both risk their lives working for Catherine Dior's resistance network in Paris during World War II. I was under the spell of this novel from page one!"

—Renée Rosen, bestselling author of *Park Avenue Summer*

"Beautiful and compelling, Christine Wells's *Sisters of the Resistance* skillfully weaves a story of ordinary women rising against the Nazis in the harrowing final days of World War II Paris, and the complex legacy of their choices. This tale of Catherine Dior's women spies is as inspiring as it is thought provoking. Full of nuanced characters, remarkable bravery, and surprises, the pages of this novel all but turn themselves. A must-read!"

—Kristin Beck, author of *Courage, My Love*

"*Sisters of the Resistance* is a breathless roller coaster of love, suspense, and danger—all spiced with the timeless glamor of the launch of Christian Dior's New Look. This story of two courageous sisters caught up in the perilous vicissitudes of war and passion in a vividly imagined Nazi-occupied Paris will have you turning the pages at light speed!"

—Anna Campbell, award-winning author

SISTERS *of the* RESISTANCE

SISTERS
of the
RESISTANCE

A NOVEL OF CATHERINE DIOR'S PARIS SPY NETWORK

CHRISTINE WELLS

WM

WILLIAM MORROW

An Imprint of HarperCollinsPublishers

P.S.™ is a trademark of HarperCollins Publishers.

HarperCollins books may be purchased for educational, business, or sales promotional use. For information, please email the Special Markets Department at SPsales@harpercollins.com.

FIRST EDITION

Designed by Diahann Sturge

Title page and chapter opener illustration © John Kichote/stock.adobe.com

Library of Congress Cataloging-in-Publication Data has been applied for.

ISBN 978-0-06-305544-5
ISBN 978-0-06-309191-7 (international edition)

21 22 23 24 25   LSC   10 9 8 7 6 5 4 3 2 1

For Allister and Adrian, with all my love

SISTERS *of the* RESISTANCE

Chapter One

Paris, February 1947

YVETTE

Paris was freezing. Even colder than New York. Yvette waited while the young lawyer's clerk who had met her at the Gare Saint-Lazare patted his pockets and muttered to himself. Monsieur LeBrun was small, neat, and brilliantined, with round black spectacles like bicycle tires framing his dark eyes.

For mercy's sake, stop fussing and let's get somewhere warm, she begged him silently. But with such men, one must be patient.

"Ah!" He fished out a paper from an inner coat pocket with an expression of mild triumph. "You will be staying at . . ." He frowned at his itinerary as if it confused him. "The Ritz."

Yvette nearly dropped her suitcase. "*Vraiment?*" She peered over LeBrun's shoulder to check, but there it was in black and white. Louise Dulac had hauled her all the way across the Atlantic to testify at her trial. Knowing the film star, Yvette had not expected simple gratitude, much less accommodation fit for a king.

Perhaps Louise was sending her a message: *You were complicit. You were there, too.*

"If you will follow me, mademoiselle." LeBrun took Yvette's suitcase and they stepped into the thin light of a wintry Parisian afternoon.

Yvette's last memories of Paris were of sweltering heat and evening thunderstorms. For a moment, the sight of this brittle, frigid metropolis disoriented her. Then she looked up and saw the delicate strength of the Eiffel Tower standing tall above the tree-lined boulevards, caught the faint strains of an accordion from a café down the street, and the city swept her up in its embrace.

Half-laughing, Yvette closed her eyes, lifted her shoulders, and inhaled deeply. The air was so cold it burned her lungs, but it was ripe with those old, familiar smells. As in any city, there was exhaust mixed with the whiff of wet rubbish and urine, the chemical tang of printer's ink from a nearby newspaper stand. But she caught the phantom scent of baking bread, the earthy sweetness of Gauloise cigarettes, and the faint, complex notes of French perfume.

"How I have missed you," she whispered. New York, for all its excitement and challenges, had not been Paris.

A sharp *crack-ack-ack* made her jump and duck her head, her heart beating wildly. It was only the clatter of the metal grille being pulled shut in front of a jeweler's shop—she saw that almost at once—but she couldn't stop the images that flooded her mind. It all came back in a rush of constant vigilance, of hunger and fear. In New York, she had tried so hard to forget . . .

"Mademoiselle?"

She started, blinking, then her heart gradually slowed. The war was over and she was safe. The lawyer's clerk was waiting. "Sorry, monsieur. It is being back again, you understand." She fastened the top button of her heavy coat, pulled her gloves out of her pocket and tugged them on, then followed Monsieur LeBrun to a waiting Renault.

If only she had her bicycle! She longed to reacquaint herself with her delivery routes, her old friends and haunts. First, she ought to visit Gabby and Maman . . . But LeBrun shepherded her into the car, settled himself beside her, and ordered the driver to go.

When Louise Dulac's summons had come, Yvette's first instinct had been to refuse. Reliving her wartime experiences, particularly the treatment she'd suffered at the movie star's hands, was something she'd wished never to do. But the chance to return home to Paris, all expenses paid, was so very tempting, and when she'd discovered that by leaving a week earlier than proposed she could arrive in time for Monsieur Dior's first-ever fashion show, that clinched the matter.

She had obtained some catalog work as a mannequin in New York but the American designers had wanted a strong, wholesome, sporty look. Yvette's high cheekbones and masses of curling, honey-brown hair could not compensate for her ethereal thinness, the pale translucency of her skin, or the disconcertingly catlike shape of her hazel eyes. Besides, everyone knew the true home of haute couture was Paris. If she could be part of Monsieur Dior's first show, even in some small way, or, even better, if she could talk Monsieur Dior into giving her a job as a mannequin at his new fashion house, testifying for Louise Dulac would be worth it.

Inevitably, thinking of the couturier brought memories of his sister. *Catherine.* Guilt uncoiled inside Yvette, spreading its tentacles, enfolding her in its grip. If not for her impulsiveness, if not for the foolish mistakes she'd made—

Monsieur LeBrun's pedantic, clipped speech interrupted her thoughts. "The charges against Louise Dulac are very grave, mademoiselle." He described them and her stomach clenched.

"Treason?" She had expected they would prosecute Louise for collaboration only. *Collaboration horizontale,* they called it. Sleeping with the enemy. The authorities must have discovered more about Louise's activities than Yvette had anticipated. Suddenly, her own position turned precarious.

She caught the edge of LeBrun's query: "Does that suit?"

He was waiting for her answer. "I beg your pardon, monsieur. I was not listening."

LeBrun frowned. "The trial begins in less than two weeks, mademoiselle. I will let you get settled tomorrow, but the next day, we must meet to begin preparing your statement. Shall we say, one o'clock?"

Yvette tried to pay attention as he outlined the judicial process, but his voice soon slipped from her mind's grasp, became mere background noise. She gazed out of the window, drinking Paris in, its tree-lined boulevards and sidewalk cafés, its grand stone terraces with their blue tiled roofs. Plenty of military vehicles and troops still about, but friendly ones. And not a swastika in sight.

As they headed toward La Madeleine church, her heart gave a sudden, hard thump, but the driver turned left, then right, zigzagging toward the Place Vendôme. Her shoulders relaxed.

Before anything else, she must see Gabby and Maman. But if merely driving in the direction of their tiny apartment on the rue Royale made her sick and dizzy, how would she bring herself to face her sister? She had not opened a single one of Gabby's letters, much less answered them.

It had been enough to know they were alive, Catherine and Gabby and Maman. She'd needed very badly to put the war behind her, to move on. If she'd allowed even one of those memories to seep in through the wall she'd built around herself, it would have become a flood. She would have drowned in them.

Now, because of the trial, she would be forced to relive it all. Had it been a mistake to return? But what else could she have done?

Forcing her thoughts elsewhere, Yvette said to LeBrun, "I hear rationing is still in force." There was no masking tape on the shop windows or sandbags stacked against the walls anymore, but the effects of war were still apparent from the queue outside the butchery they passed, the small pâtisserie whose display window stood empty, the scant vegetables for sale at the grocer's stall.

"You will not have to worry about rationing at the Ritz," said LeBrun dryly as the Renault swung into the Place Vendôme and pulled up outside the hotel entrance.

Guiltily, she acknowledged that of course, this was true. Ah, but what memories this hotel brought back! She had been there many times before, but she felt even more out of place as a guest than as a shabbily dressed delivery girl from the House of Lelong.

The foyer, with its high ornate ceilings dripping chandeliers, its elegant Louis XVI furniture, marble columns, and potted palms, had welcomed royalty and movie stars to this home away from home for decades. The reception desk was tucked beneath a circular window, almost out of sight of the foyer, adding to the illusion of a private residence. While Monsieur LeBrun conducted a low-voiced conversation with the superior-looking individual at the counter, Yvette approached the concierge. "Good day, monsieur. I was hoping you could help me. I hear that Christian Dior has opened a new atelier. Could you please tell me where it is?"

The concierge smiled. "Yes, indeed, mademoiselle. It is on the avenue Montaigne, number thirty. In fact, monsieur's premiere is tomorrow."

Excitement fizzed inside her. "Isn't it marvelous? I can't wait."

The concierge looked apologetic, no doubt inwardly shaking his head at this strange creature who thought she could waltz into a couturier's first-ever fashion show. "I'm afraid it's invitation only, mademoiselle."

"Oh, yes, of course," Yvette replied. "I didn't mean I expected to go." And of course she could never command an invitation. She'd only been the delivery girl when Monsieur Dior worked as a designer at the House of Lelong, after all. But that didn't mean she couldn't slip in behind the scenes. She would manage somehow.

With a sense of living in a dream, Yvette followed Monsieur LeBrun up to her suite. Moving through the sumptuous hotel room, she tried to glance about casually, as if she was accustomed to residing in such a place. A far cry from the dingy Brooklyn apartment she shared with two other girls from the modeling agency.

As LeBrun oversaw the disposal of her suitcase and dealt with the tip, Yvette wandered around, running her hand along a cream silk sofa, inspecting the painting above the marble mantelpiece—a portrait of a lady from the Belle Epoque. The sitting room window overlooked the Place Vendôme. Yvette paused in the embrasure, staring vacantly at the activity below. She felt overwhelmed and wary, off balance in a way that she could not explain.

The door clicked behind the porter and she turned to Monsieur LeBrun.

"You must be hungry, mademoiselle." He indicated the ivory and gold telephone by the sofa. "You are to order whatever you wish."

Yvette closed her eyes, imagining a piping-hot meal delivered by two waiters, silver domes whipped away with a flourish. Gleaming lumps of caviar, a steak *grillé sur planche*. To finish, crêpes Suzette, which the chef would prepare before her eyes, flaming the orange sauce with all the dazzle and drama of a Broadway show.

It was far, far too much for someone who had subsisted mainly on soup from a can for the past two years and on wartime rations before that.

"Perhaps later. Thank you." She paused, then indicated the suite with a wave of her hand. "I did not expect such generosity. Despite her arrest, Louise Dulac still has deep pockets, it seems."

LeBrun shifted slightly, as if to disagree. Yvette raised her eyebrows. "Or perhaps it is not mademoiselle who has the deep pockets."

He pressed his lips together and did not reply.

Regardless of who was footing the bill, even the wealthiest person would not pay for Yvette to cross the Atlantic and stay at the Ritz without good cause. Louise must be desperate.

Yvette's head jerked up. "Tell me, monsieur, am I Mademoiselle Dulac's only witness?"

The clerk fixed her with his worried, earnest gaze. "Mademoiselle Foucher," he said, "you are her only hope."

When Monsieur LeBrun had gone and Yvette had freshened up a little, she left the Ritz on foot, passing through the colonnade and out onto the Place Vendôme with a shiver that was more due to nostalgia than to the winter air that frosted her lips and made her eyes water. If she had her bicycle, she could get to the rue Royale faster. But perhaps she did not wish this reunion with Gabby and Maman to be upon her so soon. Stepping out briskly to ward off the cold, she sank her chin into her scarf and hunched her shoulders against the icy wind.

Yvette's stomach growled. She should have taken Monsieur LeBrun's advice and ordered something at the Ritz. She thought of those feasts laid out in Louise Dulac's suite during the war, even though Louise's diet seemed to consist mainly of cigarettes and champagne cocktails. So much food wasted while French citizens went hungry.

Paris was bleak in the winter with the plane trees leafless and grey. While the bombings had not touched the part of the city in which Yvette now hurried along, the place had the air of a beautiful, damaged creature still licking its wounds. Now that winter had come, all its scars were laid bare.

In a dream, Yvette wandered Paris, traveling those old routes she used to take when she was a delivery girl for the House of Lelong. How many of the couturier's wealthy clients still led the same hedonistic lifestyle as they had during the war? Most of them, she supposed. But not Madame Abetz, the German ambassador's wife, nor his young mistress, Corinne Luchaire. And neither did Louise Dulac. The movie star was locked up in Fresnes, the prison where the Nazis had incarcerated foreign spies and members of the resistance, before sending them away to unspeakable fates.

It had grown dark without Yvette's noticing and the streetlamps were lit, giving out their rosy glow. She turned down the rue Royale, and her steps slowed as memories came rushing back. Music from the café where she had first met Liliane Dietlin floated out to the pavement and wrapped itself around her in a slow, mournful caress. Yvette squeezed her eyes shut. Despite the hardships of her journey to Spain and of her first lonely months in New York, the sweltering July day Liliane helped her leave Paris had been the worst day of her life.

And yet, how could she dwell on her own pain, when Catherine's suffering had been so vast as to be incomprehensible?

She stopped before she reached the apartments at number 10, where Gabby's life probably went on much the same as it had before Yvette left. A storm of emotions—fear and grief and searing guilt—hit her so hard, she began to shake and gasp for air, her head swimming, her heartbeat rapid and hard in her chest.

This faintness could overtake her if she didn't bring it under control. "*Breathe,*" she told herself. *Deep breath in; long, slow breath out.* The dizziness receded, but she couldn't make herself take one more step toward the apartments at number 10. She couldn't face Gabby and Maman. Not yet. Not after the damage she'd done.

She'd try again tomorrow. Maybe. Wrapping her arms about herself, Yvette turned on her heel and walked away.

Chapter Two

Paris, February 1947

YVETTE

Sometime after three in the morning, Yvette paced up and down the pavement outside the House of Dior at number 30 avenue Montaigne. There was much activity at the new couturier, despite the early hour. Few who worked there would sleep tonight, that she knew from experience. Lights glimmered between cracks in the draped windows of the ground floor. In the rooms above, shadows bustled back and forth. Behind the curtainless windows of the top-floor ateliers, white-coated seamstresses were still putting finishing touches to Monsieur Dior's creations mere hours before the show.

Yvette hugged herself and rubbed at her arms, trying to keep warm as she observed the comings and goings. She hoped to glimpse someone she knew from the old days, when Christian

Dior had been one of the *premier* designers at the House of Lelong.

Her teeth chattered. Despite her heavy coat, the winter chill bit into her skin and her feet were blocks of ice inside her smart boots. She checked her watch. The mannequins would arrive soon. Perhaps she could slip inside with them. At the house of the famous couturier Lucien Lelong, she'd run errands during the shows. The mannequins had been kind. Some had even bothered to remember her name.

The wind picked up, slicing through her outerwear as if it were made of gauze. Maybe this had not been such a grand plan. She'd freeze to death if she stayed out here much longer. But it was better than lying awake at the Ritz, haunted by ghosts, fretting about Louise Dulac's trial. She was no closer to judging the movie star's guilt than she had ever been. Yvette stamped her feet to awaken the circulation, clapped her gloved hands together, held them to her cheeks to warm her face.

A car pulled up, disgorging two young women who were laughing and talking excitedly. Mannequins, by the look of them, a blonde and a brunette, but Yvette didn't recognize either. The dark-haired girl paused to give Yvette a long, appraising look. "Are you here to see the show?" she said. "You're early."

The other smirked. "*Le patron* is not hiring, hadn't you heard? All the positions are filled."

"But no, I—" Yvette faltered to a stop. Suddenly, it seemed like one of her more ill-conceived ideas to try to get into Dior tonight.

"Cat got your tongue?" the dark girl taunted.

"Maybe she is a burglar," said the blonde. "Or a spy, come to steal *le patron*'s designs."

"Of course not! I would never do such a thing."

Just then, she heard the click of heels on the pavement approaching. Another girl come to join in the teasing?

"Goodness, Yvette, is it you?"

She recognized the accent at once. It belonged to one of the most beautiful women in the world. "Tania!"

The Russian mannequin emerged from the shadows to embrace Yvette, kissing her warmly on each cheek. "Ah, but you are a woman now," exclaimed Tania, stepping back to look her up and down. "So pretty. And so thin!"

Yvette blushed and stammered like an idiot, praise from her idol reducing her to an awkward delivery girl once more. The two women who had been so quick to ridicule her seemed to melt away. No one was foolish enough to get on the wrong side of Tania.

"Come!" said the mannequin, taking Yvette's hand. "Inside, out of the cold."

Seeming to take Yvette's presence as a matter of course, she swept her into the relative warmth of the house. Yvette jumped at the sound of banging overhead. Tania laughed and waved an elegant hand. "They are still laying the carpet. Can you believe it? Ah! Here is Madame Raymonde."

"Oh good, Tania, you're here." A woman dressed in black hurried down the staircase toward them, her large, bright eyes brimming with excitement. "I need to talk to you about the Bar Suit."

Leaving the two women to an intense conversation, Yvette took the opportunity to explore a little. In a nook off the foyer, she spied a miniature boutique, the most charming little kiosk imaginable, papered in *toile de Jouy*. Accessories cluttered every surface—hats and scarves and feathers, belts and purses, silk flowers and velvet bows, satin cushions studded with jeweled hat pins, necklaces of jet and pearls and brooches of marcasite. An apprentice stood on a ladder, filling a high shelf with hatboxes and rectangular garment boxes, all in pristine white, with "Christian Dior" printed on them in the palest shade of grey.

A tug at her elbow pulled Yvette from this delightful oasis. "Come!" said Tania, shepherding her toward the stairs. "We must make sure everything is ready."

She hustled Yvette up to the *cabine*, where several mannequins were having their hair styled and various attendants buzzed around to assist them.

"That is Madame de Turckheim," said Tania, indicating an imposing woman with large bright eyes who presided with calm good nature over the mayhem. "She is the *chef de cabine*. The senior staff call her Tutu but we call her La Baronne." Tania dumped her makeup case and purse on the section of mirrored dressing table allotted to her, then stood on tiptoe to check through the hats on the shelf above her head.

"Do you need me to do anything?" Yvette asked.

But the mannequin seemed to have forgotten her existence already and began sorting through accessories, her attention dagger-sharp.

Well, that was Tania. One would be stupid to take offense. Every inch the artist that any couturier might be, she approached her work with complete focus and dedication.

Tania had gained Yvette admittance to the House of Dior. Now Yvette must make the most of the opportunity.

The *cabine* was slowly filling with mannequins undressing and donning their robes, white-coated apprentices bringing gowns and outfits to hang on designated racks. It was a wonder that so many people could work efficiently in such a small space. The ravishing gowns and ensembles held Yvette transfixed. Fabric and femininity seemed to have been Monsieur Dior's watchwords when he designed this collection, the full calf-length skirts and nipped waists creating an hourglass shape supremely flattering to the female form. Yvette had not seen hemlines this low since before the war. Had they lifted the fabric restrictions here in Paris?

A leopard-print dress with a straight skirt, belted at the waist, caught her eye, then a white halter-necked evening gown with a ruffle at the bosom. Exquisitely soft and effortlessly chic, these were truly the designs of a master.

But she must remember why she was there. She watched for opportunities to help and soon joined the swim of people moving back and forth between the *cabine* and the workrooms, until it was as if she had always been a part of La Maison Dior.

"I don't think we've met." Yvette started, turning to see Madame de Turckheim standing behind her, a gleam of challenge in her eye.

"I am Yvette Foucher, madame," she said, awkwardly plaiting her fingers together. "I used to work at the House of Lelong, so I offered to come tonight and lend a hand." She hoped madame would not demand to know precisely who had authorized Yvette to be there.

La Baronne's thin eyebrows lifted. "That is kind." She gave Yvette a quick, appraising scan from head to toe. "Monsieur would approve of your look, mademoiselle. Have you worked as a mannequin before?"

Every cell of Yvette's body danced with excitement. "But yes, madame. For almost two years in New York."

La Baronne nodded. "Come and see me after the show. There might be work for you here."

Yvette gasped. "Really? Oh, thank—" She broke off. La Baronne had already turned away to resolve a small crisis over shoes.

Though giddy from madame's praise, Yvette did her best to focus on the tasks she was given. What was Monsieur Dior doing right now? While his creative force pervaded every corner of the *maison*, she had yet to set eyes on the man himself. He was holding aloof from the madness, it seemed, which was probably wise. He must be riddled with anxiety at this moment. Anyone in his position would be, but from what Yvette had seen of the collection he was about to present, *le patron* had nothing to fear.

Would he approve of her look? Or would he still see the ragamuffin tomboy with windblown hair who used to fetch and carry for him at Lelong?

Come, Yvette, she told herself. *This could be your big break.*

The hours flew by. Nothing mattered but dresses. Not the war, not the Nazis, not the testimony that would surely break Yvette if she thought about it too much. She could hardly believe it when Madame de Turckheim said they had started letting guests in. The salons were slowly filling; the excitement in the *cabine* reached a fever pitch.

"You can stay for the show if you promise not to get in the way," La Baronne told Yvette. The offer was too good to pass up.

As she waited for the show to start, she noticed that one of the mannequins was shaking so hard, she could not fit her lipstick back into its tube. Yvette went over to her and removed the lipstick from her grasp, slotted it back together. "All is well," she said softly. "You will be perfect."

"Is everything good with you, Marie-Thérèse?" Ever vigilant, Madame de Turckheim hurried over.

"Just nerves," said the blond mannequin, trying to laugh off madame's concern, but the laugh became a hiccup and then a shudder. "I—I don't know if I can do it. All those people. And I am so very tired, Baronne." Tears filled her eyes, but she tilted her head back and pressed a handkerchief carefully to each corner, blotting them before they ruined her face.

Yvette eyed her in astonishment. Imagine *weeping* over taking part in such a triumph. Tired? What did this girl know of true exhaustion, the kind that made you wish to die on your feet before you took another step? But she said nothing and left Marie-Thérèse to madame's soothing.

The next time Yvette entered the *cabine*, the mannequins had shed their white coveralls and were being dressed. So many bodies in such a small space—they didn't need Yvette crowding them further. She just managed to glimpse Monsieur Dior as he addressed a comment to Madame Raymonde over his shoulder, then turned back again to adjust the fit of a jacket, tugging and tweaking at the fabric to make it sit smoothly over the mannequin's torso.

At last, it was time for the show to begin. In the narrow corridor that led to the first salon, Yvette watched with mingled envy and pride as each mannequin passed her, then stepped through the pale grey curtain and entered the show. This was as much as Yvette would glimpse, but she could hear the *compère* announce each model, and the reaction of the crowd was as appreciative as Monsieur Dior might have wished.

The curtain twitched aside, and Marie-Thérèse stormed through, her hand to her mouth. Tania hissed, "What's wrong?" But the mannequin shook her head and ran past. Yvette stared after her. Marie-Thérèse was a nervous one, that was for sure.

Putting the incident out of her mind, Yvette watched for any last-minute problems she might solve. She was helping one of the mannequins adjust her hat when Madame de Turckheim caught her by the wrist. "Oh, thank goodness! There you are, Yvette," she said. "Come quickly."

"What is it?" She followed Madame de Turckheim back to the *cabine*, where a glance told her that Monsieur Dior sat in a corner with his fingers in his ears, only taking them out to listen to the returning mannequins' reports on the acclaim his designs had received.

Yvette yelped as Madame de Turckheim practically fell upon her and began unbuttoning her jacket. "Madame?"

"There is no time," the older woman muttered. "No time at all."

"Wait! Please, what are you doing?" Madame wrenched the jacket from her shoulders, spinning her around with the momentum, ignoring her protests. Her jacket hit the floor.

Hope blossomed inside Yvette. "I can undress myself, but only tell me why." Moving out of reach, she unhooked her waistband and stepped out of her skirt.

Madame spoke rapidly in a low voice. "Marie-Thérèse stumbled on her first walk. She is having hysterics and vows she cannot go back out there. But *you* . . ." Madame set her hands to Yvette's waist and nodded, as if she had sized up her figure to pinpoint accuracy. "Yvette, you must take her place."

GABBY

Gabrielle Foucher hurried along the rue Royale, the wooden soles of her shoes clipping the pavement, her breath puffs of vapor in the freezing air. If she never accomplished anything else in her life, she must reach the House of Dior in time for the fashion show. It was a twenty-minute walk to avenue Montaigne. She needed to be there in ten.

She sped past old Abelard, who was sweeping the sidewalk under the red awning of Maxim's, cap pulled low over his forehead, a cigarette attached to his lower lip. Answering his good-morning wheeze with "Sorry! I'm so late," she did not stop for their usual banter.

Even now, at nearly ten in the morning, delicious scents from the famous restaurant filled the air, following her up the street. They were baking something sweet—pastries, perhaps, or brioche? Her stomach murmured. She hadn't even drunk her morning tisane. There'd been no time for that.

She'd crammed a full day's work into a few hours, rising well before dawn. Gabby's duties as concierge of the apartment building at number 10 rue Royale did not stop for a fashion show, of course—not even the premiere of Christian Dior's first-ever collection. But her mother could take over for the couple of hours she was away. All that was left to be done was to peer out the window of their little ground-floor apartment, see who desired admittance, and press the button that released the street door to the building. Maman could manage that much. She'd been concierge there for many years until Gabby took up the reins.

The tall, pointed obelisk at the Place de la Concorde loomed ahead, spearing into the sky. Gabby turned the corner. She would cut through the gardens to the Champs-Élysées to save time.

Then she spied one of her tenants, Madame Vasseur, leading her apricot poodle out of the gardens and turning toward her. Ah, no! Madame would be certain to delay her with endless complaints, from the state of the plumbing in her apartment to the state of the nation under de Gaulle. Gabby put her head down and veered left, taking the long way around. The long way would be quicker than an encounter with madame.

The Champs-Élysées stretched before her, stripped and bleak, its leafless trees reaching skeletal fingers toward the dirty white blanket of cloud overhead. Far in the distance, at the end of the avenue, stood the Arc de Triomphe. Gabby's chest gave that familiar clutch of panic and her stomach began to churn.

"Stop it!" she muttered. It was 1947. They were free. Yet, every time she glimpsed the monument, a vision would fill her mind's eye: the spiderlike swastika flying from Napoléon's triumphal arch, mocking France's celebrated military power.

She clutched her purse tighter and squared her shoulders. This morning was about beauty and glamor, not past ugliness. At the House of Dior, she would revel in the shining promise of the future, even if her own reality would never match those silken dreams.

An ordinary woman like her would never wear Dior. But she was alive. She had a job and a roof over her head. She hadn't suffered in any significant way during the war—not like countless others who had been rounded up, sent away, some never to be seen again. Not like Catherine Dior.

Had it not been for Catherine, Gabby never would have been invited to witness the first showing of her brother Christian's premiere collection.

Had it not been for Catherine, Gabby might now be content. Mademoiselle Dior had tossed a challenge into Gabby's existence like a resistance fighter lobbing a hand grenade. For that brief period in 1944, Gabby's world had exploded into danger. But when the dust had settled, she'd found herself completely alone.

As she hurried down the avenue, weaving in and out of other pedestrians, Gabby glanced again at her watch. Ten o'clock already!

She was supposed to be there now. Lungs burning from the cold air and exertion, she put on an extra burst of speed.

At last, she reached avenue Montaigne and her shoulders sagged with relief. The pavement outside the House of Dior teemed with people still waiting to get in. She need not have worried she'd be turned away at the door for being late.

Slowing as she approached, Gabby looked up, scanning the impressive structure as she tried to catch her breath. Monsieur Dior had chosen a most elegant building for his atelier, constructed of that buttery limestone peculiar to Paris. The tiny foothold balconies outside its long windows were girded with iron railings so delicately wrought they looked like black lace.

As she came closer, she saw the pale grey awning over the entrance with the name "Christian Dior" printed in white. Vicarious pride flooded her chest with warmth. He had done it! Of course he had. And there was monsieur's name again, carved into the stone walls on either side of the door, speaking of quiet confidence in its permanency.

Unable to stop the stupid grin that spread over her face, Gabby joined the waiting crowd. Guests were being admitted in an orderly fashion, in groups of three.

She knew a little about what happened at shows like these. They would all be packed together like sardines in a tin. She did not expect to be given a good vantage point. Those were reserved for far more important people than she.

Today, everyone who was anyone would be there. And she was there. She, who was no one at all.

Covertly, Gabby studied what the other women were wearing under their sleek fur coats. Mostly black suits like hers. Although, not like hers, really. Even she could tell the other women's clothes were of a superior cut, their hats infinitely more fashionable than her simple beret. Their hair was cropped or pinned up, not worn long down the back and rolled up at the front as she'd styled her thick black tresses today.

She lifted her hand to her lapel, rubbed the pad of her thumb over the pin that nestled there. It was a bird made of platinum, with a diamond-dappled breast and a small, round sapphire for an eye.

With a nervous half smile, Gabby showed her invitation and was waved through. The salons of number 30 avenue Montaigne were filled to bursting, and by the time Gabby entered, every one of the chairs provided for guests had been filled.

It was like stepping into an expensive cloud, she thought, peering around her. Monsieur Dior had outfitted his domain as elegantly as any of his beautiful mannequins. The walls were the most exquisite shade of pearl grey, the moldings picked out in white, like piped icing on a cake. Swathes of grey satin at the windows whispered of luxury; crystal chandeliers and brass light fittings shimmered and gleamed. Everywhere, there were flowers—white lily of the valley (monsieur's favorite), sweet peas, roses, blue delphiniums. The beauty was almost overwhelming and somehow utterly right.

And through it all, the salons breathed a new fragrance, a most exquisite scent, fresh and floral. The one Christian had named after Catherine. He had called it "Miss Dior."

Remembering Catherine as she had been before the war, so joyous and full of life, Gabby's throat swelled with emotion. The perfume was a fitting tribute to her spirit. Gabby accepted the program the attendant handed to her and looked about for somewhere to sit.

As she edged through the throng of people greeting each other like long-lost friends, Gabby tried not to gape. There were so many famous faces here, she did not know where to look first. She recognized Jean Cocteau and Henri Sauguet and an extremely stylish woman who might have been the British ambassador's wife.

And there was Catherine herself, seated in the very front row. Gabby stood on tiptoe and tried to wave, but Catherine didn't see her, and Gabby had to keep moving with the flow of the crowd or risk being trampled.

There was no getting a chair in the salons at all now. People were beginning to sit on the stairs that led to the ateliers above. The staircase was a work of beauty, its bannister supported by a wrought iron fantasy of scrollwork. Having picked her way up, stepping over the guests already seated on the lower steps, Gabby perched as elegantly as she could on a vacant tread. The step was cold and hard beneath her bottom, but she didn't care.

A very businesslike woman with a notepad and pencil took the place beside her.

With a little nod of acknowledgment, and feeling pleasantly businesslike herself, Gabby took out her little sketchbook and flipped to the next blank page. Drawing gowns and costumes was something she had never done before. She had only ever illustrated little stories for the children in the apartment building. But it was for her own pleasure, after all. This was an experience she was never likely to repeat, so she wanted to capture it on paper.

Excitement bubbled up. The show was about to start. Gabby gripped her pencil tightly and waited for the magic to begin.

Chapter Three

Paris, June 1944

GABBY

I don't want you to be disappointed, that's all," said Gabby's mother. She sat in her armchair by the window of the *loge*, a tiny set of ground-floor rooms at the entrance to the grand apartment block at number 10 rue Royale. Many years after her husband's death, Danique Foucher still grieved for him, dressing all in black with her salt-and-pepper hair scraped severely from her forehead and pinned in a bun. "The tenants will never treat you like an equal, no matter how much you do for them."

Gabby didn't answer. She peered into the bubbling pot of chicken soup. The broth was almost clear; the scrawny black-market chicken carcass had been picked bare last night and rendered little in the way of further flavor. Only a pitiful few strands of cabbage bobbed here and there.

She had queued for hours that morning, clutching a raft of coupons from her family and several of the tenants, but by the time she'd reached the front of the line, there had been only cabbages left. The meal was little more than a gesture, but the soup was hot and would warm the bones of the old lady in apartment twelve.

"This is so typical of you, Gabby," said her mother with a tired smile. "You are a concierge, remember. The tenants are supposed to give you favors, not the other way around."

"It is no trouble," said Gabby. "Madame LaRoq has always been kind to Yvette and me." When they were little girls, their mother was always working, with no time to spare for them. Madame had invited them into her pretty apartment and played games and sung songs and told them fairy tales. As they'd grown older, she'd listened to their woes and dispensed wise, shrewd advice. Now madame was frail and ill and alone in the midst of war, and it was Gabby's turn to be kind.

She ladled soup into a blue bowl, set the bowl on a tray and a faded checked cloth over the bowl, put a spoon beside it. Then she hurried across the courtyard to the east wing.

On the stairs, she passed Madame Vasseur with her poodle. Madame closed her eyes as if in great pain. "I wish you would not cook so much in that apartment of yours," she said to Gabby. "It stinks up the whole place."

"One must cook to eat, madame," said Gabby. "Often cabbage is all there is." Madame might exist on cigarettes and acorn coffee, but others needed a little more sustenance.

"Hmph! You'd think we lived in the slums."

Bidding madame a determinedly cheerful good day, Gabby reached number twelve and set the tray down on the floor beside the door. Out of politeness, she knocked, but madame was bed-ridden. She would not come to answer it.

Gabby took out her big iron ring of keys and found the right one. The door opened with a creak. She would like to oil that hinge, but of course there was no oil to be had.

Madame was propped up in bed, a lace shawl about her shoulders, her soft white hair plaited in a long braid and a white linen cap on her head. She looked like the grandmother in a fairy tale, but her smile held a youthful radiance that belied her infirmity. "Good day to you, child." She held out her hand in welcome.

Gabby set down the tray and went over to grasp madame's hand and kiss her cheek. "I've brought soup. It's a little weak, I'm afraid."

Not even the hint of a wince crossed madame's features. With so much to complain about, she never said a word. Gabby laid the tray carefully across madame's knees.

"I wish it was cassoulet," said Gabby, beginning their game.

"Or caviar."

"Crème caramel."

"Calvados!"

They both chuckled. Gabby's stomach growled. Rationing had been in place for so long, she'd become accustomed to doing without. Sometimes, when another of the tenants, Catherine Dior, came up from her farm, she brought fresh produce with her. She would sneak Gabby eggs or butter. Sometimes even salted pork or sausage. And there was the black market when they could afford it, but that was not often.

"How is the little Yvette?" madame asked, spooning up her soup and taking a careful sip.

"Oh . . . She is Yvette."

"Any more incidents?"

"No, madame."

The older lady raised her eyebrows. "Tell me."

Gabby shrugged. "She is impulsive and reckless. She burns with hatred. It is dangerous."

"And yet, there are many who would lie down and let the Boches have their way with us." Madame gave a grim smile. "Don't look so shocked. We need people like Yvette. It is time for France to stand up and fight."

"France does not need hotheaded young idiots who go about spitting in Germans' eyes."

"Is that what she does?"

Gabby threw out a hand. "Metaphorically." She lowered her voice. "Yvette is mixed up with that Jean-Luc and his communists. But as far as I can see, they never actually do anything useful for the cause. She'd be better off queuing for rations or helping me around here than delivering leaflets for those bags of wind."

"She has a job at Lelong. That is something."

"Of course." Madame was right. Gabby sighed. "It is just that I worry about her."

"I know you do. You are a good sister. But she is not a child anymore. And to live a full life, one must take some risks, you know." There was a glint in madame's eye that told Gabby she wished she could be out there taking risks, as well.

Gabby said nothing. When the war was over, there would be time enough for Yvette to spread her wings. With the Allies already landed in Normandy and fighting their way south, surely the occupation would soon be at an end. They all needed to keep their heads down, stay out of trouble, until then.

She waited until madame had finished the pitiful meal, then she removed the tray from her lap. She performed the other nursing duties necessary for the bedridden patient, then washed her hands and returned to the boudoir.

"I hear Catherine Dior arrives today," said madame.

"Yes. Monsieur is very excited."

"Ask her to call on me when she arrives, will you? At her convenience."

"Yes, madame," said Gabby. She hesitated, curiosity stirring. Whenever Madame LaRoq wanted someone to do something at their convenience, it meant "straightaway." What did she need from Catherine Dior?

Madame held out a hand. "Come. Kiss me, my dear."

Gabby smiled and bent to the frail figure to kiss her soft cheek. "I'll stay and read to you if you like." Madame's sight was still good but she had mentioned once or twice that her eyes became dry if she read for too long.

"I can read to myself, but thank you. Off you go." Madame smiled at her warmly and made a shooing movement with her hands. "You have work to do. I'll be fine."

As she left the east wing, Gabby stopped in the courtyard to check on her seedlings. The planter boxes on either side of the entrance used to contain bright red geraniums, but she had dug them up in order to plant vegetables. Green shoots peeked out from the soil, making her heart lift. Her carrots and turnips would be fully grown in a few weeks. Then they would have a feast.

The street door opened, and a voice called a cheery good day. It was Catherine Dior, carrying a small suitcase, a shopping bag, and a hatbox.

"Let me help you." Gabby hurried over to take the suitcase from her hand.

Catherine gave her a weary smile and relinquished the suit-case. "Thank you, my dear." She was a slender, dark-haired young woman, very like her brother. Not beautiful, it was true, but she had a subtle charm. Even in a suit that had seen better days, she managed to look elegant.

They went upstairs to Monsieur Dior's apartment, which was down the hall from Madame LaRoq's. The apartment had an un-expectedly masculine ambience, with dark red velvet drapes and mahogany furniture. So unlike his deeply feminine gowns, Gabby always thought. But then he was a man, after all. She could not expect him to decorate in florals.

"How was the journey?" Gabby handed the suitcase to Sabine, the maid. Catherine removed her hat and gloves and handed them over also.

"Oh, it was fine." Catherine never complained but Gabby sensed something troubled her. Not that she would ever expect Made-moiselle Dior to confide in her. They did not have that kind of rela-tionship. Gabby couldn't help wishing for more, despite Maman's warnings about getting involved with the tenants.

Catherine set her shopping bag down on the hall table and dug around in it. She came up with a package that smelled of garlic and squished a little as Gabby accepted it from her. "Sausage! Oh, thank you, mademoiselle. Thank you!"

The savory reek of small goods made her stomach give a loud growl. Heat rushed to her face, but Catherine laughed, extracting her cigarette case from her purse and opening it. "Enjoy that, won't you? It is the last one for a while, I'm afraid."

Gabby was about to leave but remembered her message and turned back at the door. "Oh! Madame LaRoq wishes to see you."

Catherine paused for a couple of heartbeats, then shut her

cigarette case with a snap. "I will go to her now." She called to the maid that she was going out.

"Do not be late for dinner, Mademoiselle Catherine." Cook emerged from the kitchen, wiping her hands on a cloth. "Monsieur Dior expects you. He has been planning the menu for weeks, saving up the sugar ration especially."

The somber look vanished and Catherine chuckled. "Heaven forbid I should keep dear 'Tian from his food."

YVETTE

There you are, Yvette!" Madame Péthier beckoned imperiously as Yvette entered the mail room at the House of Lelong the next day. "Monsieur Dior wants to see you right away."

Madame sounded stern. Jean-Luc, who also made deliveries for the fashion house, gave Yvette a warning glance as he limped past with a pile of packages in his arms. Together, they had been distributing leaflets for his resistance group while on their rounds for months now, without the knowledge or permission of Monsieur Lelong. If the Gestapo caught them, they would be arrested, perhaps shot. Yvette's conscience had begun to smart because perhaps Monsieur Lelong himself would be blamed for their crimes. "Then don't get caught" was all Jean-Luc had said.

Before going up, Yvette paused to tidy her hair a little in the cloakroom mirror. Monsieur Dior would not like to see her disarranged from cycling all over Paris, no matter how urgent his need for her.

She found him up in the studio and hovered on the threshold, not wanting to disturb his train of thought. Bathed in a shaft of sunlight that streamed through the window, he looked more like a priest than a fashion designer, with his balding, egg-shaped head and his gentle, almost reverent, manner.

He was arranging and rearranging sketches on his desk, muttering to himself. The new season's designs, perhaps? She tried to catch a glimpse but couldn't quite see from the doorway. He held one drawing to the light and viewed it with a dissatisfied grimace. Ripping it up, he caught sight of her in the doorway.

His frown turned to a smile of welcome. "Come, *petite*. I need you to deliver this package to my sister."

He reached for a box, exquisitely wrapped in silver paper and tied up with white ribbon. It was not a Lelong package, but Yvette did not mind at all running errands for Monsieur Dior.

"Is your mother well?" murmured monsieur.

Yvette made no answer, holding her breath as he retied the bow on the small gift, his fingers tugging and working with deftness and precision. He liked to say he had the hands of a laborer, but that was silly. He was an artist in the truest sense of the word. Yvette had learned so much from being near him—not least of which was how to tie a bow.

He finished with the ribbon, but still his mouth turned down at the corners. For Monsieur Dior, even the presentation of this small trifle for his sister must be perfect. Then his face lightened, his hooded eyes sparking with an idea. "Go to the workroom and fetch me some lily of the valley. The smallest sprigs you can find."

She dashed to the ateliers, which were always well supplied with these flowers, as monsieur often had them sewn into the hems of his designs. Careful not to bruise the delicate white blossoms, she hurried back to monsieur and spilled them into his hands.

He selected a sprig and threaded its stem beneath the white bow. The deep green of the leaves and the purity of the bell-like flowers struck the perfect note of elegant whimsy.

"There," he said. "Now it is worthy." He placed the box carefully into her hands. "Take this directly to Mademoiselle Catherine. She is meeting Lili Dietlin at the Café de la Madeleine." He lowered his voice as if to share a secret. "I heard them talking about it the last time she was here."

Yvette grinned at him, pleased to be included in the surprise. "With pleasure, monsieur."

Yvette cycled toward the rue du Faubourg Saint-Honoré with the scent of lily of the valley filling her nostrils. Such small pleasures were precious these days. As she rounded the corner, a German patrol goose-stepped toward her. Their heavy boots struck the cobbled road in perfect unison, a soulless, inexorable beat that haunted her nightmares. The street was narrow at this point, so she stopped outside an empty boutique to wait for them to pass by, before continuing on her way.

As she cycled by the church of La Madeleine, she noticed a woman collecting for the Red Cross. Two German soldiers stopped to drop coins in her little bucket. The woman smiled and nodded, as if she was genuinely pleased to receive their money. Did none of them see the irony?

At the café, Yvette propped her bicycle against the wall and scanned the outdoor tables for Catherine. The place was full of German officers, reading the paper and sipping ersatz coffee beneath the café's bright red awnings. A couple of young soldiers gave a jackknife salute to their superiors as they passed.

Yvette frowned. Why would Mademoiselle Dior want to eat here, surrounded by the enemy? Yvette did not see her but noticed

Catherine's friend Liliane Dietlin sitting by herself at a table, smoking a cigarette. She was a lively, elegant creature, with a quick mind and a ready smile.

Catherine would undoubtedly join her friend soon. Yvette started toward Mademoiselle Dietlin with her delivery. As she approached, the man at the next table stood up to go, folding his newspaper and tossing it onto the seat between him and Liliane.

The man brushed past, face averted, as Yvette sidled between the tightly packed tables. When she looked beyond him, Liliane was tucking a newspaper into her shopping bag. Yvette blinked. It was the man's discarded newspaper that Liliane had taken. Well, that was the rich for you. They tried not to pay for anything. Even a newspaper, it seemed.

On closer inspection, Liliane's neat jacket was fraying a little at the cuffs, the same as every other honest Parisienne's clothing during this dreadful war. It made Yvette feel a kinship with her, even though their situations in life were miles apart. Mademoiselle was highly educated and worked at the Carnavalet museum, while Yvette was a mere delivery girl whose schooling had been cut short by war.

"*Bonjour*, Mademoiselle Dietlin," said Yvette. "Forgive me for disturbing you, but are you meeting a certain someone here today?"

Liliane stared back very hard, for so long that Yvette wondered what on earth she'd done to offend her. She held out the elegant package. "I-I have a present for Mademoiselle Catherine. Monsieur Dior told me to bring it to her here."

Liliane's face broke into a delighted smile. "Oh, that dear 'Tian! It is just like him. But I am sorry, *ma petite*, Catherine is not here today. Just me. I think Monsieur Dior must be a little confused."

"He seemed quite certain," said Yvette. "I think he overheard Mademoiselle Dior discussing a meeting with you."

"Well, we are to meet tomorrow, so that might be the cause of his confusion," said Liliane, picking up her purse and her shopping bag with the stranger's newspaper inside it. "Will you excuse me? I must be going now."

"Of course." At a loss and irrationally embarrassed, Yvette turned to leave.

"Wait!" said Liliane. "What is your name again, my dear?"

"Yvette Foucher."

"And you run deliveries for Monsieur Dior?"

"For the House of Lelong, mademoiselle, but sometimes for monsieur." Liliane seemed to expect Yvette to say more, so she added, "I live at the *loge* in Monsieur Dior's apartment building."

"Ah! That's where I've met you before." Liliane nodded. "Well, Yvette, perhaps I will see you again sometime."

Yvette wheeled her bicycle toward number 10. She would try at the Dior apartment. She did not want to let monsieur down.

She did not stop at the *loge*. Maman would want to know what was in the package and worry about her running errands for the Diors when she should be working, and valuable time would be lost. Yvette went up to the Dior apartment and knocked, grinning when their maid, Sabine, opened the door. "Good day, my friend. Is Mademoiselle Catherine here?"

"With Madame LaRoq," said Sabine with a jerk of her chin. "Mademoiselle Dietlin has been visiting the old lady the last few days, too. Is madame not well?"

Yvette blinked. "No worse than usual, as far as I know." A twinge of guilt made her press her lips together. She ought to visit madame more often, not leave it all to Gabby and Catherine Dior.

Sabine nodded. "You have a delivery for mademoiselle? I'll take it."

"No, I want to give it to her myself." Yvette showed her the package. "Monsieur Dior wants a full report on her reaction when she opens it, I think."

"She is a lucky woman," said Sabine, shaking her head. Then she lowered her voice. "You know she is living with a married man down there in Callian. They say—"

"That is none of our business," Yvette interrupted. Sabine could be such a gossip sometimes. Yvette knew about the Baron des Charbonneries. Apparently, the arrangement was amicable on all sides—the baron's wife had her own affairs—but Yvette did not intend to share that with Sabine.

When Mademoiselle Dior did not reappear for some time, Yvette went along the corridor to knock at Madame LaRoq's door. "It is I, Yvette. Will you let me in please, Mademoiselle Dior?" She did not have her own key to Madame LaRoq's apartment, like Gabby did.

There was no answer and Yvette worried that Madame LaRoq might be sleeping, so she did not like to try again. She slipped back to the Dior apartment.

Yvette set the package on the sideboard. She had nothing pressing to do back at the fashion house, so she would wait for Catherine to return.

"Hand me one of those, will you?" Yvette caught the cloth Sabine threw to her and began dusting the ornaments on the mantelpiece.

She liked this work, caring for pretty things, speculating about how Monsieur Dior had come by them. She covered her fingertip with the dust cloth and carefully traced the intricate lines of a gilded clock, paying special attention to the detail on the sinuous nude figure that held the clock face aloft. There was a portrait of monsieur above the mantelpiece. It did not flatter him at all but captured the sensitivity behind what some might say—and many did say—was a very average appearance.

Monsieur Dior did not look like a fashion designer, not like the debonair Lucien Lelong, but even though he did not have his own fashion house, the name of Christian Dior as a *premier* designer at the House of Lelong was becoming known. Every time a chic member of the Paris élite wore one of his gowns to an event, more clients flooded in. It was as if to these people, the war did not exist. They went to horse races and receptions and drank champagne in the company of high-ranking Nazis, while their countrymen suffered and starved.

Monsieur Lelong had explained to Yvette that couture was a vital industry to France, one that bolstered the economy. It was imperative to keep it operating, even if that meant clothing people one might not personally admire. Though he did not say it, Yvette knew that Monsieur Lelong had resisted the Germans as much as anyone. As president of the Chambre Syndicale de la Haute Couture, he had blocked several attempts to move the entire Parisian fashion industry, its couturiers and artisans, to Berlin.

"Yvette?" Sabine's voice sharpened. "Are you listening to me?"

"But of course." Sabine had been prattling on about her latest boyfriend, as usual.

"He is so nice and polite," said Sabine, "you'd never know he was a German at all. And very handsome, don't you think?"

"*Pfft.* I suppose so. If you like that sort of thing." Yes, Sabine's German was handsome, but that hardly made up for the rest.

"I know you don't approve," began Sabine, "but—"

"There are no 'buts,' Sabine," Yvette said, setting her jaw. "The only good Nazi is a dead Nazi."

"If you knew any, you might not say that. Many of them are ordinary soldiers, caught up in the war against their will, just like us."

Yvette bit her tongue, knowing it was futile to argue. You never knew what might happen, these days. If she thought herself so in love, Sabine might report on Yvette's opinions to her Nazi boyfriend.

Yvette gave a little laugh. "Don't mind me. I'm just jealous."

Sabine smirked. "You said it, not me."

Rolling her eyes at the mantelpiece, Yvette replaced the candlestick she had been dusting. Perhaps she was a little jealous. Not of having a German sweetheart—she would starve in a ditch before she consorted with the Boches—but she had never had a boyfriend. France had been at war ever since she might have taken an interest in young men, and unless she counted the occupying forces, which she did not, the pickings were very slim. Frenchmen were all in work camps, dead, incapacitated, or old. Or they were collaborating with the enemy. The odd, experimental embrace with Jean-Luc did not count. They had both agreed there was simply no spark of attraction between them. They were more like brother and sister.

Sabine lowered her voice like a conspirator, and that made Yvette concentrate again on what she was saying. "There were some funny goings-on here last time Catherine visited. I heard voices in the night."

"What is so strange about that?" Monsieur Dior often had unconventional friends come to stay. He was an intimate of Jean Cocteau and Salvador Dalí, and many others in the avant-garde world of Parisian literature and art.

Sabine went to a potted palm by the window and began to wipe dust from each spiky frond. "Well, no one was here when I came out in the morning. Whoever it was had left before dawn."

"You must have dreamed it," Yvette said. These days, curfew was set at one in the morning and lifted again at six. Ordinary Parisians did not dare to break it.

Catherine Dior let herself into the apartment then, putting a stop to the conversation. "Yvette? What are you doing here at this time of day?" She eyed the duster in Yvette's hand and smiled. "My brother will have to start paying you wages."

"I came to find you." She told Catherine about the Café de la Madeleine. "But Mademoiselle Dietlin told me your meeting with her was for tomorrow, so I tried here instead."

Catherine's eyebrows drew together. "Christian sent you there? How odd of him to do that."

"A misunderstanding, but never mind. Now I've found you." Yvette handed Sabine her duster and fetched Catherine's package. "From Monsieur Dior." She presented the gift, bouncing a little on her toes, as excited as if she were the one receiving the present.

Catherine, who had been looking pale and drawn as she came in, laughed with true pleasure. "Dear 'Tian!" She shook her head fondly and lightly touched the floral decoration. "I am spoiled, am I not?"

"Yes, indeed," Yvette said. "But it is such a pleasure for Monsieur Dior to spoil you, I think it is equally a gift for him as well. You will note how carefully he wrapped your little present."

"Lily of the valley." Catherine raised the package to her nose to sniff. "How it reminds me of home." She held the box but made no move to open it. Yvette did not like to insist that she do so, even though she was dying to see what was inside. Catherine's mind seemed to be elsewhere, her dark eyes clouded with worry.

"Is it very beautiful in Callian?" Yvette asked, trying to stretch out the conversation so that she might glimpse monsieur's gift. She had never been to the flower fields in Provence, where seas of blossom covered the countryside throughout the warmer months. Often, she had envied Catherine, living in the rural south, where surely one might grow one's own food to eat and restrictions had not been as harshly enforced as they had been in the capital. But of course, Yvette would not have left Paris for anything in the world.

Catherine nodded, setting the pretty box on the mantelpiece. "You must visit sometime." But both of them knew that would never happen. Yvette was a delivery girl, the daughter of a concierge. Catherine was the sister of a tenant, the daughter of a factory owner. Yvette would never be a guest at her house in Callian.

"Well, I must be going," Yvette said reluctantly, as it did not seem Catherine intended to open her gift. "Do you think Madame LaRoq would like me to call in later?"

Catherine's gaze darted toward the door. "I think not, my dear. She is tired today. Perhaps you might attend her with your sister tomorrow?"

"I'll do that," Yvette said, and with one last glance at the gift she had taken such trouble to deliver, she made her farewells and left.

Chapter Four

Paris, February 1947

GABBY

Gabby's pencil flew over each page as she raced to keep up with the mannequins, craning to catch the fall of a hemline or some interesting detail at a cuff or collar before each model disappeared from view. She tried to evoke the essence of a garment with a few bold strokes, much in the manner of the original sketches she'd seen lying about Monsieur Dior's apartment, labeling each creation as she heard the *compère* announce its name.

The sheer volume of fabric in the collection was shocking—frightening, even, when they'd all become so accustomed to rationing and regulations dictating shorter skirts and plain tailoring. Would Monsieur Dior be in trouble with the authorities? How on earth had he managed it?

"It's a revolution!" murmured a woman behind her, and Gabby

knew what she meant. But with all the beading and billowy skirts; nipped waists; full, padded hips; and accentuated bosoms, perhaps it was not so much a revolution as a revival. From the décor in the salons of the atelier to monsieur's "figure eight" and "flower" dresses, wasn't his new offering a modern interpretation of pre-revolutionary France?

The instant the first mannequin had stepped into the salon, Dior made every other style redundant. The masculine, blocky torsos and short, straight skirts of wartime were an abomination next to these deeply feminine creations. But was it also a signal for women to return to their function as ornaments now that their men had come home?

Gabby was uneasy in a way she could not explain. She did not want things to go back to the way they were before the war. But then, for her, wasn't that precisely what had happened? She smudged a line of skirt with her finger to soften it until it was just right, then flipped the page of her sketchbook.

A gasp from the audience made her look up, staring intently at the creation that was causing such a stir. The jacket was made of cream silk shantung, nipped in at the waist and flaring at the hips over a pleated black crêpe *corolle* skirt.

Gabby captured the ensemble with quick, emphatic lines before the mannequin glided out of sight. She ignored the next model as she filled in remembered detail—the buttons, the black gloves, the shoes, the tilt to the hat, a suggestion of the pearl choker at the mannequin's throat.

Finishing the last bit of shading on the Bar Suit, Gabby raised her head again to watch the next outfit: a more fitted dress this time, black, with a sweetheart neckline, small puffed sleeves, and long black gloves. From this angle high above, the mannequin's face was obscured by the brim of her hat. Yet, there was something familiar about her, a way of holding her head, that made Gabby's heart quicken. Then the mannequin performed an elegant turn, one hand hovering near her hip, the other not quite touching her hat, as if to announce, "*Et voilà*. Here I am."

A jolt of shock made Gabby drop her pencil. *Yvette?* Her heart hammered; her body turned first hot, then cold. Gabby's pencil rolled off the tip of her shoe and slipped down behind the back of the woman on the step below. The woman flinched, shifted awkwardly to fish the pencil from underneath her, and handed it back to Gabby with a displeased frown. Too astonished to do more than murmur an apology, Gabby blinked and craned her neck to see better.

Oblivious, Yvette gave another smooth twirl, then passed through the crowded landing and into the salon. She walked with an arrogant tilt to her head, as if she was born to be a mannequin. As if she'd never been a naughty toddler who had gotten powdered sugar through her hair, or an awkward twelve-year-old, all gangling limbs and big feet. As if she'd never come home after curfew with her clothes torn and eyes wild and her hands covered in blood.

But how could it be? Yvette was supposed to be in New York. Gabby's mind cast about for meaning in a situation that was clearly impossible. Her sister was in Paris. In Monsieur Dior's show . . .

Yvette. Here. And she had not even bothered to visit her sister and mother. Since the resistance had smuggled her out under the Germans' noses three years before, Yvette had maintained complete silence, ignoring Gabby's letters. Did she resent her so much for trying to keep her safe?

Suddenly, a great wave of nausea rose up, and Gabby's vision swam. She couldn't think. She certainly couldn't sketch. She couldn't rest inside her own skin until she spoke to her sister again. She wanted to stumble down through the crowd on the staircase to accost Yvette and wrap her in a tight embrace.

Even had she wished to make a spectacle of herself, Gabby could not have reached Yvette, not with several rows of people sitting on the steps below her and several more rows of them seated on the landing as well.

As the parade went on, shock and yearning gave way to growing anger. How could Yvette simply turn up like this, after all this time, without a word to her family? To be included in this show, she must have attended weeks of fittings . . . But no, that could not be. Monsieur Dior would not have failed to mention it, had Yvette appeared at his atelier.

Gabby could not even imagine how Yvette came to be at Dior at all, much less in the show itself. But then, hadn't Yvette always possessed diabolical good luck? Or perhaps, rather, an instinct for being in the right place at the right time, for grabbing every opportunity with both hands, always asking for more.

Despite everything she had been through during the occupation, Yvette had achieved her dream, to walk among the best mannequins of Paris in an haute couture parade. And not just any parade. The first showing of the first collection of the most ingenious couturier in the world.

The collection had moved on to cocktail wear, and the next mannequin wore a deep-midnight-blue gown that made Gabby gasp with longing. Almost without conscious thought, she took up her pencil to sketch, her hand a little unsteady. She made sure to suggest the intricate detail in the full-bosomed, tight-waisted bodice and the way the skirt bloomed around the model's hips.

Yvette came out again, this time supremely confident in one of the flower dresses, a pale, strapless gown, with a bell-like skirt and large silk flowers at the breast. Her long throat rose elegantly from her pure white décolletage. The neckline of the gown cut across her lovely bust, and her waist seemed impossibly tiny, emphasized by the cinched-in bodice. Slipping her hands into the pockets of her skirt, she sauntered off toward the salon.

Later, she made another queenly entrance in an indigo evening gown with a skirt of tightly pleated silk. The audience gave loud applause. Yvette looked so poised and chic that Gabby's heart ached with pride and her eyes burned with unshed tears. She smiled and shook her head. Where was the sense in being angry or upset? Her sister was alive and in one piece. And in Paris. That was all that mattered.

Gabby's fingers were covered in shiny grey splotches of lead pencil and her hand was throbbing by the time the show ended. Yvette had carried herself with poise and aplomb, never stumbling, never appearing awkward or self-conscious. How Gabby envied her. What must it have been like to wear those creations, to feel so beautiful?

At last, Monsieur Dior appeared to humbly accept his clients' acclaim. Watching him, Gabby's heart overflowed. So much work, such brilliance and dedication—it had all come to fruition in this triumph of a show.

When it was over and the staircase began to empty, Gabby put her sketchbook and pencil away and rubbed her aching wrist. It had been an emotional morning. But the time . . . She checked her watch. Oh, dear! She must get back to work.

There was no hope of talking with Yvette. The mannequins were all busy posing for photographs in each of the outfits they'd modeled in the parade. Monsieur Dior was mobbed by the press and clients alike, so there was no opportunity to congratulate him, but there would be time later to express her admiration and wonder. Gabby spotted Catherine in a small cluster of guests. A waiter was serving them champagne. She might slip away. She did not wish to impose . . .

"Gabby!" Declining champagne, Catherine excused herself and hurried toward her, taking Gabby's hands and squeezing them. "Did you see her? I nearly fell off my chair."

Gabby's throat tightened. "It was . . . a shock."

"Thoughtless of her not to come to see you first, but knowing Yvette, there is some wildly random series of events to account for it." Catherine searched Gabby's face and her expression softened with sympathy. "Why don't you slip into the *cabine* and say hello?"

Gabby shook her head. "She has a job to do. I'll just get in the way." Besides, it was not the kind of reunion she could imagine taking place in a crowded dressing room.

Why hadn't Yvette come home at the first opportunity? She hadn't answered any of Gabby's letters, so perhaps she was still angry with Gabby for her harsh words that horrible summer's night. Or perhaps, like so many French people, Yvette wanted desperately to forget . . .

Forcing herself to smile, despite the ache in her heart, Gabby embraced Catherine, kissing her on both cheeks. "Will you please tell monsieur everything was beyond perfection? Thank you for inviting me."

Resisting Catherine's urging that she stay for champagne, she made her way to the door. Approaching the threshold, she hesitated. Her feet felt heavy. Once she left the Maison Dior, the spell would be broken for good. By contrast with this wonderland of exquisite and extraordinary beauty, her ordinary life seemed to yawn before her like a desert canyon. Yvette's attainment of her long-held dream only underscored how static and banal Gabby's life had become.

She stepped out onto the pavement and forced herself to turn toward home.

GABBY'S SHOULDERS DROOPED when she reached the apartments at number 10 rue Royale. Maman's pale little face, with its thin eyebrows and worry lines, stared out the window of the concierge's *loge*. Gabby waved and motioned for her mother to let her in. A buzzer sounded. The latch clicked and Gabby pushed through.

The vestibule was like a short, cavernous tunnel, but beyond it, pale sunlight illuminated the square, uncovered courtyard around which the apartments had been built. The garden beds were bare. She must plan for something pretty in the spring.

Gabby hesitated, staring at the door to the *loge* that gave onto the vestibule, as if lost. To return to the drudgery of her work as concierge after the glamor and beauty of the Dior fashion show seemed a travesty. At least she had her sketches to remind her.

She looked down. The fat mailbag squatted by the wall beneath the tenants' pigeonholes. Gabby sighed. She had not even taken off her hat and coat, and here was work to be done.

"What took you so long? There is still the mail to sort." Maman stood at the door to their tiny apartment, her chapped hands gripped together.

Gabby followed her mother inside, dragging the mailbag with her. She shrugged off her coat and put her hat and scarf on the hook by the door. "The work will get done, Maman. I do not take too many mornings off, you will admit."

She opened her mouth to tell her mother that Yvette was back, but the words didn't come. She took out her art satchel from the armoire by the window and slid her sketchbook and pencil inside. She owned a fine drawing set given to her by the mother of a little girl Gabby used to look after from time to time in apartment number eight. Before the war, she wrote fairy stories and illustrated them, too. Elisabeth had loved those tales and begged for more.

But Elisabeth was a little girl no longer. She was fourteen now, away at a convent school in the country, and too old for picture books in any case. Gabby put away the satchel and went to get ready for work.

She exchanged her suit for warm work clothes and a housecoat. Then she poured the mail over the floor, kneeled among the drifts of envelopes, and began sorting through.

She liked to deliver some of the post herself to a few select tenants, to exchange a few words with them here and there and hear all their news. The rest of the mail would go into each tenant's pigeonhole for collection. Short of time as she was today, it would have been more efficient to distribute everyone's letters that way.

But there was post from Avignon for Monsieur Gerard. Gabby gasped in delight. His daughter must have had her baby. She would hand that to him personally. Monsieur had been so anxious for news.

And then, of course, Madame Vasseur would be affronted if Gabby did not deliver her correspondence to her door.

Another piece of mail looked important, and she slipped that into her stack as well. There was quiet pleasure in seeing friendly faces each day, even if it was not as exciting as working as a mannequin at Dior.

Gabby was a very ordinary person, even if she had done one

quite extraordinary thing during the war. All of that was over now. Had circumstances not happened in quite the order they had, had the cause not been specific and personal, she never would have possessed the courage to risk her life in such a fashion. She did not believe in dying for an ideal. She was not Yvette.

Yvette. So elegant and haughty in her couture clothes. The mannequins had moved through the salons at Dior like empresses, swishing their skirts with impunity, deliberately knocking over the slim ashtray stands scattered throughout for use of the guests. If only Gabby had one-tenth of the confidence those women had shown . . .

She sorted through the rest of the mail and came across a thick cream envelope. She sat back, eyes wide. It was addressed to her. It looked like . . . Frowning, she picked up her letter opener and flipped over the envelope.

Her heart stopped. It was. Just like the one she'd received two months ago. The same seal. A red one with a crest and the printed letters "OHMS" on it. British. Important. Dread crashed through her like an avalanche. The letter opener fell to the floor with a clatter. Official news was never good.

Almost without thought, she shoved the envelope among her drawing materials, scooped up the letter opener, and thrust that inside, too. She shut the portfolio away in the armoire. She couldn't think about it. She needed to get back to work.

In Paris, people were accustomed to concierges knowing their business. Monsieur Gerard invited Gabby inside and read his daughter's letter to her. She exclaimed and congratulated him on the birth of his new grandson, felt the lump in her throat when he announced with simple pride that the infant's parents had given the child his name.

The news of the baby, though expected, lifted her spirits. After the devastation of war, new life was particularly precious. One might always have hope while there was still such joy to be found.

When she got up to go, monsieur gently squeezed her hands. "Thank you, Gabby. We are lucky to have you."

She laughed and demurred, but the small compliment was a balm. She liked nothing more than to help people. That was its own reward, of course, but it was nice to be appreciated. Particularly in light of her mother's constant reminders that she would never be accepted by the tenants as their equal.

No thanks would come from Madame Vasseur, however. She made Gabby wait while she perused every letter at length, squinting down at the words through her pince-nez. The old lady complained about all the bills she received as if Gabby were personally responsible for them. Out of habit, Gabby murmured placatory nonsense, while wondering what on earth she had to apologize for. It was this kind of behavior her mother chided her about, and she was right. How had Gabby never learned to draw the line?

"Wait." Madame lifted a gnarled finger as Gabby tried to leave. "I want you to take Chou-Chou for a walk. I'm not feeling well."

In spite of her uncharitable feelings toward the cantankerous tenant, Gabby regarded her with concern. Madame always took her apricot poodle for a stroll twice a day, even in bitter weather like this, when the poor animal shivered and trembled at her side.

Gabby was sorry for the dog and for madame as well, but she could not spare the time to take Chou-Chou for a walk. She had too much else to do, and caring for tenants' pets was not part of her job.

"I am sorry, madame, but I am very busy today. Perhaps when

Léon comes home he can walk the dog for you? He should be back from school for lunch very soon."

Madame paused in her knifing of the envelopes and looked up at Gabby, astonished and affronted. "It is not often that I ask you for a particular favor, mademoiselle."

This was such a barefaced untruth that a snort of surprise escaped Gabby. She put her hand to her mouth as if to snatch it back. "I am sorry. I must be getting on."

Madame's expression hardened. "Well, be off with you, then, if your work won't wait. I'll find someone else, but not that naughty Léon. He is not responsible enough to take care of a sensitive animal like Chou-Chou."

Unfortunately, this was true. Gabby sighed. "Perhaps a compromise? I will take him on my rounds and maybe a little way up the street and back. But I'm afraid that is the best I can do today."

She studied the gaunt, wrinkled face with its heavy application of blue eye shadow and rouge and tried to gauge whether madame's illness was of the body or the spirit. Madame Vasseur had been indomitable throughout the war. There had been a certain kind of strength in her relentless self-centeredness. The only creature madame truly loved was her dog.

Gabby stooped to attach the poodle's lead to his glittering collar and took him out with her. The poodle seemed to perk up at the promise of a walk, even if not with his favorite human. He trotted along beside her, his nails clicking jauntily on the polished floor.

Monsieur Dior had mail, so Gabby went to his apartment and handed the letters over to the new maid. Sabine was long gone. Monsieur had helped her leave Paris before the terrible reprisals against the women who had consorted with German soldiers began. Poor, silly Sabine, Gabby thought. It was a high price to pay for falling in love.

That brought her letter to mind, but she banished it and doggedly carried on with her deliveries. With all the mail distributed, she would make good on her promise and take Chou-Chou for a short walk.

"I cannot believe you are doing *that woman* favors," said Maman, eyeing the poodle when Gabby went to the *loge* to get her coat. "But I see you can't help yourself."

Gabby grimaced. "I know, I know. But the way I see it, it is Chou-Chou I am doing the favor, not madame." She pulled out her beret, coat, and scarf and swaddled herself against the chill February day.

Outside, the rush of relief that flooded her when she left the apartment building was an unwelcome sensation. Had her mother's fears come to pass? Had she been spoiled forever by that one morning at Dior?

Walking the dog, she reflected on the fashion show. It had been like a dream, and yet so much more nourishing and substantial than simply gazing at pretty gowns. She had felt her own creativity firing in response to the challenge of capturing on paper not just the appearance of an ensemble, but its movement and mood.

She ought to take up drawing again. But with no cleaner or handyman to help her anymore, there were never enough hours in the day to do all that needed to be done, and when she finished in the evening, she still had chores to do around their little apartment. She fell into bed every night, exhausted. That was not always such a bad thing, as it gave her little leisure to dwell on the past, but it also gave her little leisure to dream or to draw.

Perhaps she could change that. Perhaps she might steal just

twenty minutes a day so that she could work on her art. In twenty-four hours, was that so much to ask? And perhaps it was time to stop coddling her mother. Papa had died many years ago now. The war was over. It was time for Danique Foucher to resume living. Yes, and perhaps working a little, too.

That night, after an afternoon spent mopping and dusting the common areas, fixing small problems in the apartments and opening the street door to visitors, making dinner and cleaning up afterward, Gabby was heavy eyed with fatigue. But once her mother was asleep, she took out her pencils and sharpened them carefully, one by one.

As she pulled out a sheaf of paper, the letter with the official seal dropped out, skittering along the floor. Gabby stared at it, heart pounding. She was afraid to pick it up, as if the envelope were searing hot. She had to force herself to retrieve it, to hold it between forefinger and thumb. After a moment's hesitation, she shoved the letter back into her portfolio.

Gabby was quite certain that she did not want to know what that letter contained. As long as he was alive somewhere in the world, she could be content. Well, not content perhaps, but . . . What? Was there a word for the absence of crushing grief?

She made herself turn to her drawing. She needed to do something fun, something to escape. A picture book, perhaps. Yes. She stared at the wall and let herself lose focus. Soon, the story was forming in her mind, a tale about a little girl in ragged clothing who is swept into a magical wonderland of lace and satins and silks.

But no matter how hard she tried to escape through her own creations, her mind kept wandering back to that letter with its official seal, and the little girl in her sketches looked exactly like Yvette.

YVETTE

On the evening of the Dior premiere, Yvette greeted the door-man at the Ritz and tried to disguise her limp as she headed toward the grand staircase. She had walked all the way from Saint Germain and the blisters on her feet were indescribably painful.

After the show, there'd been official photographs, and all the dressing and undressing repeated several times more. Monsieur Dior had been startled to see Yvette among his mannequins, but as always, he was kind, praising her look and the way she wore his opera dress, though he chided her for letting her hair grow too long. Yvette vowed to get it all chopped off at once.

The show had been an unmitigated success, but by midday, she was weary and a little cross, the excitement and nervous tension of the parade giving way to exhaustion, a feeling of running too hard on too little fuel. However, with the end of the parade, the mannequins' day had only just begun. Yvette had to stay and show clothes in private viewings for buyers and special clients. When she began to flag—she had not slept for the past forty hours or so—she reminded herself how much she longed to be part of this world and that she had managed to work her way into this position only by the most outrageous luck imaginable. She could not afford to waste this chance.

"You need to *sell* the clothes to them," said Tania, touching up her makeup while Yvette tried to do something with her overly abundant hair. "Make them cry for wanting each dress. Can you do that, Yvette?"

Unsure what she meant, Yvette wished she could watch what

Tania did and copy. But she was whisked away to the salon and the madness began again. They did not stop with the buyers until late, and then, while most of the models went home with their husbands, Yvette and a couple of other girls let some rich men take them dancing. Hence the limp she tried to disguise as she crossed the foyer of the Ritz.

All she wanted was to remove her clothes, pour herself a nightcap, and tumble into bed. Tomorrow would be a big day. She had to meet with Monsieur LeBrun about the trial, and she must see Gabby and Maman. Then, too, she needed to see Madame de Turckheim about a more permanent role at Dior. They'd both been too busy to discuss the matter in all the bustle after the show.

Oh, but the grand staircase seemed insurmountable. "Come on, Yvette." She had climbed mountains in espadrilles; she should be capable of ascending a hotel staircase with blistered heels.

When she reached the corridor of her floor, she kicked off her shoes and carried them, relishing the plush carpet beneath her poor feet. Letting herself into her room and locking the door behind her, she switched on the light and looked around the suite with renewed awe. She would never get used to this. That was probably just as well.

A man stepped out of the shadows. With a hoarse cry, Yvette dropped her shoes and fell back against the door.

Chapter Five

Paris, June 1944

GABBY

"Do you need some help, Gabby?" said Yvette. "I have time to spare." The night had been too hot to sleep and Gabby had risen at first light.

"Really?" Had Madame LaRoq put a gentle word in Yvette's ear?

"Yes, of course." Yvette gave her a funny look. "I do help sometimes, don't I?"

Gabby wasn't stupid enough to argue with that statement. She handed Yvette one of her dusters and a spare apron. "The bannisters need a dust and polish. That would be a big help."

They set off across the courtyard, leaving their mother snoring. Yvette began to hum a jaunty version of "The Marseillaise" under her breath.

Gabby felt the corners of her mouth lift. Yvette could be willful and impulsive, an impractical dreamer to hanker after glamor and fame as one of Monsieur Dior's mannequins. Yet, sometimes, she could be just the tonic to lift the spirits.

At the flower beds that flanked the east door, Gabby stopped short. "My vegetables!"

She dropped her mop and bucket and ran to make sure. Both beds were nearly devoid of produce, soil carelessly scattered over the flagstones around them.

With a cry, she fell to her knees, scrabbling in the dirt. "The carrots! They would have barely grown to the size of my finger. The beans were only sprouts!" Someone had stolen them all.

Yvette touched her shoulder. "People are hungry and desperate."

"People are stupid and greedy! If they had only waited, they could have shared in a much larger crop." Tears started to Gabby's eyes. She sat back on her haunches, biting her lip savagely so as not to cry. The war had been one long struggle, one step forward, two steps back.

"It was always going to be hard," said Yvette.

Gabby knew what Yvette was thinking. There were many tenants in this building and her small harvest would not have been nearly enough to feed them. Plus, they risked the Germans finding out and confiscating what little they had.

Gabby gave a shuddering sigh. She tried so hard not to be hopeful of anything in this godforsaken war, but she had been hopeful of this. She had imagined providing a nourishing little feast for all their friends, and now her plans were ruined.

"Look!" said Yvette, skirting the edge of the garden bed and bending to peer closer. "Here are some they've missed."

Gabby scrambled to her feet and joined Yvette. She was right. At the edges of each patch of soil, green shoots peeked out.

"Not for want of trying, I'm sure." Gabby set her jaw. "Whoever it was will probably be back for those. I'm going to stay up and keep watch tonight, that's what I'll do. Catch him in the act."

"Him?" Yvette said. "Do you suspect someone in particular?"

"No. I don't know. It could easily be a woman." She brushed the soil from her hands and knees.

"I'll keep an eye out for someone with dirt beneath her finger-nails," Yvette promised. "Perhaps we should line everyone up for an inspection, like Madame Bertold used to do at school."

Anger flashed through Gabby. It was just like Yvette to make it all into a joke. While Gabby struggled to ensure their survival, her sister stepped so lightly through life. And everyone simply let her. You could get away with much if you were beautiful and young.

She was about to make a sharp retort, but Yvette put out a hand and squeezed her arm. "Gabby, don't stay up. You need your sleep." She hesitated. "I worry about you."

Gabby's anger melted. She patted Yvette's hand, grateful for her concern, but still, she shook her head. "I won't be able to sleep, knowing someone is helping themselves to all my hard work."

"Maybe we should take turns, then," Yvette said. "Wake me up and I'll do the second shift."

But of course Gabby wouldn't do any such thing. Yvette was pedaling about Paris on her bicycle all day. She shouldn't be doing that on a few hours' sleep.

That night, once her mother and Yvette had gone to bed and all was quiet around the apartment building, Gabby took a little chair outside. The blackout meant there was not a glimmer shining from any of the windows, but a full moon shed a pale wash of light over the courtyard. She positioned the chair so that her back was to the wall, her silhouette blending into the shadows. Whoever had been bold enough to plunder her gardens would not notice her. She settled down to wait.

As the minutes passed, then hours, without incident, she repeatedly fell into a doze, only to start awake again. She hadn't considered how hard it would be to remain alert without coffee. She tried all kinds of tricks to ward off sleep, but as the night deepened, she eventually lost the battle.

A noise woke her. She jerked to alertness and planted both feet on the ground, ready to spring into action. Pain shot through her neck as she tried to pinpoint the cause of the sound. She didn't know what it had been, only that something on the edge of her dream had pulled her out of slumber.

But there was no one in the courtyard at all, much less bending over the garden beds.

Gabby rubbed her eyes. She must have dreamed the noise. For the first time, it seemed like a stupid thing for her to have done, to sit snoozing in a chair outside in the dark. No wonder Yvette had stared at her as if she were crazy.

Her neck ached. She'd be very sorry for this when she had to scrub the floors tomorrow. Feeling sheepish, now that her fury had cooled, she stood and picked up the chair and walked toward the vestibule.

There came a stifled giggle from the blackness of the vestibule just inside the street door. "Oh lala, we are discovered!"

"Shhh!" More low laughter, a female snort.

"Who's there?" Gabby said sharply.

A low, calm voice said, "It's I, Catherine Dior. And some friends to stay. I beg your pardon, Gabby. I hope we did not wake you."

That must have been the noise Gabby had heard. Catherine and her friends coming in through the street door.

There were three people with Catherine. The woman who must have giggled—for one could not imagine Catherine Dior ever giggling. Two larger figures Gabby guessed to be men, though she couldn't see their faces, one swaying drunkenly, the other man's arm around him, holding him up.

Gabby wasn't sure of the time, but it must be well past curfew. That was dangerous. This recklessness seemed quite unlike Mademoiselle Dior. But Gabby said nothing. It was not her place to chastise tenants for their nocturnal activities or the risk they courted by flouting Nazi edicts.

"Don't let me keep you," she murmured. "Good night."

She turned to let herself into the *loge*, but a deep disquiet filled her. She hoped Catherine Dior didn't mean to make a habit of late nights while she was in Paris. The last thing they needed was to have the Gestapo sniffing around.

"Gabby, wake up!" It was Yvette, shaking her shoulder, but sleep dragged Gabby back.

"Mmph, go away . . ." Then she gasped and sat bolt upright. "What is the time?"

"Don't worry. I've done the bannisters and the floors, too," said Yvette. "You should have woken me last night. Did you catch our thief?"

Gabby pressed her fingertips into her temples, fighting the druglike stupor. "No."

Something altogether more shocking had occurred. Now that she thought about it in daylight, she was more worried than ever about Catherine Dior.

Gabby plucked at the neckline of her nightgown. Catherine was far too sensible to risk being discovered breaking curfew for the sake of a night out. The more she considered, the more likely it seemed there was some other explanation for her behavior. But did Gabby really want to know?

"Will you be all right now, Gabby?" Yvette was being very careful around her. "I have to get to work."

"Yes, yes, of course." The words came out as a snap, and she bit her lip. "Thank you, Yvette. It was kind of you to let me sleep."

Later, when Gabby was sweeping the courtyard, Catherine reappeared, dressed in a smart suit and pumps and a jaunty little hat.

Gabby straightened to greet her. "I trust your friend has recovered, mademoiselle."

She had meant it as a semi-joking reference to the man's inebriation but it came out in a tight, accusatory manner that made her inwardly cringe.

"Good morning, Gabby." Catherine's dark eyes held a question. "I am sorry we disturbed you last night."

"You did not disturb me. I was . . ." Gabby almost laughed to think she could have been so crazed about a mere vegetable thief. "I was already up."

Catherine's gaze sharpened. "You get up in the middle of the night often, then?"

"Not often. Hardly ever." Where was Catherine heading with this?

After a hesitation, Catherine said, "My dear, I might have more visitors arriving late tonight."

Gabby's chest tightened. "You mean, after curfew again?"

Catherine met her gaze steadily, as if willing her to pass a test. "Yes."

The trickle of fear that there was more to last night's episode than Catherine had let on burst into a flood. Catherine Dior working for the resistance? Gabby would never, not in a million years, have guessed.

Seeming to take her silence for acquiescence, Catherine leaned toward Gabby and continued in a rapid undertone. "I will let them in myself. You have nothing to do with it. If you hear anything at all, stay where you are, don't look, and don't worry. All will be well."

"But . . ." It was a terrible risk. If a German patrol caught Catherine admitting people after curfew, they'd haul the lot of them in for interrogation, maybe worse. Gabby did not want to get mixed up in this. Not even passively.

Catherine gripped Gabby's shoulders and met her eyes in a long, charged look. "Do you understand me?"

Gabby hesitated, then nodded. What else could she do?

"And Yvette?" said Catherine, releasing her. "Do we need to warn her?"

"No." Definitely not. She'd never put her sister in such danger. It would be her secret. Hers and Catherine Dior's. The thought gave Gabby a tingle of pride, though her body was vibrating with anxiety and her chest was so tight, she could hardly breathe. "Both Yvette and Maman sleep like the dead—don't worry."

Catherine nodded. "Thank you, my dear," she said. "I am greatly in your debt."

Gabby wanted to say something significant, something meaningful and brave. But she couldn't think of the right words. "*De rien*," she murmured. *It is nothing.* What a trite thing to say.

YVETTE

That afternoon, Yvette returned to Lelong to pick up her last load of deliveries for the day. It was so hot outside, the very air seemed to shimmer, and it was a relief to enter the comparative cool of the fashion house.

Tiny though the mail room was, Yvette loved Madame Péthier's domain. It was so orderly and neat, with its high zinc-topped counter in front of a wall of floor-to-ceiling shelving. On those shelves sat boxes of every conceivable size and shape, covered with the distinctive coffee-and-cream Regency stripe of Lelong. On the counter sat all the accouterments of wrapping: scissors and ribbon, tissue paper and brown paper, envelopes, labels and paste, stamps and string.

"What's wrong?" said Yvette, realizing that Madame Péthier stood at her counter looking haughty and affronted and Jean-Luc was scowling back. The two of them could not have been more different—madame dressed to the throat in unrelieved black, her dark hair exquisitely styled into a chignon, her makeup expertly applied; Jean-Luc, stocky and short, with patches of sweat in the armpits of his grubby white shirt and his untrimmed hair tousled by the wind.

"There you are, Yvette!" said madame, her shoulders relaxing slightly.

"About time." Jean-Luc snatched up his satchel and a stack of parcels from the counter. "Maybe you will take the next delivery. I certainly won't."

"Why? What is it?" asked Yvette.

"You tell her, madame." Jean-Luc shouldered past Yvette and limped toward the door. "I can't stomach much more of this."

Yvette stared after him, then turned to Madame Péthier. "What is the bee in his bonnet?"

Madame licked her lips and smoothed her skirt. "I wonder what is taking Clothilde so long?" Strangely, she was avoiding Yvette's gaze as well as her question. "Go up and see, Yvette." When Yvette stayed where she was, her eyebrows lifted in inquiry, madame sighed. "Mademoiselle Dulac needs that cloak for this evening's reception. It is getting late."

"Dulac?" Yvette echoed, impressed in spite of herself. "Not the—"

"Yes," snapped madame. Lowering her voice, she added, "And if you want to keep your position here as well as your freedom, you will not mention the lady's morals, or that she is mistress to one of the most powerful men in the German air force. You will not gawk or ask for her autograph or spit in her face and call her a dirty collaborator. Understand?"

"Yes, madame." Truthfully, she felt no such impulse. For years, she had loved to watch Louise Dulac on the silver screen, worshipped her in the way young girls worship glamorous movie stars. She was not a flesh-and-blood person; she was a goddess. Yvette could not believe what they said about her was true.

Excitement bubbled up within her. Would she actually get to meet the famous Dulac?

Yvette went up to the workrooms, where the afternoon sun slanted through the long, rectangular windows set into the sloping attic roof. Seamstresses in white coats hummed about, pinning models made of toile onto dummies, correcting a seam here, adding a pleat there, under the watchful eye of Monsieur

Balmain. In the corner, two seamstresses sorted through bolts of fabric, searching for the particular rose silk Monsieur Lelong had ordered for the spring/summer collection and disagreeing most politely with each other about who had handled the fabric last.

Yvette sidled past this pair and made her way to the end of the room, where three seamstresses sat on stools around one of the high tables, embroidering crystals and tiny pearls on a luxurious white silk cape, their needles flitting in and out like dragonflies. Shaded lights hung from long cords to illuminate their intricate work, but Yvette noticed Diane rubbing her eyes and blinking, as if to focus better on her task.

"Excuse me, Clothilde, but Madame Péthier needs that cape immediately," Yvette said. "Is it nearly done?"

"It would be done quicker if she stopped sending people to check whether it is done," said Clothilde, snipping off a thread.

"Where is Monsieur Dior?" Yvette asked. "Has he approved it yet?"

"Monsieur will not be back this afternoon," said Léonie, selecting a crystal and holding it up, winking, to the light. "He has taken his sister to lunch."

Yvette smiled. "The two of them are very close."

Diane and Léonie exchanged knowing looks. Yvette gave an inward sigh. Usually, she tried not to mention that she lived in the same apartment building as one of the head designers at Lelong, nor that she knew him quite well. Sometimes these things slipped out. She shut her mouth and waited.

One by one, the seamstresses finished. Clothilde checked every inch of the cape for marks or stray threads. An imperfect crystal was removed and another stitched in its place.

An apprentice brought out the dummy that had been made

to mademoiselle's exact measurements, and Clothilde settled the cape around its shoulders. She stood back, eyeing the garment. "Perfect. Take it down."

Yvette put on her white gloves and removed the garment from the form.

"I'd like to spit on it," muttered Diane as Yvette walked past.

"Or stick it with pins," said Léonie.

"That's enough!" Clothilde wouldn't hear of compromising any of her creations, even to avenge France. "Off you go, Yvette."

Taking great care not to snag the cape on anything, Yvette carried it downstairs to Madame Péthier, who wrapped the garment in tissue and laid it in its box as lovingly as a *maman* might lay her sleeping infant in his cradle.

"You will deliver the parcel to Mademoiselle Dulac in suite twelve at the Ritz with the patron's compliments," said madame.

Yvette stared at her. "But aren't you going to come with me?" Ordinarily, a *vendeuse* would attend to ensure the garment fit properly and was to the client's satisfaction. Yvette had fetched and carried for the *vendeuses* before but she'd never delivered a garment to a client on her own.

"I regret we are too busy with the new collection to spare anyone else," said Madame Péthier, folding the tissue paper away, avoiding Yvette's gaze. "There is a war on."

"I see." Monsieur Lelong might be obliged to dress the mistresses of Nazi occupiers, but there were some small rebellions his employees could make in the name of France. Despite Yvette's loyalty to the nation and her disgust at dirty collaborators, she could not suppress the excitement that flooded her veins. A shameful double standard, it was true.

"Hurry now," said the *vendeuse*, handing the parcel to her. "It would not do to be late."

"I'll be as quick as I can." Yvette dashed outside, stowed the box in the deep basket of her bicycle, and pedaled toward the Ritz.

The rue du Faubourg Saint-Honoré was lined with tall white buildings with red awnings over their doors. Many of Monsieur Lelong's rival couturiers were to be found on this street, and even though several ateliers lay dormant now, the air still reeked of luxury.

The street was narrow and she had to concentrate as she weaved in and out of traffic and pedestrians, but she could never pass the empty president's palace without a pang of shame. The French government had abandoned the city to the Germans and fled in the night, leaving Parisians like her family to carry on as best they could under the new regime.

A shout and a scuffle further up the street caught her attention and her chest tightened. What this time? Since the Normandy landings, the Boches had become even more brutal than before.

She pedaled slowly toward the commotion. There were tall men in black uniforms on the sidewalk across the road. Gestapo. Her stomach turned over. Raids usually took place under cover of darkness. It was unusual to see a disturbance in a genteel street at this time of day.

A small crowd had gathered on the pavement opposite. Yvette dismounted and wheeled her bicycle over to them. Nodding to a bright-eyed woman who carried her rations in a string bag, she asked, "What is happening over there, madame?"

"Someone informed on her," said the woman in a low voice. "She's the concierge of that building. They say she's been giving aid to Jews."

The front door to the apartments slammed open and two Gestapo officers muscled a thin, middle-aged woman out of the building. She was struggling, protesting her innocence at the top of her voice. A fist rammed into her stomach, cutting off her cries. She doubled over and the two men dragged her into their waiting car.

Yvette winced and sucked a breath through her teeth. "What sort of aid?"

"Hiding people. Moving them from place to place until she could arrange safe passage to Spain."

They watched as the big black Citroën sped off. Through the back windscreen, Yvette made out the woman fighting still. Yvette admired her spirit, but perhaps she ought to save her strength for whatever would come next. "Did she do what they say?"

The bright-eyed woman shrugged. "What does that matter? She has been accused. These days, that is enough."

Inside Yvette, a deep anger bubbled up and threatened to boil over. She closed her lips tightly and breathed through her nose until the urge to release a torrent of abuse against the Nazis passed. "Thank you, madame."

She rode away, furious at how powerless she'd been to help that poor woman. Much as she railed against the Nazis, she had done nothing at all to fight them. Distributing propaganda leaflets for a ragtag band of communists did not count.

Mademoiselle Dulac's parcel slid sideways in her basket as she dodged around a horse and cart. Yvette felt stifled, almost suffocated with rage. Her legs pumped and the wind whipped her hair so that it flew like streamers out behind her. Everywhere she went, the swastika loomed above, its ugliness a constant reminder of scenes such as the one she had just witnessed.

She was going too fast. These days, to appear in any great

hurry was dangerous. The slightest deviation from the ordinary, and you could end up like that poor woman, dragged off to an unknown destination, never to be heard from again. She applied gentle pressure to the brake to slow down as she entered the Place Vendôme.

Outside the Ritz, the square was littered with German vehicles, the shining black motorcars that transported high-ranking Nazis from place to place. Swastika flags hung from the entrance, proclaiming that the hotel was under Nazi command. The Luftwaffe had commandeered half the hotel—the side that faced onto the Place Vendôme. Civilians had been corralled into the rue Cambon section.

At the Place Vendôme entrance, Yvette hesitated. Should she take the parcel up to mademoiselle's suite herself? That was what the *vendeuses* usually did.

Always make the bold choice, as Madame LaRoq would say. She would walk in by the front entrance and up the grand staircase as if she had every right to be there. If anyone questioned her, she need only name her client and show the box from Lelong.

She propped her bicycle against the wrought iron gate that opened onto the colonnade outside the hotel. She explained her mission to the doorman, pointedly ignoring the German soldiers who stood sentry at the door. Of course, given the occupants of the hotel, security was tight.

The doorman waved her in, but one of the soldiers held out his hand for her to halt.

Stomach tightening with apprehension despite her innocence, Yvette froze, gripping the package from Lelong as if it would protect her. Trying to appear confident, she said, "I have to deliver this package to Mademoiselle Louise Dulac. It is most urgent."

Did they even understand French? Well, at the least they recognized the screen idol's name. There was a widening of the eyes, a sideways glance, and a smirk, hastily repressed. Yvette's tension eased a little. These men were not much older than she was. They were not to be feared. She *refused* to fear them.

One soldier, the blond, gestured to the box. "Open it." He spoke in French.

"Are you crazy?" she said. "What do you think will happen if you rummage about in a parcel belonging to the special friend of Oberst Gruber?"

With a lift of one eyebrow, as if he didn't quite believe her, he took the box and turned it over.

"May I have your names and ranks?" Yvette lifted her eyebrows, imitating Madame Péthier at her most supercilious.

The blond openly laughed at her. He tilted his head and said something in German to the other soldier. The gazes of both men wandered over her body, and it felt as if their hands crawled over her bare skin.

Her stomach flipped over, but she made herself be calm. There wasn't much they could do to her at the entrance of a luxury hotel. Flushing, she made herself go on. "I want your names so that I can tell Oberst Gruber who ruined this very expensive garment mademoiselle was to wear to the reception tonight."

That brought the blond's attention back to her face. He said something to the other soldier, weighing the package in his hands, then he gave it back to her. "On your way, mademoiselle."

Nerves jangling with relief and a strange exhilaration, Yvette continued into the grand hotel. A small victory, true, but a satisfying one.

The foyer was light and airy, with high ceilings supported by marble columns and the most breathtaking chandeliers Yvette had ever seen. Here and there, the floor was strewn with rugs that looked plush and priceless, and the furnishings made her think of a palace, rather than a hotel. But then her only experience with hotels had been at a very shabby bed-and-breakfast in London, when the family had visited cousins there before her father died.

Were it not for the concierge desk by the staircase, she might well have imagined herself in the midst of a fairy tale. A lady dripping in diamonds arrived with a small dog tucked under her arm and the most preposterous hat Yvette had ever seen. As she brushed past Yvette, the little dog snapped and Yvette jumped back with a gasp, nearly dropping her parcel.

Feeling foolish and exposed, she followed the woman with her dog. The distance to the grand staircase and up to the second floor seemed endless. She was certain every eye must be upon her, cataloging each shabby detail of her appearance: her windblown hair, the many darns she had made to her blouse, the seat of her skirt, which was shinier than the rest due to the rub of the bicycle on her behind.

She ran that gauntlet, only to be leered at by the elevator boy as he took her up to mademoiselle's floor. Yvette shifted as far away from him as she could in the small space.

The elevator hit the correct floor, and the boy opened the door with one hand and pinched her backside with the other as she walked past him. Ugh. She wanted to lift up her parcel and beat him over the head with it. She would have done it, too, if she hadn't felt an obligation not to disgrace the House of Lelong. More dignified to ignore it and be on her way.

A gaunt, sour-looking maid with her blond hair braided around her ears opened the door to Dulac's suite. She spat out something in German and made as if to snatch the parcel. But now that she was there, Yvette did not mean to give up her delivery before she set eyes on the movie star.

"Excuse me, but I am to make sure everything is to mademoiselle's satisfaction before I leave."

The maid eyed her suspiciously and seemed about to refuse her entry, when a voice behind her said, "Let her come in."

Chapter Six

Paris, June 1944

YVETTE

The voice that instructed the maid to admit Yvette was cool, husky, and bored. She repeated the command in German.

With a sniff, the maid stepped aside. Suppressing her excitement, Yvette walked into the sumptuous suite. She had an impression of opulence such as one might find in the home of a prince: paintings and gilded mirrors and richly upholstered Louis XVI furnishings. But there was a light and airy ambience, perhaps lent by the color scheme of lemon and cream and pale blue, and by the breeze that flirted with the muslin curtains at the long window—as if even the weather catered to the comfort of patrons of the Ritz.

But all of it faded to a mere stage set in the presence of the woman standing before her. Dulac was tall, slender, and full breasted, with the palest white skin and waving platinum hair.

Her lips and fingernails were painted scarlet. Her eyes were silvery grey and heavily lashed. She was dressed in a column of pure white, a color no ordinary woman chose in these hard times because it showed every bit of wear. The movie star's ensemble was, of course, immaculate. Dior's white cape, embroidered all over with seed pearls and crystals, would set the seal on her magnificence.

Dulac's gaze flickered over Yvette, reminding her of every frayed seam and scuff. She hardly looked like a true representative of a famous couturier. Not that any of his employees could afford to wear Lelong's creations, but still . . .

Well, at least I came by my clothes honestly. Yvette returned the other woman's stare. Had she sought favors from the occupiers, perhaps she might dress in Lelong and live at the Ritz, too.

"You are extremely pretty," Mademoiselle Dulac said finally.

That was the last thing Yvette had expected. She made a strangled sound in the back of her throat. Not knowing how to respond, she muttered, "Thank you, mademoiselle."

The movie star gestured to the Lelong box. "Is that for me?"

"Oh! Yes. I beg your pardon." Yvette placed the box on the sideboard, lifted the lid, and peeled back the tissue that wrapped the garment. She stepped back to let the other woman see.

Dulac's eyes widened and a smile of genuine, blinding delight broke over her face. "Ah, it is superb. Help me, will you?"

Yvette took out the white cotton gloves she kept in her pocket and put them on. She often helped with fittings, so she knew what to do. The cape should be straightforward, at any rate.

Carefully, she lifted the garment from its wrappings and turned, to find that mademoiselle had opened the door to her bedroom and gone in.

Yvette supposed she was to follow. She carried the cape, heavy with beading, glittering like ice crystals in her hands. The actress stood in front of a full-length mirror while Yvette settled the cape around her. "Mmm." She raised her shoulders and closed her eyes. "It's like being wrapped in a cool cloud."

"The lining is silk." Tentatively, Yvette indicated the wide satin and velvet ribbons that dangled loosely past Dulac's bosom. "If you will permit?"

Dulac nodded.

Hardly daring to breathe, Yvette came around to stand between the actress and the mirror and tied the ribbons in a lopsided, artless, yet perfect bow, just the way Monsieur Dior did it—or at least, she hoped so. As she worked, she smelled something sweet and alcoholic, spiked with peppermint, on Dulac's breath. Was mademoiselle drinking and trying to mask the evidence? Did her conscience torment her? *No.* Her imagination was running away with her.

Yvette looked up and Dulac's gaze seemed to pin her in place. It was a disconcerting feeling. There was something there. Some message in those silvery eyes. Or again, did she imagine it? Jean-Luc always said she was an idealist, wanting to believe people had hidden depths when they were all as shallow and venal as anyone else. He'd be disgusted to see her falling under Dulac's spell.

Yvette stepped out of the way so that the film star could see herself in the mirror.

Louise touched the bow lightly with a flash of painted red nails. "But this is charming." She turned side-on to survey her profile and Yvette gasped as she caught a glimpse of another figure in the reflection. A large, stocky man stood framed in the doorway behind them. He wore civilian clothing, but Yvette knew who he was. Oberst Gruber. A colonel in the German air force.

He was of above-average height, fit looking, with thin lips and a high forehead and cheekbones. He was not the typical Aryan in coloring, being dark haired and almost swarthy in complexion. Perhaps that was why he'd chosen a blond goddess for a mistress.

At the Ritz, it was the rule that German officers did not wear their uniforms in the public areas. Had she not known this man to be cruel, sadistic, and callous—after all, he would not have risen so high in rank if he were not—would she have sensed the evil behind those dark eyes all the same?

Dulac turned, her smile as brilliant as a diamond, and in some way, hard like a diamond as well. In a low, breathy voice unlike the one she'd used with Yvette, she murmured something in German.

She moved to Gruber and held out her hand. He clasped her fingers, turned her palm upward, and kissed her wrist. Bile rose to Yvette's throat. How could she?

Louise's gaze met Yvette's, then flicked to the door. That was her cue. Yvette sidled out of the room and left them to it.

In the elevator, the same smarmy youth who had pinched her bottom smirked as she got in.

"If you touch me again, I will hurt you," she said, calmly and clearly, before stepping in.

"Hold the door." A tall man entered the elevator, his broad shoulders seeming to occupy most of the available space. He looked between Yvette and the youth she had just threatened but said nothing.

Yvette stole a sidelong glance at the newcomer. He was young and dark and very good-looking. She didn't dare turn to peer directly up into his face. When they alighted, she made herself stare straight ahead but sensed his large masculine presence keeping pace with her.

As they approached the front entrance, the man said to her, "Was that lad in the elevator bothering you, mademoiselle? I could have a word with management." He spoke impeccable French with a Parisian accent.

Now that he addressed her, she had an excuse to pause and look directly into his face. He was a handsome devil, she'd been right about that, no more than midtwenties, at a guess. But what was a young, able-bodied Frenchman doing at the Ritz? A collaborator, perhaps? What a pity that would be.

"Thank you, but it is nothing, monsieur."

"If you say so," he replied, indicating that she should precede him out of the hotel.

In the arcade outside, Yvette stopped short. Where was her bicycle? It was not by the wrought iron gates where she'd left it. "No, no, no," she muttered. She looked up and down the arcade, then out to the square, but the bicycle was not there.

Someone must have stolen it. She cried out in dismay.

"What is it?" Again, the man from the elevator. "What's wrong?" When she didn't answer, he prompted, "Mademoiselle?"

There was a note of command in his voice that made her give the stranger her attention. "Someone has taken my bicycle." Her voice shook. She was trying very hard not to give way to panic.

The man frowned. "Are you certain this is where you left it?"

"Of course." She hurried back to the doorman. "Excuse me, sir. Did you perhaps move my bicycle?"

"No, mademoiselle."

"Did you see anyone move it or take it?"

He shook his head. "I've been busy."

Yvette put a hand up to her temple. "I can't believe it. It's been stolen right outside the Ritz!"

She went out onto the square, scanning the Place Vendôme, but it was hopeless. Her bicycle with its distinctive basket, all threaded through with scraps from the workroom floors, was nowhere to be seen.

Despair yawned inside her. That bicycle was her work, her independence, her freedom. All gone! A secondhand one would cost more than a month's salary. She could never afford that. She would be dismissed from Lelong. She would have to stay at the apartments and fetch and carry for Gabby and Maman.

A sleek black automobile of a make she did not recognize pulled up at the curb and a driver got out. The stranger glanced at the car and said, "If you'll permit, I'd like to help." He paused. "I know where you can get a bicycle."

Hope lifted her chest, just for a moment, then deflated like a fallen soufflé. "Thank you, monsieur. That is kind, but I cannot afford it."

"Never mind about that." He waved a hand, a gold cuff link flashing. "The owner of the bicycle owes me a favor."

As simple as that? It must be nice to be rich and have men owe you such large favors. Yvette eyed the stranger, her native wariness nagging at her. "But why should you help me?"

He shrugged. "I don't know. Boredom, perhaps."

Boredom? In this war? She studied him intently. He had a slight golden tan to his skin, the kind rich people acquired on Swiss ski slopes. Beneath a pair of high cheekbones, laughter lines bracketed his lips. One might have written him off as exactly the kind of European playboy his fine suit and manner suggested, except for one thing. His dark eyes were perceptive and kind, and shadowed by something . . . Suffering? Loss? Something that made Yvette want almost desperately to delve into his thoughts, into his past, attempt to erase the pain she saw there.

His height and his broad shoulders might, in other circumstances, have been intimidating. And yet he was offering to give her something vital to her well-being. She sensed that whatever else he might do in this war, in this moment, she could trust him.

She tilted her head. "I don't even know your name."

He grinned. "I'm a diplomat. Swedish legation. Vidar Lind, at your service."

He didn't look Swedish. Weren't all Swedes blond? "Staying at the Ritz?" she said doubtfully. Half the hotel was occupied by Nazis, the rest by displaced foreign royalty, collaborators, and spies. She had heard that most diplomats were spies, so that seemed to fit.

"Just visiting, I'm afraid." He indicated his motorcar. "Will you trust me? I promise you won't come to any harm."

Yvette bit her lip. She wanted to see this place where it was possible to get bicycles at a moment's notice. And it seemed churlish to refuse when he was doing her such an enormous favor. Undoubtedly, she would be reckless to go anywhere in a motorcar with a strange man. But then she saw that his driver was not a man in chauffeur's livery, after all, but a competent-looking woman dressed in a neat grey suit. Women were capable of evil, it was true, but Yvette really needed that bicycle, and the presence of a female was sufficient reassurance to take the risk.

"Why don't you wait here, then," said Vidar Lind. "I'll bring the bicycle back to you."

"No. Thank you, monsieur. I'll come."

He held the door open for her to slide into the backseat, got in next to her, and gave instructions to the driver. Then they were off, cruising through the streets of Paris.

Yvette tried to appear relaxed. "I have not ridden in a motorcar for a long time." She was still alert for any indication that Lind had plans for her that he had not yet disclosed, but although he smiled at her attempt at small talk, he made no answer. Instead, he lifted an attaché case from the footwell and laid it on his lap. Flicking it open, he sifted through the papers inside it, then began to read one, his concentration absolute.

She took the opportunity his distraction provided to peer covertly at what he was reading. One never knew; it might be important. But the document was in English, so she gained little from her snooping except a word here and there. She could speak English passably well. Reading what appeared to be quite a technical report was another thing altogether.

She decided on the direct approach. "What are you reading, monsieur?"

"Something terrifically dull, I assure you, but rather pressing, nonetheless. But never mind that," he added, slipping the document back into his case, snapping it shut. "This won't take long."

They had stopped at a brasserie on the rue de la Pompe, practically in the shadow of the Arc de Triomphe, a monument the Nazis had gleefully spiked with the swastika as soon as they'd stormed into the capital. Yvette couldn't look at those flags without a shiver of hatred and fear.

As his driver opened the door for him, Vidar said to Yvette, "Wait here." She would have argued, but he was gone on the words. The soft thump of the door closing punctuated his command.

She wanted to know more about the transaction this Vidar Lind was making on her behalf. A restaurant full of German soldiers seemed an unlikely place to obtain a bicycle. Perhaps someone here was an agent for the black market, like the local bookseller, Monsieur Arnaud. But then, Monsieur Arnaud could never have laid hands on something as significant and valuable as a bicycle. A little cheese here, a little soap there, that was more monsieur's level.

"Do you know whom he is going to see?" she asked the driver, who had reached into the glove box to retrieve a packet of Gauloises.

The driver held it out to Yvette. "Smoke?"

Clearly, she wasn't going to answer Yvette's question. "No, thank you."

The woman shrugged, as if to say, *Suit yourself,* and got out of the car. Yvette bent her head to watch through the window as the driver leaned against the car door, facing away from the brasserie as she lit her cigarette.

Now was Yvette's chance. Quietly, she opened the opposite door and slipped out onto the pavement. With a quick glance at the oblivious driver, Yvette headed for the alley down which Vidar Lind had disappeared shortly before.

The narrow space, enclosed by brick walls, was dingy and smelled of urine and rotting food. Yvette's heart beat hard, even though it was broad daylight.

She didn't enter the alley—she might as well admit to herself that she was too afraid—but she watched for some minutes before what appeared to be the door to a garage opened with a clatter and Vidar Lind emerged from it, wheeling a bicycle.

He stopped short when he saw her, throwing a quick glance over his shoulder. "I told you to stay in the car." He jerked his head. "Come on. You can't be seen here."

But her attention was fixed on the bicycle. It was a little large for her but it looked brand-new. Hardly able to believe he had so quickly and easily solved her problem, she trailed after Vidar Lind as he wheeled the bicycle out onto the pavement.

No. These things did not simply happen. Particularly not in wartime. There must be a catch.

As they approached the motorcar, Lind's driver threw down her cigarette and stubbed it out, coming around to open the car door for him. It was odd, that reversal of roles, and Yvette stared at the woman curiously, but she seemed to think nothing of it.

Lind was still frowning, as if Yvette's attempt to follow had seriously disturbed him.

She said, "I'm sorry for disobeying you, but it's because I wanted to know . . ." She swallowed. "Did this bicycle come from the black market?"

He gazed down at her and began to open his mouth, but she blurted out, "Please. I-I can live with not having a bicycle, but I could not bear it if it turned out that this one came from someone . . ." From a Jewish person, she wanted to say. Or a dissident, someone the Nazis had sent to the camps. She was plaiting her fingers together, trying to think of a way to phrase it without insulting her benefactor.

Instead of being affronted, he smiled faintly. "You are concerned that this is confiscated property? Don't be. I give you my word on that."

Perhaps she was wrong to trust the sincerity in those compelling dark eyes, but she believed him.

He had done this incredible thing for her, and now they would part ways. The entire exercise had taken less than half an hour and yet she felt as if she'd known him longer. Reluctant to accept that they might never meet again, she said, "I don't quite know how to thank you."

An expression she couldn't identify crossed his face. "There is no need, mademoiselle."

They stared at each other and the silence stretched too long. Yvette cleared her throat. "I must be going," she said, conscious that they were standing like statues on the busy pavement with people jostling to get past and his driver looking on. "Thank you for helping me." She wheeled her new bicycle about. *"Au revoir, monsieur."*

"Wait." His hand gripped hers, trapping it around the handlebar, and she felt a strong jolt, like electricity, shoot through her. She stopped and looked up at him.

He was intent now. "How old are you, mademoiselle?"

"Nineteen. Why? I'm almost twenty."

His eyebrows rose. *"Almost twenty?"* He gave an odd, harsh laugh and stepped back, as if to dismiss a notion that had occurred to him, and it felt like a loss when the warmth of his hand left hers.

"So?" she demanded as he busied himself lighting a cigarette. "You are, what, twenty-five? You are not so much older than I am."

"Twenty-seven, but close," he admitted, glancing around, then turning his focus back on Yvette. The hand that held his cigarette moved restlessly, then he rubbed his chin with his thumb and sighed. "Perhaps we will meet again, mademoiselle. When you return to the Ritz someday."

She shrugged and tried to match his sangfroid. "Perhaps. It is true that I am often there."

One side of his mouth quirked up and he gave a slight nod, as if he read her all too easily beneath the pretense of sophistication. "Goodbye, mademoiselle. Keep that bicycle safe."

Chapter Seven

Paris, June 1944

GABBY

Catherine's visitors would come tonight. If only Gabby's duties occupied her thoughts as well as her hands. She'd been going over and over what Catherine Dior had said to her that morning. Visitors after curfew. Visitors Catherine did not wish anyone to know about. Worries revolved around Gabby's mind. The danger to her mother, to Yvette. The Gestapo. The last thing they needed was a raid on number 10 rue Royale.

All Gabby had to do tonight was to turn a blind eye. She might well have slept through it anyway, if Catherine hadn't warned her. If only she had remained in blissful ignorance! In the politest way imaginable, Catherine had thrust this complicity upon her. And Gabby, always desperate to please, had been too flustered and flattered to say no.

The night was silent and moonless, so that was a relief. Gabby lay beside her sleeping sister and listened intently for a telltale sound. The tick of the mantel clock and her mother's snores were all she gleaned from the deep darkness of the blackout.

She was beyond tired, and only wished she could forget about Catherine and go to sleep. She'd been tempted to accept the glass of black-market calvados Maman had offered her as a nightcap, but she needed all her wits about her in case something went wrong with Catherine Dior's mystery guest.

In bed next to her, Yvette sighed and rolled over in her sleep. Though grateful that her sister had been able to replace her stolen bicycle so quickly, Gabby was worried about the incident with this Swedish diplomat. Yvette was growing more beautiful every day, an exotic orchid flourishing among weeds, defying the lack of nourishment and attention that would have withered a lesser specimen.

If only she had more sense! Had she really come by her new bicycle in the manner she'd claimed? The story was so bizarre, Yvette couldn't have made it up. But why had that Swedish diplomat taken such an interest in her in the first place? Gabby didn't believe in altruism. Certainly not the altruism of strange young men.

However, she couldn't see a way to approach the subject with Yvette without making her storm off in a rage. And Yvette enraged did reckless things.

What was that? Her heart gave a sharp pound. There it was again. A faint scuffling outside.

The street door opened with a click and a long, thin creak. No voices. No footsteps. No other noise at all. Gabby got out of bed and crept through the small parlor to the window. Carefully, she eased the drapes open the merest fraction and pressed her eye to the gap. The street was bare. No one outside. No one to see the late arrival of a guest at number 10.

She resisted dashing to the other window, the one that gave onto the vestibule that led to the courtyard. The less she knew, the better. Catherine was right about that.

She listened. Had they removed their shoes? The apartment building was silent.

Gabby waited several more minutes, heart drumming, ears straining, but no other noise came.

Realizing she'd been holding her breath, she exhaled slowly. Catherine Dior had carried it off. Gabby rubbed her hands over her face, trembling with relief.

She lay in bed, staring at the ceiling. The incessant tick of the clock scraped her nerves. After what seemed like an eternity of wakefulness, she jerked out of a doze to see sunlight streaming through a crack in the drapes.

Yvette sat up, rubbing her eyes. "What time is it?"

Gabby looked at her watch. "You don't have to be up for another hour. Go back to sleep."

"I can't once I'm awake." With an energy Gabby heartily envied, Yvette leaped out of bed and padded over to the window to open the drapes. Golden light bathed their room.

"Sometimes I wake up and I forget," said Yvette as she looked out to the street. "Just for a second."

Gabby nodded. Occasionally, after a deep sleep, she woke disoriented, thinking she was free, that the war had never happened. She was young and life was full of possibility, and Didier was still with her. Then the truth would slam into her, flattening hope, dragging her under. Would there ever be an end to this war? And when there was an end, would France be free?

"I despise them," said Yvette in a small, hard voice, without turning around.

"The Boches?"

Yvette shook her head and began to dress. "Our soldiers. Our men. They were arrogant. They didn't train properly, they didn't prepare to fight, they gave up before the battle began. And I have done nothing to fight the Boches, either. I am just as bad."

Gabby closed her eyes. She didn't want to hear it. Didier had fought and died for France. For nothing. She could not lose her sister, too. Gabby had learned not to argue when Yvette was in this mood, however. She threw back the coverlet and got out of bed, padding out to the kitchen to boil water for a tisane while Yvette dressed for work.

When her sister had gone, Gabby dressed slowly and tied a scarf, turban-style, over her hair, then went to the kitchenette to prepare a little meal for Madame LaRoq. She sliced off a piece of bread that probably owed much of its structure to sawdust and added a tiny scrape of precious butter, courtesy of Monsieur Arnaud. She poured the tisane into two cups and arranged them with the plate of bread on a tray to take to madame.

In the courtyard, she stopped short, observing with a dull sense of the inevitable that while she had been too scared to look out the window of her apartment, the vegetable thief had been at work once more. Dirt was scattered all around the flower beds. The few shoots that had remained after the last raid were gone. So that was that. She would clean it up later.

As she moved down the corridor, she thought she heard the rumble of a masculine voice coming from madame's room. Hurrying forward, she pressed her ear to the door but heard nothing more. Perhaps she'd imagined it, or perhaps it had come from the next apartment. Monsieur Dior, maybe? But monsieur's voice was a light tenor, not nearly so deep.

She knocked. "Madame LaRoq? It is me, Gabby." She was much earlier than usual. She had not thought to check the time before she came up.

Silence. Then a thud and a scraping sound.

A long pause. "Enter."

Gabby balanced her tray on one arm, unlocked the door, and went in, half-expecting to see that madame had company. But there was no one. She went through to the older lady's bedroom and laid the tray on the dresser. "Is everything well, madame? Is someone here?"

"Not a soul but the two of us." Madame's voice was even, but her eyes were bright.

Gabby handed madame her tisane, then took her own cup and sat in the easy chair near the bed. The two of them sipped in silence, then Gabby said, "I could have sworn I heard a man's voice in your room." She chuckled in what she hoped was a convincing manner. "You're not stashing a secret lover in here somewhere, are you?"

"If only I were." Madame shrugged, lifted her gaze to the ceiling, and laughed. "What fun I had when I was your age. My mother was aghast."

That brought to mind Yvette's strange encounter with the Swedish diplomat. She related the story and madame's eyes sparked with interest. "A Swede, you say? Staying at the Ritz."

"That's right," said Gabby. She wrinkled her brow. "Actually, I'm not sure if he was staying there. It's where she met him, at least."

"Did Yvette get his name?"

"It was something-or-other Lind, I believe. Why do you ask?"

Madame tilted her head, her eyes tracking back and forth, as if she were sifting through information in her mind. "Oh, no reason. I must tease her about it when I see her. But I know she is busy and works so hard. Please pass on my love."

The tone of this speech and the nod that accompanied it indicated dismissal. A little disappointed to have her visit cut short, Gabby collected their cups and got up to go. Madame had not touched the bread and butter, so she left that on the bedside table.

Outside the apartment, Gabby nearly collided with Catherine Dior, who approached from the other direction with a plate of her own. It was covered with a cloth and Gabby wondered what delights lay beneath. She was sure it would cast her meager slice of bread and butter into the shade. Not that she begrudged madame anything. She simply wished she could do more.

"Good morning, Gabby," said Catherine. Her smile was a little strained. "You are early on your rounds this morning."

Gabby nodded, watching Catherine carefully. "I am ahead of myself today."

Catherine's glance darted to the door. "Is everything . . . Is she well?"

"As well as she ever is, I believe," said Gabby. "Madame never complains. Actually, she seemed very bright just now. Almost as if she's had exciting news."

"Well, wouldn't that be nice?" said Catherine. "There is so much bad news, these days."

She seemed to be waiting for something. "Oh, would you like me to let you in?" Gabby felt in her pocket for her keys.

"That is quite all right," said Catherine. "I have a key to madame's apartment, too. See?"

Gabby stared at the key in Catherine's hand, surprised. Then she said, "Of course." Lowering her gaze, she went on her way.

But when she heard the door close behind Catherine, she crept back down the corridor and put her ear to the door. She hated herself for acting like a typical nosy concierge, but something wasn't quite right about madame that morning and Catherine was hiding something, too. Surely, Catherine wouldn't embroil madame in her resistance work?

Gabby didn't hear a masculine voice as she'd half-expected after the mutterings she'd caught earlier. But she did catch Catherine Dior's pleasant tones. The words were enunciated quite clearly, even though she said them in a low voice.

"How are you feeling today?"

Gabby frowned. Not because of the words themselves. It must have been the most common question Madame LaRoq was asked. But why had Catherine spoken in English?

GABBY TOOK A dustpan and broom out to the courtyard to clean up the mess the vegetable thief had made. She set down the dustpan on the raised edge of the flower bed and began to sweep. First Yvette and her communists; then the man who had given her sister a bicycle and might want something in return; now Catherine Dior's secretive behavior, perhaps involving Madame LaRoq in her activities . . .

Even she, Gabby Foucher, the most cautious person in the world, had agreed to turn a blind eye to whatever Catherine Dior was doing in these apartments at night.

All she wanted was a peaceful life. Her mouth twisted. *Peace!* What a stupid thing to wish for in wartime. And yet, after the shock of Didier's death, she had managed to get through the occupation without any major disasters. Now it seemed danger lurked in every corner.

One thing was certain: She was not going along with any more of Catherine's schemes, even passively. She would simply tell her she did not want to know.

As if the thought had conjured the woman herself, Catherine Dior emerged from the east wing and hurried across the courtyard toward Gabby, a pretty blue scarf flattering beside her cheek.

Catherine stopped, eyeing the dirt and debris. "What's all this, Gabby? As if you don't have enough work to do."

Gabby tried to brush off her concern. "It is nothing, mademoiselle," she said in a formal, distant tone that made Catherine's fine eyebrows draw together.

Catherine tilted her head and fixed Gabby with an intent, searching stare. "What is the matter, my dear? You do not seem to be quite yourself today. Has something happened?" Catherine glanced about them and lowered her voice. "If it's about last night . . ."

Gabby shook her head. "It's not that." She wanted desperately to tell Catherine that she could no longer take any part in her schemes. But when it came to the point, she could not bring herself to speak her mind to this woman she had always admired, who was clearly working for France in some secret capacity. Doing something noble and right.

"Pardon, mademoiselle," mumbled Gabby. "It is a family problem. I cannot talk about it."

Catherine's shoulders eased and she exhaled a long, slow breath. *Relieved,* Gabby thought. *She is relieved that I am not going to report her, that my troubles are all my own.*

Ah, but she was being unfair, since Catherine knew nothing of Gabby's troubles, save those Catherine herself had created. Still, there was the matter of madame. "I hope Madame LaRoq is safe. I would not want her to be . . . involved."

"Madame knows what she is about." Catherine hesitated, catching her bottom lip between her teeth. "However, it might be best if you only visit her at set times each day."

"If you say so," said Gabby, unable to hide her annoyance that Catherine should dictate to her when she saw the woman who had been like a grandmother to her all these years. But clearly, something secret was going on in that apartment, and hadn't Gabby just moments before vowed not to have anything more to do with risky undertakings? She ought to be pleased. She set her jaw. "I will visit madame each day at nine o'clock, and at midday, and again at six."

Their gazes locked and Gabby sensed the steel in the other woman, her grim determination. She could not help but admire it and long for some steel of her own.

Catherine gave a curt nod, as if to accept a tacit rebuff. "Very well, my dear."

There was a long pause and Gabby lowered her gaze, feeling herself redden under Catherine's scrutiny. Something shifted then, and with a long sigh, Catherine put out her hand to grip Gabby's arm—a bracing hold, yet a comforting one.

Gabby's gaze met Catherine's and she wondered at the warmth and compassion she saw in her face. Catherine said, "I hope that whatever family matter is troubling you may be resolved. Let me know if I can help, won't you?"

Feeling petty and small, Gabby managed a nod and a whispered *Thank you*, and turned back to her sweeping once more.

YVETTE

When Yvette returned to the *loge* that evening, her sister greeted her with a chore.

"Oh, good. You're here. Will you watch the door for me?" Gabby collected her tray from the kitchenette and headed for the door.

Yvette sighed. For pity's sake, she had only just walked in! Pointedly, she said, "Good evening, Yvette, and how are you after your long day at work?"

But clearly, Gabby was in no mood for banter. "Maman is lying down and I have to check on Madame LaRoq and do my evening rounds."

"Let me check on madame," Yvette said. "I haven't visited her this week."

"No, I need to see her," said Gabby quickly, whisking herself out the door before Yvette could argue further.

With a shrug, Yvette went to sit by the window, tucked her legs beneath her, and settled in to watch the passersby.

It was too early for the usual clientele to arrive at Maxim's restaurant a little way down the street, but she had often sat at this window before, watching the parade of well-dressed guests go by. She'd dreamed of dining at Maxim's herself one night, wearing a gown designed by Monsieur Dior, with diamonds glittering around her throat. Now she found herself imagining an evening there, escorted by a tall, handsome man with dark, world-weary eyes . . .

The buzzer broke her reverie and she saw Liliane Dietlin pressing the bell to number 10. Jumping up, Yvette released the street door and went out to greet her.

"Good evening, mademoiselle." Yvette indicated the parcels Liliane carried. "May I help you with those?"

"That is kind." Liliane handed her a shopping bag and Yvette followed the other woman up to Monsieur Dior's apartment.

It was Catherine who opened the door. Sabine must have the evening off.

Mademoiselle Dior seemed to have been expecting Liliane. She handed her a liqueur glass of amethyst liquid as soon as the other woman put down her parcels on the console by the door. Yvette set the shopping bag next to the parcels, then hovered in the background, wanting to say hello to Catherine but unsure of her welcome.

"Thank you. I needed this," said Liliane, taking the liqueur. She did not sit but downed the drink in one gulp. Her hand trembled as she gave back her glass. Silently, Catherine poured another.

"Will you join us, Yvette?" said Catherine, lifting the decanter in offering.

"Me?" Yvette retreated toward the door. "Oh, no, thank you. I shouldn't. I need to get back."

She wasn't sure why she was suddenly so shy. Not just shy but apprehensive. Maybe it was the look on Catherine's face, a press of the lips and a slight dent between her eyebrows, as if she was reluctant but determined to carry out an unpleasant task. A task that seemed to have something to do with Yvette.

"I think the door can wait awhile," said Catherine. "Your mother will hear anyone wanting admittance, will she not?"

Yvette didn't answer. What could she say? That Maman would slumber through a herd of elephants breaking down the door?

"We have a very important question for you," said Liliane. She took a deep breath. "We want you to do a small errand for us."

"No. Stop." Catherine pressed her fingertips to her temple, as if to try to clear her thoughts. "I think we must not do this."

"You know it is the only choice we have," argued Liliane. "It has to be tomorrow. And there is no one else."

Catherine said, "They are not watching me. I can go. It is not right to ask Yvette. I won't do it."

"Don't be a fool, my dear," countered Liliane, her voice gentle but firm. She gestured toward Yvette. "You know she is the perfect choice. Yvette is on her bicycle making deliveries every day for the House of Lelong. She knows Paris. She is smart and capable and she can ferry messages to and fro without raising suspicion. She has the perfect cover."

Catherine sliced the air with her hand, as if to cut off the conversation. "No. It is not right. She is too young."

Yvette looked from one woman to the other as they argued back and forth. What was this? Were they actually talking about her joining the resistance? If what Yvette suspected from their conversation turned out to be correct, she was going to play her part in the liberation of France. That would be worth any risk.

"I will do it," Yvette said, making both women's heads snap around to look at her. "I am ready." She had been ready to do something important and dangerous for her country since the beginning of the occupation. How wonderful that there were brave women doing important and dangerous things right under her nose and she had never even suspected it.

"I want to help," Yvette said. "Please. Use me."

Catherine gazed at her for a long time. "Gabby will never forgive me," she murmured.

"It is my life, not Gabby's," Yvette said. "I am not a child." What a childish thing to say! As soon as the words were out of her mouth, she could have cut her tongue out.

Catherine gave a short, broken laugh, making Yvette flush hotly, but the older woman sobered again almost at once. What had happened to make her so upset and afraid?

Catherine shot a glance at Liliane. "Don't you see? She *is* a child at heart. You cannot ask it of her."

Liliane's beautiful face hardened. "There are boys fighting in the trenches who are years younger than she is."

"Tell me what to do," Yvette begged, "and I will do it."

Liliane took her hand and drew her to sit beside her on the sofa. "Tomorrow, when you are on your rounds, cycle past Monsieur Arnaud's bookshop—you know the one?"

"Of course."

"Good," said Liliane. "If you see a potted geranium in the window, go inside and ask monsieur for a book on birds."

She waited, searching Yvette's face to see if she comprehended. Yvette gave a slight nod.

Liliane's shoulders relaxed slightly. "Monsieur will give you the bird book and you will then take that book to this address." She rattled off an address in the eighth arrondissement and added, "Memorize it. Do not write it down. Do not tell anyone where you're going, or look behind you, or cycle too quickly, or do anything that could arouse suspicion. For you, it is a day like any other and you are simply making your rounds."

"Yvette, know this." Catherine leaned forward in her chair and fixed Yvette with her gaze. "The message you will carry is for the resistance. If you're caught, we cannot help you. No one can. Think very carefully before you agree to take this on, my dear."

To be caught by the Gestapo would be the most terrifying thing imaginable. But what about the brave young men who fought and died for the Allies, the men and women of the resistance who risked their lives every day? For years, she had fretted and fumed at her helplessness, longing to make a contribution beyond distributing the communist leaflets Jean-Luc gave her. She could not fail to act now that she had the chance.

Besides, she was quick and nimble and good at talking her way out of difficulties. And who would suspect her? What was one more delivery among so many? Liliane was clever to think of using her.

"I'll do it," she said quietly. "I understand the risk." She held Catherine's gaze, trying to convince her without words that she accepted the gravity of her position. "I would never betray you," she promised them both. "I will not even tell Gabby or Maman."

Liliane nodded, clearly satisfied. She believed Yvette. She believed *in* her, which was even more important.

Catherine still seemed uncertain. She muttered under her breath, "It has come to this. We are using children to do our work."

Yvette wanted to protest again that she was nearly twenty years old but stopped herself. She lifted her chin, waiting for Catherine's final verdict. Any more pleading on her part would probably hurt her chances.

The silence wore on, and Catherine sipped her apéritif and gazed out of the window, her troubled thoughts making creases on her brow.

Unable to stand the suspense, Yvette blurted out, "I know enough now to get me into trouble. I know about the two of you. Why not trust me further with this message?" She licked her lips. "Besides, it sounds as if you have little choice but to use me."

The women looked at each other. Catherine said, "The reason

we need you, Yvette, is that the last courier we used is dead." The sentence came out baldly. If it was intended to shock, it worked. All the oxygen left the room. Yvette couldn't catch her breath.

"She was tortured before she died," Catherine added.

Yvette felt sick and hollow, as if she'd been punched in the stomach. She had not been treating this as a fictional adventure. She knew that she would be taking a risk, but Catherine's words brought the danger sharply home.

Did she really want to do this? She could still back out. Her pride might be hurt, but at least she would be alive.

But the very fact that they lived under a regime that would torture and execute people like this courier meant that she, Yvette Foucher, must stand up and fight, whatever the cost.

"Geranium in the window. Book on birds." She recited the address Liliane had given her. She pictured the Paris map in her mind and the route she would take to get there, then back to Lelong. Or better yet . . . "I will make a few deliveries in between, before I deliver the book. That way, if anyone is watching the bookstore they will not see me go straight from there to the destination you gave me."

Liliane nodded approval. "Yes, that is a very good idea, Yvette. But do not hold the book for too long. If you are found with it, that is reason enough for them to arrest you." She smiled. "Thank you for doing this, my dear. And good luck."

Yvette got up to go before Catherine could raise more objections.

Liliane stood, too. With a worried glance at her friend, she tucked her hand in the crook of Yvette's arm and went with her to the door. In a lowered tone she said, "Leave Catherine to me. I will persuade her. If you do well with this, there will be more work for you."

Yvette left the Dior apartment with her head spinning. It wasn't until she got back to the *loge*, to be scolded by Gabby for her neglect of the front door, that she was yanked back to the present. With that, the realization hit her anew. Finally, *finally*, she was working for the resistance. At last, she would be doing something to make a difference in this war.

Chapter Eight

Paris, February 1947

YVETTE

She had thought about him so often in the years since she'd left Paris, it was as if a figment of her imagination had turned to flesh. He must have picked the lock of her suite. Either that, or convinced one of the maids to admit him. He could be very persuasive.

All the fatigue and aches of the long day disappeared in a rush of adrenaline. The cool metal edge of the room key dug into her palm. She should unlock the door, get out and run.

How had he found her so quickly? Did he have an informant among Dulac's defense team? But if her lawyers could have called him as a witness, why would they need Yvette?

A hundred thoughts chased through her mind in those few

seconds of silence. Images of their shared past flashed before her eyes like the numbers flicking at the end of a newsreel.

How could he be in Paris like this? Surely, it was dangerous.

"Yvette." Her name, spoken in that low rasp of his, made the hairs stand up on the back of her neck.

"*Don't.*"

He was dressed in white tie, which might have made him stand out in another milieu, but at the Ritz at this hour, it was practically a uniform. Was he staying in the hotel as well? Yvette shivered, then began to tremble.

Perhaps he was here to silence her. But then she'd be dead already. She swallowed hard, struggled to find her voice. "What do you want?"

He hesitated. Then he spread his hands, palms up. "I need your help, Yvette."

She laughed, a pathetic sound that scraped her throat. "Do you know how crazy that is? I am the last person you should turn to."

His straight black eyebrows drew together, as if he were genuinely puzzled. "Believe me, you and I are not enemies. We never were."

She made no reply, simply waited. She wanted to hear this. She wanted to know how he could justify what he'd done. Perhaps he would sing the same tune as those unrepentant Nazis at Nuremberg: They were under orders. They weren't aware of what was happening in the death camps of Ravensbrück and Auschwitz and the rest.

He did not elaborate. Perhaps he needed goading. "I was right all along. The only good Nazi is a dead one."

His nostrils flared. "I am *not* a Nazi." Another lie. He had pretended to be a Swedish diplomat by the name of Vidar Lind. All the better to worm his way into the resistance networks, no doubt.

"I suppose that explains why you are still at large," she said. "Shall I call the *gendarmes* and tell them you are here? I doubt you have many friends left among the authorities in Paris."

"Yvette, listen. I need you to—"

"Why me?" She hated how weak that sounded, but she had to know. "I was young and stupid, of no possible use to you. Why spin me your lies?"

On the surface, he was so elegant and cool, black hair neatly trimmed, the set of his coat across those broad shoulders utter perfection, handsome features composed. But there was a banked fury in his eyes. She had touched a tender spot. Could she make that anger boil over if she needled him in the right place? Enough to tell her what had really happened, back in 1944?

He broke eye contact, flicked something from his sleeve. "You are here to testify in the trial of Louise Dulac." Back to business. Well, a man who consorted with Nazis and hardened criminals would not crack in the face of her abuse.

"How do you know that?"

He simply stared at her, as if expecting her to do the math. Her eyes widened. *He* was the man with deep pockets funding Dulac's defense—not to mention paying for Yvette's travel and accommodation at the Ritz. The idea was like a kick to the ribs.

"It is important in this case that certain things do not come to light," he said. "What do you intend to say about your involvement with her?"

"What is your real name?" she countered. If he would not answer her questions, she would not answer his.

He sighed. "Yvette." He had remained where he was by the window since her arrival, but now he moved toward her.

"Don't." She held out her hands to ward him off. "Don't come any closer."

He stopped. Then a gleam lit his eye and he started toward her again, until he stood close enough that she could reach out and touch him.

She didn't feel threatened—not physically. At least, not with violence. The threat of a different kind of contact made her blood race. "Why should I tell you anything?"

As he stared down at her with such intensity, she became acutely conscious of their surroundings. There was a bed only meters away, a couch even closer. A door at her back, if it came to that. Then he said, "Vidar Lind will do. Why complicate things?"

"Fine. Have it your way. Are you here to—what do you call it— tamper with the witness?"

There was a wry twist to his lips, perhaps acknowledging a double entendre she had not intended to make. "Only in one respect. You must not mention my involvement with Louise."

"Why would I?" She shrugged. "No doubt Dulac had many lovers."

There was a change in his expression, a mere flicker, but it was there. How to interpret it, she wasn't sure. In another man, she would have said it was surprise. Did he think she was an idiot? "Don't bother to deny it. She told me herself."

"And Louise Dulac always told you the truth."

That was a knife-thrust to the gut. "All right," she said in a low, shaking voice. "I was stupid. I was naïve. But at least I tried to do the right thing." *And how did that turn out, Yvette? What about Catherine Dior?* The space between them seemed to contract. Softly, she said,

"All those shades of grey, the compromises and accommodations, all that playing along and biding time." The words tasted bitter on her tongue. "At what point does it become collaboration? At what point treason? Do we judge by someone's actions or by their intentions?"

His jaw hardened. "Or do we judge them by the damage they've done?"

Her eyes burned with unshed tears. She was damned if she'd cry in front of him. "Get out." She fumbled with the key, turned to unlock the door. Opened it, flung it wide. "Get out or I'll scream for help."

He stared at her for a long, hot moment. Then he seemed to close in upon himself.

There was a pause, and perversely, she groped for something to say to open him up again, to make him stay.

Too late. He inclined his head. "It was good to see you again, Yvette."

Before she could find a response, he was gone.

GABBY

The fairy tale Gabby was writing had transformed into an adventure, taken on a life of its own. She couldn't move her pencil fast enough to get it all down. A little girl, spirited and brave, with an ability to talk her way into and out of trouble—one who looked suspiciously like Yvette as a six-year-old—is locked in the Louvre overnight. She discovers that when no one is there to see, all the artworks come to life.

Epic battles are waged, men and gods do amazing and terrible things. With the help of a boy from a Renoir painting, the little girl works her way to a basement vault, where her family treasure is hidden. She takes it and . . . Gabby frowned. What happened next? Did she take the boy with her? Was the boy killed and the Renoir forever altered, a blank space where the boy should have been?

She chewed the end of her pencil. It was a children's story, after all. Should it be that grim? But then again, every fairy tale she'd ever come across was pretty gruesome in one way or another. Children liked that, didn't they? Perhaps they could handle such things better than adults.

And why she was worrying about the audience for her little tale, heaven only knew. It wasn't as if Elisabeth would want to read children's books anymore. And naughty Léon never sat still long enough for stories.

With that single, negative line of thought, the story magic evaporated. Gabby threw down her pencil, frustrated with herself, both for daring to dream and for giving up before her little project was finished. She leafed through the frenzied sketches she'd made. Some of them were not bad. Maybe . . . maybe she'd feel better about it in the morning.

Maman's gentle snore seemed to dispute that hope. Gabby glanced at the clock. Midnight. She had to be up in five hours. Rubbing her eyes, she gathered her papers and opened her portfolio.

And saw the envelope. The unopened letter she'd somehow managed to forget.

Her insides trembled, ripples of anxiety flowing through her veins. Gabby set her papers aside. Lower lip gripped between her teeth, she made herself reach into the depths of the leather case and take out the letter.

She hesitated. If she burned the letter without reading it, she could go on pretending. One fine spring day, he would walk through the door. He would make her laugh, pick her up and swing her around in his arms and kiss her. Just like they did in the movies.

That stupid, irrational hope kept her going. If she read this letter, all hope would be destroyed. Why else would she receive correspondence from the British government sealed with His Majesty's coat of arms?

Curiosity, her besetting sin, gnawed at her insides. Had she not been curious about what went on behind closed doors in this building, the entire course of her life would have been different. Giving in to her baser nature now was likely to shatter her peace once more.

There was only one way to remove temptation. She picked up the letter, went to the tiny kitchen, and found matches. Lighting a match, she stared at the flame for so long, it singed her fingers. "Ah!" She shook out the flame, dropping the charred remains of the match into the sink.

Again, Gabby took out a match and struck. She held the letter up so that its corner was near the flame. She drew a deep breath, let it out. *Truly, I do not want to know.*

The envelope was stiff and smooth between her fingers and thumb. She felt the heat as its corner caught and flared, smelled the acrid scent of burning paper. The flame crackled; the envelope's edges browned and curled into blackened bat's wings, then floated down. The red seal burned brighter, melting and dripping like real wax. She held the envelope as long as she could before the flame crept dangerously close to her hand.

Sucking a breath through her teeth, she dropped the last remnant into the sink and shook her smarting fingers, watched until that final, pale corner turned to ash. The flame sputtered and died. The last glow of the embers went out.

There. She'd done it. She didn't need to feel the excruciating pain of yet another loss. She could go on pretending he still lived somewhere in the world, desperate to get back to her.

Maybe tomorrow, or the next day, he would come.

YVETTE

Yvette was so shaken by the encounter with Vidar, she needed a drink or two to settle her nerves. The brandy at the Ritz was, of course, excellent.

The liquor brought a warm, slow calm that seeped through her body like butter through a hot baguette. She was exhausted, wrung out, but despite the physical relaxation brought on by the drink, arguments and worries still zinged through her mind.

She replayed her conversation with Vidar in her head, trying to judge who had won that round. Reluctantly, she conceded the loss. She didn't doubt she would have an opportunity to turn the tables, however. Damn the misplaced sense of loyalty that prevented her from reporting him! After all that had happened, was she still hoping he was not the man she took him to be?

If only she could confide in someone. In Gabby. The thought made her insides twist. Seeing her sister again would be even more wrenching than a visit from Vidar.

Well, maybe she would write to Gabby first. Her sister had written every two weeks after Liliane Dietlin had told her Yvette's New York address. She should have sworn Liliane to secrecy.

Yvette had been so ashamed of her own behavior that summer, so riddled with guilt over Catherine, she could not bring herself to write to Gabby or to read her letters. She'd burned every one. Now she wished she'd kept them.

She took some stationery and a pen from the handsome desk by the window and climbed into bed with her drink. She only managed a few lines before she fell asleep.

Yvette woke to someone banging on the door and abusing her loudly for being a lazy slugabed. She opened one bleary eye and cursed when she realized she had managed to drool on her letter to Gabby, smearing the ink on what was undoubtedly a masterpiece of diplomacy.

She frowned. Who could it be out there? Few people knew where she was staying. And why would anyone be yelling at her?

A glance at the clock told her she had slept ten hours straight. It was well past noon.

She crept over to the door to listen, her ear pressed to the panel. Then she realized that there was an ingenious invention, a little spy hole in the door, through which she might see who was there. She put an eye to it and squinted. Her face distorted by the spy hole, Madame de Turckheim glared back.

Yvette blinked. What was La Baronne doing here? *Please, don't tell me I damaged one of Monsieur Dior's gowns yesterday!*

Cautiously, she opened the door.

Madame barreled past her. "Honestly, Yvette, what do you think you are doing?"

"Good morning, madame." Yvette's head had begun to pound. "I'll ring for coffee."

"What's the matter with you?" La Baronne demanded. "I've

been trying to find you all morning. Even your sister did not know where you were."

"My sister?" Yvette closed her eyes, unable to imagine Gabby's reaction to madame's demands. She must see Gabby immediately and make it right.

"You are to report to La Maison Dior by three o'clock," said madame, bustling over to open the curtains, letting in sunshine that was winter pale and yet for Yvette, far too bright.

"Oh, but why?" No one had told her they needed her today. She'd intended to ask for more work once the trial was over.

"Because *le patron* wills it, of course. Good God, Yvette, what happened to you last night?"

She caught sight of her reflection and frightened herself. "Oh, dear. You are right. Pardon me, madame, for receiving you like this, but I do need that coffee."

By the time Yvette had tidied herself a little, the coffee had arrived. While Yvette poured each of them a cup, madame explained, "Monsieur Dior wants you to continue to work for him. Only Tania sold more of the models to the buyers yesterday. You were a hit."

The ache in Yvette's head seemed to vanish. "Really?"

Just at that moment, the telephone rang. It was reception. A Monsieur LeBrun was waiting for her downstairs. "Oh, dear!" She'd forgotten their appointment. "Give me five minutes, please. Then send him up."

"Your first appointment is at three, Yvette," madame called after her as she hurried to the closet to rummage for something appropriate to wear.

"I'll be there." Guiltily, she acknowledged it would mean putting off her visit to Gabby and Maman, but this was the chance of a lifetime. This was Dior.

When Madame de Turckheim had gone, Yvette turned into a minor whirlwind, making herself presentable before the clerk arrived at her door. She was just jabbing the last pin into her chignon when the doorbell chimed.

The clerk declined coffee but perched on the couch opposite Yvette and placed his attaché case on his knees. He snapped it open, extracted an official-looking document, and handed it to her. "I have taken the liberty of preparing a draft statement, based on my interviews with Mademoiselle Dulac. Please read through it. If you disagree with anything or if you remember any details that you would like to add, tell me and I will make a note."

Yvette's head started to throb again and her heart to pound. She took the statement and tried to read, but the neat black type swam before her eyes. *Breathe,* she told herself. *You need to breathe.* She closed her eyes and exhaled, letting the statement fall from her hand.

As her pulse slowed and her mind cleared, the answer came. She knew what she must do. In a quiet, firm tone, Yvette said, "I need to see her."

LeBrun furrowed his brow, dark eyes wary behind the thick lenses of his spectacles. "Well, I don't know if that's wise . . ."

The more Yvette thought about it, the more convinced she became. Their interactions during the war had been so charged with emotion that it was impossible to judge the situation fairly. If Yvette could see Louise, talk to her again with a cool head, she could decide once and for all.

Was Louise Dulac a traitor? Or was she a heroine of France?

Chapter Nine

Paris, February 1947

YVETTE

Having extracted a promise from Monsieur LeBrun that he would arrange a prison visit to Louise Dulac before the trial began, Yvette made it back to the House of Dior in plenty of time for her three o'clock appointment. Afterward, she saw Monsieur Dior on the landing outside the workrooms, muttering to himself, his brow furrowed. No doubt, he was thinking of a hundred things at once.

When he saw Yvette, his expression lightened. "How are you getting on, little one? Are you liking the work as you always hoped?"

"Oh, yes, monsieur! It is a privilege to wear your creations."

"Good. That is very good." He was a modest man and swiftly changed the subject. "You have seen your sister."

It was more a statement than a question. Yvette bit her lip. "It has been such a whirlwind since the moment I arrived in Paris. I have not had the chance . . ."

That made *le patron* frown. Family was of the utmost importance to him. "Then you must go to her immediately."

"But I have a fitting—"

His soft *tchut-tchut* told her he would brook no argument. "I will make all right with madame. Off you go."

Thanking him, Yvette did as she was told, walking briskly to keep off the chill, fear deepening with every step. Her failure to correspond with Gabby since she'd left Paris had not sprung from petulance or anger. Each time a letter arrived for her from France, she relived that awful night. The shots, the blood, her own betrayal of Catherine, her pleading with Louise came back to her in vivid detail.

She paused at the big street door, then pressed the bell with shaking fingers and made herself stand her ground. It felt strange, waiting to be admitted to what used to be her home. She expected to glimpse the sharp, pale little face of Maman at the window, but the door simply buzzed open. Had Monsieur Dior telephoned ahead? Were they expecting her?

When she entered the vestibule, she gave a cry of surprise. Her bicycle—the one Vidar had given her when hers had disappeared from the Ritz that day—was propped against the wall of the *loge*. "Hello, my friend." She ran her palm over the handlebar, touched the ragged scraps of silk and velvet she'd threaded through the basket weave in an attempt to make this bicycle her own. The memories of Lelong and the workrooms where she'd scrounged these bright favors swirled through her mind, only to be drowned in apprehension.

Gabby. Maman. What on earth was she going to say to them?

The urge to hop onto her bike and pedal away as fast as she could nearly overpowered her.

No. She had to do this. Putting it off was the work of a coward. And deep down, she longed to see her sister and mother again. But her entire body was trembling and her throat felt swollen and sore.

Really, it was odd that someone hadn't come out by now. The Foucher women were such busybodies, they had to know about all the comings and goings at number 10. Maybe someone else was filling in as concierge today? Yvette rapped on the door to the *loge* with one crooked finger.

She waited, half-hoping no one was home, but also knowing that she would have to return once again if they were not, and that would be worse.

She knocked again, before finally the door to the *loge* opened and Gabby stood there, wiping her hands on her apron, an old habit that gave Yvette a stab of regret. Gabby was thin. Thinner even than during the war, her eyes too large for her face.

Those eyes widened and lit up with surprise. "Yvette!" she cried, starting forward. Before Yvette could stop her, Gabby wrapped her in a tight, desperate hug. Yvette closed her eyes and felt the pain and loss of their last time together flood her entire being. She couldn't—simply could not—hug her sister back.

GABBY

Just as someone rang the street doorbell, the telephone in the *loge* began to shrill.

Gabby shot up from the bureau where she'd stolen a few minutes to complete her drawings, pressed the button to release the street door, then dived for the telephone. A phone call was still a rare occurrence at the *loge* and every time the instrument rang, it seemed like a life-or-death imperative to answer it before the caller disconnected.

"Hello?"

The line was bad but she could just make out the words the man on the other end spoke. "Hello? Am I speaking with Mademoiselle Foucher?"

Gabby gasped and dropped the receiver. English. The man had spoken in English.

She stood frozen, poised to flee, staring at the phone. Then she scrabbled for the receiver, got a firm grip on it, and hung up, leaping back from the telephone as if it might rise up to bite her.

She only dimly heard the knocking at first, but eventually, it registered. Heart still drumming against her ribs, she went to open the door.

And there stood Yvette, her brandy-colored eyes fierce against the pale milk of her skin. She was the last person Gabby had expected to see, and yet so very welcome for so many reasons. Gabby practically fell upon her sister, hugging her so hard, Yvette yelped. The years dropped away and it was just the two of them once more.

Moments passed before she realized Yvette did not return her embrace quite so eagerly. She was rigid, unyielding. Almost three years, Yvette had been gone, and no word from her. Was she still angry after all this time?

Grief crushed Gabby's heart. She had to set her jaw and summon all her strength not to crumple. "It is good to see you looking so well, Yvette," she managed, dropping her arms and stepping back. "Would you like some tea?"

Yvette walked inside. "Where is Maman?"

"She is visiting Madame Everard," said Gabby. "She will be sorry she missed you."

Yvette merely blinked at that, then peered about her as if she had never seen the apartment before. Gabby looked around as well, at the scant, shabby furniture, the faded curtains, the clutter of knickknacks her mother had received as gifts from various tenants over the years. There was still a shortage of almost everything in Paris. But perhaps Yvette had forgotten all that while living the high life in New York. America had grown more prosperous while Europe starved.

She gestured to the settee. "Will you not sit down, at least? Tell me what you have been doing, why you are here."

Yvette stayed where she was. "I'm here to testify for Louise Dulac." She was speaking slowly and carefully, as if she had half-forgotten her native tongue. "There is not much else to tell."

Gabby stared. A journey down through France, across the Pyrenees to Spain, and then all the way to the United States of America was so far out of her range of experience that Yvette might as well have been to Jupiter. And that wasn't taking into account her stint as a mannequin in the Dior show.

Gabby wanted to tell her she'd been there, seen for herself, that she'd been proud of her, but the words stuck in her throat. Instead, she said, "I should have realized you were here for the Dulac trial. It's all over the papers. The most hated woman in France, they say." She hesitated. "I thought you hated her most of all."

"I do."

"Then why come all this way? Why testify?"

Yvette's face remained impassive but her eyes burned with emotion. Not anger. Was it pain? Slowly, she said, "I am not at all sure that I should."

Gabby resisted the urge to question her further. That cryptic answer was all Yvette seemed prepared to give.

Her gaze made another circuit of the room, then snagged on Gabby's folio. "What's this?" Ignoring Gabby's half-hearted protest, she crossed to the table and picked up page after page, examining the sketches of Dior dresses with close attention. She looked up. "You were there."

Gabby wanted to snatch the drawings back, but she made herself stay where she was. "Yes. I saw you."

Yvette stared at her intently. Then she lowered her gaze to the page. "These are . . . superb, Gabby. You always did hide your light."

"Take that one," Gabby blurted out. "It's of you." It was the *corolle* dress that Yvette had shown off so well, her waist impossibly tiny, her bosom and neck rising, swanlike, from the low-cut bodice.

For the first time, Yvette's face relaxed, just a little. "Thank you. That is kind." The words were quietly spoken, through pale lips. Yvette seemed engaged in some momentous inner struggle. She placed the rest of the sketches on the table with great care, as if they were precious and delicate. Gabby noticed that her hand shook. "I—I must be going."

The telephone rang out like an alarm and Gabby jumped. The tremble in her limbs became a weakness. She groped for the back of a chair to steady herself. Seconds went by before she realized Yvette was saying her name.

"Gabby? Aren't you going to answer it?" Eyeing her askance, Yvette reached out and lifted the receiver.

"No, don't!" Gabby started forward to stop her. But it was too late.

Blood drummed in her ears so loudly that she couldn't hear her sister's murmured responses. Yvette turned to grab one of Gabby's sketching pencils and a scrap of paper to write something down.

Heat and cold washed over Gabby in alternating waves. This was it. The news she'd been dreading. There was only one reason an English person would want to contact her.

Jack was dead.

As she watched Yvette calmly take down the details, she knew it with a certainty that left her strangely numb. She had feared this day for so long, a constant looming presence, like an impending avalanche. Yet, now that disaster engulfed her, she felt nothing at all.

Yvette put down her pencil and set the receiver back in its cradle. Then she turned to Gabby with a somber expression.

"Don't say it. *Don't.* I don't want to know." Gabby was amazed at how calmly the words came out of her mouth.

"But, Gabby, you must—"

"No, no, *no*," she whispered, hardly hearing what Yvette said. This should be a joyous, wonderful occasion, their reunion. And now she would have to accept a truth so awful, she couldn't face it. Gabby sank onto the couch, staring straight ahead. Then she put her head in her hands, kneading at her temples in an effort to massage her brain back into order.

A hand squeezed her shoulder. Yvette's voice, soft now, said her name. Said it several times. The sound was muffled, as if they were separated by a wall of glass.

"Gabby!" This time, Yvette's tone was as sharp as a slap. "Listen to me. It is *not* bad news, do you hear?"

It took a full minute for Gabby to digest what Yvette had said. She froze, scarcely able to believe she'd understood correctly.

Yvette shook her gently. "It is *good* news. Understand?"

Gabby took a deep, shuddering breath and lifted her head. "What is it? Please don't lie to me, Yvette. Please."

Yvette stroked a lock of Gabby's hair back from her forehead. With the smallest quirk of a smile, she said, "Gabrielle Foucher, the British government wants to give you a medal. How about that?"

Chapter Ten

Paris, June 1944

YVETTE

Yvette made several deliveries before turning toward Monsieur Arnaud's bookshop. First of all, she cycled straight past the store without stopping, glancing at the window as she went by. There was no geranium displayed there, so she rode on.

She did not have any deliveries for the Ritz, but she went there anyway, cruising along the edge of the Place Vendôme, eyes sharp, in the unlikely event that she might spot Vidar Lind.

It was not that he was so attractive—well, not *only* that he was attractive; he was an enigma. With Maman and Gabby, even with Jean-Luc, everything was concrete, black-and-white. But Vidar Lind was different. Sophisticated, yet damaged in some way. She could not be sure where the loyalties of such a man might lie, nor where she stood with him. He fascinated and intrigued her.

But today, Yvette had more important business than mooning after some man, no matter how compelling he might be. She went back to Lelong and picked up more deliveries, plotting her course so that she would need to pass the bookshop again. She didn't register the geranium until too late. It was a poor specimen with only one limp crimson flower to its name. Easily missed if you weren't looking for it.

Instead of turning around and going back, Yvette made another delivery, then approached the bookshop again. This time, she stopped, dismounted, and rested her bike against the wall. Her heart seemed to expand until it knocked hard against her rib cage. Careful not to go too fast or too slowly, she approached the bookshop, pausing with her hand on the doorknob.

What she glimpsed through the web of masking tape that laced the glass door made her snatch back her hand. A large man stood over Monsieur Arnaud, a wooden stick like a policeman's baton in his grip. The two men seemed to be arguing, though she couldn't hear what they said.

The big man turned, raised one booted foot, and kicked over a table, sending books flying. Monsieur Arnaud retreated behind the counter, his hands raised defensively. Rotund, balding, and bespectacled, half the other man's height, the bookseller was no match for this ruffian.

What to do? The bully with the baton was huge, not someone she could even think of fighting. Catherine had instructed her not to involve herself in anything that would draw attention. Yet here was this thug, clearly threatening Monsieur Arnaud. The bigger man was not in uniform, so it was not an official visit. Could it be about monsieur's black-market trade?

The stranger surged toward Monsieur Arnaud, baton raised,

and smashed it down on monsieur's shoulder. Yvette cried out, cringing in sympathy.

She couldn't stand by and do nothing. She wrenched open the door, setting the bell jangling. "Stop! Stop that! He is an old man."

The bully turned to glare. "Store's closed," he snarled. "Get out."

Yvette glanced at Monsieur Arnaud, who was struggling to his feet. "For God's sake, do as the man says, Yvette," he panted.

"I will call the police!" It was the only thing she could think to do.

The big man showed his teeth in a horrible grin. They were capped with gold, glittering with menace. "I *am* the police." His gaze sharpened, and the grin turned into something more appreciative as he eyed her up and down.

"Leave her out of it, Rafael," said Monsieur Arnaud, growing even more agitated. He glared at Yvette. "Damn it, girl, just go!"

She swallowed hard, wishing with all her heart that she could see a way to fight this Rafael and win. But the way that man was looking at her . . . What he'd already done to Monsieur Arnaud . . .

Rafael feinted a step toward her and laughed when she skittered back toward the door.

"Run!" said Monsieur Arnaud. "You silly girl, get out!"

This time, Yvette did as she was told. She darted out the door, making the bell clang wildly, and swung onto her bicycle. Pedaling as if all of hell's demons were at her heels, she shot toward the Place de la Concorde.

She turned the corner and nearly collided with a boy who was dashing across the street. He yelled at Yvette and made a rude gesture.

"Sorry, sorry," she called, slowing her pace. Just in time, too. A couple of Gestapo officers in their evil black uniforms rounded the corner, making her heart beat harder, but they scarcely glanced in her direction.

The image of Rafael striking Monsieur Arnaud played again and again through her mind. Had that been an interrogation? Had he somehow suspected Monsieur Arnaud of resistance activities? He'd said he was the police. What had he meant? At least it wasn't the Gestapo or some other German official. Small comfort, that.

Yvette was supposed to avoid trouble. That's what Catherine had told her. Stay alert and watch for anything out of the ordinary. The slightest indication that something might have gone wrong and she was to disappear. That was all very well, but what if Rafael killed Monsieur Arnaud or injured him seriously? Monsieur was all alone in that place.

The bookseller had not wanted her help, but she could not rest until she knew he was safe. Then, too, she refused to let her first mission for Catherine and Liliane result in failure. As soon as she'd reloaded with parcels from Lelong, Yvette headed straight back to the bookstore.

Having scouted the area carefully before approaching the establishment, she peered inside, to see that the shop was empty. "Monsieur Arnaud?" she called as she pushed open the door and walked in.

A soft moan drew her attention, and she found him lying on the floor behind the counter, a trickle of blood issuing from his temple, his glasses askew. His blue eyes were dazed.

"Oh, monsieur!" She kneeled down to help him up, but the bookseller waved her away.

"Leave me," he panted. "Let me catch my breath."

"But why was that awful man here?" she demanded. "Why would he treat you like that?"

"I'm an old fool," muttered Arnaud. "That was one of Friedrich Berger's men. Berger is a big player in the black market. He was content to let me run my little side business while I paid him protection money, but lately, he has demanded more and more. Takings have been down. I couldn't pay the full amount this time. So he sent Rafael."

He grunted, then groaned as she helped him stand. "Thank you, my dear. But you shouldn't have interfered. Now you might well have made yourself a target." He took out a handkerchief and dabbed at the blood on his temple. "What were you doing here, anyway?"

Yvette hesitated, thinking that it was hardly the time to ask for the book on birds. However, that was her mission and she was determined to show Catherine Dior she could carry out her instructions. She made the unusual request.

Monsieur Arnaud stared at her, then rasped out, "Have you any idea how close you just came to betraying us both?" He exhaled a breath. "That man, Rafael. He is not just a thug and an extortionist, he is a *gestapiste*."

Yvette went cold. She had not come across this term before, but it sounded like a diminutive of "Gestapo," the most hated and feared organization in Paris. That told her most of what she needed to know.

"Rafael runs with the Berger gang," said Monsieur Arnaud. "The Nazis have given them policing powers. To search premises for Jews and dissidents, to arrest and interrogate. They are criminals—smugglers and murderers—running amok, all with the might of the Third Reich behind them."

"But . . . but he was a Frenchman," Yvette said. "Surely he would not betray his own country like that."

Monsieur Arnaud grunted. "That sort would betray his own mother. You have a lot to learn about people, Yvette." He looked troubled. "How did you get yourself mixed up in this?"

"Never mind that," said Yvette, trying to sound businesslike, even though monsieur had just exposed her ignorance and lectured her as if she were still the little girl who used to curl up with her favorite storybook on the window seat of his shop. "Please. Give me the book on birds."

He stared at her hard, as if willing her to back down, but she simply stared back at him. He was taking a much bigger risk than she was if he had dealings with these *gestapistes* while also working for the resistance. Finally, Monsieur Arnaud gave a cross between a grunt and a sigh. "Give me a moment and I will get it for you."

While he went to the back room, Yvette did her best to tidy the mess Berger's henchman had made of the bookstore. She hadn't made much progress before the bookseller returned.

"Here you are." Monsieur handed her a package.

The book was very small, wrapped in brown paper. Yvette shoved it into her satchel.

"Will you be all right now, monsieur?" she asked, reluctant to leave him in this state. "Would you like me to fetch someone to sit with you?" He'd suffered a head wound, after all.

"Get out of here," growled the bookseller, waving her away. She hoped his snappish retort meant he was feeling better. "And stay out of trouble!"

HAVING DELIVERED THE book on birds to the address she had memorized, Yvette arrived back at Lelong, still shaken by the violence she had witnessed and by how close she had come to danger, both to herself and to Catherine's resistance cell. She jumped when Madame Péthier said, "About time! You're late. You've completely missed Louise Dulac's fitting. She asked for you particularly—" Abruptly, madame stopped scolding and caught Yvette's chin in her hand, turning her face to the light. "What is it, little one?"

Yvette told her that she had seen a man in a shop being beaten and tried to help.

Madame's brow furrowed. "You are a good, kind girl, Yvette, but you must stop interfering in things that don't concern you." She made a helpless gesture. "I am sorry for your distress, but we don't have time to waste. We've made the alterations to Mademoiselle Dulac's suit and she wants you to deliver it to her personally. She has the de Noailles party tonight and desires you to help her dress. Quick! Tidy yourself. There's a car waiting."

Yvette stared. How could she even think about fashion and movie stars and parties when such people as this Rafael were allowed to terrorize innocent citizens?

"Here." Madame produced a silver flask and held it to Yvette's lips.

She reared back a little as the fumes hit her nostrils. "What is it?"

"Brandy. Medicinal. Just a small sip, mind."

Yvette obeyed, and madame let her sit quietly for a few minutes, before she said, "I am truly sorry, my dear, but you must get moving. Mademoiselle was not happy when you were not here to attend her today."

Reluctantly, Yvette obeyed. Within minutes, she was on her way to the Ritz. The doorman who stooped to let her out of the car was the one who had been on duty when her bicycle was stolen. Having directed his minions to carry the movie star's packages up to her room, he tipped his hat and smiled at Yvette as if he remembered her. "Good afternoon, mademoiselle." He winked. "Not with your boyfriend today?"

Whatever else about Paris might change, the tendency of its citizens to believe that everyone was in love had not. Yvette flushed at his teasing but repressed the urge to deny any interest in the Swede. "Is he not here already?"

The doorman shook his head. "I haven't seen him, but I only started work ten minutes ago. He is often in the Little Bar at this time of day."

Yvette showed her papers to the guards, then went into the hotel and up the grand staircase. The youth who had pinched her last time was not there. The old man who had taken his place operating the elevator seemed completely uninterested in her, for which she was grateful. She had more important things to do than fending off wandering hands.

What did Dulac want with her? If this mistress of a high-ranking German officer did intend to make Yvette into a pet, was there some way that could be used to help the resistance? Delivering messages for Catherine Dior was one thing; getting close to the Germans for the purposes of espionage was as risky as openly opposing them. Yvette would need to be careful, curb her temper and conceal her disgust.

Outside Mademoiselle Dulac's door, she hesitated, listening. The movie star seemed to be entertaining guests in her suite. There was a murmur of voices—masculine ones. Friends of Gruber, perhaps?

Ordinarily, Yvette would scorn to eavesdrop. Now every cell of her body strained to hear what was going on in that room. She frowned. They were speaking in French, that much she could glean, but their voices were too low for her to discern more than a word here and there.

She knocked and the maid answered, her expression repelling. Yvette smiled sweetly. "Mademoiselle Dulac?"

The maid grunted and shook her head. "*Nein. Sie ist nicht herein.*"

"She's not here?" Yvette waved a hand. "Oh, I do not mind waiting. Monsieur Lelong has put me at the disposal of mademoiselle for the afternoon." She craned her neck to see who was present, but the great lump of a maid had not moved an inch from the doorway. Was she hiding something? Perhaps whoever was in the suite didn't want anyone to know they were meeting there?

A male voice, probably Gruber's, snapped, "*Wer ist's?*" The maid turned her head to answer in a stream of guttural language, but Gruber cut through her speech with a curt response.

"Hmph." The maid stepped aside, allowing Yvette to enter.

Yvette tried not to appear interested in the group of men assembled in mademoiselle's sitting room as she followed the maid to the boudoir. On a quick glance, she had an impression of three middle-aged men: Gruber plus two men in civilian clothing.

The cold good looks of one of the civilians made Yvette steal a second glance. At first, she'd mistaken his slicked-back blond hair for silver, but now she realized he was younger than the others, perhaps in his late thirties. He possessed an air of command, however, and it would not surprise her to learn that he was the most important man in the room.

"Wait, mademoiselle. Will you come over here?" The blond man spoke in flawless French.

She halted and turned slowly, fixing a vapid expression to her face.

Officiously, the maid grabbed Yvette's upper arm and yanked her toward the men, who were grouped around the fireplace, their booted legs stretched before them, glasses of brandy in hand. The remnants of a lavish luncheon lay on the supper table by the window. Yvette could not fail to note the sharp contrast between this genteel scene and the brutality of Rafael's attack on Monsieur Arnaud—all sanctioned by the Nazi occupiers. Masking her feelings when in the presence of such men was never easy, but now Yvette struggled to hide her revulsion.

"Come here, little one," said the blond man, again in French.

Yvette tugged free of the maid's grasp and walked between two sets of booted feet, over to where the blond man sat by the fireplace. He tilted his head and his bright blue eyes surveyed her in a considering way she didn't like.

"But you are a beauty," he remarked softly, as if he wanted only her to hear. "Where did you come from, hmm?"

"I am from the House of Lelong, monsieur," she replied. He raised his eyebrows and she added, "I beg your pardon, but I do not know what rank to call you. I do not mean to offend."

A gleam of humor came into his eyes, warming them. "They call me King Otto," he said, flinging out a hand. "The king of Paris."

His arrogance made her blood boil, but she forced herself not to react.

"This is the Third Reich's ambassador to France, you ignorant hussy," snapped Gruber. "You call him 'Your Excellency.' Show some respect."

The ambassador rubbed the side of his mouth with his fingertip. "No, no, don't yell at the child, Gruber. She wasn't to know. How could this little slip of a girl have any regard for ambassadors and the like?" He eyed her over his glass. "You find mademoiselle away from home. What shall you do now?"

The third man remarked testily, "What does it matter? Get rid of her. We have important matters to discuss."

Her eyes widened. The man spoke with a Parisian accent so idiomatic and perfect that he must be a native. A dirty collaborator, right here in mademoiselle's suite, probably a high-ranking one, too, if the company he kept was any guide.

The ambassador did not seem to mind the Frenchman's rudeness. He said, "Why don't you go down and find mademoiselle at the bar? Tell her our meeting should end in half an hour."

"Yes, Your Excellency." What could she do but obey?

There was more than one bar at the hotel, but when she inquired after Mademoiselle Dulac, Yvette was directed to the Little Bar. Intimate and clublike, with wood-paneled walls and leather chairs, the Little Bar was one of those places where it always seemed to be night—to encourage drinking, she supposed. Even at this hour, it was well patronized, mainly by men with a military bearing and an arrogance that led her to believe they were probably officers of the German air force, but a few perfectly coiffed and dressed women smoked cigarettes in ebony holders and leaned in to hang upon the men's every word.

No one paid Yvette any attention, yet she felt awkward and conspicuously out of place. The harsh accents of the Germans seemed to bombard her from every direction. At a glance, she could see that Louise Dulac wasn't there, but she lingered, thinking hard.

The meeting upstairs . . . What had that been about? Something of interest to Catherine Dior and her friends? If only she'd had the chance to overhear.

She was about to try her luck elsewhere when Vidar Lind came in, heading for one of the small circular tables in the darkest corner of the room. Yvette's stomach lurched, as if she'd jumped from a great height.

Her first instinct was to get away before he saw her. But that was foolish. At the least, she ought to acknowledge him when he'd been so kind about replacing her bicycle. Hadn't she hoped to run into him here? But now that she was faced with the reality of speaking with him again, it did not seem like a simple thing to do.

She made herself move toward his table. "Good day, Monsieur . . . Lind?" As if his name wasn't emblazoned on her memory.

There was a moment when she thought he had not recognized her and would tell her to get lost. If he did that, she would sink through the floor with embarrassment. But after a quick scan of the room, a corner of his mouth quirked up. Rising, he gestured to the empty chair at his table. "Please. Join me."

She hesitated. She was supposed to be looking for Louise Dulac. But this man intrigued her, and if he was a diplomat, he was almost certainly also a spy. And if he was a spy, then he might be able to . . . what? Help her. Guide her. Tell her how to be useful.

She glanced around. A few minutes one way or the other would not matter. She took the proffered seat.

As if he sensed her heightened state of excitement, Vidar leaned in, his eyes alight with interest. "Is something wrong, mademoiselle? Not your bicycle again."

"No, monsieur." She lowered her voice. "An encounter with a high-ranking Nazi. The German ambassador."

"Really?" He seemed unimpressed. "Sounds like you could use a drink." Rather than call over a waiter, he rose in his leisurely way and went to the bar, slipped the white-jacketed bartender some-thing, and ordered. Monsieur Lind seemed to be at home at the Ritz, as if he was accustomed to this kind of life. She noted his tall, elegant frame encased in a perfectly fitted suit, his collar and cuffs showing crisply white. While he waited for the bartender to pour a drink from a sweating cocktail shaker, he seemed to survey the rest of the patrons. Looking for someone, perhaps? Had she preempted a rendezvous?

He returned with two martini glasses filled with clear liquid, an olive on a cocktail stick bobbing in each. The table was so small and his legs were so long, his knee brushed Yvette's when he sat down again. He seemed not to notice. She noticed it very much.

Setting the glasses down, he turned to her. "Tell me all about it."

Yvette sipped her cocktail and wrinkled her nose, fighting the urge to cough. It was very strong. "Well, it is Mademoiselle Dulac, you see. She is a client of Lelong, where I work, and today, she called me to her suite. But when I got there, she wasn't in. Just Gruber, the ambassador, and another man."

He nodded. "And Herr Abetz seemed pleased with you?"

Why did he put the question that way? She hesitated. "He—he made me uncomfortable."

"Ah. He *was* pleased with you, then. I gather the feeling was not mutual."

"Of course not." She lowered her voice. "I am no collaborator, monsieur." She watched him closely, and when the statement of defiance only produced a slight crease between his eyebrows, she added, "You needn't be worried for me, though. I am good at pretending."

He smiled. "I am sure you are infinitely discreet. What is your name, by the way?"

"Yvette Foucher."

"A delivery girl with important connections. Tell me what happened upstairs just now to make you all . . ." He waved a hand. "Bright eyed."

Was she that obvious? She felt heat rising to her cheeks and quickly sipped her drink. Her voice a little husky from the strong martini, she replied, "There were three men. Gruber, the ambassador, and another man. French. A round face and bushy moustache. Dark hair. I'd say midfifties, middle height." She shrugged. "I didn't get his name."

"He was French? How do you know?"

"The accent, monsieur. It was definitely Parisian."

There was a faraway expression in Vidar's eyes. Did he recognize the description? Perhaps this encounter meant something to him.

She stirred her drink with the spiked olive, waiting for him to respond or prompt her for more. When he didn't, she reluctantly pushed her glass away. "I must continue my search for Mademoiselle Dulac. But it was very pleasant to see you again, monsieur. And thank you once more for the bicycle. I . . . It is the nicest thing anyone has ever done for me."

"Must you go?" He rose as she did. "We have barely become acquainted." He hesitated. "Mademoiselle Foucher, might I take you to dinner one evening?"

Dinner? He wanted to take her to dinner! She cleared her throat. "I'd like that very much, monsieur." She gave him her address and telephone number for the arrangements, then a glance at her watch told her the half hour the German ambassador had given Louise was up. "I had better be going. If I am not needed here after all, I must get back to Lelong."

Vidar took her hand and bowed over it in a way that was charmingly casual rather than courtly. She had never met a man like him, so elegant yet so unaffected.

"As for Louise Dulac," he said, releasing her hand, "try the lounge. If you really do want to find her, that is."

Chapter Eleven

🌿

Paris, June 1944

YVETTE

Yvette could not locate the actress anywhere in the hotel, so she decided to return to the suite to ask Gruber to dismiss her, only to catch Louise entering the Ritz from the Place Vendôme. "What a lucky chance, running into you down here," Louise said, quite as if she had not demanded Yvette's attendance. "Do come up."

"I have been here some time, mademoiselle. I went to your suite, but when I found the ambassador with some other gentlemen there, they sent me to find you in the bar."

"I see," said mademoiselle. Her face was inscrutable, but Yvette had the impression she wasn't pleased.

Perhaps mademoiselle did not wish it to be known she had left the hotel. "I will say that I found you in the bar if you like."

The actress said slowly, "It is wisest not to offer to lie so easily when you don't know why you're doing it. After all, you don't owe me anything."

"And yet, mademoiselle, I have the feeling you are going to ask of me a great deal," Yvette murmured, watching for a reaction.

The actress stared at her for a moment. Then she set her shoulders back, as if to shake off the comment. "We will return to the suite and hope that the men have finished their important business by now." She smiled. "They'd better have, because I need to get ready for tonight's soirée."

"And soirées are of far more importance than politics or war," Yvette agreed, with only a hint of irony.

"You speak the truth without knowing it, child," replied mademoiselle, giving her a sidelong glance.

Yvette wished people would stop calling her a child. Vidar Lind had as good as told her she was too young for him when they'd first met, although the dinner invitation seemed to indicate he had changed his mind. Well, at least when people underestimated you, you could sometimes catch them off guard.

"I must look spectacular tonight, Yvette," murmured Dulac as they entered the elevator. "You will see to it, won't you?"

"Yes, mademoiselle." Yvette made herself smile. "It should not be at all difficult."

The de Noailles party would indeed be the event of the season as far as she could tell from the gossip at Lelong. Monsieur Dior and Monsieur Balmain were dressing many of the ladies present.

To work in haute couture during the war was to split into two selves. There was the self that delighted to see such exquisite creations shine, who understood that in France, fashion was not trivial but a key contributor to the nation's economy. However, her deeper self, the one that gave her so much trouble now, was the young woman who loathed Nazi oppression, who risked her life as a courier for the resistance, the girl who had seen her compatriots starve while people like Gruber and Göring and their cronies gorged themselves at Maxim's and the Ritz. How could she be both of those people at once?

By telling herself she was getting close to Dulac in order to help the resistance. How, she didn't know yet, but she would try.

They arrived at the suite to find Gruber and his guests about to depart. The German ambassador smiled broadly. Yvette hovered a pace behind the actress, trying to melt into the background, as Dulac gave her hand to the ambassador to kiss. He bent to press his lips to the back of her knuckles and did that click of the heels that always sounded like a threat.

Having spoken smooth platitudes to Dulac, he cocked an eyebrow and glanced at Yvette. "Bring the girl with you to Chantilly, won't you? She is an original."

"Refreshing, is she not?" mademoiselle responded. "But sadly, I do not think it will be possible. She is not my maid, you understand, Otto. She is employed by the House of Lelong."

The ambassador waved his hand in an airy gesture, as if the obligations of lesser mortals hardly ranked with one of his whims. "Bring her anyway. I am sure Herr Lelong will be happy to accommodate us."

When he had gone and Yvette was alone with mademoiselle in her boudoir, Yvette asked, "When is your visit to Chantilly, mademoiselle? Do you really think Monsieur Lelong would let me go?" She tried to sound like a vapid young girl excited at the prospect of a treat. In fact, she was thinking about her resistance work and wondering if Catherine would prefer her to be here in Paris delivering messages or there in Chantilly with access to high-ranking German officials. Catherine would urge caution, Yvette felt sure. But what would Liliane say?

The actress inhaled deeply, smoothing the fabric of her dress as if to make more room for air in her lungs, then blew it out. "The house party at the Château de Saint Firmin is not for another week. Who knows? Herr Abetz might well have forgotten you by the time he leaves the hotel. If he insists, however, Monsieur Lelong will hardly have a choice but to let you go."

Mademoiselle Dulac went to the window and gazed out, contemplating the Place Vendôme, with its towering monument and its traffic and its luxury shops. Did she also notice the military vehicles parked in the square, the barbed wire beyond it, tethered by wooden hurdles that looked like fallen crucifixes in an ugly patch of dirt? "This is all moving very fast. I don't know whether it is wise to bring you with me."

Yvette tensed, her senses on high alert. Surely mademoiselle was referring to something besides stealing away an employee from a fashion house. She had not scrupled to do it for an afternoon, after all.

This more serious, contemplative side to the screen goddess was new and intriguing. Could it be that Louise Dulac was more loyal to France than anyone knew? That she had a strategy of some sort and was wondering how Yvette might fit into it? The better course might be to remain silent and wait for more.

"He seemed very taken with you, didn't he?" said mademoiselle at last.

A feeling of unease crept over Yvette, but she didn't respond, unwilling to break the line of reasoning in case the actress stopped ruminating aloud.

Dulac's gaze dropped to the ring on her finger as she turned it around and around, making the diamonds flash in the sunlight, and Yvette wondered if Gruber had given that ring to her. It was not on the engagement finger, of course. Men like Gruber did not marry women like Dulac. He was probably already married to some loyal German frau.

"If I go," Yvette said quietly, with a seriousness to match the movie star's mood, "what would I have to do?"

The actress shrugged, her somber air lifting. "Let's worry about that when it happens. For now, I need you to help me dress."

GABBY

Gabby was on edge, her temper frayed by lack of sleep, constant vigilance, and the abominable heat. The Allies had landed on the beaches of Normandy a week ago and were still fighting their way south. Paris was so close to salvation, and yet for their family, the dangers of the occupation had never loomed so large.

Yvette erupted into the *loge* like a whirlwind, eyes burning with excitement. "You will never guess what happened today."

Gabby braced herself.

It all tumbled out, one alarming event after the other. The gold-toothed *gestapiste* at Monsieur Arnaud's shop, the encounter with the Swedish diplomat, and the invitation from the German ambassador to his château.

Gabby's attention snagged on the most immediate threat. "You should not have confronted that horrible villain, Yvette! He might have hurt you, too." What if he made it his business to find out who Yvette was and came after her? Gabby's blood turned cold at the thought.

"You would not have stood by, either," said Yvette. "Monsieur Arnaud is an old man, Gabby. And it turned out all right, so don't nag at me now." She twisted to peer down at the back of her skirt. "I knew it. I must have torn my hem in my haste to get away." Unhooking her skirt, she stepped out of it to reveal a half slip full of darns, then went to the bureau to take out the sewing basket. "Come and sit down. I'll fix this while we talk."

Gabby did not like the way Yvette seemed to have become both more mature and more reckless overnight. How did she always seem to be at the center of events? Witnessing violence from a *gestapiste* was one thing; an invitation from Otto Abetz was a threat on an entirely different level.

"Poor Monsieur Arnaud," said Maman. "He has always done his best to get along with the Germans. What has he ever done but keep his head down?"

Yvette gave a little snort, but she was rummaging in the sewing box and Gabby couldn't see her face. "What?" demanded Maman.

"Well . . . selling things on the black market *is* a risk, you will admit." Yvette found a needle and threaded it, then began to darn her hem.

"Tell us more about this invitation from the ambassador," said Maman. "Can he be serious? When would you have to go?"

"Oh, not for another week," Yvette said. "It will probably come to nothing. These things so often do."

Getting too close to the Germans might be as dangerous as spitting in their eyes. Besides which, to be seen as a collaborator by French patriots would be equally harmful to Yvette. "The place will be crawling with Boches," said Gabby. "Can't you get out of it?"

"I could hardly refuse, could I?" said Yvette, her needle working in and out with speed and delicacy. She might pretend to be absorbed in her work, but Gabby knew better. The excitement came off her in waves.

"For someone who hates the Germans so much, you seem awfully keen to go," said Gabby.

"I am looking forward to a change of air and a decent meal, that's all." Yvette tied off her work and broke the thread with a nip of her teeth. "I am following in your footsteps, Gabby, along the path of least resistance." She put away her sewing box, slipped back into her skirt, and left the room.

Such passivity seemed unlikely in someone who had chafed to do her bit for France since the occupation began. However, Gabby decided to approach the subject with caution. She passed an uneasy night before she mentioned it again.

"It is a great honor, being asked to the Château de Saint Firmin," she said as her sister was getting ready for work the next morning. "You will meet many interesting and wealthy people."

"I suppose so." Yvette coaxed her thick, curly hair into a rough chignon and began securing it with pins.

"And you said it was the ambassador himself who invited you?"

"That's right."

"I hope your head is not turned by these visits to castles and such." The words came out more sharply than Gabby intended, but Yvette seemed to be thinking of something else.

Gabby tried again. "I am worried for you, going to that place."

Yvette stuck the last pin into her hair, then turned to put her hands on Gabby's shoulders, those cat's eyes of hers grave and steady. "I am worried for me, too, Gabby. But I must do what I can. We all must."

That alarmed Gabby even more, but before she could reply, Yvette kissed her cheek, grabbed her satchel, and left.

Gabby needed to get moving, too. It was time to visit Madame LaRoq. She took out some black-market cheese from the larder and cut it in half. Spearing one piece with the point of her knife, she brought it to her nose and sniffed. It had the pungent smell of sweaty feet, the scent of good aged country Brie.

Gabby had been tempted to surprise Madame LaRoq with a visit outside the hours she'd given Catherine Dior. But curious as she might be to discover what was going on in that apartment, it was safer not to find out. She wanted to know, but she did not want the responsibility of knowing, and it was impossible to separate the two.

The show of good behavior the Germans had put on when they first arrived in Paris had not survived D-Day. As it began to look as if the Allies must win the war, the Nazis became more vicious, like cornered rats. Every day, resistance workers were being rounded up, tortured, and shot, their loved ones sent to work camps. Simply knowing of resistance activity and failing to report it was enough to get Gabby arrested, and possibly Yvette and Maman, too.

There was no going back once Gabby became a party to the secret Madame LaRoq and Catherine kept. As matters stood, she could plead she had been their dupe.

Madame would probably laugh if she heard how concerned Gabby was for her safety these days. "But already, I am dying, my dear," she would say. "Best go out with a *boom*, no?" During the occupation, a certain recklessness had overtaken some of the old as well as the young, it seemed.

But the sudden distance between Gabby and the woman who had been like a grandmother to her all these years could not help but hurt her feelings. The hurt became harder and harder to hide.

Gabby arranged the cheese and a slice of bread to go with it and poured a cup of weak dandelion tea.

She left the *loge* and went through to the open courtyard. The sun smiled down today, warming the cobblestones beneath her feet. The wind had died and all was quiet. No leaves had whirled through the space to gather in drifts for her to sweep. No one had dug up vegetables in the night—there were no vegetables to dig anymore. She must beg Catherine to bring her more seeds to plant the next time she returned from Callian.

The quiet felt almost eerie in the summer heat, like the high street in an American western when a shoot-out is about to start. This courtyard used to be a cheerful place for neighbors to meet and chat or even sit and enjoy an evening apéritif, but now it remained deserted. Residents kept to themselves in their apartments if they had not vacated them altogether and journeyed south as soon as the Germans marched on Paris. Many suites stood empty. Such a waste, but what could one do?

Sliding the teacup onto the plate, she opened the door to madame's wing. The bannisters needed dusting again, she noticed as she made her way up. It seemed as if she was destined always to be dusting. Was that all her life would ever be?

Of course, a life of drudgery was preferable to the tense nights she'd spent waiting for telltale sounds of Catherine's visitors or living with the fear of Yvette's strange encounters with *gestapistes* and German ambassadors.

Gabby reached Madame LaRoq's apartment and opened it with her key. She was expected, after all, and it was nine o'clock on the dot.

What she saw in madame's bedroom made her drop her plate and cup and stumble forward, her arms outstretched. There, leaning over madame in a menacing fashion, was a large, fair-haired man.

Chapter Twelve

Paris, June 1944

GABBY

"What are you doing? Get away from her!" Gabby charged forward, gripped the stranger's arm and tugged with all her might, then shoved him away. With a groan, he staggered back, crashing into the dressing table. Panting and clutching at the edge of the vanity, he struggled to right himself. There was something wrong with him. She shouldn't have been able to do that to a man of his size. At a glance she could see that he was weak—sick or possibly injured. But once she realized he was not a threat, her attention was all for madame.

"What happened? What's wrong with her?" Gabby reached across the bed to take madame's hand. It was slack in her grip. Madame's eyes were staring straight ahead. Before she even felt for a pulse, Gabby knew what this meant.

"Ah, *no!*" Pain flooded her chest. There she had been, thinking only of herself and her hurt feelings, when madame lay lifeless in her own bed. She couldn't stop the ragged keening that came from deep inside her chest.

"Please. Please don't," said the man hoarsely, panting as if speaking were a huge effort. "Please. Quiet. Fetch . . . Mademoiselle Dior."

He had his back to the dresser, and he was sliding down it, his legs crumpling beneath him. His face had turned a pearly grey at odds with the fierce blue of his eyes.

She could not deal with him now. All she could think was that madame was gone. That enchanting smile would never strike warmth into Gabby's heart again.

She bent her head and pressed it to the old lady's temple and wept.

Everything else seemed to fall away and there was only Gabby and madame and her grief. She sobbed and held on to that lifeless hand, feeling the papery skin, the wrinkled knuckles, and the wasted palms.

If only she could have had just one more day. She would have used it wisely, had she known the end was so near.

After some time like this, Gabby heard the man rasp out, "I am sorry. She was a remarkable woman."

Gabby was silent. In a distant part of her mind, she knew what the man was, that she risked her life simply by staying in this room with him. Yet her sorrow was too overwhelming for her to react.

Anger swelled deep inside. She wanted to accuse him, blame him. But despite what it had looked like when she'd entered the room, she knew that this had not been a violent death. The man—whatever he was doing here—had not murdered madame.

Slowly, thoughts came to her, drifting through the fog. The man who sat on the floor with his eyes squeezed shut was very ill indeed. Deathly ill. She regarded him dully. His breathing was labored and his color was ashen. His lips twisted as if he was in pain. She'd had the impression he was large and it was true that he was tall, but now that she saw him better, he appeared painfully thin. He looked like some of the French soldiers who had returned from the war, broken and starving.

So, this was madame's secret. Madame's and Catherine Dior's.

"Frightfully sorry," the man mumbled in English, "but I rather think I'm . . ." Then he slid into a dead faint and narrowly missed hitting his head on the knob of the lowest dresser drawer.

Gabby bit back a cry. She ought to do something for him. But what could she do? She doubted she could move him on her own.

And Madame LaRoq? How could Gabby bring an undertaker here, with this man occupying the room? She drew a deep breath and tried to order her scattered thoughts.

Madame first. Gabby reached forward and gently closed the lids of her eyes and whispered a quick prayer. She bit her lip to hold back more tears. She couldn't afford to indulge herself now.

Reluctantly, Gabby left madame's side and went to bend over the unconscious Englishman. On his shoulder, she saw a red stain seeping through his shirt. He must have a wound that had opened when he fell. Trembling with shock and grief, she hunted around for something to staunch the bleeding and came up with a towel from madame's bathroom.

Kneeling beside him, she put a hand around his neck to support his head, then pressed the towel to his shoulder.

"Come on," she muttered under her breath. He wasn't regaining consciousness. He was wedged between madame's dresser and the bed, impossible to extricate without help. "Monsieur?" Gently, she patted at his face with her fingertips. Maybe he'd rouse sufficiently to move himself. But it was no good. He was out cold.

She should fetch Catherine Dior. He was Catherine's problem, after all, one she had never intended to share with Gabby. She slid her hand out from under his head and then used her scarf to bind the towel firmly in place. He gave a soft groan. She'd hurt him.

"So sorry," she whispered. He was white to the lips, but even pale and sickly, he was a good-looking man.

When she eased her arm from beneath his shoulder, he immediately slid sideways, so she lowered him gently and shifted him so that he lay flat on the floor. "I'll be back as soon as I can," she told him, though why she bothered when he was unconscious, she didn't know. She felt sick, not at the sight of the wound, but at the danger the man's mere presence represented.

Gabby went to the bathroom to wash her hands and saw her face in the mirror. Her eyes were wide and wild, her cheeks flushed. She looked guilty of something. She tried to tidy her hair, repinning the wispy black tendrils that had escaped from her chignon when she'd pulled off her scarf. She splashed her face with water, then gripped the sink, breathed in, breathed out, attempting to steady herself.

Get Catherine. Leave it all to her. Gabby made herself move. She cleared the broken crockery from the threshold of madame's bedroom, locked up, and hurried down the corridor to Monsieur Dior's apartment. She took a deep breath, then tapped on the door.

Sabine answered, feather duster in hand. She looked so normal, so untouched by danger in her perky little apron and cap, that Gabby wanted to shake her and yell at her to wake up.

"Is your mistress at home?" She tried to sound casual but her voice trembled.

Sabine didn't seem to notice her distress. "Mademoiselle Dior is in Callian."

"*What?*" Gabby stared at the maid. Of course! What an idiot. She'd forgotten Catherine had left already. Oh, good God, how would she possibly manage this situation without help?

Sabine frowned at her, curiosity dawning, but then she gave a start. "One moment, I have something for Yvette. Will you take it to her?" She left the room without waiting for an answer.

Gabby squeezed her eyes shut. She felt as if the ground had been whipped out from under her. How could Catherine leave the Englishman in madame's apartment like that and not arrange for his care? She might have let Gabby know who had taken over in her absence. Whom could she possibly trust to help her now? Not Sabine with her German boyfriend, that was for sure.

Who would know, then? Monsieur Dior? But if he wasn't aware his sister was working for . . . *them*, it wasn't Gabby's place to endanger him by revealing that information. The wounded man was British. A pilot, maybe, or perhaps a spy. Simply knowing about him could get all of them arrested, tortured, and killed. With a huge effort of will, she pushed the panic away.

If only Simeon, the handyman, still worked at number 10, she could ask for his help in moving the injured man. Could she wait until Yvette came home? She didn't think so. And anyway, she couldn't involve Yvette. It was too dangerous.

The Englishman must be hidden before the undertaker could be called. Gabby ran through the able-bodied men of her acquaintance, but she could not think of one she might trust.

An inkling of an idea was forming in the back of Gabby's mind. One so abhorrent, she did not truly wish it to flourish and grow into a fully fledged thought.

Sabine came back into the room and handed Gabby a small, light package. "Stockings," she said with a wink. No doubt a gift from her German soldier.

Bemused by the great chasm between Sabine's concerns and her own, Gabby blinked, then shoved the package into the pocket of her housecoat. Yvette would throw them on the fire.

"Are you feeling well, Gabby?" said Sabine. "You look as if you're about to faint."

That made Gabby pull herself together. "No, no, I'm fine." She hesitated. Should she ask Sabine to alert her if anyone called for Catherine? But no, she could not afford to raise any suspicions, particularly not Sabine's.

"When will Catherine be back?" She tried to sound casual rather than desperate.

The maid shrugged. "She does not keep me informed of her movements. I believe there was some problem at home and she had to dash away. Perhaps she will be back tomorrow. Perhaps not."

At a loss to know what to do next, Gabby turned and almost collided with Liliane Dietlin.

"What is this?" demanded Liliane, walking into the apartment and stripping off her gloves. "Catherine not here? I didn't know she was going away."

She sounded most put out. Gabby could identify with the sentiment. On closer inspection, Liliane's ordinarily cheerful demeanor had deserted her this morning. She looked pale and drawn.

Gabby hated to add to her troubles, but if anyone knew what Catherine was up to, it would be Liliane. And Gabby desperately needed her help.

As Sabine repeated what she had already told Catherine's first visitor, Gabby watched Liliane closely. If only there were some secret handshake or password Gabby could use to test whether Liliane was a part of Catherine's resistance group. There was no way around it; given the situation in madame's apartment, Gabby had to take the chance of revealing her own involvement. But she would do it away from the inquisitive Sabine.

Liliane hesitated, as if debating a difficult decision. Then she thanked Sabine and turned to leave.

Gabby followed Liliane out of the apartment. When the door shut behind them, she whispered, "Mademoiselle Dietlin! I must speak with you." Before Liliane could respond, Gabby boldly gripped her wrist and drew her toward Madame LaRoq's suite.

Meeting Liliane's astonished gaze, she murmured, "Are you aware of Catherine's . . . er . . . nighttime activities?"

Liliane smiled. "Nighttime activities? That sounds mysterious. What on earth do you mean?"

Gabby licked her lips, glancing down the corridor. "A few nights ago, Catherine asked me to ignore certain visitors who arrived after curfew. I did it, of course. But now things are a little precarious. She has gone, and she has left behind a . . . a difficulty, shall we say."

"A difficulty." Liliane stared hard at Gabby, as if she were calculating the odds. Then she said, "I don't know what you're talking about. It is dangerous to make insinuations like this, Gabby. I'm surprised at you. Catherine is a sensible woman. She just wants to get along with the Germans like the rest of us."

Gabby could not tell anything from Liliane's demeanor. Had Catherine truly kept this secret from her friend? Or was Liliane Dietlin just a very good actress?

With Catherine gone, Liliane was her only chance. "I found something in Madame LaRoq's apartment," she said, trying to put as much meaning into her words as she could. At least if Liliane were not a resistance worker, no harm could come to madame now. She shuddered inwardly at the cold pragmatism of that thought.

"Something?" said Liliane.

"Some*one*," said Gabby. She gripped Liliane's elbow. "Please, Mademoiselle Dietlin, you must come."

Liliane's gaze darted toward madame's apartment. "What is it? What's wrong?"

In a low voice, Gabby said, "It is madame. She has passed away in the night. And there is a—a person in there, wounded. He fell down and I cannot move him."

Liliane's quick nod said she comprehended the implications. "It is broad daylight," she whispered. "I cannot bring anyone in to help until nightfall. We will have to see what we can do ourselves."

They slipped inside Madame LaRoq's apartment and went through to her bedroom. Liliane took in the situation with one cool glance. She put her purse on the dressing table and bent to the injured man. "He has stopped bleeding," she said, "but he is unconscious. We need to get him back to his hiding place before we can arrange for the undertaker. Help me."

Careful of the wound, Liliane hooked her hands under the man's armpits, which made him groan in pain but did not rouse him fully. Gabby took him by the ankles and together, they hefted him up. "My goodness, he is heavy," said Gabby.

When they'd half-carried, half-dragged him out of the boudoir and shuffled into the sitting room, Liliane said, "I have to stop for a minute." She jerked her chin toward the sofa. "Over there." Panting, they carried him over to the sofa and lowered him onto it. With quick, gentle hands, Gabby raised him and placed a cushion behind his head.

They took a few moments, staring down at their burden. Gabby's heart pounded—from both fear and exertion. "Where are we taking him?"

"Come and see."

The maid's room was not much larger than a cupboard. There was space only for a cot and a bedside table inside.

Liliane waved a hand. "All we had to do was pull something in front of the door, and it's as if there is no room there at all."

Gabby gazed in wonder. "So that's why madame had the cabinet put there!" The glass-fronted armoire was enormous, made of burl walnut and cluttered with madame's family silver. Gabby had been so preoccupied lately that she'd scarcely questioned Madame LaRoq's decision to rearrange the furniture.

"Catherine had casters fitted to make it easier to move. See?" Liliane pressed her palms flat on the side of the cabinet and pushed. The cabinet stuttered to the side, silver rattling.

"It seems Mademoiselle Dior has thought of everything." Gabby could not help but admire Catherine's ingenuity. She had achieved all this right under Gabby's nose. She looked to the tiny room again. "There is no way out for him if there is a raid."

"That is true," admitted Liliane. "But you can't have everything, can you? Believe me, it is safer and more comfortable than many other places he might be at this moment."

Just peering into that room made Gabby's throat close over with anticipated panic. She hated small spaces. "Must we put him back there? Could we not hide him in the spare bedroom while the undertaker comes?"

"I've been thinking about that," said Liliane. "He needs treatment and we need easy access to him. I think putting him in the spare room should work in the short term. Now that you are in on the secret, it will be easier."

"I can nurse him," said Gabby. "Just until Catherine comes back." The quicker he got better, the sooner she would be rid of him. "Do you have any medical supplies?"

"In here." Liliane went to the bathroom and fetched bandages, ointment, a solution for cleaning the wound, and a precious vial of morphine. "It might not seem like much, but we can ill spare it."

Given the apparent seriousness of the man's condition, it would not be enough. He must be important for Catherine and Liliane to bring him here, to take such a risk. She burned to ask who he was, but it was safer not to know.

Gabby drew up the coffee table beside the sofa and perched on its edge. She took the scissors and carefully snipped away the bandages, laying the shoulder wound bare.

She sucked air between her teeth. "That does not look good." The wound was ugly, jagged and wet, the skin surrounding it striated with red, as if infection had set in. She saw other evidence of infection. Smelled it, too. "I'll do my best, but I am untrained, you understand."

"You have experience?" said Liliane.

"A little." She had nursed Didier through the long, painful weeks leading to his death.

"Then you are the best we have at this moment."

While Gabby worked to clean and dress the wound, Liliane went to see to the spare room. The man had more than just this wound wrong with him, Gabby suspected. His breathing was shallow and rattling. She hoped he wasn't going to die.

She wished she could bring a doctor to him, but that was far too risky. People were being arrested and shot for helping Jews and dissidents escape capture. She, Catherine, and Liliane were giving aid to the enemy. If she approached the wrong person and he informed on them, it would mean their arrest, followed by weeks of interrogation and torture. They'd be shot or transported to Germany to be worked to death in the camps. Yvette, Maman, perhaps even Monsieur Dior might be rounded up as well.

"Help me bind the wound again," Gabby said when Liliane returned. Liliane hefted the man up while Gabby passed the bandage around his torso and secured it in place.

"There," she said. "That is the best I can do." She eyed the Englishman again. His breathing had grown more regular.

"What next?" said Gabby when they'd washed up and put the medical supplies away. "Look, Mademoiselle Dietlin, I made it clear to Catherine I didn't want to get involved in this." What was Gabby doing now, aiding and abetting these resisters without so much as a second thought? With madame lying cold and alone just a few feet away?

A fresh wave of grief broke over her. She dashed the tears from her face with the back of her hand.

"Madame LaRoq is dead," said Liliane with unwonted brutality. "That changes things." She rose and paced the room. "Now that madame is gone, we must be rid of him. He is a millstone around our necks. I told Catherine this from the start."

Despite Gabby's reluctance to get involved, this seemed callous. She ought to be glad to be freed of this liability as well as the burden of his care. But he was her patient now. She felt a duty to him. "You can't. He is in no fit state to be moved."

"Let me worry about that. But you do need to keep quiet about his presence here. You must." Liliane's gaze drilled into her. "You are in it now, too, you know."

"Of course, I know that." Gabby was torn. On the one hand, every cell in her body urged her to nurse her patient back to health.

On the other, her family's safety would be in jeopardy every second the man remained in this apartment.

For the moment, however, what could she do but be practical? Only a true coward would leave Liliane to deal with all of this on her own. Gabby gathered up the bloody bandages and put them in the fireplace, set them alight.

"Right. Let's get him into bed," said Liliane. "He'll have to stay here until I can make arrangements."

They hefted the wounded man over to the spare bedroom and muscled him onto the mattress. Gabby checked that his wound had not reopened due to their clumsy handling, then tucked him in. The simple act of smoothing the covers over him produced a strange feeling of tenderness.

The man's dark blond hair was a little long; the darker stubble covering his jaw gave him a rakish look. English, behind enemy lines, and wounded. She couldn't imagine how frightening that must be.

When she had closed the spare-bedroom door behind them, Liliane said suddenly, "What happens to the apartment, now that Madame LaRoq has gone?"

Gabby flinched. The question was indecent, with madame silent and still in the next room.

She blew out an unsteady breath. "Usually, I would need to find a new tenant, but I already have several vacancies I can't fill."

"In that case, we have time." Liliane grabbed her purse and tucked it under her arm. "I'll meet my contact and request instructions and make the arrangements for madame. Back as soon as I can, all right?"

Gabby nodded. Alone again, with the immediate problem resolved, loss bloomed in her chest. She forced back the threatening tears. She didn't want to weep in front of this petite woman with her steely resolve and her unnatural composure in the face of danger and death.

"Oh, my dear." Liliane laid a hand on Gabby's arm. "You were most fond of madame, I can see that." She sighed. "The war has hardened me in many ways, of a necessity. It is not always a good thing."

Liliane turned to leave, then looked back. "Madame LaRoq . . . She had the heart of a lion, you know. She might have been bedridden, but she did much for the cause. Everything she could. You should be proud."

Gabby nodded and closed the door after Liliane. She looked around at the apartment, empty now of that charming, warmhearted spirit.

Now that there was no one to see her, Gabby could let herself fall apart, but the desperate bout of weeping that had threatened to overtake her seemed to have vanished. She might not be as brave as Liliane or Catherine or Madame LaRoq, but she could gather the courage to face this challenge. She took a few moments to collect herself. Then she put her shoulders back and went to make madame presentable for the undertaker.

YVETTE

Yvette had delivered books on birds several times without incident when a greater challenge presented itself. This time, it was an envelope monsieur handed her, rather than a book. She delivered three packages from Lelong before following Catherine's instructions, crossing the Pont des Arts and cycling toward the Luxembourg Gardens.

"You have done well, Yvette," Catherine had said when she had briefed her for this new mission the night before. Catherine did not call them missions—she called them little jobs—but that was how Yvette liked to think of them.

Catherine had ceased to waver about whether she ought to employ Yvette in such dangerous work. Now she was all business. "I leave for Callian in the morning. I'm sorry I won't be here to check on you afterwards, but I trust you, Yvette. I know you won't let me down."

"What's the address?" Yvette had a little trick for remembering where to deliver the messages, using the digits of the street number to make a word or a silly phrase that stuck in her memory better than a number ever could.

"It is not an address, as such," said Catherine. "This time, it will be what we call a 'dead drop.'"

A chill skittered down Yvette's spine. That sounded ominous. But she remembered what Liliane had said to her. "When you are most afraid, smile. It will distract others and relax the rest of your body." So she smiled. And she breathed in and out and tried to stay calm while they practiced what she would do the next day.

The following morning, Yvette did an awful lot of smiling as she went through her routine at Lelong, until finally, the time came to make the dead drop. Her entire body trembled as she cruised past the Institute of France toward the Luxembourg Gardens.

Much of the park was barred to the public. Not content with requisitioning half of the Ritz hotel for the Luftwaffe, Göring had taken over the Luxembourg Palace and much of the adjacent parkland, surrounding his fiefdom with high railings and German guards. As instructed, Yvette took the long way around and entered the section of the gardens still open to the public from the boulevard Saint-Michel.

She made her way along the leafy avenues, where the dappled shade provided a blessedly cool change from the baking heat of the Paris streets. When she heard music, she headed in that direction and soon came to a clearing dominated by a bandstand and a large crowd of people, either standing, fanning themselves with their hats or newspapers, or seated on folding chairs.

Incongruously, the sweet strains of the music were produced not by Parisians, but by a string quartet of German soldiers, each sawing away at his instrument as if the performance was his sole reason for being in Paris. And here gathered Parisians and Germans alike, shoulder to shoulder, united in their love of music.

Never had Yvette felt so keenly the difference between her own situation and the attitude of so many Parisians. To them, this was a rare and wonderful opportunity to enjoy live music for free (if one didn't wish to pay for a seat). If they had to mingle with Germans for the privilege, so be it. To Yvette, it was like diving into a pool full of sharks. She was literally surrounded by the enemy.

Too nervous to even think of appreciating the music, Yvette dismounted. As instructed, instead of paying two francs for a folding chair, she wheeled her bicycle toward an unoccupied bench some distance from the bandstand. She soon saw the reason the bench remained empty. It was covered liberally in something nasty and yellow that looked like vomit.

She took the newspaper from the basket of her bicycle, removed an inner sheet, and used it gingerly to wipe off whatever concoction had been used by the resistance to deter other patrons from taking that spot. Then she took another sheet of newsprint, laid it on the bench, and sat down upon it. A fitting use for Nazi propaganda, she thought. Opening what remained of the newspaper, she stared blindly at the print, while fear became a hard pulse in her throat.

How long would she have to sit there waiting for the concert to end? She made herself leaf through the newspaper slowly, scanning each article. Occasionally, someone would pass by quite close, and she tried not to look up in case she caught a German soldier's eye and somehow betrayed her guilt.

Finally, the concert wound to a close. As the audience showed their appreciation in applause, Yvette took the large envelope out of her satchel and slipped it inside the folded newspaper in a movement she had practiced over and over with Catherine. She put the folded newspaper with the envelope inside it on the bench, then picked up her messenger bag and fastened the clasp.

Who would collect the newspaper she left behind? Catherine had told her she was not to linger or be anywhere in the vicinity when the other person came. That was the whole point of a dead drop.

As Yvette stood up, a German soldier accosted her. "Hey! What are you doing here?"

Chapter Thirteen

Paris, June 1944

YVETTE

The hairs on the back of Yvette's neck rose and her skin turned cold and clammy, despite the heat. The soldier had seen her make the drop. She was cornered. Her gaze darted left and right. There was no way to escape without running into more Germans.

Calm, Yvette. Smile!

She spread her lips and tentatively showed her teeth, wishing she was a better actress. But she must have fooled the soldier, because he smiled back at her, touching his cap in a greeting that was clearly benign. He was young and fresh faced and he seemed to mean her no harm, but she couldn't risk his noticing the newspaper she'd left behind. Releasing a breath, she moved toward her bicycle, trying to draw his attention away from the bench.

He spoke to her in German, and she thought he'd only inquired after her health but couldn't be certain. "Pardon?" she said, playing for time. "I don't understand."

"Good morning, mademoiselle," he tried in French. "What is a pretty girl like you doing here all alone on such a beautiful day?" He chuckled, as if aware he spoke a well-worn cliché.

He seemed harmless, but one never knew with the Boches. They liked to toy with their prey. "I love this park." It was the truth, although she did not love it so much when it teemed with Nazis. "I was lured here by the music, but now I must get back to work."

If she walked off, would he notice that she'd left her newspaper behind and try to return it to her? That would be disastrous. It might be better to humor him, to draw him away from the scent.

"I, too, am a lover of music," said the German. His grin widened, as if he was enjoying a joke at her expense. "You do not recognize me, mademoiselle?"

"No, I . . ." She really looked at him then. "Oh!" She laughed from relief. "Sabine's friend." They had only met once, briefly, at a café. She had been rude to him, but he did not seem to remember that.

"And you are . . . I am sorry. I have forgotten your name," he returned, glancing back toward the park bench where she'd been sitting, as if he might find a clue to her identity there.

Before he could notice the newspaper she'd left, Yvette tucked her hand into the crook of his arm, obliging him to turn away from the park bench. "Why, it is Yvette, of course! Will you perhaps take a little stroll with me or do you have to get back to your important duties?"

He seemed like a nice enough young man for a Nazi. Yvette

could see why Sabine liked him. He was pleasant, well mannered, and not terribly bright.

"Yes, of course." He gestured for her to precede him, a guiding, familiar hand on the small of her back.

"As her very good friend, I want to be sure that your intentions toward Sabine are honorable," Yvette said. "So I intend to interrogate you mercilessly. Would you bring my bicycle, please?" He would need both hands to wheel it. Thus, they would be occupied and not pawing at her. She hoped very much that he didn't take her invitation to stroll as encouragement to pursue a romance. She had no intention of poaching on Sabine's territory.

They ambled through the tree-lined paths, carrying on a stilted conversation. Although Sabine's boyfriend was very good at French, he seemed rather tongue-tied. Yvette began to relax, though her heart was still beating hard.

"I think here we must part ways, monsieur," she said, reaching out to take her bicycle from him when they neared the park entrance. "Thank you for the walk."

"Can I offer you lunch, mademoiselle?" said the young man, retaining custody of the bicycle.

Food! Her stomach cramped at the thought, her mouth filling with saliva. No doubt this young man ate well. All the Germans did. The temptation was great, but she could not compromise her principles for the sake of nourishment. And besides, he was looking at her in a way she was sure Sabine would not like. She checked her watch and gasped. "Is that the time? So sorry! Truly, I must go."

With hurried thanks, she yanked her bicycle from his slackened hold, hopped onto it, and called to him as she pedaled away, "Be good to my friend, monsieur!"

∗∗∗

Back at Lelong, Yvette was immediately summoned by Madame Péthier. "*Le patron* wants to see you."

A spurt of guilt about her detour to the gardens made her exclaim, "Oh, dear! What have I done?"

"Don't joke about it," said madame. "He looked very serious when he asked for you."

Not the gardens. Dulac's invitation. That must be it. Yvette's stomach gave a queasy roll. Did she really want to go through with her visit to the château? Her encounter with Sabine's German friend in the middle of her dead drop that morning had been a very close call indeed.

She reached the studio and walked in, to find Monsieur Lelong putting the finishing touches to one of his models, tugging and pushing the mannequin about as if she were a dummy rather than a flesh-and-blood person. The girl looked bored and tired as she put her arms up and her arms down and allowed herself to be swiveled this way and that.

Yvette remained quiet, waiting until finally, monsieur dismissed the mannequin. He turned to beckon her inside.

"Ah, Yvette," he said, smiling a little. "It seems you have been very busy of late."

"Yes," she said cautiously. "Busy" did not begin to describe it. "Well, no more than usual, monsieur."

Now his brow furrowed, but he appeared concerned rather than angry. "I have had a request—a rather unusual request—from Mademoiselle Dulac."

"Yes, sir."

"Sit down, my dear." He indicated one of the chairs in front of his desk and she complied.

Monsieur Lelong perched on the edge of the desk, looking down at her as a fond uncle might, with a rather exasperated affection. "What have you been doing to get yourself into that woman's good graces?"

She grimaced. "I am not sure." She told him about her encounters with the movie star. "She is surrounded by Germans. I wonder if she likes to have a young French girl with her who does not despise her for the way she lives."

Lelong raised his eyebrows. "And do you not despise her for it?"

Yvette shrugged. Her feelings on that subject were complicated in a way that Monsieur Lelong would probably understand. He, too, was obliged to work for people he might privately despise. "I keep my opinions to myself. When I visited mademoiselle, I thought of what Monsieur Dior always says: he wants to make women feel happy and beautiful. I thought that if a woman wears a Lelong creation at all, she must be made to feel special. Certainly, she must not be insulted."

Monsieur Lelong's expression was enigmatic as he studied her. She couldn't tell whether he approved of her statement. "This invitation to the Château de Saint Firmin," he said. "I will not conceal from you that I do not like it."

"I am sorry that you have been placed in this position, monsieur." She was ready to argue her case, but that was difficult because she could not pinpoint the reason for Monsieur Lelong's disquiet. "Is it not a benefit to stay in your clients' good graces?"

His dark eyes shadowed. "There is a limit. And besides, we have enough business without touting for more from those quarters."

He sighed and ran a hand over his high forehead. While he was always point-device, she noticed dark circles beneath his eyes. As president of the Chambre Syndicale de la Haute Couture, he had worked tirelessly to secure the future of Paris fashion.

He said, "I feel a responsibility to you, Yvette, since you have no father to guide you. I hope you understand what might be asked of you if you go with Louise Dulac to the château." He hesitated. "You are aware that she is Oberst Gruber's mistress, I presume."

Such things were hardly a source of embarrassment to a French woman, and yet, she felt awkward talking about it with Lelong. She nodded. "But there is no danger to me in that, is there, monsieur?"

He smiled a little at that, as if he could not help being amused at her naïveté, and she felt herself redden. He bent his head to look into her eyes. "If you wish me to forbid you to go, I will."

"But it is the ambassador . . ." She spread her hands. "And Gruber as well. I think it is not a good idea for you to stand against them."

"You let me worry about that."

It warmed her heart to hear him say this, even though the reason for his concern set her insides churning. "No, monsieur. Thank you, but I do not want that."

She hoped her voice sounded firm and decided. She would not burden him with the knowledge that she intended to spy for France while she was at the château, but she wished she could make him understand that her motives were far from frivolous.

His heavy frown lightened a little. Undoubtedly, he had not relished the task of confronting the German ambassador, particularly not over a delivery girl. But there was a slight catch in his voice when he said, "Be careful, Yvette. If a woman like Mademoiselle Dulac is kind, there is always a reason."

Did he suspect, as she did, that Dulac was a spy? No. That was not it.

Yvette didn't like to question him, and he didn't elaborate. "Sleep on it. Whatever you decide, you have my support. But I'll need your final answer in the morning."

She left the fashion house that day with her mind full of this conversation. She wasn't sure what she might find out at the house party. She only knew that it was an opportunity she could not afford to miss.

After work, Yvette was stowing her satchel in the basket of her bicycle when Jean-Luc returned, dismounting from his bicycle and wheeling it toward her. "You keep avoiding me," he said, grabbing her arm. "Are you having second thoughts?"

"Let me go!" She pulled free, then lowered her voice, glancing around in case anyone overheard. "All you ever do is talk, talk, talk. I am tired of handing out leaflets. Tired of listening to hot air while nothing ever gets done."

He moved close to her, eye to eye. She could smell the faint sourness of his breath. "We are expecting a parachute drop of guns any day now," he whispered. "Then you will see action."

She stared at him. This was crazy. It was too early to begin fighting in the streets. Without the Allies to sweep in and take advantage of a local uprising, the insurgents would simply be crushed under the Nazi jackboot. Arrested. Tortured. Executed. A complete waste of lives.

She understood why these men were so filled with the need to act, but she no longer wanted to join them. "I don't want to be involved anymore."

"You think you're too good for us, is that it?"

"I just don't agree with the plan," she said. "Let me know if they come up with something sensible. In the meantime, count me out."

Jean-Luc was shaking his head at her. "I thought you were a patriot. You've changed, Yvette. Now that you have movie star friends, you've become a dirty collaborator, just like the rest." He jerked the handlebars of his bicycle around and rode off in the other direction.

GABBY

Perhaps the lowest point of Gabby's day—and there had been many candidates for this honor—had been assisting Liliane and the undertaker to smuggle Madame LaRoq out of the apartments in a laundry bag. The horror of it, the gross indignity perpetrated on that lovely old lady, had made Gabby's insides flail with shame.

But then Liliane had whispered to her, "I expect she would have thought it a very good joke, don't you? And something of an adventure," and Gabby could not help but agree.

The undertaker treated his burden with tender care despite the circumstances, thank God. As the laundry van drove away, Gabby said, "What will happen to her?"

Liliane said, "Best you do not know. We must remember her spirit, Gabby, not all of this. She would want that, I think."

They had decided on a course of action that had Gabby praying fervently for forgiveness every time a new wave of guilt tumbled through her. They would keep Madame LaRoq's death a secret so that Gabby could continue to visit the apartment with food and supplies without raising suspicion.

"I have made contact with the network, but we can't move your patient yet," said Liliane. "Besides, you were right. He is in no condition to go anywhere." She frowned. "We might well have to dispose of another body."

Not if Gabby could help it. Squeezing her eyes shut to block out the echo of Liliane's words, she let herself into Madame LaRoq's apartment.

She didn't bother to knock but fitted the key in the lock, balancing the meal tray on her forearm as she had done so many times before. This time, however, there would be no enchanting smile to greet her, no grandmotherly interest in all her doings, no calming words of wisdom about her squabbles with Yvette.

Gabby paused for a moment to gather herself, then carried the tray to the second bedroom, where the injured man lay.

"Oh, you have more color in your cheeks now." She set the tray on the dresser and felt his forehead, which was a little warm. His eyelids were heavy and he gave a faint, muzzy smile. He must still be feeling the effects of the morphine she had given him.

"So sorry to trouble you," he murmured, his voice deep but threaded with pain. "I do apologize. I seem to have suffered a relapse." He spoke French like a native but his excessive politeness was all British.

"What happened this morning?" The shock of seeing him bending over Madame LaRoq was still imprinted on her mind.

"I heard madame cry out." He winced and shifted a little on his pillows, then winced again. She would check the wound, but she wanted to hear this first.

He sighed and settled his head into the pillow, looked up to the ceiling. "I went to help, but by the time I'd managed to shift that blasted cabinet out of the way, I was too late. And I nearly fell right across the poor woman when the dizziness came. Clumsy oaf," he muttered.

"You could have ruptured your stitches."

He nodded. "To no avail." He made a helpless gesture. "I am sorry."

Gabby blinked and clenched her hand into a fist, trying to keep her grief at bay.

He tilted his head. "You were close to madame, I gather? My deepest condolences."

Gabby pressed her lips together and nodded. She tried to sound clipped and practical, like Liliane. "I was very fond of her, yes. But she was old and in pain. It was only a matter of time." Did that sound stoic or heartless? She hoped he would not offer her more sympathy.

"I must thank you for what you've done here," he said, gesturing down at himself. "Binding me up."

"It was nothing," said Gabby, smoothing the sheet and giving that activity all her attention. His eyes were the clear, stunning blue of the sky, and difficult to meet with any confidence.

"But it is everything, is it not?" said the man softly. "You risk your life, harboring me."

Something inside her opened like a flower, basking in the light of his admiration. But she didn't deserve any accolades. She made herself look at him. "Truthfully, I had no choice in the matter, monsieur."

His expression dimmed and she realized how ungracious she sounded. "But I am glad I have the chance to do something for the cause."

And I am glad to have met you, she thought. He was so very . . . masculine. Even weakened by injury and drowsy from the drug, he had that aura about him of a young, virile man. She'd almost forgotten what it felt like to be in the presence of a man like this, and the intimacies of the sickbed brought back memories of Didier, and other intimacies she had shared with her fiancé. When she helped the Englishman sit up so that he could eat, she was acutely aware of the heat of his body, of his breath stirring stray tendrils of hair against her neck as she bent over him. Once he was settled, she quickly turned away, conscious of the blush that had risen to her cheeks.

At her patient's bedside, she arranged a carafe of water and a glass, and brought the plate of food. Bread and a sliver of cheese and a bowl of watery vichyssoise.

"Oh, no," said the man. "I am not hungry in the least. The morphine dulls the appetite, I expect. Please." He gestured to her. "You have it. I cannot take your rations."

"They are madame's rations, not mine," Gabby lied. "We thought it best to . . ." She trailed off, hoping he would understand what she meant without her having to admit they were covering up madame's death because it was expedient. The shame of it would always haunt her.

"Ah." She was both intrigued and a little pleased to see that briefly, he looked appalled. Almost immediately, his expression turned blank. Even drugged and wounded, he was good at masking emotion.

"May I?" She lifted the bowl of leek soup and the spoon, ready to feed him.

A tinge of color edged his cheeks. "Thank you, but I can manage."

She'd embarrassed him. She bit her lip and set the bowl and spoon on the tray, then carried the tray over to him.

He ate his soup without slurping or spilling it. He had excellent manners. "Will you share the cheese with me?" He cut the small slice in two and looked up at her, a smile in his eyes that was difficult to resist.

She ought to refuse. Instead, she found herself saying, "Thank you, I will."

When they'd finished, she took the tray. "Can I get you anything else, Monsieur . . . ?"

"Jacques." His smile warmed her to her toes. "I'm sure you have other duties. Thank you for taking such good care of me."

Jacques. In English, his name would be "Jack." If that was his real name, which she supposed was unlikely. However, it suited him. She thought of Jack, all alone up here, in pain and with nothing to occupy him.

He was right. She should get back to work. However, she said, "Madame has many books. Would you like me to stay and read to you for a while?" Didier had always enjoyed it when she read to him. She would like to do that for this man, to show him he was more than a chore to her. More than a danger and a burden.

"I would like that very much," said Jack.

"Do you have a preference?" she asked him, moving to the door.

"Something with a good story to it." She knew what he meant. It was the kind of novel she liked, too.

Gabby went to madame's bookshelves and retrieved a well-worn copy of Alexandre Dumas's *Queen Margot*. It was a bloodthirsty tale of epic romance, and Gabby would enjoy losing herself in it for a while. But when she returned to her patient, she saw that his eyes were closed. He had drifted back to sleep.

That was what he needed, of course. Silly to feel disappointed.

She set the book by the bedside, covered him with the bed-clothes, and slipped out of the apartment with her tray.

YVETTE

Yvette stared at her reflection in the spotty mirror over the mantelpiece and wished she had never agreed to go to dinner with Vidar Lind. She was so nervous, she thought she might be sick. "I don't feel well, Gabby. Maybe this wasn't such a good idea."

Her sister inspected her closely. "You are a little pale. I'll fetch you my rouge."

Surprised, Yvette stared after her. Gabby's precious rouge. She was entering into the spirit of the venture, despite her misgivings about the diplomat's intentions.

Gabby returned, unscrewing the lid of the rouge pot. Frowning with concentration, she patted her third finger in the scraping of rouge powder that still lined the little pot and deftly dabbed some color along Yvette's cheekbones.

"Thank you." Yvette admired her sister's handiwork in the mirror. Gabby had always been good at makeup.

Out of the corner of her eye, Yvette caught Gabby inspecting the residue of rosy powder on her fingertip. With a small smile, almost instantly repressed, she leaned in to the mirror beside Yvette and applied a dash of the color to her own cheek. After a moment's hesitation, she dipped her fingertip into the pot once more and smoothed a little on the other cheek, as well.

Yvette's eyes widened. It was not like Gabby to waste anything, much less the last remnants of her makeup when she wasn't going anywhere special.

"Gabby?" Yvette whispered, conscious of their mother's presence nearby. "What is happening with you? You look . . . different." There was a gentle glow about her sister that owed nothing to rouge.

Gabby's eyes flared, then she laughed and gestured to her cheeks. "What, this? I suppose I am excited for you, and perhaps a little envious." She didn't meet Yvette's gaze. "I wonder where he will take you tonight."

Maman came in with a hairbrush and pins. "Here, Yvette. Let me do this for you." Gabby made room and Maman stood behind Yvette, brushing her hair with long, gentle strokes. "Up, I think." Maman separated out thick hanks of Yvette's long tresses and began to twist and pin them into a complicated chignon. "This will make you look more sophisticated," she said.

"I'm not sure if that is such a good idea," Gabby began, but Yvette gasped when she saw the finished product. She might not wear couture or expensive jewelry, but the hairstyle made her look almost chic. Even if Vidar Lind considered her too young for him, he might be brought to think differently if he got to know her. The chignon was bound to help.

"Liliane Dietlin came by earlier and brought me this for you," said Gabby, handing her a small box.

"Oh!" Yvette opened the box to find a jeweled hair barrette. It was very pretty, enameled in shades of topaz and bronze.

"She thought it would go with your hair," said Gabby. "Do you want me to put it on?"

"How lovely. Yes please." She handed Gabby the pin. "You told Liliane of my dinner appointment? Why?"

Gabby shrugged. "It is not every day my sister has a young man come to call."

But Yvette wasn't convinced. "Since when have you become friends with Mademoiselle Dietlin?"

"I'm not," said Gabby. "I hardly know her. There," she said, putting her hands on Yvette's shoulders as if to cut off further questioning. "You are ready."

Yvette stared at her reflection and felt an odd sensation, as if a stranger stared back. Gone was the ragged tomboy of the windblown hair, patched jackets, and threadbare skirts. In her place was an elegant creature worthy, she hoped, of a night out with a Swedish diplomat.

She turned around, looking over her shoulder to make sure her dress fell correctly at the back.

It was Gabby's, kept in tissue paper and only brought out on special occasions. Yvette had outgrown all her nice dresses and hadn't had any new party clothes since before the war began. The dress was black and simple, with a scoop neckline and a fitted bodice, the skirt flaring a little past the hips. Though longer on Gabby, it fell just past Yvette's knees, so she didn't flout the clothing restrictions by wearing it.

"You look enchanting," said Gabby. "Doesn't she, Maman?"

Maman nodded, blinking away a sentimental tear. "She takes after her sainted papa."

Finally, the buzzer rang. Maman spied out the front window. "He's here!" She pressed the button to release the street door.

When Gabby admitted him to the *loge*, Vidar seemed to fill

the tiny apartment. He had not appeared quite so large at the Ritz.

When he turned and saw Yvette, his gaze seemed to intensify. She hoped he might compliment her on how she looked, but he said only, "Good evening, mademoiselle."

She had spent the last couple of days trying to conjure Vidar's face specifically in her mind but failed every time. Now that he was here, she was startled all over again by his magnetism. He was all edges—the set of his shoulders, his lean face with its high cheekbones and blade of a nose, the hard line of his jaw, the sharp, precise cut of this dinner suit. Only the warm expression in his dark eyes as they rested on her lent him the least hint of softness.

The burn of a flush began at Yvette's décolletage and swept over her face. With a start, she remembered her manners and made the introductions. Vidar exchanged a few words with Gabby and Maman, but she hardly heard what he said. He wore a dinner suit. They must be going somewhere special.

"Mademoiselle," he said, and held out his hand to her. "Shall we?"

She'd expected his driver to be waiting outside but was not disappointed to find they would walk. As it turned out, they did not have far to travel, only a few paces down the rue Royale.

She laughed. "Maxim's? I have always wanted to go here."

He raised an eyebrow. "It is not too familiar, then? I wasn't sure."

"Of course not. Who can afford to go to Maxim's?" A silly question. Clearly, Vidar Lind could afford to go there.

He drew her closer, tucking her hand into the crook of his arm as they strolled inside. While he dealt with the *maître d'hôtel*, Yvette stared around her. The art nouveau wonderland was an enchanted garden made of wood and stained glass. The lighting was dim and romantic, and the setting, with its swirling sylvan décor, was so beautiful, she held her breath in case it all disappeared. It was as if a magical new world enveloped her in its scented embrace.

She tried not to stare as they were led to their table. The Nazis had replaced all the principal staff at Maxim's with Germans, and looking around, Yvette could see that the majority of the patrons were German officers and their guests. That dimmed her mood, but it was only to be expected. One could not eat at a fine restaurant in wartime without meeting the enemy.

"You look very pretty tonight, Yvette," said Vidar.

For some reason, the word "pretty" made her think of little girls with ribbons and bows, not a grown woman. "So do you," she said, then laughed. "Very pretty, indeed."

In fact, in his immaculately tailored suit, he attracted the attention of every woman present.

A group of German officers laughed raucously at the next table and Vidar leaned in to her. "Perhaps this was not the right place to come, but I wanted to give you a treat. The food here is very good."

She had heard that at Maxim's they were not bound by rationing restrictions. She wondered what Vidar would say if he knew that on some days, she did not eat at all.

With her permission, he ordered for them both. The wine, a crisp Chablis, was brought, tasted, and approved. Yvette took a sip for courage but resolved not to drink too much. She needed to keep her wits about her for the conversation she intended to have with him. "I look forward to the meal."

He smiled. "Perhaps next time we will dine at the Ritz. You go there often, I understand."

"I find myself there frequently of late, it is true," she said, wondering if he was fishing for information about Louise Dulac. "Mademoiselle Dulac seems to have taken a liking to me." That brought her to the question she'd been wanting to ask him. "She has even invited me to go with her to Chantilly. To the Château de Saint Firmin."

Vidar's eyebrows rose. "Indeed?" His face seemed to harden, as if he didn't like the thought of her visiting King Otto's castle.

"Is something wrong, monsieur?"

He shrugged. "It is an honor, I suppose." He met her gaze, then glanced away. "I would have thought your mother wouldn't allow it."

She wanted to tell him she did not consider an invitation to a German ambassador's country house to be any kind of honor. She considered it an opportunity. Among such influential people, she might find out something significant.

"You disapprove of my going?"

"Disapprove?" He gazed at her with those world-weary eyes and she couldn't tell what he was thinking. "What right do I have to disapprove of anything you do?" After a pause, he added, "I trust you will be careful. It is a very . . . sophisticated crowd."

And I am not sophisticated at all, she thought. It was true and she ought not to be offended by his pointing it out. Clearly, one needed more than a fancy hairstyle to prove one could move in such circles.

He sipped his wine and lowered his voice. "The war will be over soon. What do you intend to do with yourself then?"

"I will continue to work at Lelong," she said. "Maybe I can convince *le patron* to make me a mannequin."

"A worthy ambition," said Vidar, his tone dry. Was he being sarcastic?

"Those girls work hard," she said. "You have no idea what it takes."

"Clearly not," said Vidar, amused. "But with your intelligence and resourcefulness, would it not be better to do something more worthy of your talents?"

"Like what?" Other than teaching or secretarial work, there were few options open to women, and she had not even completed her schooling before the occupation ruined everything.

He sipped his wine. "Let's see how you do at Chantilly. Then we'll talk about it again."

Her gaze snapped to his. One minute, he had been against her going; now he seemed to imply it was some kind of test. Before she could question him, the waiter came with their food. Vidar sat back in his chair as the appetizer was laid down before them. Pâté de foie gras and crisp, paper-thin triangles of toast.

Yvette had to restrain herself from falling upon the food like swine at a trough. She made herself take another slow sip of wine before dipping her knife into the pâté and spreading some on a piece of toast. But the urgency she felt made her clumsy. The toast cracked in half in her hand. "What do you do in your job as a diplomat, Monsieur Lind?" she asked, hoping he hadn't noticed. She selected a piece of shattered toast and nibbled on it. The pâté was gamey and smooth, laced with cognac. Sublime.

"Please. Call me Vidar." He waved a hand. "My duties are quite unexciting. Paperwork, mostly."

"Really?" She didn't believe it. He was too vital, too quick-witted, to spend this war sitting behind a desk. "And how does it come about that someone who does mostly paperwork can lay his hands on a bicycle at a moment's notice, and from a rather shady-looking establishment, too?"

He sat back in his chair and fiddled with the stem of his wine-glass. "There was nothing shady about that alley—except in the literal sense, mademoiselle."

"Then why did you tell me to stay in the motorcar?" countered Yvette.

His eyes crinkled at the corners and he nodded, as if happy to be caught out, the master with an apt pupil. "I did, didn't I?" He reached for a point of toast and spread pâté on it. "If I tell you why, will you promise to keep the bicycle?"

As he ate, Yvette hesitated. "You gave me your word that it wasn't confiscated property. So in that case, I will promise to keep the bicycle, monsieur."

He leaned toward her. "The bicycle was police issue. It was acquired by an associate of mine. And, since he owed me a favor, he was happy to hand it over."

She gasped. "Police issue? But—"

He held up a hand. "Remember your promise." He smiled, a little grimly, she thought. "It wasn't stolen, I assure you. My associate has connections. He managed to purchase a surplus supply."

Yvette stared at him. Whoever heard of there being a surplus of anything in this war? Lowering her voice, she asked, "Is your . . . *associate* part of the black market, monsieur?" She thought of Monsieur Arnaud and the thug, Rafael, who had beaten him. Clearly, there was a hierarchy of black marketeers. Someone who could lay his hands on a shipment of bicycles was probably more in Friedrich Berger's league than Monsieur Arnaud's.

"One comes across many different characters in my line of work," said Vidar, as if reading her thoughts. "One deals with people one doesn't necessarily like. It is all a question of expediency."

"I suppose it is expediency that forces such people to extort and beat up elderly men," she hissed. "I saw a gold-toothed ruffian creating havoc in a bookshop the other day. A fellow by the name of Rafael. He was from the Berger gang, or so the bookseller told me."

Vidar nodded. "Protection money. Berger's men collect a fee from the local businesses every month, in return for not raiding them or smashing up the premises." He eyed her for a moment, then explained in a low voice, "The Germans have deputized several criminal gangs to do their dirty work. They round up resistance workers, then torture them to give them names of more people in the network."

"I have heard about this." She shivered at her own narrow escape. On the very day she had encountered one of Berger's men, she had been acting as a courier for the resistance. "What happens to these agents after that?"

Vidar's eyes burned like hot coals, though he kept his face neutral. "Some die of the torture. Some are sent to Fresnes or one of the other local prisons, then shipped off to Germany to work in the camps."

Suddenly, their opulent surroundings took on a nightmarish aspect. All around them, fine ladies simpered and preened, gentlemen laughed. Did they know what went on right here in Paris, not too far from where they all sat, quaffing wine and sampling delicacies as if rationing had never been invented?

Yvette pushed her plate away. She had lost her appetite. Vidar cleared his throat. "My apologies. Hardly appropriate dinner conversation."

The waiter removed the appetizers and set new plates before them. Some kind of fish in a delicate lemon sauce. New potatoes tossed in butter and parsley. Yvette couldn't eat a bite.

She leaned in to continue the conversation. "Berger's men, they are French, aren't they? How can they cooperate with the enemy like that?"

Vidar touched a napkin to his lips. "They might be French but they are first and foremost criminals. The Germans have let them run amok, importing goods and selling them on the black market, rounding up Jews and dissidents and stealing their property. All of it is officially sanctioned. They are untouchable."

"But how much longer can they continue to operate?" She glanced around to check no one was within earshot. "Surely the war is almost over. The Allies are marching through France."

An impatient shake of the head told her she did not understand. "Listen to me, Yvette. Now that the Allies are so close, it is even more dangerous for people like you. The Germans will want to leave as much destruction as they can in their wake. There will be no mercy for those who resist."

Her attention snagged on one phrase: *people like you*. What did he mean by that? What did he know about people like her?

She made herself fork a morsel of fish into her mouth, chew and swallow, playing for time, but the tender flesh stuck in her throat. She sipped her wine. "All I want to do is to work in fashion and mind my own business until it's all over."

He raised his eyebrows. "Is that why you have been visiting Monsieur Arnaud's shop and leaving newspapers in the Luxembourg Gardens?"

Chapter Fourteen

Paris, June 1944

YVETTE

Her gaze flew to his, a surge of fear filling her chest. Had she got him all wrong? Would he denounce her in the middle of Maxim's with all these German officers looking on?

He smiled. "Oh, I know all about you, Yvette Foucher. But you needn't look so terrified. I'll keep your secrets. You have nothing to fear from me."

That did not reassure her very much. Carefully, she set her fork on the edge of her plate and did her best impression of Gabby. "I don't know what you're talking about. I keep my head down. I don't make trouble. I just want to get through the war."

Vidar nodded but his eyes seemed to bore into hers, as if to read the thoughts behind them. "That is a very good plan, Yvette. But you should not go to Chantilly, in that case."

She licked her lips. "It is already arranged. It's too late to back out now."

He seemed to accept the rebuff and changed the subject. Dessert came next, but she was so agitated by his sudden revelation that she hardly noticed what she ate. Suddenly, her life was in the hands of Vidar Lind, and she did not like that sensation at all.

As they left the restaurant, he offered his arm. "Perhaps we might take the long way home?"

Despite Yvette's misgivings, a delicious thrill of apprehension shot through her. Did he intend to kiss her tonight? His manner had hardly been romantic. He seemed to find her amusing more than attractive, and his warnings about Chantilly showed he thought her incapable of looking after herself.

Nonetheless, she tucked her hand into the crook of his arm and let him turn her in the direction opposite to number 10. The evening was sultry, and thunder rumbled in the distance. She felt a confusing mixture of excitement at his closeness and terror at the knowledge that a word to the right quarter and he could have her arrested. "Where are you taking me?"

"I have no idea," he said. "Isn't it nice not to have a plan?"

Although it was late, they passed many other people along the way, out strolling after an evening on the town. Yvette was in a strange, reckless mood, her attraction to this man heightened by the danger of their shared secret. He had not referred to it again, but it was there, vibrating between them like a tuning fork, a constant hum in the air.

"*Ricky, mein lieber Freund! Wie geht's?*" A large man in a German officer's uniform lumbered toward them, opening his arms wide.

Vidar's arm tensed beneath hers. In French, he said, "I'm afraid you have confused me with someone else. Excuse us." His grip was firm on Yvette's elbow as he guided her past.

She was too surprised to resist. "What was all that about?"

"Keep walking," answered Vidar. The grim note in his voice made her shut her mouth and do as she was told. They continued at a steady, brisk pace toward the Place de la Concorde.

Questions bombarded her brain. Was Vidar a spy? He must be if he had found out about her dead drop in the Luxembourg Gardens. Was he working undercover? Was that why that German had greeted him by a different name?

She followed his lead as he slowed to a meandering stroll. They stopped to peer through shop windows, at the empty shelves inside. They doubled back, turned abruptly down quiet alleys, changed direction once or twice. She recognized the same countersurveillance techniques Catherine Dior had taught her.

Vidar's grip on her elbow was not tight, but it felt inexorable. She said, "That German officer knew you. He called you Ricky." He had also called him "friend."

"He mistook me for someone else," said Vidar.

That was so blatantly untrue that she opened her mouth to probe further, but he cut her off. "Let it go, Yvette." His tone made it clear; he was implacable. No matter how persistently she interrogated him, he would never tell her the truth.

When they passed La Madeleine, she realized they had essentially walked in a circle. She was nearly home again.

Relief and disappointment mingled in her chest. Would she see him again? Would he kiss her good night? As they approached her front door, she slowed her steps in hope.

But they'd no sooner reached number 10 than the buzzer went on the street door, signaling that someone—Maman or Gabby—

had seen them and released it. With a rueful smile, as if his thoughts ran along the same lines as hers, Vidar took a card case and pencil from his pocket and jotted something down. "If you ever need me, call this number."

That sounded very much like a final farewell. "All right, then," she said, taking the card he offered. She lifted her chin, hoping he didn't read the disappointment in her eyes. "Goodbye, Vidar."

She was about to turn away when suddenly, he gripped her shoulders as if he would either shake her or kiss her. But he did neither. He stared down at her with those deep, world-weary eyes and said, "Don't go. Chantilly is not the place for you, Yvette."

But of course, that only made her more determined to prove him wrong.

GABBY

The evening after Yvette left for Chantilly, Gabby waited until her mother was asleep and snoring before she crept across the courtyard to visit her patient. She eased into the building and tip-toed upstairs and along the corridor, careful to be especially quiet as she passed Madame Vasseur's apartment, so as not to wake Chou-Chou.

She unlocked the door to Madame LaRoq's suite and eased it open, then went to the spare bedroom. Since the day she and Liliane had carried their patient there, she had not had the heart to move him back to his original hiding place.

At first, Jack had seemed to improve. The wound to his shoulder was healing. He would talk to her about his home in the English countryside and ask about her childhood on the farm before Papa died. But after a few days, his eyes seemed to glaze over and his cheeks grew flushed. When pressed to describe his symptoms, he admitted to a sore throat and headache, and it was clear that breathing was becoming a struggle. A hand pressed to his brow told Gabby he was feverish, burning.

Gabby soaked towels in water and gave him sponge baths to try to cool him down, but the effects didn't last. He needed medicine, but who could come by medicine in times like these? There was no doctor she could trust. Perhaps Yvette's Swedish diplomat could help, but Yvette had left for Chantilly with her movie star friend and Gabby didn't feel she could visit the consulate to inquire.

She perched on the edge of Jack's bed and took his hand in hers. His eyes opened and slowly focused. Then he smiled and her heart grew warm and soft in her chest.

She had to save him. She simply had to.

His eyelids seemed too heavy to keep open. He sighed, and her name was just a whisper on his lips. He fell into a fitful doze.

She did not like the sound of his breathing. She tried pressing her ear to his chest. There was a distinct, rattling wheeze. Might it be a chest infection rather than the wound that was making him feverish? How could she tell? If only Catherine Dior would come back. But Gabby wouldn't relinquish this burden now, even if Catherine offered to take it from her.

Jack grew hot again, restless, as if he were trying to find a cool place on the pillow to lay his head. His blond hair was dark with sweat, plastered to his forehead. She ought to give him another sponge bath. It seemed such an inadequate measure, it made her want to cry.

Would Jack die here, alone in a foreign country? The Allies were fighting their way through northern France, but not fast enough. If only he could hang on until they took Paris. If only she might save him.

A knock fell on the door, a faint *rat-tat . . . rat-tat-tat.* Liliane.

"I've found a doctor. He'll come tomorrow," she said in a low voice. "It's all right. He is one of us."

Relief flowed like alcohol through Gabby's veins. "You are sure he can be trusted?"

"Yes. I'm sure. As sure as anyone can be, these days." Liliane checked on Jack and her expression darkened. "I hadn't banked on this fever. It is taking too long for him to get better, far longer than I'd thought. We need him to walk out of here on his own two feet."

"There is not much I can do with homemade remedies," said Gabby. Even herbs were hard to come by. "I try to keep the fever down, give him fluids." She spread her hands. It was far too little.

"I'm sure you're doing everything you can." Liliane licked her lips. "There are more men like him," she said. "Not injured, but needing sanctuary until we can get them out."

All these people needing sanctuary . . . The implication was clear, but Gabby's instinct was to protest and deny. Wasn't one secret enough? She risked her life for the man in madame's spare bedroom, but she'd accepted that because she'd had little choice, and . . . well, because she had a tenderness for him, if she was honest with herself. But a stream of strangers putting not only her but her mother and sister, possibly everyone in the building, in grave danger? No. Too much could go wrong.

"Think about it," said Liliane, pressing her shoulder. "You said there were more spare apartments around the building. I know it is a risk, but we must all do what we can."

⤺

WHEN THE DOCTOR attended Jack at last, he confirmed Gabby's fears. "Pneumonia. His right lung is very congested."

Taking off his coat, he rolled up his sleeves and showed Gabby a technique she could use to break up the congestion, pummeling the man's chest, kneading it like bread dough. Gabby winced when the action made Jack moan in pain, then clamp his teeth down hard on the wad of cloth the doctor had shoved in his mouth.

"His wound!" gasped Gabby. "Please be more careful."

The doctor grunted as he worked. "I am being as gentle as I can."

"Is there no cure?" Gabby asked. "No medicine for this?"

He rolled down his sleeves and shrugged into his coat. "Sulfa pills. If by some miracle you could get hold of some, they would inhibit the growth of bacteria." He jotted down the dosage for her. "In the meantime, rest, plenty of fluids, and use that massage technique I showed you once a day."

"But without the medicine . . ." Gabby struggled to form the words. "Will he die?"

The doctor looked grave. "He is malnourished and weak. You must prepare yourself for the worst."

"How do we get our hands on those pills?" But the doctor only shook his head and left.

Liliane set her jaw. "I will ask my contacts about these sulfa pills, but unfortunately an escaped English spy is not a high priority."

"Escaped?" repeated Gabby. "How did he get caught?"

Liliane raised her eyebrows. "I thought you wanted to know nothing about it."

When had she said that? She wanted to learn every last detail. Liliane was regarding her with a knowing smile but Gabby refused to rise to the bait. "Either way, I am doomed if they find him. Tell me. You know I can be discreet."

So Liliane explained. "He was operating north of Paris. One of the captains in his circuit was caught and betrayed him under torture. He should have run as soon as he heard the members of that circuit were taken but he insisted on carrying out his last mission in Paris. He was shot in a melee, then taken to a place on rue Lauriston and tortured there. Somehow, he managed to escape and evade capture until one of our people found him half-dead at a safe house nearby. There was nowhere else to take him at that time, so in desperation, Catherine brought him here."

By the end of this recital, Gabby was struggling to hold back tears. Of pride in Jack's bravery and of horror at what he must have suffered. "So, the marks on his body—"

"Are thanks to those thugs who held him," said Liliane. "The pneumonia is probably a result of the *baignoire*. They plunge their victims into an icy bath, almost drowning them, over and over, until they talk."

Gabby shuddered. A murderous rage bubbled up inside her. "The Boches, they are barbarians."

"Yes. But these were not the Germans," said Liliane quietly. "What makes it so much worse is they were Frenchmen. The Bonny-Lafont gang." Liliane's expression darkened. "But they will get what is coming to them when this war is over, mark my words."

Gabby hesitated. "Those others. The ones you want me to hide. Are they escaped prisoners also?"

"No." Liliane picked up her hat and coat. "But they need you, all the same. Think about it."

When Liliane had gone, Gabby found that Jack seemed quieter.

He was sleeping, his lashes damp spikes against his cheeks. A crop of whiskers shadowed his jaw, practically a beard now. Was it soft? She wanted to touch it.

Tentatively, Gabby put out her hand, then snatched it back when he opened his eyes. "Oh, it's you," he muttered.

"Can I get you anything?" Gabby leaned over him to feel his forehead. It was cool now, but she didn't think the fever had broken. In fact, he was shivering. "You are cold. Let me fetch the extra blankets."

But even those did not seem to warm him. She had a crazy urge to climb under the covers and share her own body heat. She had heard of such things being effective. *Don't be ridiculous,* she chided herself. *You just want to be close to him, that's all.*

She couldn't resist stroking the hair back from his forehead, murmuring a soothing stream of nonsense, like a mother to a fretful child.

Without that sulfa medicine, he would die.

She needed to get hold of those tablets. If there was such medicine to be had in Paris, she would find it. First, she would try Monsieur Arnaud.

THE NEXT DAY, Gabby managed to snatch some time to hurry over to Monsieur Arnaud's bookstore, but he shook his head when he heard her request. "Impossible," he said. "I am sorry, Gabby. I wish I could help."

She licked her lips. "It is Madame LaRoq. A matter of life and death. I . . . I would make it worth your trouble, monsieur. Surely you know people."

He spread his hands. "If I could get them, don't you think I would? But drugs like that are supplied to the military and impossible to come by without a contact there."

She believed him, and the knowledge that she had nowhere else to turn plummeted through her like a stone. Not again. She could not bear such a loss again.

I wish I'd never met him, she thought fiercely. *I wish he was someone else's problem.* And Liliane wanted her to take on more of them!

As she was about to leave the bookstore, her attention snagged on a large white ceramic cat that had sat in the window ever since she could remember. She and Yvette had called it Maude, for a reason that was now lost in the mists of time. "Oh!" said Gabby softly, reaching out. Maude was missing her left ear. She stroked the roughness along the break, feeling tears well behind her eyes.

"Oh, that." Monsieur Arnaud cleared his throat. "No doubt you heard from Yvette about that ruffian who smashed up the place."

"Yes, I was sorry to—" She gasped, whirling around to face the bookseller. Of course! Why hadn't she thought of that? Why hadn't Monsieur Arnaud? *"Berger!"* If anyone could obtain a rare commodity like sulfa pills, it was the king of the black marketeers. "You must take me to see him."

"Are you crazy?" Monsieur Arnaud stared at her. "Don't you know what they did?"

Ordinarily, Gabby would agree with his caution, but she was desperate. "You paid him what he demanded, didn't you? You're all square?"

"Well, yes, but—"

"And there is somewhere quite public we could meet, so no one gets hurt?" Gabby took Monsieur Arnaud's hand and squeezed it.

"Please, monsieur. Someone I . . . Someone I love is dying. Please, you must help me!"

"Your mother will kill me," said Monsieur Arnaud. "But I suppose nothing too terrible can happen in a public place." His eyebrows lowered. "You'd best have the money to pay, though. Berger will be furious if he thinks we've wasted his time."

Gabby threw her arms around the bookseller and squeezed his rotund form tightly. "Oh, thank you, monsieur."

"Yes, well, that's enough of that," said the bookseller gruffly, extricating himself. "Meet me at the Café de la Mer on rue de la Pompe at eight."

Monsieur Arnaud was right to be afraid. So was Gabby, but the means of saving Jack was so close, she couldn't dwell on the danger to herself. Besides, Berger might be a criminal, but he was first and foremost a businessman. Why would he hurt Gabby, as long as he was paid? Which made her pause. She didn't know what the price of the medicine might be and she had no money to pay for it.

She scanned her memory of the trinkets and valuables in Madame LaRoq's suite. The sapphire rings. They were valuable. Perhaps too valuable to trade, but then Madame LaRoq had risked her life to hide Jack. Surely she would not begrudge Gabby using her jewels to save him.

☙

BY THE TIME she met Monsieur Arnaud at the appointed rendezvous, Gabby was wound so tightly with nervous anticipation that the utter normality of the Café de la Mer came as something of an anticlimax. Tables and chairs spilled out onto the pavement beneath red awnings; people drank whatever they could afford—or persuade the Germans to buy for them—and fanned themselves against the lingering heat with whatever came to hand.

"Will Berger himself be here?" Gabby asked Monsieur Arnaud as they found a table and sat down.

"Probably not," said monsieur. "It is still early. But someone will be. His men."

All the cafés in Paris teemed with German soldiers and this one was no exception. The way they behaved, full of drink and song, with pretty girls hanging off their arms, they didn't look terribly threatening. But then, it was the Gestapo you had to watch out for, not the rank-and-file soldiers.

"Look," said monsieur with a jerk of his chin toward the back of the room. "He is here after all."

Trying not to stare, Gabby took a wide sweep of the café and thought she spotted Berger. Dressed like an American gangster in a sharp pin-striped brown suit and a wide, loud necktie, a man sat at the back of the café like a king surrounded by his subjects: buxom, pretty women and men with brilliantined hair and cigarettes behind their ears. In stark contrast to the shabby French patrons, everything these people wore was flashy and new.

Gabby tensed. "What should we do?" Now that she saw him, her bravado evaporated. She didn't have the courage to approach the leader of a criminal gang.

"We flag down one of his men and ask for some time with him," said Monsieur Arnaud.

Like courtiers requesting an audience with the king. Or rather, not courtiers, but peasants. The notion made Gabby's blood simmer. Honest Parisians like her struggled to feed their families, while villains like these quaffed champagne and smoked cigars.

"Let's get a drink." Monsieur Arnaud ordered two glasses of red wine and they settled in to wait.

The minutes ticked by. Gabby eyed Monsieur Arnaud, sitting there dressed in his Sunday best. A bead of sweat had formed on his brow—whether from the heat or from anxiety, she couldn't tell. He took out a worn handkerchief and mopped at his forehead, folded it carefully, and returned it to his pocket. "I am sorry about Madame LaRoq," he said eventually. "I know you're fond of her."

Gabby's stomach gave a hard twist. She nodded, pressing her lips together. "Monsieur, thank you for—"

"*Tchut!*" He made a quick cutting gesture with his hand. "Here he comes."

With a surge of nervousness Gabby glanced sideways. Not Berger himself, thank goodness. One of the men who had been gathered in the booth at the back of the café was sauntering over.

He smiled with a flash of gold teeth. "You are a brave man, showing your face here, Arnaud."

Monsieur stuck out his chin. "I have a request to make of your boss."

As if to draw attention to his dental work, the man produced a toothpick, stuck it between his clenched teeth, and wiggled it up and down as he considered this. He gave Gabby a pointed look that turned speculative. "Who is this?"

"Never mind," snapped Arnaud. But when the gangster's mild expression turned menacing, in a trembling voice, Gabby interposed, "I am Gabrielle Foucher, monsieur. And it is I who have the request."

"Enchanted, mademoiselle," said Gold Teeth. She thought he

might bend to kiss her hand, his manner was so courtly. To her relief, he did not. "I am Rafael."

She'd suspected as much from her sister's description of the man who had beaten up Monsieur Arnaud and threatened Yvette. Thank goodness monsieur was doing the talking, because Gabby's mouth had gone dry.

"Will you tell Berger we wish to speak with him?" said the bookseller.

Rafael laughed. "He is busy. He is always too busy for the likes of you. What do you want?"

Gabby was torn between relief that she didn't have to confront Berger and doubt that dealing with one of his henchmen would be as effective. However, at a nod from monsieur, she stumbled into speech. "I need medicine. Sulfa pills."

"Sulfa pills?" Rafael stroked his chin. "It's going to cost. They are not easy to come by."

"But you *can* get them?" Gabby leaned forward eagerly. "I am prepared to pay well."

She ignored Monsieur Arnaud's sharp glance. She knew she was going about bargaining the wrong way, but she had to get those pills.

Rafael tilted his head and scanned Gabby in a thorough and insolent manner that made her think he was not at all considering possible sources of medical supplies. "I'll see what I can do. But the price might be more than you can afford."

Gabby licked her lips. "I know I don't look like a wealthy woman, but I'm the concierge at number ten rue Royale. My tenant, the lady who needs the medicine, she can pay."

"Number ten rue Royale," mused Rafael, stroking his chin. He narrowed his eyes at her. "You have many rich tenants, no?"

Gabby saw where he was going with this. "The Germans took everything they had. No one has anything anymore."

Rafael laughed. "Somehow, I don't think that is true," he said. "Get me something interesting and I will consider your request. If you can bring me good artwork or jewels, I might be able to source some medicine." He removed the toothpick from between his teeth and jabbed it in her direction. "I assume that time is of the essence, so why don't you meet me back here tomorrow night?" He glanced at Arnaud, then added, "Alone."

The sulfa pills must not be so very difficult for him to obtain if he would have them tomorrow night, but she judged it wisest not to point this out. "I'll do that." She would use madame's sapphires. They were more portable than paintings, and unlike gold, sapphires tended to hold their value. It was not truly stealing, even if it felt like it.

"Until tomorrow," said Rafael with a flourishing bow.

Inwardly, Gabby shuddered. "Until then."

"I hope you know what you're doing," said Monsieur Arnaud as they left the café.

Gabby sincerely hoped so, too.

When she reached the apartments, Gabby went straight up to madame's suite to look in on Jack. He was still. So still that she rushed to his bedside to make sure he was alive.

Relieved to feel the warm brush of his breath on her palm, Gabby went to hunt for madame's jewelry box, which she'd kept hidden beneath a loose floorboard in her bedroom. There was a lovely string of pearls, Gabby knew, but it was a family heirloom and must go to madame's niece. Other pieces were sentimental, but madame had always said that if the worst came, there were a couple of sapphire rings she might sell.

Gabby found the jewelry box and opened it. In a little drawer, she found the two rings. She took the smaller of them, wrapped it in her handkerchief, and put it in her pocket. No doubt it was worth far more than a few sulfa pills, but she was hardly in a position to bargain.

Before she left the apartment, she looked in on her patient again. A surge of hope rose in her chest. He was going to get better now. She would make sure of it. On impulse, she crossed the room, took his hand, and told him the good news. He couldn't hear her, but it made her feel better.

Everything was going to be all right.

Chapter Fifteen

✦≫≪✦

Paris, February 1947

GABBY

A medal, Gabby! You are getting . . ." Yvette snatched up the scrap of paper with her notes on it and read: "'The King's Medal for Courage in the Cause of Freedom.' Awarded to foreign civilians who have given great assistance to British forces during the war." Her eyes glowed as she raised them to Gabby's, more like her old self than she had been since her arrival. "I'm so proud of you."

"But . . . how?" The explanation that leaped to mind only confused Gabby more.

"I would have thought that was obvious," said Yvette. "Clearly, it was an Englishman who recommended you. One of the men you saved."

"That can't be. Oh, no, that *could* not be." If Jack was alive, he'd be here. He wouldn't have arranged for them to give her this medal as some sort of consolation prize. One of the others, then? Yes, perhaps . . . This news on top of Yvette's arrival had made her dizzy. She struggled to think it through.

The tiny inkling of hope that perhaps Jack had put up her name for recommendation quickly died. If he was alive, he would have returned to Paris—to Gabby—as soon as he could. Or if . . . if he didn't feel the same . . . He would have written to her in friendship, at least, to let her know he had survived.

The insidious thought that he had simply forgotten her, that his affection had never been sincere, snaked through her brain.

No. She refused to believe it. Jack was a good man and she would not let herself suspect otherwise. To tarnish the bright memory of the time they'd shared with doubts like that was the act of a coward. She gave a shuddering sigh. She had not wanted to know what had happened to him, fearing the worst. Now it was time to change that. One way or the other, she had to know.

"Gabby?" Yvette had been speaking, and Gabby hadn't heard a word.

"Sorry, what did you say?"

With a worried frown, Yvette repeated, "The ceremony is at the British embassy next Thursday. They said they sent the invitation twice and were calling to make sure they had the correct address. Why didn't you reply? Of course you must go."

Gabby put a hand to her mouth. "Oh, no. I couldn't." Stand up in front of all those people and accept an award for doing no more than any decent person would? They didn't know what a reluctant heroine she had been.

She didn't want accolades. There were many people who deserved medals—Yvette, for example, and Catherine Dior—but

Gabby was not one of them. She had never been brave, not for one solitary second of that war. She had been scared and begrudging yet eager to help Catherine, whom she so admired. Later, her motives had been personal, not noble in any way.

"Don't be silly," Yvette said. "Of course you can! Besides, I have told them you will be there and I refuse to let you make me a liar."

Gabby gave a hollow laugh that ended on a hiccup. She grabbed Yvette's hand and squeezed it. "Will you come with me? Help me be brave?"

Yvette smiled. "I wouldn't miss it for the world."

Gabby put her arms around her sister. "Thank you, Yvette." And the feeling when Yvette hugged her back was more precious than any medal.

YVETTE

The prison at Fresnes was a vast citadel of punishment and correction, containing both men's and women's jails and a hospital as well. The subterranean corridor that led to the women's prison was sporadically lit, with alternating pools of eerie bluish light and Stygian darkness, like a tunnel into hell. Yvette swallowed hard and threw her shoulders back. There was no need to be afraid, was there? She would only be here for a meeting, less than an hour. Then, unlike Louise Dulac, she could walk free.

Nevertheless, when she and Monsieur LeBrun followed the guard up a flight of steps into the women's prison, Yvette released a long breath of relief. At least here, watery daylight filtered through the clouded glass windows at the far end of the complex.

She gazed up and up, counting five stories, gallery upon gallery of cells ranged around a central atrium. The whitewashed walls were punctuated with iron doors as grim as tombstones. The place reeked of misery. Yvette couldn't repress a shiver.

What had been an abstract idea—Louise Dulac arrested and charged—suddenly became a stark reality. But Yvette set her jaw. Hadn't Catherine Dior been incarcerated here during the war? Hadn't she suffered unimaginable torture in between bouts of questioning at rue de la Pompe? And all of it might have been prevented had Louise lifted one perfectly manicured finger.

That thought stiffened Yvette's spine as she climbed one flight of stairs and followed the guard along the landing to a small meeting room. The room had a window with a narrow sill. There was no seating; the only furniture was a rectangular wooden table. The guard left, presumably to fetch the prisoner. LeBrun set his attaché case on the table and opened it with a *click* that bounced off the bare, hard surfaces around them.

While LeBrun frowned over his documents, Yvette waited in silence, watching the door, her body humming with tension like a plucked string.

Why should she be nervous? Monsieur LeBrun himself had said that she was Louise Dulac's only hope. She ought to hold all the power in this situation. But that day, that horrible day when she had begged for Louise's help and the actress had refused her, taunting her about Vidar, and then the pain and despair of losing Catherine . . . All of it came flooding back.

When the heavy door opened and Louise Dulac stood on the threshold like a performer taking the stage, Yvette went first hot, then cold. The movie star did not wear Lelong or Schiaparelli or

Chanel this time, but a shapeless wool sweater over some kind of tunic.

Louise was thin, her high cheekbones even more prominent than before, and her hair had grown. But despite all of this, Louise Dulac's presence shone like a beacon through a stormy night. She might have been dressed in a prison uniform and fed starvation rations for the past few months, but her star power remained undimmed. It was as if she did not belong here, in this miserable fortress; she was simply playing a part.

Strangely, the sight of Dulac so poised despite her circumstances came as a relief. Had she seemed broken by her experience, it would have been much harder to hate her.

"Ten minutes." The warden shut the door on them with a resounding clang.

Before Yvette could say anything, Monsieur LeBrun darted forward, offering Louise a cigarette, lighting it.

Blowing out smoke, Dulac sauntered over to the window embrasure and leaned against it, lifting her face to the light in a sinuous movement, like a cat basking in the sunshine. Then she turned and took a long drag on her cigarette, her gaze kindling with challenge as it rested on Yvette. "Come to gloat?"

But whatever response Yvette might have made was cut off. With a brisk shake of the head, Dulac fixed her gaze on LeBrun. "So. We go to trial."

LeBrun cleared his throat. "It is fair to say that the examinations with the magistrates did not go as well as we'd hoped—"

"Magistrates!" Louise threw up a hand. "These are the very same men who condemned French patriots in Vichy, those black-robed puppets with the Nazis pulling their strings. Now they turn around and presume to judge *me*—" She broke off, straightening her shoulders as if to throw off the sudden emotion. "But in the high court, it might be different. Maybe I will get a fair hearing there."

LeBrun hesitated, as if about to disagree, but the film star took no notice. She gestured at Yvette. "And what are you doing here, if you haven't come to gloat?"

There was no point prevaricating. They didn't have the time. "I thought seeing you would help me decide."

"Decide what?"

"What to say in court, of course."

Louise removed a strand of tobacco from her lower lip, flicked it away. "I should have thought that was simple. You tell the truth."

Yvette nearly laughed. "You know as well as I that the truth can be colored in the telling. How hard should I fight for you? Should I fight at all?"

A shrug indicated an indifference Louise could not possibly feel. She turned to stare out the window, taking long, deep drags on her cigarette.

Yvette wanted to scream. She wanted to shake that arrogant, beautiful icon, to interrogate her until she spilled all her secrets. But there was no use trying. Beneath that gilded surface, this woman was pure steel.

"And if I decide not to testify at all?" Yvette didn't mean it. At least, she wasn't sure that she meant it.

That captured the movie star's attention. "Then I should be forced to call on the man you knew as Vidar Lind to take your place on the witness stand." Her gaze flickered to LeBrun. "I'm sure none of us wants that."

It was Yvette's turn to shrug. "What is Vidar Lind to me? By rights, he ought to be in the dock along with you." When Louise did not reply, Yvette struck the table with her open hand. "Tell me that is not the case!"

Louise tapped the ash from her cigarette. "If you are determined to be petty and stupid about it, there's nothing I can do to persuade you. For all that you were a clever little thing, you never learned to separate personal feelings from the work, did you, Yvette?"

That was like tinder to flame. The old Yvette would have flown at Louise in a rage. Now she forced herself to match that tone of disdain. "We are done here," she told Monsieur LeBrun. "Call the guard."

Monsieur LeBrun hurried to keep pace with Yvette as she stalked back along the dim, dank corridor that led away from the women's prison. "Will you do it, mademoiselle? Will you sign the statement? Will you testify?"

LeBrun was either obtuse or desperate. Perhaps he was both. Yvette swallowed a harsh retort. It wasn't the law clerk's fault his client did not have the sense to placate her star witness. Dulac's arrogance hadn't dimmed, not even in the face of hardship and imprisonment. Yvette could almost admire her for that.

"I'll sign the statement," she said as they emerged into the fresh air once more. Glancing back at the ugliness that had become Louise Dulac's life, she added, "I'll testify, too. But she might not like what she hears when I do."

GABBY

Gabby and Yvette were admitted through the outer gate to the British embassy on the rue du Faubourg Saint-Honoré without incident, but in the courtyard before the grand Hôtel de

Charost, which housed the embassy, Gabby balked. "I can't. I can't go in there." Other guests flowed around her, moving toward the shallow flight of steps that led to the palace entrance.

"Don't be silly," said Yvette. "You can and you will." She tugged at Gabby's hand. "We've come this far."

But it was all happening too quickly. Gabby had been so focused on Jack and the slim possibility that he might be alive, she hadn't considered the ceremony itself. Now the thought of being singled out in public and having to receive the medal, knowing what to do and where to stand . . . And good God, she wouldn't have to make a speech, would she? She would fall down dead on the spot.

"Gabby!" Yvette's voice was sharp, commanding. "Come on."

Somehow, she managed to move. They mounted the stone steps and entered the magnificent building. "Apparently, the Duke of Wellington bought this house from Napoléon's sister before Waterloo," Yvette whispered. "So, in fact, the English indirectly funded Napoléon's escape from Elba. Did you know?"

Gabby shook her head. She appreciated that Yvette was trying to distract her, but it wasn't working. Once inside the building, with its high ceilings and checkerboard marble floor, its chandeliers and gilt and ornate balustrades, the thought of getting up in front of people in such a place made Gabby's stomach churn anew.

She let Yvette steer her down a corridor and into a reception room, following the rest of the guests, who seemed to know the way. There was a handsome red Persian carpet on the floor but the room was quite sparsely furnished, with only a lectern, a few rows of chairs in front of it, and some couches by the windows.

There were already people milling about, conducting hushed conversations, checking the seating arrangements.

"Isn't this nice?" said Yvette in her normal speaking voice, drawing a few looks. She still gripped Gabby's hand, as if to stop her bolting from the room. "I wonder where we are supposed to sit."

A smiling woman with a clipboard came up to them. "May I have your name, please?"

Gabby gave it with a surge of fear that she was in the wrong place, or that they would have left her name off the list and she would be told to go home. But the woman made a checkmark next to her name and said, "You'll find designated seating in the front row. I'm afraid your companion—"

"My sister," Gabby said.

The woman smiled apologetically and nodded to Yvette. "Your sister will have to sit behind."

"Oh . . . Yes. All right," said Gabby, clutching Yvette's hand tightly.

"Good luck!" said Yvette, extricating herself, then adding in a whisper, "You'll be fine. Your fear will evaporate when it's your turn. The anticipation is always the worst."

And it was true, Gabby found, once the ceremony started and the official speeches were made. She did not catch the title or the name of the dignitary who awarded them the medals—she did not think it was the ambassador himself—but his words about courage and sacrifice made her heart swell in her chest.

She could not help peering around from time to time, to see whether Jack had come. As soon as the ceremony was over, she stood and turned around, surveying the room.

He wasn't there. He hadn't come.

Disappointment sank like a stone to the pit of her stomach. But how likely was it that he would be there, after all? If he had wanted to see her, he would have come to the rue Royale long ago. She ought to have known not to hope. And yet, she had hoped. Stupid, stupid, stupid.

On to plan B, then. She would go to London, find whatever records office there might be, and try to discover what had become of him. She would never be ready for the news of his death, but it was time to face the truth. She had earned a medal for courage. Well, she would try very hard to deserve it.

Light refreshments were served: cucumber sandwiches—such an odd, bland combination—and an abundance of strong, hot Indian tea. Gabby took the tea Yvette pressed into her hands and they found themselves congregating with a handful of other Frenchwomen who had been honored that day. They spoke of everything but the war, and Gabby tried to listen, but her mind kept wandering. She felt honored to be part of this ceremony, and yet, she felt like a fraud.

Catherine Dior had been decorated by the French and British governments, a heroine on both sides of the channel. Gabby turned to Yvette and pressed the velvet case into her hand, whispering, "This is for both of us, Yvette. You deserve it, too."

Yvette's eyes widened, then glazed with tears, but she gave a curt shake of the head. "No, Gabby. I don't."

Before Gabby could explore the subject further, someone touched her shoulder. She turned, to find the most quintessentially British woman she'd ever seen smiling down at her.

The stranger was dressed in good-quality tweed and a battered brown hat with a limp pheasant feather curling over its brim. She was about Gabby's age, attractive in that slightly horsey way some Englishwomen were.

"Is it really you?" the woman said, peering into her face as if to better identify her. Then she drew back and stuck out her hand, adding in English, "Mademoiselle Foucher, I am so glad to meet you!"

Bemused, Gabby shook the proffered hand. It was bare and cold, and she noted the lady carried her gloves and a small, compact purse in her other hand. "*Vraiment?* Pardon, I mean, really? But if you please, madame, to whom am I speaking?"

The woman laughed. "Oh, how silly of me! I'm Audrey Miller." When Gabby still looked nonplussed, she added, "Jack's sister."

"Jack's . . ." And then she saw it. The fair coloring, those blue, blue eyes, and something about the expression . . . Gabby clutched at Yvette to steady herself. Her sister's arm came around her, strong and comforting.

"It is *such* a pleasure to meet you." Audrey chattered on about her eventful trip to Paris. Due to several hitches along the way, she almost hadn't made it to the ceremony in time.

Gabby felt sick. She was going to be sick. She had looked for him, thought of nothing but him, yet she had not been prepared for this. "But tell me!" she burst out. "Please tell me. What happened to Jack?"

"Silly old thing stayed home." A flick of her gloves brushed off his behavior, but Audrey's eyes were watchful and anxious. She made a comical moue. "Please don't be offended. He has turned into a positive recluse these days."

"Then he's . . . he's not dead?" The room was starting to spin.

"No! Oh, *no!*" said Audrey. "Oh, my poor dear. You didn't know? I'm so sorry, I—"

"Why don't we sit down?" suggested Yvette, steering Gabby over to a group of chairs by the window. She perched on the arm of Gabby's chair and addressed Audrey in English. "Please. Will you tell us where Monsieur Miller is? Gabby would very much like to see him again."

"Ah, no, Yvette! We must not . . ." Gabby didn't know the word in English. *Intrude.*

"Nonsense!" said Audrey. "Of *course* you must come to stay with us. I insist. The sole reason I came to Paris was to bring you back with me, I assure you."

She'd so feared hearing news of Jack's death that the invitation to stay at his home, extended so matter-of-factly by his sister, bewildered Gabby. She wanted to leap at the chance to see him again, but Jack hadn't been in touch all this time. Did he even want her to come?

This was all too much on top of what had already proven to be an emotional day. "I . . . I don't know."

Audrey tilted her head, her brow furrowed in concern, and glanced at Yvette, as if seeking an explanation.

"Yes, but of a certainty, she will come," said Yvette. "I will arrange it all. Gabby will be ready to leave tomorrow."

"But . . . the tenants . . . Maman . . ." Gabby stammered.

"If I might have a word with my sister in private, Madame Miller?" Without waiting for an answer, Yvette pulled Gabby to her feet and dragged her into a quiet corner. "If you are worried about your concierge duties, don't be," said Yvette in a low voice once they were out of earshot. "I'll fill in for you if Maman won't."

"*You?*" Her sister, the glamorous Dior mannequin, scrubbing floors and sorting mail?

Yvette shrugged. "Why not? I won't do it half as well as you, of course, but I'll keep things going until you get back. All right?"

Gabby wavered. Yvette was likely to do any number of impetuous things if left to her own devices at the apartment building.

She'd probably give Madame Vasseur a piece of her mind, for example, or fail to keep the common areas up to Gabby's standards.

Oh, but to see Jack again! To touch him. To put her arms around him. It was too much temptation. Then she recalled another objection. "But what about Dior?"

Yvette shrugged. "Now that the show is over, the mannequins are only required between three and five in the afternoon each day. Surely Maman can manage for that long without me."

This casual generosity was so typical of Yvette. Fighting back tears, Gabby took a deep breath. "Very well, then."

"You will do it? That's wonderful, Gabby!" Yvette clapped her hands, oblivious to the stares she was getting from others in the reception room. She looked wistful. "What a pity I can't go with you. And what a pity we cannot beg Monsieur Dior for something for you to wear."

"Don't you dare!" Gabby shuddered to think of such presumption. "Besides," she added in a whisper with a glance around her, "the English dress so shabbily, I will hardly stand out over there."

"I suppose you're right," said Yvette with an impish twinkle. "You would not wish to shame them too much with your elegance."

A warm glow spread through Gabby, then bubbled up into excitement at the thought of seeing Jack again. They moved to where Audrey now stood by the window, clutching her purse handle with both hands, her eyebrows raised as if in hope of a good outcome.

"Thank you for your kind invitation, madame," said Gabby softly. "I would very much like to come."

"Oh, but that's simply marvelous!" said Audrey. She placed her large hands on Gabby's shoulders and kissed her soundly on each cheek.

A little overwhelmed by this heartiness, Gabby added, "But I can only be gone a week at the most. Is that enough time, do you think?"

Audrey seemed to consider for a moment, then said, "Well, at any rate, it's a start."

What she meant by that, Gabby couldn't tell, but her longing for Jack banished everything else from her thoughts. Who cared for medals or receptions or cucumber sandwiches? Jack was alive. Her Jack. And she was going to see him again.

Chapter Sixteen

※

Paris, June 1944

GABBY

When Gabby arrived at the Café de la Mer at the appointed time, Berger's usual booth was empty and Rafael was nowhere to be seen. Upon inquiry, the waiter handed her a note with an address: 180 rue de la Pompe. "Monsieur Rafael left word that you are to go there, mademoiselle." He eyed her for a few seconds before he added, "But I wouldn't. Nice young lady like you doesn't belong in a place like that."

A place like what? A den of thieves and black marketeers, no doubt.

But she had to go. If she didn't, Jack would die. "Thank you, monsieur."

She did not have too far to walk to the gang's headquarters, but a woman alone at this time of night had to be vigilant, and she was on edge as she hurried along, burningly aware of the sapphire ring in her pocket. She ought to have put it in her shoe or sewn it into the hem of her skirt or something. Why hadn't she thought of that?

Panic welled up to choke her. Every man she passed was a threat. She couldn't do this. She simply couldn't. She almost turned back, but the thought of Jack made her go on.

All too soon, she arrived at Berger's apartment building. Music and laughter blasted from an open window on the upstairs floor, so unexpected in light of her grim imaginings that, for a moment, she was disoriented.

A large man holding a machine gun across his body stood guard at the door. "State your business."

She handed him the note Rafael had left. "I-I'm here at the invitation of Monsieur Rafael. It is about—"

The guard jerked his head, which she took as permission to enter. Cautiously, Gabby opened the tall, solid door and stepped into the foyer, a large, imposing space with a marble floor and a concierge desk beside the staircase. She was about to ask the concierge to direct her when a sharp voice called from above, "Who's there?"

Gabby looked up to see a woman, young and red haired, with a supple body and hard eyes, pause halfway down the stairs. She raked Gabby with her gaze and curled her lip, as if she'd sized her up and found her wanting.

Gabby repeated her business and the woman shrugged. "Upstairs. Come."

The woman gestured for Gabby to precede her. As she went up, the redhead followed so closely, Gabby smelled the sweet odor of wine on her breath.

A shout came from somewhere below. Another, more like a muffled scream this time.

Gabby halted, her head snapping around. "What was that?" But silence fell again. The woman rolled her eyes and gave Gabby a shove between the shoulder blades. "Move. I don't have all night."

At the top of the stairs, Gabby's escort brushed past and let her into the apartment. Berger's quarters were large and spacious, even bigger than the suites at number 10 rue Royale. Through an open door, Gabby caught a glimpse inside the drawing room.

That was where the music was coming from. A couple of sharp-suited fellows smoked fat cigars, puffing thick grey clouds toward the ornate plasterwork ceiling. A young woman in a slinky gown was draped across an armchair, one long, bare, white leg swinging, marking out the beat. Another sang along to the record in between swigs from a bottle of champagne. Rafael was there, too, doing tricks with a pack of cards, while two other men sorted through boxes—contraband, she assumed.

Gabby started in that direction, but the redhead yanked her back, her fingers wrapped tightly around Gabby's upper arm. "Not that way." She jabbed her finger toward the next room along. "In there." Then she stalked into the drawing room and slammed the door in Gabby's face.

So she wasn't to see Rafael? What did that mean? Was it Berger behind that door? Gabby wiped her palms on her skirt and licked her lips. *This is for Jack,* she reminded herself. Then she took a deep breath and approached the room the redhead had indicated.

Before she could knock, the door opened and a Nazi officer in a uniform she did not recognize loomed before her. He was large, of middle age. Not Gestapo, but not a military man, either. Was he there for her? She stumbled back, heart hammering.

His eyes narrowed. They were a cold, lucent green and she couldn't help but feel he read her mind. Then he smiled and courteously stepped aside to let her pass. Tossing a laughing comment in German over his shoulder to Berger, the officer left.

"Well, don't just stand there. Come in." Berger's lair was vast, with a high ceiling and the kind of gilt-edged paneling you saw in palaces. Still shaken from her encounter with the German officer, Gabby crossed the polished parquet floor toward the enormous desk at which Berger sat, her footsteps echoing through the space.

Berger might have been cast as a gangster in a movie. His eyes were narrow and sunken beneath black brows, his nose had been broken at least once, and his lips were thick and laced with a sneer. He leaned back in his chair and threw down his pen. "The concierge from the rue Royale."

Nerves jangling, Gabby clutched her purse tightly. "I think Rafael must have told you about the medicine I need. He promised to get it for me." She licked her lips. "I—I can pay."

"It is true, mademoiselle," said Berger, "that there is very little I cannot obtain." He took out a gold case, drew a cigarette from it, and stuck it in his mouth, then offered the case to her.

She leaned across the desk to select a cigarette, equally from politeness and from a hope that the nicotine might calm her nerves. From a distance at the café, the gang leader had seemed affluent and smooth as oil. Only up close did she note the unsettling void behind his eyes.

When he snapped the case shut, she saw that it bore a coat of arms. Not his, she presumed.

A cry split the air. This time, there was no mistaking the noise from below. It was definitely a masculine scream. Gabby's hand shook so hard as she raised it to get a light that Berger grabbed her wrist to steady her.

His gaze lifted to hers and the lighter flame danced in his dark eyes. The cigarette tip flared to life and Gabby drew smoke deep into her lungs, fighting the urge to cough. Berger released her wrist. "Are you here to waste my time, mademoiselle?"

"Of course not. Please, I . . ." She fished in her purse and brought out a small velvet bag. "I have—"

"Put that away." He seemed annoyed at her. "I don't trade with the likes of you. Sit down."

She did as she was told, sinking onto a chair opposite him.

"What I need," said Berger, steepling his fingers together, "is not some little trinket from your grandmother's jewel box, but information. As the concierge of a large apartment building, surely you see things. Hear things, too."

An icicle pierced her chest. He wanted her to inform on her tenants. Did he mean to torture the truth out of her? She thought of the screams she'd heard and inwardly shuddered.

She tried not to let her terror show. "My tenants are a dull, solidly bourgeois lot, Monsieur Berger. Anyone who is left in that building is either too old for intrigue or too comfortable with the occupation to make trouble."

After a pause, Berger asked, "You are a patriot, mademoiselle?"

"I am a survivor, monsieur. And there is one very dear to me who needs that medicine. Name your price. I will do anything, inform on anyone, but I cannot make things up or tell you what I do not know."

Had she been wrong to offer him nothing at all? Could she not have reported the way Madame Vasseur had violated the blackout restrictions on too many occasions to count, or those who secretly listened to the British wireless broadcasts when they visited a certain restaurant on the rue de Rivoli?

But Jack would never forgive her if she traded some innocent person's safety for his. She would never forgive herself. She had to find another way.

"I can't give you what you want," she said. "Believe me, I wish I could." She leaned forward to stub out her cigarette in the ashtray on his desk and rose, unsteadily, to her feet.

Berger shrugged. "Until you bring me information of value, Mademoiselle Foucher, I am afraid I cannot help you." He flicked a hand in dismissal. "Now get out."

As soon as Gabby left the apartment, her knees went. She grabbed the bannister for support. Her legs were like jelly, but she had to get out of there.

No more screams now. Why had they stopped? Had the victim passed out? Had they killed him? She eased down the staircase on tiptoe, like a child in a storybook afraid of waking the monster. At the foot of the stairs, she made a beeline for the street door, but she didn't quite reach it. A hand gripped her arm in a bruising hold. Sheer terror shot through her. She opened her mouth to scream, but a gloved hand clamped down upon it.

"Apologies for scaring you, mademoiselle," drawled a voice in her ear, "but I think I have what you need."

Chantilly, June 1944

YVETTE

The day Yvette left for Chantilly, there were a few German patrols but little other traffic north of Paris on the roads. The atmosphere was tense inside the motorcar. Yvette was still stewing over Vidar. His warning about Chantilly played on her mind, chiming as it did with Monsieur Lelong's reservations—and, of course, with her own fears. Had she made a mistake coming along?

But Catherine Dior had been called away to Callian for an indefinite period. There was no courier work for Yvette without Catherine. She couldn't remain idle in Paris while this opportunity presented itself, could she? Even if she achieved nothing in Chantilly, she couldn't be worse off than she was in Paris.

Louise Dulac's German maid was coldly furious at Yvette's accompanying her mistress on this jaunt. However, the actress did not seem to notice. She made Helga sit up front with Gruber's driver, while she and Yvette occupied the back, deepening Helga's displeasure.

The movie star did not speak but sank into reverie, gazing out of the window from behind white-framed sunglasses. Yvette had no choice but to do the same. At least Gruber had not come with them, having business in Paris to conclude before motoring up later.

Acting as a courier should have been enough of a challenge for any girl. Why hadn't it been enough for Yvette? Was it the glamor of the movie star and her wealthy, powerful friends that drew her? Maybe at first. But really, it was the opportunity to use her brain, the chance to actually understand the information she passed along, the chance to make a real difference instead of remaining a small cog in a large machine. Vanity, Gabby would say. Perhaps she'd be right.

They approached the Chantilly hippodrome, slowing to a crawl behind a queue of vehicles that were cruising toward the racecourse, searching for parking. Yvette peered out at the top-hat-

and-tailed gentlemen, the ladies who stepped daintily over the lawns in their exquisite ensembles: floaty summer dresses or suits with flaring peplums and straight skirts to just below the knee, their hats sporting large bows or feathers or netting. All were drifting toward an arena that looked more like a small kingdom than a racecourse, with its ornate stone grandstands and view of the magnificent Chantilly Castle beyond.

Did these people ever think about their starving compatriots, who had been reduced to eating horse meat in the days when there was any to be had?

"Some things never change," murmured Dulac, and Yvette wondered if she detected irony in her tone. "I'll be attending the races tomorrow. Yvette, I rely on you to help me look my best."

"It will be my pleasure, mademoiselle." The words scraped her throat. She hoped the actress had more important tasks in store for her than choosing her accessories.

"At last," said Louise Dulac as they turned off the main road, onto an avenue of chestnut trees. Ahead, Yvette saw a formal gatehouse with an armed patrol of German soldiers.

As the guards checked their papers, Yvette craned her neck to catch a glimpse of their destination. Beyond a stream with a pretty stone bridge lay the Château de Saint Firmin. It was not a vast, fortified palace like Chantilly but an elegantly proportioned mansion with white walls and a blue roof dotted with dormer windows and chimneys. The house was surrounded by lush green countryside, and it felt like the most peaceful place in the world—if you didn't count the sentries with machine guns, of course.

The guards waved them through. Yvette's anticipation built as the tires of the big black Citroën crunched discreetly along the avenue, before rolling to a stop outside the front entrance to the château. Might she discover something here that would make a real difference? Surely at such a time, with the Allies having landed at Normandy, the German ambassador would not plan a gathering at his country house solely for pleasure?

A lady Yvette thought must be the ambassador's wife came out to greet Louise, but Herr Abetz himself was not there. As the driver came around to open the door for Louise to get out, Helga remained where she was, so Yvette followed suit.

When the hostess and her guest had moved into the house, Helga alighted. Yvette slid from the car and stretched, looking around with interest. The wide shutters on the doors and windows lent the house an elegantly casual air. A peaceful retreat from the tension in Paris. She could see why King Otto chose to spend time here.

"Let me take those." Yvette took a couple of hatboxes the German maid had been struggling with but received a withering stare in return. The housekeeper, a tall, buxom woman with an air of command, met them at the entrance and exchanged some conversation with Helga in German as she showed them into the house.

As they moved through the hall and up the staircase, Yvette noticed gilt-framed portraits crowding the walls and more gilding swirling in bas-relief semicircles above pocket doors. It was all very grand yet somehow casual, too. A couple strolled past them in the corridor, dressed all in summer whites, as if on their way to a game of tennis.

Entering the movie star's bedchamber was like stepping into a mermaid's grotto, with its sea-foam walls and clamshell bed with oyster satin sheets. A fitting setting for a screen goddess, perhaps, but not to Yvette's taste.

The room had a spectacular view that stretched over lawns and woods to the rooftops of Chantilly Castle. Yvette opened a window and inhaled deeply the fresh country air, then chuckled to herself. Definitely a distinct whiff of manure, so perhaps not so fresh. They were close to the Chantilly racing stables, after all.

A table was set up on the terrace below, and guests milled about, playing *boules* on the lawn or refreshing themselves with champagne cocktails from the bar cart. Everyone was dressed in cream or white, like the couple they'd passed in the corridor. They looked as if they hadn't a care in the world, as if the war didn't exist. Perhaps she'd been wrong to imagine that important business might be transacted here.

When Dulac's trunks were delivered to the room, Yvette helped Helga unpack. She slid a glance at the other woman, who was roughly sorting through Dulac's couture garments as if they were burlap sacks. A far cry from the reverence with which the seamstresses and *vendeuses* at Lelong treated the creations of Balmain and Dior. Yvette curled her lip at the Chanel costumes mademoiselle had brought. Everyone knew the famous designer had taken a German officer as a lover.

However, she refrained from comment, and the two of them worked in silence for over an hour before Helga stabbed a finger at an outfit and gabbled at Yvette in German.

Yvette blinked at her. "I don't understand."

Scowling, Helga repeated what she had said, only louder, as if that would help. This behavior was particularly annoying when Yvette knew Dulac spoke to the maid in French half the time and Helga seemed to understand everything her mistress said.

Eventually, Yvette figured out that Helga was asking which costume Dulac should change into when she came upstairs. "This one, I think." Yvette pointed to the grey silk, a perfect cocktail gown. "Show me what jewels she has brought."

They went on like that for more than a week, dressing and undressing the movie star. Yvette had begun to think she had misjudged the situation entirely. She had done her best to watch the guests in her spare moments, but her German was almost nonexistent, so she was forced to admit that she was not much use as a spy in this setting. She tried to memorize the guest list and to observe who conducted private meetings with whom, but that was about all she could think of to do while she waited for Louise Dulac to put her to good use.

She was a little surprised that Herr Abetz had not asked for her, since it was at his request that she had come to Chantilly in the first place. However, when she raised the issue on one of the rare occasions she and Louise Dulac were alone, Louise replied, "His Excellency has a lot on his mind. He seems to have forgotten about you, for the moment. I'd like to keep it that way."

One evening, Yvette laid out an ice-blue gown, designed for Louise Dulac by none other than Monsieur Dior himself, and chose a spectacular parure of diamonds to go with it.

"Too showy," said the actress when she saw the jewels Yvette had chosen. "I want to wear the pearls tonight."

With a smirk of triumph at her rival, Helga swapped the diamonds for the pearls. Yvette wondered why the actress had brought the diamonds if she didn't intend to wear them, but she was almost past caring what Louise Dulac wore. She wanted to go home. This had all been a waste of time.

Louise went to the mirror and checked her reflection, smoothing her finely plucked eyebrows with her little finger and touching up her lipstick. But as she began to undress, her manner underwent an abrupt change.

She snapped at Helga over trivialities. Hadn't she laundered yesterday's linen yet? She was a lazy good-for-nothing. Where was her tourmaline ring? "And just look at this gown. It's crushed!" She held up one of the sleeves of the gown they'd laid out. It was riddled with creases.

The maid stammered, "*Aber—*"

The actress put up a hand. "Don't give me excuses. You must take it downstairs and press it properly." As the maid, flushing with mortification, snatched up the cocktail dress, the actress said, "Run my bath first, you stupid girl."

Yvette couldn't help feeling sympathy for Helga. She had seen Dulac deliberately crush the sleeve of the gown in her fist while Helga had bent to pick up the clothes the actress had been strewing around the floor.

Completely unself-conscious, Louise stripped naked and put on the green silk dressing gown Helga had laid out for her.

When the bath was running, the maid took the cocktail gown and draped it over her arm.

"Oh, and press the cream blouse for tomorrow while you're there," ordered Dulac over her shoulder as she stalked into the en suite. "Come in, Yvette, and shut the door. Here, take my robe." Yvette held the garment for her as she slipped out of it and stepped into the tub.

Yvette folded the robe neatly and placed it on the vanity. As Dulac sank down low in the deep, luxurious tub, bubbles billowed and fluffed around her, but she did not relax. She appeared on edge, her jaw tense.

Yvette reached for the taps to turn off the flow but Dulac said in a low voice, "Keep the water running. We need to talk."

She obeyed, hope surging. Here it was. The moment she'd been waiting for.

Fixing her gaze on Yvette's, Louise said, "There's something I need you to take back to Paris. There is a bicycle for you in the stables, ready to go—" She broke off as the door to her suite opened and shut. "That was quick."

However, it was not Helga who entered the steamy en suite but Gruber. He glanced at Yvette. "Out." He said it in German, but there was no mistaking his meaning.

Dulac assumed her brilliant, glittering smile. "Thank you, Yvette. You are dismissed."

Chapter Seventeen

Chantilly, June 1944

YVETTE

When Yvette returned to Dulac's bedchamber to help her dress for dinner, Gruber was still there, lounging at his ease, a cigarette burning in the same hand that held a glass of amber liquid.

Dulac was already dressed. Perhaps she had not summoned Yvette again because of Gruber's presence. The movie star sent a quick glance her way, but she didn't need to signal a warning. Yvette wasn't about to betray her to that Nazi.

When Helga had finished with her mistress's hair, she brought the pearls she had chosen to wear. The maid opened the diamond clasp and secured the rope of lustrous gems around Dulac's throat.

"Not like that!" snapped Dulac, her earlier bad temper resurfacing. "I want them wound three times, like a choker."

The maid unclasped the pearls and began winding them around the movie star's elegant neck.

"What are you trying to do, strangle me?" Louise slid her index finger between her throat and the pearls and gave a sharp tug.

The string broke. The necklace flew from Louise's neck, landing on the polished wood floor with a clatter. A couple of the pearls came loose and rolled beneath the couch. Louise swore with amazing fluency, using words Yvette had never heard a lady say before.

With a cry, Helga bent to snatch up the fallen necklace. Luckily, each pearl was secured with an individual knot, so only two of them came off. Yvette felt around beneath the couch until she found them.

As she stood up, Yvette glanced at Gruber, but he seemed preoccupied, as if their small crisis was of little consequence compared with what was on his mind. He finished his drink, stubbed out his cigarette, and left the room.

Louise Dulac said, "Yvette, you must take these back to my jeweler immediately to get them restrung. I want particularly to wear the pearls with the black Balmain the very night I return to Paris."

"You want me to go now?" said Yvette. "But how will I get there, mademoiselle?"

"I don't care how you get there! You can walk for all I care." She blew out a breath. "Borrow a bicycle. You can ride, can't you?"

Conscious that Helga was enjoying this exchange, Yvette put a whine into her voice. "But if I leave now, I will still be riding after curfew, mademoiselle."

"I'll get the ambassador to give you a travel pass. You can show that to anyone who tries to stop you."

After the pearls had been safely decanted into the case, Dulac said, "I'll have the travel pass for you after dinner. Then you can be off."

WHILE HELGA WENT down to the servants' hall for her evening meal, Yvette lay fully clothed in their shared attic bedroom, trying to rest. There was a long bicycle ride ahead of her and it would be a wonderful thing if she could catch some sleep before she left. However, of course it was impossible to calm herself enough to doze.

When the door opened, she started upright, heart thudding in her chest. It was Louise.

Yvette blew out a breath, the heel of her hand kneading her breastbone. "You scared me."

"You are on edge. It is not to be wondered at." Dulac came over to her, sat on the bed, and took her hand. "As you've probably guessed by now, I work for the resistance." She licked her lips. "My contact has not shown up here tonight, so I must ask something more of you. I did not think I would have to do it, but . . ."

A cold finger stroked Yvette's spine. "What is it?"

"I need to get into Obersturmbannführer Werner's room later tonight, once he has dismissed his valet." Her tone grew curt. "I need you to distract him."

"Me?" Yvette reared back, instantly comprehending what Louise was asking. "Why don't you distract him while I search?"

"Oh, you can read German, then, can you, Yvette? You would know how to find what you are looking for among his papers?"

"N-no, but—"

"Besides, there is Gruber. I cannot take the risk." Her grey eyes held such intensity, Yvette felt mesmerized. "Listen to me, Yvette. There is no time to argue. You *must* do this. There is no other way."

Everything inside Yvette screamed against obeying her. Vidar had been right to warn her against coming here, after all. "I can't," she whispered. "I—mademoiselle, I don't even know how."

Louise gave a harsh little laugh. "You don't need to know how. Trust me, with a man like that it won't take much."

Yvette stared. Was that supposed to reassure her?

Dulac looked at her watch. "He is coming to see you in my suite at midnight. Now, there isn't much time. Get down there and make yourself presentable. Put on one of my negligees if you like. I've already dismissed Helga for the evening."

The thought of carrying out these instructions made Yvette's insides churn. She gripped Dulac's hands, trying to make a connection with her emotions. They were no longer the delivery girl and the movie star, but two agents working for France. "At least tell me why I am doing this. I think if I knew why, I could . . ." Actually, she was certain that she could not do it under any circumstances. Her mind was scurrying to and fro, like a mouse trapped in a maze. There must be another way.

Dulac leaned in closer to murmur in her ear. "There is a munitions store nearby. Werner inspected it today. I need to read his report and send the information back to my people."

"How long do you need for this?" Yvette asked.

She shrugged. "Twenty minutes? Half an hour, perhaps."

Yvette clutched her wrist. "It would make sense if you interrupted us before he . . . I mean, it's your suite, after all."

"He would think that strange, given I will be the one who has sent him there to be with you."

"But you could come up with some excuse. I know you could."
Yvette tightened her hold, her eyes pleading with Louise to agree.

The actress smiled, a little sadly, Yvette thought. "Your virtue is
so important to you, Yvette? Do you think God will send you to
hell if you do this?"

Yvette glanced away. Her relationship with God was none of
Dulac's business. "I do not think it unreasonable that I would prefer not to do this thing for the first time with a man I have never
met, and one who is most probably ugly and a dirty Boche into the
bargain."

"Werner is no Errol Flynn but he is not dirty, I assure you. In
fact, he is extremely fastidious." Louise fixed her with a sharp, as-
sessing gaze completely alien to the purring screen goddess she
played when Gruber was around. "All right, Yvette. I see that you
will not be persuaded. I will interrupt you as soon as I'm finished
searching his room. I'll make up some excuse."

Yvette was left feeling as if she was putting up a great fuss about
nothing. She lowered her gaze, flushing with humiliation.

Louise put a fingertip beneath her chin and lifted it, bent to look
into her eyes. "Courage, my dear. Such tasks are not pleasant, but in
this war we have to bear much that is unpleasant. I will get the information and give you the case of pearls for the jeweler with a coded
message inside. Then you need to be away as quickly as possible."

She left before Yvette could say any more. Yvette tried to calm
herself and think, but fear overtook her reasoning faculties. She
knew well enough the means Louise wanted her to use to distract
the Obersturmbannführer, but she couldn't do it. She had always
thought she could die for France. Truthfully, dying seemed preferable to letting some horrible Nazi use her like a prostitute.

She had to keep him with her for twenty minutes. Thirty, perhaps. She must think of a way to stall for that long, just until Louise came back.

DULAC'S SUITE WAS candlelit and slightly stuffy, with deep, long shadows on the walls. Yvette turned on the lights, banishing the gloom. She blew out the candles and watched the wisps of smoke curl upward from their wicks.

The large clam bed, with its mother-of-pearl headboard and rich satin coverlet, made her shudder. This was not what she'd thought she'd signed up for when she had agreed to help Louise Dulac.

The actress had told her to make herself presentable. Yvette went into the bathroom and looked about her. On the counter ranged a plethora of unguents and cosmetics, marshaled into organized rows by Helga, no doubt. With shaking hands, Yvette washed her face and tidied herself a little, but not too much. Ordinarily she would have reveled in the luxury of real, scented soap and expensive perfume, but now she felt like a leg of lamb dressing herself for dinner.

So this was real intelligence work if you were a woman. What a stupid girl she had been, abandoning her courier job for this, thinking she'd been cut out for better things.

She looked around the bedroom, searching for inspiration. The chess set? Her father had taught her how to play. She would challenge Werner to a game. Her lips twisted. Hardly a more attractive pursuit than lovemaking, she supposed—at least, not from his point of view. She would have to come up with something else.

She was still trying to think of an alternative when the door opened, making her jump. Heart thundering in her chest, she turned to see a uniformed officer in the doorway. He was lean and sharp faced, with very pale skin. His high cheekbones bore the slashing scars of the ceremonial duel. An aristocrat, then. Not one of Hitler's bourgeois bullies.

Something flickered in his pale eyes as they contemplated her. Contempt? Yvette flinched, though the contempt of such a man should not have hurt her. Her mind warred with itself. Perhaps she ought to have put on one of Dulac's negligees. She didn't want him to leave immediately in disgust, after all.

He stepped into the room, then turned to shut the door behind him. He did not seem inclined to speak, so she felt compelled to say something, to break that awful, tense silence.

"Good evening, Herr Obersturmbannführer." She turned to indicate the game set up in the window embrasure. "May I offer you a game of chess?"

He frowned. "I did not come here to play chess." He looked very grim for a man who anticipated an evening of pleasure.

"I am quite good," she lied. "Can it be, *mein Herr*, that you are afraid of being beaten by a girl?"

He didn't even react to the pert jibe. His gaze swept her body. "I am a busy man, mademoiselle. I did not come here to play games. Of *any* kind. If you will be so good as to take your clothes off, we can begin."

His French was very good. Yvette was shaking inside, but the only choice was to be bold. If she did not go on the offensive, she would have to submit entirely. The way he behaved, the entire encounter might be over before the twenty minutes was up.

She gave him an arch look. "I do not know what the custom is in your country, but here in France, we do not rush these things. We drink wine, we converse a little." She indicated the board again. "We play some chess. It, er, it builds anticipation, you see."

A muscle twitched at the edge of his mouth. Whether it was

amusement or anger at being instructed on lovemaking by a girl half his age, she couldn't tell. Probably the latter. "Not interested, mademoiselle." He started toward her.

Her throat contracted but she managed to say, "A drink, at least?" She glanced at the champagne in its sweating silver bucket.

He hesitated, then relented, crossing to the sideboard and yanking the champagne out of its nest of ice. He fiddled with the cork. "You want anticipation?" With a wave of his hand, he gestured to the bed, where Louise had laid out a lacy white negligee. "Why don't you put that on? Then we drink champagne."

Yvette could not help it. She glanced at the clock. The seconds seemed to drag by.

She had scorned to make herself attractive for him, but this might be the only way to stall a little longer. "All right." She snatched up the negligee and fled to the en suite before he could stop her. She had to force herself not to slam the door.

This had not been a good start. Gripping the marble counter of the vanity, she tried to calm herself. He was even worse than she'd expected. So utterly cold, so intent on his purpose. No big-bellied, slobbering drunk, who might have been easier to hoodwink. Nor did he seem likely to be charmed by any woman, much less one who did not know the first thing about seduction.

She stared into the mirror. Her face was flushed dark pink—so much for keeping cool under pressure. She crushed the negligee in her hand, then turned and hurled it at the door. It dropped in a limp heap on the floor. Kneading her forehead with her knuckles, she paced the small room, trying to think.

There came a heavy tread outside the door. "Don't be too long, mademoiselle. The champagne is waiting. As am I."

With trembling fingers, slowly, Yvette unbuttoned her blouse.

Chapter Eighteen

England, February 1947

YVETTE

As it happened, Yvette's noble sacrifice was not required. Maman scoffed at the notion that she could not manage very well as concierge while Gabby was gone. Observing Gabby's nervous vacillations over whether to go at all, Yvette decided to ask Monsieur Dior for Friday off so that she might accompany her sister as far as London and then return to Paris on Sunday. She politely refused Audrey's invitation to join them in the country, however. She needed to be back for Louise Dulac's trial, which would begin on Monday. Besides, she did not at all wish to intrude on Gabby's reunion with Jack.

London was grim and falling down around them, still blackened and shattered from the Blitz. The winter had been bitterly cold, which they'd discovered firsthand the night before, when they ran out of coins to feed the meter that operated the radiator in their rented room. Audrey had told them the coal heaps had frozen and there were rolling power cuts across the nation.

And now, here they were, shivering outside their bed-and-breakfast in Baker Street, snow squeaking beneath their boots as they stamped them to keep warm. Yet, hope shone like a beacon from Gabby's face. Audrey was coming to collect Gabby and whisk her off to the family home.

"I can't believe you're abandoning me," said Gabby. She held her hand out, palm downward. "See how I am shaking!"

Yvette pulled her in for a swift, hard hug. "You will be fine. Better than fine."

Gabby bit her lip. "Audrey said you were most welcome."

Yvette smiled at that and linked her arm through her sister's. "No, my mind is made up. I wouldn't have come at all, but it was clear that you needed me to stop you from jumping into the channel and swimming back to France."

Yvette did wonder why, if he was in love with her, this Jack had not come to the medal ceremony himself. Indeed, why had he not come to Paris the second he was able?

Having gained a little experience with men while in New York, Yvette wanted to urge caution but held her tongue. It would be decidedly out of character for hers to be the voice of reason, and in this mood, Gabby would not thank her for it.

Love makes us all stupid, Yvette said to herself. *But it is good to be stupid once in a while.*

Finally, Audrey arrived in a car so small, it looked like a toy, and Gabby picked up her suitcase.

Yvette kissed her warmly on both cheeks. "You will telephone to let me know you have arrived and that you are well, yes?"

"I'll try. Oh, but I wish you would come," said Gabby for the millionth time.

"No, and no, and no," Yvette said to her. "Be brave, sister. Remember, you have that medal now."

When Gabby hugged her in a final goodbye, a tightness in Yvette's chest she hadn't been aware of until now seemed to fall away. She hoped with all her heart that her sister would find happiness with Jack. She and Gabby were both making new beginnings now. They could never leave the past behind, but they could try to focus on the road ahead.

Once her sister left, Yvette had no desire to linger in the tiny room they'd rented. Despite the bitter cold, she dug her hands into her coat pockets and went for a walk.

A fine drizzle had begun to fall miserably from the iron-grey sky. The power cuts meant that many businesses and tea shops had simply shut their doors, so there were few places to find warmth and shelter. Yvette wandered the city, growing increasingly dispirited, and after nursing a glass of foul-tasting wine in the one pub she found open, she turned back toward the bed-and-breakfast. She was nearly there when she spied one attraction that seemed to be operating: Madame Tussaud's. She shrugged and paid the admission.

The wax museum was lit only with candles and gas lamps that cast spooky shadows over the displays. Yvette looked around her with a creeping feeling of unease. Even the wax models of perfectly pleasant people seemed macabre, like effigies that might at any moment come to life.

She stopped in front of the hated image of Adolf Hitler, modeled, so the guidebook told her, before the war. As Yvette stared into those fanatical eyes, she could not repress a cold shiver of fear and loathing. She had a sudden wish for a furnace, so that she could shove him in and watch him melt.

"If you keep staring at him like that, you'll turn into a statue, too," murmured a low voice in her ear.

She started, put a hand to her chest. Vidar! What on earth was he doing, following her to another country? She turned to face him. The dim lighting created shadows, deepened the lines that bracketed his mouth. He looked older than he had back at the Ritz, and twice as grim.

"Shall we?" He offered his arm. "I know a snug little place in Mayfair."

Yvette ignored his arm and walked on. "But the ticket was expensive. I want to get my money's worth."

She stopped in front of the display of the Terror. Before the war, the models that re-created victims of the guillotine might have chilled her, but she had seen real death, real suffering, and the pretend beheadings of aristocratic women seemed to belong to a fairy-tale world far away.

"Madame Tussaud herself barely escaped the guillotine," said Vidar. "A resourceful and enterprising woman."

"Really? I didn't know." Yvette hesitated. "I'm not sure why, but creating wax figures seems a tawdry skill compared with sculpting marble, say. And yet I suppose there must be skill involved."

"Hm." Vidar scanned the room, expressionless. "It's not to my taste, certainly. I prefer art to be more abstract."

"Of course you do," she muttered. And if it came out as a criticism, she didn't care. It was cool but stuffy among the exhibits and she wanted to leave very much, but as long as they wandered between the waxworks, she could stave off the conversation Vidar clearly wished to have with her.

Eventually, she could no longer pretend the wax statues of people she'd never heard of interested her in the slightest. They emerged into the biting fresh air. The rain had stopped for the moment, leaving the footpaths slippery and the gutters filled with dirty slush. Their breaths clouded and the clouds mingled. She turned away. "I'm famished," she said briskly. "Where did you say this place is?"

SITTING SIDE BY side in a corner booth in a candlelit dining room at an exclusive gentlemen's club, Yvette and Vidar ate Dover sole and game pie and a dessert called Eton mess that contained more sugar in one bite than Yvette had consumed throughout the entire war.

"Ordinarily, they use fresh strawberries," said Vidar with a wryly apologetic twist to his mouth. "Tinned cherries don't quite measure up."

She put down her spoon, unable to eat any more of this dessert that made her teeth ache. What a waste. And what a luxury not to have to consume everything on her plate in case she didn't get to eat again for some time. In New York, the food had been abundant but her finances had not. Often, she ate soup from a can or tinned beans for her supper.

The restaurant was dim and cozy and Vidar had plied her with wine, so she was feeling quite mellow when finally he said, "You wanted to know why I can't testify for Louise." He dabbed at his mouth with a napkin. "It's because I am still working undercover."

She stared at him. "But the war is over."

"And a new one has begun."

That made no sense. True, Yvette had been in New York, but

she would have heard if fighting had broken out again in Europe. "What are you talking about?"

"It is a silent war, but no less deadly." He leaned closer, his hand on the table beside her plate. "Do you think the Russians were ever truly our allies? The day the war was won, they became the new threat."

Even as he spoke these frightening words to her, she was so acutely aware of him it became painful to breathe. His clean, masculine scent stirred her body and softened her brain. How she wanted to believe every word he said to her. But she had fallen into that trap before.

This intimacy could not continue. She made herself sit back, and it was like pulling two magnets apart. "I think it comical you talk of all this 'our' and 'we.' You will only ever be 'them' and 'they' to me."

He sighed. "How many times must I say it?"

She rolled her eyes. "You are Austrian. Yes, yes, I know." She waved her spoon, then dug it into the sugary mess in front of her. "But you were a Nazi just the same."

"Clearly whatever I say on that subject, you won't believe me," he said. "But believe this. What I'm doing now means I must keep what I did in the war a secret. I cannot be a witness in a trial that is attracting enormous media coverage. It is Louise Dulac, after all."

Her name on his lips was like a stab in the gut. "I am not likely to forget."

He stared into Yvette's eyes, giving her that warm, sincere look that used to sweep away all her fears. "What she did to you was not kind. But she did it in service of a higher cause. In the cause you nearly gave your life for. Can't you understand? She was a complicated woman, living with unimaginable stress for months on end."

To hear him defend Louise was to feel claws raking her chest cavity. "She did not have to throw me to the wolves. I had a plan that would have saved me. She agreed to it, and then she did not come."

Vidar took her hand in a warm clasp. "Did it never occur to you that she might have believed you capable of saving yourself?"

Yvette narrowed her eyes. It was a strange thing that even the cleverest of men did not understand relationships between women. Particularly not between the women who were rivals for that man's affections. "Louise Dulac meant to degrade me. And she refused to help Catherine Dior." She would never, ever forgive her for that.

"There was nothing she could have done for Catherine," said Vidar. "Don't you know Gruber was part of the plot against Hitler? The one that failed? He managed to escape retribution by the skin of his teeth, but after that, he was finished, powerless to stick his neck out for anyone."

She wanted to shut out Vidar's reasonable arguments, to put her hands over her ears like a child. She realized, with a hollow laugh at her stupidity, that she had hoped this evening would go a certain way. A candlelit dinner. Back to his place, and then . . . But he was defending the woman who had treated her like garbage and begging Yvette to save her.

She twisted in her seat so she could face him fully. "Tell me, once and for all, Vidar, what is Louise Dulac to you?"

He clenched his jaw so tightly, a small muscle seemed to pulse there. She saw at once the steel in him, the utter exasperation of a man who is urging a woman to do a thing that to him is wholly logical and necessary, something in which emotion should play no part.

And she agreed that what lay between Louise and her should have no bearing on her decision whether or not to testify on her behalf. But Louise had used her as if she were nothing, a scrap of dirty rag to sop up a mess. And on top of that, she had taunted Yvette with the truth about Vidar.

Yvette sat back. "I suppose it is your gentlemanly code that keeps you silent."

At first, he didn't reply. In a gesture that he often used to buy himself time, he took out a cigarette and lit it. Then he blew out smoke. "Louise and I were not involved romantically at any stage, either before or after you and I met."

Yvette raised her eyebrows. She didn't believe him.

He returned his cigarette case to the inside pocket of his coat. "Do you think either of us would have risked it? If Gruber had caught her with another man, he'd have had her killed."

Again this appeal to logic, when all Yvette wanted was for him to reject Louise and choose her. "And yet," she said, "in time of war, the risk might have been worth it. We were all going to die sometime." She retrieved her purse from the banquette beside her and stood. "Will you excuse me? I must powder my nose."

Their eyes met, and in his, she read a challenge. He knew she was not going to use the facilities, that she would find another exit, circle back to the front door to retrieve her hat and coat.

The question: Would he be there, waiting for her when she left? Or would he let her go and find another way to save Louise?

GABBY

Gabby liked Audrey immediately, but as much as she enjoyed her company, she couldn't help wishing for Yvette. She squinted down at the little bird pinned to her lapel, its diamonds winking in the weak sunlight as they zipped along in Audrey's Aston Martin, and thought of the note that had accompanied it. *All my love.*

The bitter cold seemed to intensify as they drove deeper into the countryside. A dusting of snow frosted the tree branches and lay in patches over the ground.

"You speak English so well, Gabby," said Audrey, shifting gears with great proficiency and turning down a narrow country lane. "I was afraid you might not."

Gabby gripped the edge of her seat, which was the only thing she could hold on to in the tiny automobile. The retractable roof was tattered here and there, and icy blasts of air assaulted them from several directions. "That is kind of you to say. I lived here one summer with some cousins and learned it then. I practiced on your brother whenever I could." She hesitated. "But I suppose he did not mention it."

"No." Audrey fell silent for a few moments, lips pursed, as if deciding how to phrase her next sentence. "Jack has not spoken of you at all, I'm afraid."

The news was a punch to the stomach. Gabby held very still, as if tensing every muscle would keep the pain at bay. She ought to have expected it. Had Jack cared, he would have come with Audrey to Paris.

"How did you know I would be at the ceremony, then?" she managed.

Audrey, who seemed unfazed by anything, flushed. "Please don't be angry with me. I detest sneaks! But I happened to read some of my brother's correspondence." Audrey glanced at Gabby. "It was Jack who recommended you for the medal, you know."

Warmth flooded Gabby's chest. He hadn't forgotten her. He was simply reticent, like many men. Particularly English ones. "And yet . . . he did not attend the ceremony," she ventured.

"No. Well, he didn't know I was going, either," admitted Audrey. "He won't be happy with me for—" She broke off, but the message was clear.

Gabby's hands flexed in her lap. "He is not expecting me," she said. "And if he were, he would not wish to see me." The words were jagged in her throat. "Why?"

"Oh, please, please don't take offense," begged Audrey. "He is the stupidest man. Well, aren't they all—even the best of them?"

"Then you should not have brought me," said Gabby.

Audrey seemed about to say something, then bit her lip. She glanced at Gabby, her eyes worried and apologetic. "Just promise me you will see him. You've come all this way."

And she had, too, assuming she would be welcome. As Audrey drove too fast down these narrow country lanes for Gabby's comfort, she had the sensation of hurtling inexorably toward her doom.

She shifted her weight on the hard, low seat and closed her eyes as they whizzed around a bend. When had she stopped listening to her innate caution? Before the war, she would no more have agreed to come on this journey without assurance that Jack would welcome her than she would jump off a cliff.

Audrey's hand lifted briefly from the gear stick and pressed hers. "Please don't worry. His bark is worse than his bite."

All of a sudden, Gabby wondered if they were talking of the same man. Her gentle, amusing Englishman now sounded like the beast in the fairy tale.

Bad enough that she'd felt tentative about throwing herself at him after all this time, even if his sister had invited her to stay. Now it sounded as if he might actually be hostile toward her.

They turned off the road onto a gravel drive. The little car shot through the trees and they drove for some distance along a winding avenue, until, with another turn, Gabby saw it. Jack's house.

"*Bon Dieu*," she muttered, trying to take in the massive building that loomed before them. In France, they would have called it a château. He owned all of this? No wonder Jack had little interest in seeing her again.

"Shocking old pile, isn't it?" said Audrey, cheerfully oblivious of Gabby's awe. "Place is falling down around our ears."

To Gabby, it looked magnificent. A sprawling mansion made of cream stone, bare-branched trees, rolling hills blanketed with snow.

They swept around an enormous fountain with a central figure of mermaids and gods. The fountain lay dormant, like the countryside around it. There was a feeling of hibernation about this house that had nothing to do with the season—or was that her overactive imagination?

Gabby wanted to order Jack's sister to turn back, to take her to the nearest train station. If only she could click her fingers and be back home again. If only she had Yvette.

They puttered to a stop at the front steps and a servant came to take their bags. Feeling untethered and exposed, Gabby followed Audrey inside. While Audrey paused to exchange a few words with the servant, Gabby stared around her.

The entrance hall was wide and cavernous, running almost the full breadth of the house, with a gallery above. It was glacial inside, even colder than it was outdoors.

"Through here," said Audrey, taking her deeper into the house, where a grand oak staircase took them up to the second floor. "I've had the pink room prepared for you. I hope you like pink. Only, it's the closest to the bathroom in this wing, which I thought you might appreciate. Here we are."

She nudged open a door and Gabby followed her in.

The bedroom was bigger than the *loge* at rue Royale. An enormous four-poster bed dominated the room, its pink canopy swagged with dusty silk roses. There was a pretty Queen Anne dressing table with a stool covered in worn pink velvet, a burl walnut desk at one window and a cushioned window seat in the other. A group of Louis XVI chairs surrounded the fireplace. The furnishings were tattered and shabby, it was true, but altogether too grand for her.

"Ah, *c'est magnifique!*" Gabby set down her suitcase and went to the window.

"It's cold in here, but there'll be a fire laid for the evening," said Audrey. "Or perhaps you'd prefer the radiator?"

Gabby was scarcely listening. "Whatever you think best," she murmured, stopping short before one window. Her view was of the lake. She saw sheep on a distant hill. As she stepped closer to the window and looked down, she caught sight of a man crossing the terrace below, a pair of dogs ambling alongside.

Jack. Her heart did a slow, hard flip.

"Gabby?"

Gabby flushed, turning away from the window. "I'm sorry, I was not attending. The view is so . . ."

"I was just saying you must be hungry," repeated Audrey with an understanding smile. "Tea in half an hour, shall we say?"

After giving Gabby directions to the parlor, Audrey left her to freshen up. There was a dry washstand in the corner of the room with a pitcher of water and a china bowl, and a silk screen painted with trees and birds of paradise.

The mirror showed Gabby a windblown mess of a woman, and her mood plummeted further. She washed, then tidied her hair and brushed lint from her jacket. She reapplied her lipstick and touched up her rouge and tried to feel better. But the grandeur of the house was starting to oppress her, as if its walls were closing in. Ironic, since it was so large and spacious.

Jack had talked often of his home in the country, but she had pictured a house near the northern town of Burnley, which she'd carefully located on a map. Not that Jack's "Burnley" was the name of an enormous estate near Cambridge. What if he had not returned to her because he thought she wasn't good enough for him? She *wasn't* good enough for him. One glance at this place made that clear.

Oh, dear God, what was she *doing* here?

Gabby glanced at the mantel clock. How had the time passed so quickly? She had to go down. She looked her reflection in the eye and said, "You are here as the woman who took him in and kept him safe during the war. As a . . . a friend. That's all."

There was a squall of nerves in her stomach as she went downstairs and tried to find the way to the parlor. She had begun this trip to England with such hope and delight. For once in her life, the part of her that always doubted her worth and her welcome had not held her back. She ought to have known better.

So when she first met Jack again after more than two years apart, she would not let herself laugh and run to him and throw her arms around him as she so longed to do. She would be friendly but distant, as his failure to contact her all this time warranted.

She would stop making excuses for him and face the hard reality. Facing hard realities had always been her specialty, after all.

He did not care about her. Perhaps he never had. He did not want her here. And he certainly did not want her in his life.

She straightened her spine and straightened her skirt and marched across the hall.

The house was laid out with cheerful illogicality. Having not caught half the instructions Audrey had given her on how to get to the parlor, of which there seemed to be many, she soon got lost. Finally, after several wrong turns, she heard a murmur of voices and realized she'd found the spot. Hovering on the threshold, Gabby surveyed the cozy scene.

It was the quintessential English parlor, complete with a roaring fire and hunting dogs on the hearthrug. Brother and sister both had their backs to her. They were seated in chintz-covered chairs at a small round table by a large picture window with a view of the lake. The table was set with white linen, china, and silver. Audrey's hand rested on her brother's arm and she was speaking to him in a low voice, bending her fair head close to his. Gabby couldn't hear what she said and didn't want to. She cleared her throat.

"There you are!" Audrey jumped up and came to clutch her hands and draw her toward the table. "Did you get horribly lost? I ought to have come up to fetch you."

"It is nothing, madame," Gabby murmured, her gaze straying to the man who had risen and turned to look at her. The movement was slow; Gabby would have called it reluctant, but she saw at once a blaze in his eyes as they caught hers. The corner of his mouth lifted, as if in defiance of the stern set to his jaw.

She wanted to run to him, to throw her arms around him, but she made herself simply nod in his direction. "Good afternoon." She enunciated each word as if she had never spoken English before.

"*Bonjour*, Gabby," he said quietly. "*Bienvenue chez moi.*"

"Oh, in English, please, brother, or you will be in danger of losing me." Audrey flopped down in the chair opposite his and rang a little silver bell. "Gabby's English is *parfait*! Much, much better than my French. Do sit down, my dear."

Wrenching her gaze from Jack, Gabby sat where Audrey indicated, in the chair opposite the window. The view beyond a low stone balustrade was of an ornamental lake, woods and fields patched in snow. It all looked like a postcard, as if it weren't real. She didn't feel real, sitting here with him like this, like a stranger.

One of the dogs, a glossy chocolate hound with a plumed tail, scrambled up and trotted over to her, sniffed, then put his head firmly in her lap as if it belonged there. He looked up at Gabby with a longing in his eyes, eyebrows twitching as he searched her face.

She laughed and scratched him behind the ear. "Ah, *t'es un bon chien, n'est-ce pas?*" she murmured to the dog, immensely comforted. The animal had accepted her even if his owner was unlikely to do so.

"Jupiter. Off!" said Jack with a gruff note of command to his voice.

The dog snapped to attention and sat back on his haunches, his gaze shifting from her to his master and back again.

"But no, leave him be," said Gabby, laughing down at Jupiter and reaching out to rub his chest. "I love dogs." She lifted her gaze to Jack's face. What she saw there made her smile falter. He was annoyed at something. Angry, even. Surely not that she had made friends with his dog?

Determined to persevere, she said, "What breed is he?"

"Pointer."

Gabby waited, but apparently he was not going to elaborate. She sat at right angles to Jack, almost beside him, yet he seemed as distant as the church spire that peeked above the woods.

"Is that the village over there?" she asked, forcing the conversation in spite of the disappointment that lodged like a block of wood in her chest. He had told her often of his childhood adventures, and the village had featured heavily in them. In fact, despite her surprise at the magnificence of his home, she began to recognize many of the places he'd described. How stupid of her not to guess.

Jack remained silent. With a frowning glance at her brother, Audrey filled the breach. "Yes, that's right. I'll show you the village tomorrow if you like. The church is very old."

"That is kind," murmured Gabby with a glance at Jack. Audrey didn't seem inclined to include him in the outing. She went on to talk about the local parish and some of its quirky inhabitants. Jack did not utter a word.

As the conversation limped along, with Jack contributing nothing except the curtest reply when directly addressed, Gabby felt sick to her stomach. This was horrible. She had to leave. She would apologize to Audrey, but she couldn't stay here like this. Not with Jack so unresponsive and cold.

Almost with a sense of defiance, she said to him, "It is such a pleasure to see you, after all of this time. I cannot quite believe I am here. I . . . I wondered about what happened to you after . . ."

His jaw clenched. He looked away. Audrey rushed into another village anecdote, but Gabby felt crushed. Squashed beneath his foot like a bug.

Gabby wanted to unpin her beautiful jeweled bird and throw

it at him. She couldn't bear this. She was going to disgrace herself if she didn't get out of here. She scooted her chair back, making Jupiter give a very human groan of affront.

But before she could get up to leave, a servant appeared with the tea tray. Audrey said, "Ah! No doubt you are famished, Gabby."

Gabby kept her seat, sagging inwardly at the prospect of having to force down some food. The silver tea service and the tiered cake stand full of sandwiches and scones did not seem to impress Audrey. She took one sandwich and sniffed. "Not fish paste again. Good Lord, what will Gabby think of us?"

Jack inspected his own sandwich with a raised eyebrow, then shrugged and kept eating.

Audrey rushed on. "We are still suffering from rationing, Gabby, but try the scones and the strawberry jam. At least that is homemade. The cream is from our own dairy, of course."

"We also have rationing still," said Gabby. "One hardly remembers what real food tastes like."

Gabby had not tried scones before and put one on her plate, following Audrey's instruction to dollop the jam on first. "Like this, see?" With a decided flick of the wrist, the jam plopped on her scone. The same treatment for the cream, which was so thick, it was the consistency of butter. "And *wala!* as your lot say. Try it. Go on."

Feeling self-conscious, Gabby did as she was told, with Jupiter following her every move. When she bit into her scone, Jupiter's head jerked up, butting the table and upsetting her teacup.

"Ah!" The tea went everywhere, all over the table and into her lap, scalding her thighs. Gabby dropped the scone and jumped up, peeling her sodden skirt away from her legs.

"I'm sorry! I have to . . ." Half-blinded by tears, she turned and ran from the room.

Chapter Nineteen

Paris, June 1944

GABBY

G abby scrutinized Jack with the eagle-eyed attention of a personal physician. "How do you feel today?"

The sulfa pills had been as effective as the doctor had promised. Within twenty-four hours, Gabby saw improvement, and a few days after that, Jack swore he was on the road to recovery. She only wished she could serve him more nutritious meals, but she did what she could, giving up her own rations without telling him.

"I'm all the better for seeing you." He smiled, his bright blue eyes crinkling at the corners. "You are looking *particularly* fetching today, mademoiselle. Have you done something different with your hair?"

She chuckled. "Not a thing." It was true that she did take more care with her appearance these days, but she wasn't going to admit that. "Clearly you are getting better if you are thinking about hair-styles and such." Her pleasure in this circumstance was dimmed only by the fact that once he was well enough, Jack would have to leave her.

He struggled to sit up and she hurried over to plump the pillows behind his head. "Weak as a cat," he muttered. But he caught her busy hands in his, stilling them, and she felt a strength that belied his words.

Gabby's heart gave one hard thump. Without a thought, she returned the pressure of his grip, met his steady gaze with a soft gasp of recognition and wonder. She wasn't alone in this. He felt it, too.

"Gabby," he said softly. Slowly, he pulled her down to him. Their lips touched, tentatively at first, then he speared his fingers through her hair, pressing her to him, kissing her as if she were the only thing that mattered in all the world.

Choking back a sob, Gabby lifted her head and took his face between her hands. "I thought I was going to lose you. I never want to feel that way again."

It had been a very close thing. He'd been out of his mind with fever and for the first couple of doses, it had taken all her strength and ingenuity simply to administer the sulfa tablets. She had ended up crushing them and mixing them with honey because he couldn't seem to swallow them with water, no matter how hard she tried to make him understand that it was vital for him to do so.

She thought of his inner strength, despite his weakened physical state, of all she had been through trying to make him well again, of the intimacies she had performed.

He was not one for dwelling on his own suffering, so another kiss was the only answer he gave her. Their embrace grew more passion-ate and more physical, until Jack's hiss of pain made Gabby jerk back, a hand to her mouth. "Your wound! Oh, it's too soon. We shouldn't."

"Too soon? I've been wanting to do that since the first moment I set eyes on you," said Jack, reaching for her again with a gleam of humor in his eye. "You don't know how I've suffered."

"No, really, we mustn't." Feeling oddly shy, Gabby moved out of reach, coiling her hair back into its chignon, pinning it into place.

Jack sighed. "Will you sit with me awhile?" he asked. "Do you have time?"

She didn't, but she nodded and sat on her usual chair beside the bed. "Shall I read to you?"

"Not today, if you don't mind." He inhaled a long, deep breath, which was mercifully clear of that horrid rattle, and turned on his side. "Come here." He pulled open the bedclothes and made room for her to slide in next to him.

Willing, but shy, Gabby stepped out of first one shoe, then the other. After only a slight hesitation, she climbed in and lay on her back beside him, her head propped up on her crooked arm. The space was tight. It was a single bed, and a hot day, but she didn't care. She loved the feel of him beside her. She would stay there forever if she could.

"I wish I could go outside," said Jack. "Or even look out a window." He trailed a fingertip down her cheek and tilted her chin. "Will you describe to me what is happening out there, my dear Gabby, in the most beautiful city in the world?"

"All right," Gabby said shakily, acutely aware of him in every cell of her body.

But instead of describing Paris as it truly was, with the shops bare of produce and people queueing for hours only to find that everything had already gone, with every elegant restaurant and garden teeming with Germans and the Nazis swathing the monuments in swastikas, she spoke about Paris as it had been when she was a girl. The boulevards, wide and leafy; the simple pleasure of a walk along the Seine through rosy twilights; the fun and flair of the Moulin Rouge and the painted women there, red and black and white ruffles, rounded bosoms and legs kicking high. When the Louvre was a wondrous palace full of priceless artwork that anyone could see; when they lived with her papa on a little farm on the outskirts of Paris and kept chickens and were happy.

She was so absorbed in her tale that time passed quickly. She stopped, and the present tumbled back into place, both the ugly and the good. The good was the man in bed beside her, watching her speak as if he saw the world itself in a completely new way, now that she had described it for him.

She loved Jack. She loved him. All the doubts and the struggles and the danger had led her to take the greatest risk of all.

Their gazes caught and held. In that moment, she knew he felt the same.

His fringe was too long. It had fallen over his eyes. She reached up and swept it back from his brow. Then she pulled him down to her and let her cares fall away.

Chantilly, June 1944

YVETTE

Mademoiselle? Come out now, or I shall come in and get you." Werner's voice sounded muffled but the words held a quiet menace.

Through the en suite door, Yvette called, "I am taking my time to look nice for you, *mein Herr*. One more minute."

She slapped on some makeup, so that at least it would look like she'd done more than simply change her clothes. A slick of scarlet lipstick on her lips. Her hand was trembling too much to stay within the lines. Attempting to smooth away the excess smudges only made it worse. She picked up Dulac's mascara but decided not to risk it. Her hair . . . She bunched the thick, curling mass in her hand and twisted it into a knot, securing it with pins.

At last, she shuffled out of the bathroom in bare feet, toes curling into the carpet with each step, shoulders so hunched, her chest was practically concave. Dulac's negligee felt like cool liquid on her body. Its plunging neckline gave her the new and disconcerting sensation of being half-naked in this man's presence. Its lace edge itched her skin. She glanced at the clock. Werner had been there for fifteen minutes. With luck, Dulac would be back in five.

The German came forward and handed her a glass of champagne. Feeling the need of some liquid courage, she drank deeply. The bubbles caught at her throat, making her choke back a cough. How elegant! And how dangerous if she let herself become drunk. Just one gulp had sent a warm lassitude spreading through her limbs.

She set the glass on the table by the alcove, resolving only to wet her lips next time. What a waste of good champagne.

Gesturing for her companion to do the same, Yvette sat on a sofa in the small lounge area, as far away from the bed as possible. She would have preferred the armchair but that would be too pointed. "Come, Herr Obersturmbannführer. Tell me about yourself."

Perhaps the champagne had mellowed him, or perhaps he had

decided to play with his prey before mauling it. He complied with her request.

Like most people, Werner enjoyed talking about himself, and she took care to flatter him and ask intelligent questions, until he settled deeper into his chair and crossed one booted leg over the other, as if he now had all the time in the world.

He told her about his home in Berlin and, oddly, about his wife and children, too. He seemed to have absolutely no sense of how inappropriate that was. But then, perhaps all soldiers discussed their wives with their women. They did not think of what they did as adultery. They thought it was a purely physical thing, like eating a meal when you were hungry.

"Men are animals," her mother told her once. *Only some of them,* Yvette thought.

Nevertheless, this was good. Keep him talking until the cavalry arrived.

An age passed and still no Dulac. Yvette didn't dare even glance at the clock in case Werner caught her and took it as a cue to begin.

As if he sensed the direction of her thoughts, Werner stopped abruptly. "No more talking." He moved closer.

"Will you excuse me?" Evading his embrace, she stood up. "I need to use the convenience." Waggling her glass to indicate all the champagne she'd drunk, she put it down on the table and headed to the en suite.

On the way there, she glanced at the clock. Thirty-eight minutes. Louise should have been back by now. Had something happened to her? Yvette went into the bathroom and closed the door.

Her gaze swept the room, as if the answer to her dilemma might be hidden among Dulac's cosmetics. Maybe she could make a run for it, scuttle back to her attic and bar the door. But if Werner came after her, that would draw attention, and besides, it would make him suspicious of Louise. Yvette needed to appear willing. But there was no doubt in her mind. She could not go to bed with that man. The mere thought of him touching her made her sick . . .

Hmm. What had Louise said about him? He was fastidious. That gave her an idea.

She grabbed the tooth glass from beside the sink and filled it with water, then added some of the thick pearly liquid from the bottle of bubble bath Dulac had used earlier and mixed it a bit with her finger. Breathing hard through her nostrils, she forced herself to drink. She gulped and gagged, but by sheer willpower, she managed to keep the stuff down.

Yvette returned, all smiles, to Werner's side. As she curled up beside him and put a hand on his chest, she could already feel that noxious mixture doing its work, had to bury her face in his neck to hide a sudden retch. He smelled nice, which seemed wrong, somehow, but at least breathing in the astringency of his cologne settled her stomach a touch.

He began nuzzling her ear, roughly groping her body. That brought the nausea rushing back, until all she could think about was holding in what wanted more and more urgently to come out. Her skin grew clammy. She felt as if she might faint.

She heard a clink of metal. He was undoing his belt buckle. So much for finesse. "I'm sorry," Yvette gasped out. "I don't feel well. We have to stop."

"No more of your games." Werner bared his teeth as if he'd eat her. Then he gripped her wrists in one hand, pushed her back against the cushions, and pinned her hands above her head. With the other hand, he shoved up her negligee. The ease with which he subdued her despite her struggles made tears spring to her eyes.

Why had she let Louise talk her into this? And then it struck her. Louise had never intended to interrupt them. She'd only said she would to placate Yvette.

A surge of panic somehow made her nausea disappear when she needed it most. "Please don't," she whispered. "*Please.*" But he either didn't hear or didn't care. He undid his belt buckle and shoved down his trousers. She felt a strange, insistent weight against her thigh.

That did it. Soapy water surged up her throat. Not even attempting to turn her head, Yvette vomited down the front of Dulac's beautiful negligee. And all over the Obersturmbannführer, too.

It was two in the morning before Dulac returned to her suite. Yvette had turned off the lights and awaited her in darkness. The movie star must have thought the room unoccupied because when she saw Yvette, she gasped and put her fingertips to her breastbone. Then she straightened and held her head in that queenly way of hers to stare Yvette down.

"You should at least have the grace to look guilty," Yvette said, wishing her voice didn't tremble. She'd finished off the champagne. It had given her courage. Or perhaps bravado was nearer the mark.

Louise shrugged. "You have to grow up sometime. How was it?"

"How was what?"

The actress put on a flamboyant Chinese silk dressing gown in jade and gold. The sleeves drooped as she fixed herself a drink. "Don't play dumb. It doesn't suit you."

"Nothing happened," Yvette said. "Most unfortunately, I was taken ill. My apologies. Your negligee is ruined."

Werner had nearly wept with outrage and disgust. Due to their respective positions, he had not been as covered in sick as Yvette had wished. However, poised as he was to begin, the sudden volcanic eruption of soapy bile from her throat had so revolted him that she wondered if he would forever associate the one act with the other.

She hoped so. She hoped the image would shrivel him if he ever tried to force a woman again.

Dulac listened to her explanation. "Clever. Let us hope he doesn't suspect a ruse."

"I did warn him I was feeling poorly. Did you get what you wanted?" Somehow, despite fuming over the other woman's treachery, Yvette found that she could be all business now. Something about Louise Dulac demanded toughness from her. Yvette wouldn't forgive the actress for her betrayal, but the horrible encounter with the Obersturmbannführer would be for nothing if they didn't carry out the next part of the plan.

Louise said, "I need to encode the message. You might as well wait for it, since you're here. Then you need to be ready to leave as soon as curfew lifts. You have a long ride ahead."

"I have nothing in my stomach, mademoiselle."

Dulac tilted her head and narrowed her eyes. "You have become bold all of a sudden, Yvette." Then she smiled. "It suits you."

When Yvette merely shrugged, Louise added, "I'll send for bread, fruit, and cheese. You can eat now and wrap some up to take on your journey."

"Thank you, mademoiselle." After telephoning the order to the kitchens, Louise sat down at the desk and took out writing implements, preparing to work. Clearly, she had dismissed the incident with Werner from her mind, and Yvette wondered how a woman became so hard that she could leave a young girl to be raped by her enemy without a qualm, then calmly sit down to encode a message to her contact back in Paris.

If this was what it took to be an intelligence agent, Yvette wasn't sure she had the stomach for it.

When Louise had finished the message, she took out the satin-covered case in which she kept her pearls and removed them, dropping the loose pearls into a china bowl.

She lifted out the velvet bed from the jewel box and used a penknife to slit open the lining, just enough to slide her small note through, between the lining and the base of the box. Then she sewed up the tear with tiny stitches, fitted the velvet bed back in place, and put the pearls on top of that.

"Here." She rose from the desk and handed Yvette the case of pearls, together with the pass she'd persuaded the German ambassador to endorse. "Go safely. The bicycle is at the stables, waiting for you. Good luck, Yvette."

Her attitude left no room for Yvette's resentment. She certainly wasn't going to beg forgiveness or apologize for deceiving her, for placing her in a horrible position without her consent.

They all did what they must. There was a war on, after all.

THE JOURNEY BACK to Paris was long and arduous, made infinitely worse by the sultry weather. By the time Yvette reached the jeweler's shop in Paris, she was sunburned and soaked through with perspiration. She ached in places she had never thought about before, and when she saw the jeweler's shingle out front, she sent a silent prayer of thanks up to the good God in heaven that she'd made it at last.

In her relief, she nearly rode straight up to the shop. However,

Catherine Dior's training kicked in, and she cycled slowly past on the opposite side of the street to scope out the area first. There was no need to be subtle about her surveillance, however. Passersby were all stopping to stare.

The shop front had been smashed up, every single pane of glass missing, as if a bomb had gone off inside. The interior had been looted. With a hollow, burning horror, she set her foot down on the ground and asked a boy nearby, "What happened?"

In an undertone, he said, "It's the Bonny-Lafont gang, mademoiselle. There was a raid last night. The jeweler was arrested, then they looted his wares."

Yvette thanked him and cycled away. What on earth was she supposed to do now?

All she knew was that she needed to get home, to regroup. She was trembling all over, from muscle fatigue as well as fear. She barely made it back to the apartments before her legs gave out. In the vestibule, she got off the bicycle and collapsed to the ground.

"What is it?" Gabby rushed out of the *loge* and bent over her. "Oh, Yvette, what has happened? What have you done?"

"Is Mademoiselle Dior here?" she gasped out. "I need her."

"She is not back yet," said Gabby. "What is it? What's wrong?"

"What about Miss Dietlin?" Yvette let Gabby help her up. Her inner thighs were chafed raw and her muscles burned.

"She is gone also. I don't know where." Gabby brought her inside and sat her down. "Don't tell me you rode all the way from Chantilly?"

Yvette nodded. "Water. Please, Gabby."

Stomach lurching with anxiety, Yvette groped for her satchel, which she had slung across her body. She relaxed. It was still there, with the velvet box, the pearls, and the message inside. She lay back against the cushions and took the water Gabby handed her, gulped it down.

"Slowly, now," said Gabby. "What happened, Yvette?"

She knew Gabby would not leave her be without an explanation, so she gave her the cover story about the pearls.

"And I suppose her highness couldn't wait a few days for her necklace to be mended? She had to send you on such a journey alone? Unbelievable." But it appeared Gabby did believe it, because she didn't say any more. Untying her apron and bundling it up, she added, "A call came for you an hour ago. Vidar Lind. He said to contact him as soon as you got back." She tucked a tendril of hair behind Yvette's ear. "I have to go, but will you be all right now?"

"Yes, of course." *Vidar.* She could trust him. He knew her secret and he hadn't betrayed her. He'd know what to do with Dulac's message.

The card with Vidar's name on it was still in the purse she'd brought to Maxim's that night. She took it out and dialed the number. "I have a message for Vidar Lind."

There was a murmured conversation and then Vidar's voice came over the line. "Are you all right?"

"Yes, but—"

"I'll meet you in the suite you know at the Ritz in half an hour. Mind you go straight up and don't talk to anyone. Got it?"

A flood of relief nearly knocked her over. He knew all about everything. He was going to take care of it. It was going to be all right. "Yes."

Yvette nearly cried as she got back on the bicycle, but she clenched her teeth and pushed through the pain. Vidar wanted her to meet him at Louise's suite. That made sense. Louise wouldn't be there. How would they get in, though? It wasn't as if Louise had entrusted Yvette with a key.

That question was resolved when Yvette arrived at the door and it instantly opened. She slipped inside, saying, "How did you . . . ?"

"Never mind that." He took one good look at her, then stretched out a hand to touch her cheek. She flinched away.

"What happened?" He searched her face. "You look weary to the bone. Come. Sit with me."

He led her to the sofa, and they sat side by side, not touching. The cushions were so soft, Yvette wanted very much to curl up and go to sleep, but she had a mission to complete. She summoned the energy to tell Vidar what had happened. "I cycled all the way back to Paris. I had to deliver this." She reached into her satchel and handed him the jewel box. "I was to give the message to a jeweler on the rue . . . well, never mind where. But he has been taken by the *gestapistes* and now I don't know what to do."

"I'll take care of it." Vidar opened the jewel case, decanted the loose pearls into an empty ashtray, and lifted out the velvet bed. Then he took from his pocket a small penknife and began to unpick Louise's neat stitches.

Yvette said to him, "What are you, Vidar Lind?"

"Don't worry, I'll see the message gets to the right person." He slid his fingers between the lining and the base of the box and retrieved the coded message, held it up between forefinger and middle finger, then slid it into his breast pocket.

"You are not going to read it?"

"In a moment. I have to decode it. You can stop worrying about it now. All is well."

She sank back against the sofa cushions, closing her eyes with relief. She opened them again to find him regarding her intently.

"Is it just fatigue, Yvette? There is nothing . . . nothing else?"

It was as if he knew, she thought vaguely. She shook her head.

His shoulders relaxed. "I was worried about you."

"Were you?" She felt herself drifting again. She couldn't keep her eyes open. "I should get back to the *loge*."

"Sleep first. Then you must tell me everything." Vidar smiled at her, and his smile was tender, completely transforming his face.

After her experience with Werner, she welcomed his consideration. She did not wish to be touched just then. She did not want to leave him, either, so she curled up on the sofa while he sat down at the desk and set out his utensils.

"Can you decipher it?" she asked on a yawn.

He glanced at her. "I'll try."

He took out a sheet of clean paper, then disappeared into Louise's bedroom, returning with a large hand mirror. He put the paper on top of the glass—a piece of tradecraft she recognized—so that his writing would not make impressions on the surface beneath that could be found and deciphered later. Then he began.

She did not like to disturb him, so she kept quiet after that. Eventually, boredom overtook her nervous excitement and she fell into a doze.

When she woke, he was gone, and so were the papers. Disappointment flooded her, but then she realized there were sounds coming from the bathroom.

She hesitated, then knocked. "Vidar? Are you in there?"

The door opened and he came out, smiling. "I took the liberty of running you a bath. For your aching muscles," he added tactfully.

Yvette felt herself redden. She had cleaned up somewhat at the *loge*, but the sweat and dirt of the road needed her full attention. "Thank you. That is kind."

"You must be hungry. I'll order us something," he said, moving to the telephone. "Don't be too long in there."

That this situation closely mirrored her experience with Werner made her shiver. And yet, she felt no threat from Vidar Lind. She was fairly sure she could trust him, at least where her personal safety was concerned.

She turned the lock on the bathroom door, just in case.

As she lowered herself, inch by inch, the hot water brutally stung the rawness on her thighs, but she held her breath and gritted her teeth until the pain became bearable. The bath was not as leisurely as it might have been under different circumstances, but it was like heaven after all she'd been through.

She was gingerly toweling herself dry when she heard Vidar dealing with the waiter who had brought the room service. Stomach growling, Yvette went into the bedroom. Her own clothes were in sweat-stained tatters, so she donned one of Louise's robes and peered into the movie star's closet.

So many beautiful costumes and gowns. She rummaged through the racks of expensive, well-cut clothes for something appropriate. Trousers! She had always wanted to wear trousers—so practical for cycling around Paris—but Gabby was old-fashioned and would not let her.

She pulled on a pair of toffee-colored silk-lined culottes, paired them with a cream blouse, then added a little scarf in fall tones to complement her hair.

When she emerged from the bedroom, Vidar's raised eyebrows told her he noticed the change. He said nothing, however, but invited her to eat. They dined on real beef with *mange-touts* and new potatoes, washed down with a heavy burgundy that went straight to her head.

"Be sure to drink plenty of water," said Vidar, pouring some into a crystal goblet for her. "You will be dehydrated after that long ride."

Yvette took the glass and dutifully sipped. She felt clean and sated, though sadly unable to do full justice to the meal. "I know it is not good manners, but I shall wrap some of this up to take to Maman and Gabby." They would swoon at the mere sight of red meat.

"If you're finished, why don't we sit awhile?" said Vidar.

She left the table and joined him on the sofa. "I wish we could stay here forever."

His gaze became distant.

She cleared her throat. "I didn't mean I wanted to be with *you* forever, or anything . . ."

He laughed. "Of course not. If I looked serious, it's because I feel the same. Unfortunately, I have to get back."

"To the embassy?"

He took her hands and shook his head, still smiling. "I am not a Swedish diplomat, Yvette. My name is Rick and I work for the resistance."

Silently, she digested this. All this time, he had let her call him the wrong name, and that felt . . . as if she hadn't really come to know him at all. She looked down at his hands, which still gripped hers, and wanted to pull away. But she didn't.

"Be careful, *ma petite*," he said softly. "Do not run headlong into danger when the end is so near."

Yvette stared into his eyes and saw something there, something deep and warm. "I won't if you won't," she whispered.

"Don't worry about me. I am like a cockroach. I always survive. But you, Yvette . . . Will you stop working for them now?"

She opened her mouth to deny involvement, but his seriousness stopped her. "I know you are a courier," he said. "And I know who you work for. The war is almost won and the Germans, they are desperate. They've brought in troops from Algeria; they are letting *gestapiste* scum like the Berger gang run riot in Paris. Girls like you are being rounded up and tortured for days on end. You cannot imagine the horror."

From his face, she suspected he knew of such horror firsthand. "Keep your head down now," he urged. "You have done enough."

"I could just as easily die from a bomb blast while keeping my head down," she said flatly. If everyone had the same attitude, how would they ever win? How would they keep their friends and family safe?

His mouth had a bitter twist. "At least then it would be quick."

He would have turned away then, but she held on to him. "Would you do something for me? In case we don't meet again?"

"What?"

She took a deep breath and exhaled it in a rush. "Kiss me? Just this once." She thought of Werner's brutal assault and gave her head a small shake to dislodge the memory. "Please . . ." She had been about to call him "Vidar." "Please, Rick."

His gaze searched hers, as if he needed to make sure she meant what she said. Then something darkened in his eyes. He released her hands to cradle her face, his long fingers plunging through the thick, damp mass of her hair.

When he bent his head to touch his lips to hers, a great hunger sparked inside her. She slid her hands to his shoulders and he wrapped his arms around her, angling his head and taking the kiss deeper, until she was consumed by it, by him. Finally she felt wanted, desired. For a fleeting instant, she felt loved.

All too soon, he ended the kiss and pressed his forehead to hers. "When this hellish war is over . . ." He sighed, his breath whispering over her lips, making her shiver.

"No promises." Lightly, tentatively, she touched his cheek. Had he held out some vague assurance of the future to make her feel better about his leaving? He didn't have to. She was accustomed to living in the moment. A few weeks, or a month, could feel like years in wartime. Everything might change tomorrow.

"This is all we have," Yvette whispered. "And it is enough."

But her heart ached for him the second he walked out the door.

Chapter Twenty

Paris, July 1944

GABBY

G abby hesitated outside Madame LaRoq's apartment and looked over her shoulder to make sure no one was around. Almost a week had passed without incident since Yvette's abrupt return from Chantilly, seemingly shaken but unharmed. Jack was getting stronger every day. Despite the increasing brutality of the Nazis in Paris, the Allied bombings, and the bloody battle that waged even now in the north, Gabby's heart was as light as a dove's wing. Anticipation filled her chest as she turned the key and slipped inside.

A large hand grabbed her arm, pulled her deeper into the room. She gasped. "Jack! You should be in bed."

"My Gabby." He pulled her to him and she felt the strength of his arms, the breadth of his chest with a pang of bittersweet pleasure and regret. Part of her could not be glad to see him so strong, for then surely, he must leave.

When she could speak again, she said, "You are much better now, I see."

"Thanks to a brilliant nurse, I am well again." His chuckle turned into a dry cough.

"Don't overdo it just yet, soldier." She pushed him to the sofa and bustled to get him water.

Her cheeks burned and her blood simmered from that kiss. When she set the water on the table beside him, he pulled her down to him again. "I am fit as a fiddle. I just need to get out and about a bit. Fresh air and exercise, that's the ticket."

"The ticket?" Gabby eyed him warily. Did he mean to travel?

His eyes warmed with laughter. "When you are worried, you have a little crease, just . . . here." He brushed the place between her eyebrows with his fingertip. "Let me see if I can smooth it away."

"I worry about you more now that you are well than when you were sick," she said, a little breathlessly, because his fingers and hands had begun exploring other parts of her. *I ought to stop this,* she thought vaguely, but there was so little joy to be found in this war, and he was very, very good at what he was doing.

It seemed as if no time at all had passed when they became aware of a commotion downstairs. Jack heard it first and leaped off her as if she were on fire. Still dazed with kisses, she sat up. "What? What's going on?" Then she heard shouts and shot to her feet.

Jack was already moving. "Quick, we need to get rid of all this." He was packing up books and cigarettes, the dirty plate from the meal she'd brought earlier. Heart racing, Gabby helped, emptying the ashtrays, putting cushions back in place, taking his blanket and pillow back to the spare bedroom.

Wordlessly, they worked together until the apartment looked uninhabited. They stared at the massive cabinet that stood in front of the maid's room. "Help me shift it," said Gabby.

"No, allow me." Clearly relishing his returned strength, Jack heaved the cabinet aside, then grabbed some supplies to take in with him. Cigarettes, lighter, an old water canteen she'd brought him, a couple of novels. A pistol, which Gabby prayed he wouldn't need to use.

There were more shouts on the floor below, then a sharp, angry tirade from Madame Vasseur, who must have come out from her room down the hall to see what was going on.

Gabby turned to Jack and met his gaze. Everything that must be said passed between them in that look. She was loved. Despite the danger and the fear, a warm feeling filled her heart. He gave her one final, urgent kiss, then ducked into the maid's room and closed the door.

Gabby eased the armoire back in place, tidied her hair and clothing, then slipped out of the apartment. She grabbed Madame Vasseur by the elbow and hustled her back into her suite. "Safer for you to stay inside. I will tell you all about it later." Backing out, she shut the door on the old woman's protests, then made for the stairs.

Please, God, she prayed silently, *I know I have not been to mass much lately but I am a good person. At least, I try. Please spare him. Please. It's the only thing I ask.*

After that, there was no more time for praying. A man in a trench coat and fedora appeared in the stairwell and looked up at her. Even at this distance, in the dim light, she caught the glint of gold in his teeth. Rafael. The gangster who had sold her the sulfa pills.

She stopped short, confused. "What are you doing here?"

"Official business." He climbed the stairs until he stood eye to eye with her and held out a card.

"I don't know what that is," Gabby said, frowning down at it.

"*Gestapistes*, Gabby." Her mother's voice, sharp and clipped, called up from behind Rafael. "It's a raid."

All the air left Gabby's lungs. *Keep calm. Never show them fear.* She had to breathe deeply in through her nose before she could form the words. "And what is your business here?"

"Routine inspection," said Rafael. "Stand aside, mademoiselle."

Gabby let them pass, then turned to follow them up the stairs. *Think!* How could she distract them, divert them from Madame LaRoq's apartment?

Uncharacteristically, her mother made a terrible fuss the whole way up to the second floor. They were all respectable bourgeois at number 10, not wealthy, not political. They minded their own business here. Rafael and his men had better have good reason for storming in at this time of night.

The men ignored her, trading insults and jokes with each other in loud, coarse voices as they clattered up the stairs.

Rafael stopped outside Madame LaRoq's apartment. "This one." He gestured to Gabby. "Open it."

Moving as slowly as she dared, Gabby fumbled with her ring of keys.

"Hurry up or we'll break it down," Rafael said.

"I trust you have a warrant, messieurs?" Catherine Dior was standing in the hallway. Her voice was quiet but commanding. Her dignity and calm lent Gabby a dash of badly needed courage.

"Gentlemen?" Catherine gave a faint, ironic smile when no one answered her straightaway.

Rafael sneered and thrust a crumpled piece of paper at her. "We're here to seize the goods of one Madame LaRoq, who is believed to have been harboring enemies of the Third Reich in this very building, mademoiselle."

Catherine's eyes widened as she scanned the warrant. "Enemies . . ." She shook her head. "No, no, you must have it wrong. Madame is—*was*—bedridden. She could not possibly . . ."

Rafael shrugged. "That is our information, mademoiselle."

Danique Foucher spoke. "Sadly, madame has just passed away, so it's no use trying to arrest her."

Gabby stared at her mother. She'd known all along? But of course, somehow Maman always knew everything that went on in the building. And she had clarified an issue Gabby hadn't considered until Catherine's slight slip with the tenses. Until now, they had covered up madame's death. She would not be found in her room, however, so her very recent passing was the simplest explanation. Gabby would have to worry about what that meant for Jack later.

Rafael turned to Gabby. "In that case, you won't mind letting us into the apartment. All madame's property is to be seized."

There was a glint in his eye, just for her. The blood drained from her face as she finally understood what was happening. No information had been laid against madame. This was about the sapphire ring she had used to barter for the sulfa pills, not her Englishman. Rafael thought there was more where it came from.

This was all her fault.

"You can't do this," she whispered. "Why—where is your evidence? You can't simply go around accusing people of crimes so that you can take their things."

But even before the words were out of her mouth, she knew

how ludicrously naïve she sounded. The sneers on the men's faces told her they thought the same. They were going to raid madame's apartment and there was nothing she could do to stop them. Gabby's heart pounded. What if they found Jack?

Catherine spoke, drawing everyone's attention back to her. "I don't think you'll find anything of real value among madame's things. She owned a few paintings, some silverware, and some jewelry. That's it."

"That's right." Gabby needed to hold herself together but her breath was coming in short pants. She knew what they did to prisoners at rue de la Pompe, had heard the screams with her own ears. She couldn't let them find Jack. She'd die before she let them take him.

She took a deep breath and released it, trying to stay calm. Any more delay and obfuscation would only seem suspicious. Gabby unlocked the door to madame's apartment, and the men filed in after her. Speaking clearly, she said, "I am afraid you will not find anything much to tempt you here, messieurs. The paintings might fetch something, as Miss Dior said."

Rafael grunted. "Where did she keep the jewels?"

Gabby went to madame's bedchamber and took the jewel box from beneath the floorboards. "Here."

Rafael rummaged through the box, his big hands pawing over madame's delicate pieces, then shut the lid with a snap. "I'll take this." He tucked the box under his arm and made for the door. "Ransack the place," he ordered the other two men.

Gabby cried out, "No! Please do not destroy her things. Poor madame. She never did anything wrong."

"You seem strangely upset for someone who just pawned the woman's jewelry," said Rafael, stepping back as his henchmen rampaged about the room, tipping over furniture, slitting cushion covers with their knives, getting the stuffing everywhere.

"It was for madame's medicine," she said quietly. "She asked me to do it."

"Well, much good it did her." He shrugged. "You might as well submit with good grace, mademoiselle. You brought this on yourself. You did not come to Berger with the information he required."

So, not only was Rafael being greedily opportunistic, Berger was punishing her for not turning informer. There was no way out for Jack. If the men started on the silver cabinet, they might discover where he was hiding. Could he possibly shoot all three men with that pistol of his before they shot him? She didn't think so. And anyway, shots would be heard far and wide, and bring more trouble down upon them.

Gabby winced and turned her face away as they smashed the glass in madame's china cabinets and swept the ornaments off her mantel shelf. What was the point of all this? They seemed to take delight in needless destruction. When they moved on to the silver cabinet, Gabby yelped in fear.

"Enough!" her mother shouted. "I'll give you what you want. Just stop this at once!"

Shocked at her mother's unwonted ferocity, Gabby stared. The men halted and turned to stare at her, too.

Danique seemed to gather herself, then let out a long breath. "Come with me." She shot a look at Rafael that was as hard and direct as a bullet. "I assure you, it will be worth your while."

With a jerk of the head to his men to follow, Rafael went after her.

Before she could sag to the ground with the relief of it, Catherine's arm came around Gabby to shore her up. "Go with them," she whispered, her breath warm in Gabby's ear. "They might get suspicious otherwise. I'll stay here."

Gabby wanted more than anything to stay with Jack, but that was impossible. She nodded and stepped carefully around the debris.

"I wonder what your mother has up her sleeve," whispered Catherine as Gabby paused at the door.

"It had better be good," Gabby whispered back. She left Catherine at the apartment and continued downstairs.

GABBY HAD NO trouble finding them. Rafael's men seemed determined to make as much noise as possible. Their raucous laughter echoed through the cavernous cellars below.

The cellars? "What on earth?" Gabby murmured, descending after them.

The darkness of the subterranean cavern was profound and a damp cool pervaded the space, a contrast from the thick heat of the summer night aboveground. By feeling along one clammy wall, Gabby made her way down a corridor before she spotted the faint glow of light to her right.

The men must have brought flashlights with them. The cellars, with their row upon row of empty wine racks, stretched beyond.

But Danique did not venture as far as the wine cellars. She stopped at a large store cupboard and fumbled with a key.

One of Rafael's men snatched the key from her and jammed it into the lock. He flung the cupboard door wide. Nothing. Shelves full of nothing. "What?" he spluttered. "You'd better not be playing some sort of game here, madame."

"If you'll allow me . . ." Danique waited until Rafael yanked the bully aside, then she felt along the edge of the cupboard. There was a click and a creak. The false front of shelving swung inward and Danique stepped through. The others followed. Impossible as it seemed, they all went in, one after the other, disappearing inside.

Everyone fell silent. The room, easily as big as madame's front parlor, was stuffed full of treasure.

Gabby stared at her mother. "These belong to the tenants. The ones who were taken. The Bloms and the Gellners, and . . . *You did this . . .*"

"Hush, Gabby," said Danique. To the men, she added, "Take it," waving her hand around. "Take it all. But it's everything, you hear me? It's all we have, so take it and then leave my tenants alone."

Gabby was too shocked to speak or protest. She just stood there, gaping at the Aladdin's cave her mother had amassed without Gabby's knowing a thing about it.

"You two make yourselves scarce," said Rafael to the women. "Don't get in our way."

Shaking, Gabby turned to leave, but not before she heard him say, "Go get the van. There's more here than we bargained for."

Gabby hurried back to the *loge*. She longed to check on Jack, but she didn't dare. Not until Rafael and his men were gone.

When her mother came in, Gabby eyed her warily. How could Maman have looted those people's homes? And what did it say about Gabby that she was thankful for her mother's duplicity?

Danique's cheeks reddened. "What? You think I stole it all? I was keeping it safe for them. In case they return."

"But why hand it all over now, Maman? Why not keep the secret? Rafael would never have found your hiding place."

"And let him find what *you're* hiding up there?" Danique pointed to her own chest. "Me, I know all about it. You are reckless, Gabby. No better than your sister."

Gabby could only stare dazedly at her mother, unable to voice the many conflicting thoughts that exploded and fizzed like fireworks in her head. Danique had known about madame, about Jack, probably about Catherine, too.

But the most important thing: Jack was safe. There was no reason for the gang to return to madame's apartment now. And Maman had been looking after the absent tenants' belongings for them all this time. Was her quiet, timid mother truly a heroine underneath? Sometimes, the people closest to you could surprise you the most.

"I'd better make sure they leave once they've emptied that cupboard," said Danique, heading out. "You keep watch for your sister."

"Yvette!" Gabby gasped and looked around. In all the commotion, she hadn't realized her sister wasn't there. It was past curfew. What on earth was she doing out so late?

Nerves taut, Gabby kept watch for Yvette as Rafael's thugs looted the treasure in the cellar. The van Rafael had sent for arrived and drove past the *loge*, right into the central courtyard. Another two men jumped out.

Seconds later, a slight, furtive figure slipped through the street entrance. Gabby hurried to the vestibule to whisk her trembling, tearstained sister inside.

"Oh, God, Yvette!" Her hand came away sticky from Yvette's arm. "What in the world?"

The darkness on Yvette's hands, on her clothes ... That smell ... It was blood.

Earlier that day

YVETTE

Less than a week after her bicycle ride to Paris, Yvette heard that Louise Dulac was back at the Ritz. Yvette had arranged to have the pearls restrung and returned to the actress and hoped that would be the end of their association.

Yvette had completed her final round of deliveries for the day and did not have to return to Lelong until the next morning. The sun would not set for hours, and all around her, people complained about the heat. Would there be a storm tonight? Not if the clear sky was any indication. They would all have to sweat it out until the weather broke. Maybe tomorrow, rain would come.

She spotted Jean-Luc loitering at a newspaper stand by the Pont des Invalides, no doubt passing a message to his contact there. Yvette picked up a newspaper. As usual, the headlines heralded Nazi victory.

"Any real news?" she asked Jean-Luc when an old man had paid for his paper and moved away.

"The uprising. It is for tonight." Although he muttered the words beneath his breath, she heard the tremor of excitement. "Come with us."

"But—" She broke off because a German soldier had stopped by to purchase a paper flower on a pin for his girl. It seemed to take forever for him to pay, and then what must he do but stand there and flirt while he fixed the silly brooch to the girl's lapel.

When the couple moved off at last, Yvette said, "But it is too soon, Jean-Luc. You know this. I told you what is being said. You need to coordinate with the Allies. You don't have enough men to succeed on your own."

"You don't understand anything, Yvette," said Jean-Luc, his dark eyes alight with fire. "When we do this, all of Paris will rise up with us. There will be no stopping the will of the people."

This was crazy talk. She glanced around them, at the pragmatic Parisians going about their everyday business as best they could, trying to stay out of trouble. "Don't you think that if they'd wanted to rise up they would have done it by now?"

But then another customer came to the newsstand, and Jean-Luc jerked his head, indicating that they should leave. They walked together, guiding their bicycles along the wide pavement, toward the bridge.

Halfway across the river, they propped their bicycles against the low stone balustrade. Jean-Luc leaned out, his gaze lifted to the peak of the Eiffel Tower, which rose to dizzying heights above the Paris skyline. He looked like a man who was contemplating a lofty place in history, but he might as well throw himself into the river below as carry out this stupid plan.

"Will you look at me?" she said.

Jaw tensing, mouth a hard line, Jean-Luc turned to face her. Yvette stared into his eyes, as if she could compel him with the force of her gaze. "Don't do this, Jean-Luc. Please don't. It is suicide."

"I have to, Yvette. I can't stand to wait another day." He put his hand on her shoulder, one comrade to another. "The usual place. You know it."

She did know it. There was a cellar beneath a seedy café in the Marais district where Jean-Luc and his comrades used to meet. A secret back-alley entrance. She had never been, but he had told her about it.

"We gather there at midnight."

"Jean-Luc, no!"

But he wouldn't listen. He was no longer the boy she had grown up with at Lelong, but a man. A proud, stupid, pigheaded man.

"You said you wanted to take action, not just talk," he said. "Now's your chance, Yvette."

WHEN YVETTE RELATED this exchange to Catherine Dior, the other woman shook her head. "Fools. They risk all for no reward."

"Can't we find a way to stop them?" Yvette paced the floor of Catherine's apartment, hands clenched, fingernails digging into her palms.

"I'm afraid not," Catherine replied. "Even if I could get a message to my superiors that fast, they have no influence with this group." Her dark eyes were compassionate. "There's nothing we can do."

"I'm so sick and tired of feeling helpless," Yvette said wildly. "D-Day was weeks ago. Why don't they come?"

"Fighting is still raging in Normandy," said Catherine. "And who knows? The Allies might not plan to enter Paris at all for some time."

Yvette stared at her. "But they must! It should be their first priority." What was France without its capital?

Catherine smiled faintly. "If only wishing made it so. Strategically, the Allies might well bypass Paris altogether, fight their way to Germany."

Yvette fell silent, dumbfounded by this disclosure. News of the

Allied landings in early June had made hope leap in every Parisian's heart. But as the weeks dragged on, it seemed as if the worst of Nazi aggression was yet to come and their saviors were not even a speck on the horizon. Now Catherine was telling her they might have even longer to wait.

Catherine went to the drinks cart and poured a tiny glass of crème de cassis for each of them. "The longer the delay, the worse it will be for us in Paris." She handed Yvette the apéritif. "The Germans know they will lose. There will be reprisals, revenge, more rounding up of Jews and dissidents. The Nazis will most likely lay waste to the city before they surrender."

"We can't let that happen." Yvette sat forward and sipped her drink. The alcohol stole her breath for a second. "And if our men sacrifice themselves now, who will there be to defend us later?"

"Your Jean-Luc and his crew are not the only fighters we have," said Catherine. "Until then, we need to hold everything together and keep calm." She hesitated. "I have a job for you tomorrow."

"Yes. Of course." Anything to be active, to *do* something instead of waiting and waiting for salvation to come.

"Things have become . . . difficult for me," said Catherine. "I think I am being watched." She frowned. "It could be that I am frightened of shadows, but I'd prefer to err on the side of caution." She licked her lips. "I am to meet someone at the Place du Trocadéro tomorrow afternoon at five o'clock. I want you to go in my place."

The message was in code and Yvette was to deliver it to the contact in a "brush-past" maneuver, a little like the passing of a baton in a relay race. She and Catherine practiced the move together until Yvette could manage it without detection.

"Thank you, my dear. Let me know how you get on, won't you?"

"Yes, of course."

Before Yvette left, Catherine took her chin and tilted her face up. "I know you are worried for your friend, my dear. But we all make our own decisions. He knows the risks, just as you and I do." She sighed. "For some men, it is all about the grand gesture. It is their pride, you see. They cannot abide the waiting. But it is with patience and careful planning that we will prevail."

She smiled, took Yvette's shoulders, and kissed her on both cheeks. "Take care, Yvette. And go with God, my dear."

YVETTE SPENT THAT night tossing and turning in her bed. Finally, she opened her eyes and frowned up at the ceiling. There was no way she could sleep until she had done all she could to prevent Jean-Luc from making a huge mistake.

Maybe she should go to the café to meet him, as he'd demanded. Maybe she could talk his friends out of their plans. Anyone with common sense would understand Catherine's reasoning. The Germans needed little excuse to take out their fear and frustration on the civilian population, but in their eyes, a revolt of the kind planned tonight would give them plenty of justification to execute many innocent people in addition to the insurgents.

Ah, who was she kidding? Those men would not listen to her. She bit her lip and stared hard at the ceiling. But Jean-Luc might. Maybe she hadn't tried hard enough this afternoon. Maybe she could persuade him not to join in. If she could save him, at least, she would have done something worthwhile.

The more she thought about it, the more convinced she became. She had to make the attempt.

What time was it? She flicked on her flashlight, taking care to shield it with her hand so as not to disturb Gabby, and looked at the bedside clock. Eleven-thirty. She had to hurry. She glanced over at her sister's side of the bed, preparing to slip out without waking her. Gabby wasn't there.

Was Gabby still up? She'd never let Yvette out of the apartment if she saw her trying to leave at this time of night. Yvette got out of bed and crept through the empty parlor, checked the kitchen, but Gabby wasn't in the *loge* at all.

Was she with one of the tenants? Perhaps someone was ill and she was tending to them. Yvette thought of Madame LaRoq. With a guilty pang, she realized she hadn't visited madame for weeks. Tomorrow, she would not let Gabby put her off.

Maman's snore shattered the silence, and a choke of nervous laughter escaped Yvette—a release of tension more than genuine mirth. So Danique was in her room, then. Good.

At least with her sister gone, Yvette didn't have to bother being quiet as she dressed. She pulled on Louise Dulac's trousers and shirt and swept her hair up beneath an old beret of her father's. She wouldn't fool anyone close up, but at a distance she would pass for male. Less hassle that way.

She had time before curfew, so there was no need to worry about being stopped on the way to the café, but she carried out a few countersurveillance measures, just in case.

From her training, she knew better than to simply walk into a meeting place. It was important to reconnoiter first. But as she wheeled her bicycle toward the entrance to the alley behind the café, the *ak-ak-ak* of machine-gun fire split the air.

Jean-Luc! Glancing wildly over her shoulder, she saw citizens taking fright, ducking and running for cover, but she couldn't move. She was too late. Even now, he could be dead, they could all be dead, mown down where they stood, shot to pieces, drowning in pools of blood. As Yvette stood there, frozen, a man practically tackled her, hustling her off the street, bicycle and all, into a deeply recessed doorway.

She was too shocked to resist, and when she turned to speak, he had gone. Some anonymous hero bent on saving those too stupid or panicked to save themselves.

Someone must have talked, betrayed the group. The senseless futility of it made Yvette want to punch and kick and scream, and yet for some time she was too scared even to make a whimper or to leave her hiding place. She held still and listened, her ears straining for the next flurry of shots.

After what seemed like years, she heard signs of life, of people emerging back into the street, if only to scurry to the safety of their homes. Then the world fell silent, as if a blanket had fallen over everything, smothering all sound.

She left her bicycle where it was and crept further along the street. Two large vans rounded the corner toward her with a squeal of brakes, one after the other, and turned into the street up ahead, in front of the café where the men had met. They didn't look like army vehicles or anything she'd seen the Nazis use. Who were they?

All went quiet again. Did she dare to approach? A thin sound came from the alley that ran behind the café, a wheezing cry that turned to a whimper. Someone was in agony. Flattening herself against the wall, she peered around the corner into the alley. A figure slumped over in the gutter, clutching his chest. It looked like Jean-Luc.

"No!" She ran to kneel down beside the figure. It wasn't Jean-Luc; it was a man a few years older. Still, she had to help him. She took off her scarf, wadded it up, and held it to his shoulder to try to staunch the bleeding. The bullet was on the right side, so it had missed his heart. *It is not too bad*, she thought. *Please, let it not be too bad.* But how could she get him to safety? Were there men looking for him, even now?

"Quick, help me bind it up," gasped the young man, stripping off his kerchief and handing it to her. "Then get out of here. I'll be fine."

She did her best in the dark to bind his wound, but she could feel blood seeping through her scarf as she held it in place. "We need to get you medical attention." Gabby would know what to do, but Yvette couldn't bear this fellow's weight all the way to the *loge*. She wanted to ask about Jean-Luc but in that group, they didn't use names. "The young man with the limp. Did they take him?"

Her patient grunted. "I was late. I ran when I saw what was up. No time to see who was taken and who was killed." He sucked a breath between his teeth and struggled to his knees, leaning heavily on her shoulder. "Thank you. Now leave me. You've done enough."

As Yvette hesitated, the injured man gave her a shove. "Go, you stupid girl. It's all turned to hell but there's no reason for you to get—"

He was cut off by a shout coming from further down the alleyway. "Here's one! Hey, I've got another one!" A powerful flashlight caught them in its beam. Dazzled, Yvette turned her face away, blinking hard to get her night vision back.

"Two. There are two here."

"Alive, lads. We want them alive, remember," called another voice.

She saw the glint of the pistol in the injured man's hand before her mind switched into gear.

"Run, girl. Run!" He fired off a shot in the direction of the light. "Go!"

She didn't hesitate. She turned and bolted for her bicycle. She was already pedaling away when she heard the man's scream. She squeezed her eyes shut, feeling his pain, wishing she could have stood by his side and fought.

Then, it hit her. Those men who had hunted the injured man had not been German. She'd understood every word. They'd spoken in French. *Gestapistes.*

They wanted the rebels alive. That could mean only one thing. They meant to question them. And if their captives did not give them the information they wanted, what then? Torture?

Cold fear swept over her, even as she pedaled harder through the blackened Paris streets. She was shaking so violently, she could barely steer her bicycle. It was well after curfew now, and if she was caught with blood on her, she was done for.

But she knew the city well, and like a little mouse scuttling back to her nest, Yvette managed to avoid checkpoints and patrols on the way home. Turning at last into the rue Royale, she was almost light-headed with relief. Then she saw the great doors to the courtyard of number 10 standing open, the twin beams of a van's headlights streaming forth. With a gasp, she braked hard, her foot dropping from the pedal to the ground. What now? A raid? Had they come for her already? No. Impossible.

Yvette looked over her shoulder. She had nowhere to run, and the surge of panicked energy she'd experienced in the wake of the skirmish in the alley had left her depleted, her legs weak and limp as noodles. She hid well out of sight on the opposite side of the street and watched.

The main door to the courtyard had been left wide open and

a van was backed up in the vestibule, its headlights blazing in fla-
grant disregard for blackout restrictions. She could make out a tall
man standing beside the van, talking to the driver. Then the van
continued to reverse, right into the courtyard beyond the wide vestibule. She caught the outline of the tall man's features illuminated
briefly by the headlights as he turned away.

Her whole body turned cold. It was Vidar. Rick. She would
never get used to that name.

The van's headlights switched off, and blackness fell, and her
eyes took a few moments to adjust. She started toward Vidar, then
realized, with a swirl of confused emotions, that his intentions
might not be good. Whatever he was doing there at this time of
night, it did not seem to bode well for the residents of number 10.
Nighttime visits rarely did.

While she argued with herself over whether or not to confront
him, Vidar seemed to melt into the shadows and disappear.

When the street was clear, Yvette crossed, well out of sight of
anyone in the courtyard. She leaned her bicycle against the wall
and peered through the front window into the *loge*. She couldn't
see anyone. What was going on?

She heard first one door, then another open and shut. Peering around the corner into the courtyard, she saw that the cabin
of the van was empty now. Two men were walking away from it,
their backs to her. They were crossing the courtyard toward the
east wing with a purposeful stride. Now was her chance. Yvette
retrieved her bicycle, wheeled it in through the street door, and
rested it against the vestibule wall.

Gabby grabbed her and pulled her into the *loge*. "Oh, God,
Yvette! What in the world?" When Gabby got a good look at her,

she turned white. "You are bleeding! Are you hurt? What happened to you? Where have you been?"

Yvette looked down at herself. A deep patch of red darkened Louise Dulac's beautiful blouse. "No, no, it's not my blood, but tell me, what is going on here?"

Gabby grabbed her arm and yanked her to the bathroom. "Quick! You can't let anyone see you like that. Wash the blood off and get out of those clothes. I'll burn them when these men are gone. Hurry!"

"It's not Catherine?" whispered Yvette. "They have not come for her?"

"No! *Bon Dieu*, why should you think that?" Gabby's eyes narrowed, but all she added was "They're taking some valuables that belonged to the tenants, that's all. It's that horrible Berger's gang."

A masculine voice called from the vestibule. "Mademoiselle Foucher. A word?"

Gabby turned to go, but Yvette said, "No! Gabby, the blood." Her hand was covered in it from grabbing Yvette. "Quickly."

"Just a minute," Gabby called back. Wild-eyed, she took the soap and scrubbed at her hands. Then she dried them, briefly pressing her forehead against the wall, as if to gather courage. Taking a deep breath, she went out to see what the man wanted.

For once, Yvette did as she was told, too numb and shocked to bother about the raid, even though just a week before she would have been squaring up to these men, spitting and fighting the dirty looters tooth and nail. When she'd finished washing, she dressed and hid the bloody garments in the bottom of their bedroom wardrobe. She poured some of Maman's apple brandy into a mug, then sat in a sort of trance at the kitchen table, cradling the mug in her hands and forgetting to drink it. When the van finally left and the street doors closed behind it, Yvette waited for Gabby, but she didn't come.

Maman was the first to return. "What a night!" She frowned at Yvette. "What happened to you?"

Yvette couldn't even begin to answer. "Nothing."

Maman eyed her for a moment. "Just tell me this. Will what you have done tonight have consequences for you or this family?"

Yvette looked away. She couldn't even form the words. They might have killed Jean-Luc. But they'd wanted those men alive—for questioning, of course. If Jean-Luc had been taken, she was compromised. If it hadn't been for the injured man shooting at those men, providing cover for her escape, she might well have been captured herself. "I have to see Catherine Dior." She gulped down all the brandy, and the fire of it racing down her gullet gave her courage. She stood.

"Dior, Dior," grumbled Maman. "All of our troubles can be traced back to that family. Every single one."

Yvette was too tired and overwrought to ask what her mother meant. Aching in heart and body, she went up to see Catherine, to confess what she'd done.

Chapter Twenty-One

England, February 1947

GABBY

Away from Audrey's kindhearted curiosity and Jack's stony indifference, Gabby felt more alone than she ever had before. Even with Yvette in New York, Gabby had still had her work and her mother, and the hope of seeing Jack again. That hope had kept her going through the pain of losing Yvette and the worry over Catherine. It had given her the courage to hide those other men.

She had been right not to open that cursed envelope, not to listen to that British voice on the phone.

She curled up on the window seat, defeated. Dully, she inspected the dark patch in her lap. She should wash the tea out before it stained, but the will to do anything but sit there had left her completely.

If only she knew the way to the nearest train station, she would have set out with her suitcase that minute. As it was, she would have to ask Audrey to take her there. She grimaced. Audrey had been so kind, and the last thing Gabby wanted was to be overly dramatic about her departure.

No, much as she wanted to run from this, she couldn't go until the appointed time. She'd have to brazen it out, ignore Jack's hurtful behavior.

Why had he been so cold to her? As if he resented her presence, thought it an imposition. She hoped Audrey would tell him Gabby hadn't simply invited herself, but she wouldn't bank on it. Audrey was a treasure, but she did not seem an overly sensitive sort of person. Would she even suspect there had been deeper feelings than friendship between Gabby and Jack—at least on Gabby's side? Gabby could not bring herself to explain it. Bad enough to have those feelings. A hundred times worse to be obliged to speak them aloud.

But what had happened to him? The man she had fallen in love with had been courteous and considerate. Had she been a stranger, the Jack she knew would have treated her better than he had treated her that afternoon. She was the last person to wish for plain gratitude—that would have hurt almost as much as this silence—but why couldn't he at least be civil? Where was the tenderness he had shown her back in Paris? Had it all been a lie, calculated to keep her sweet so she wouldn't betray him to the Germans? No. That couldn't be.

The piping on the window-seat cushion was fraying at the edges. She rolled the ragged fabric between her fingers, trying without success to repair it. Wartime romance was notoriously fleeting and fickle. But Jack had spoken so often of his plans for them when the war was over. He did not seem the kind of man to make promises he had no intention of keeping.

Maybe his feelings for her had been genuine at the time, but they'd faded once he was safe home in England.

Or had something happened to change him? What had he been through after he'd escaped Paris and returned home?

She would ask Audrey on their excursion tomorrow. Gabby turned her head to gaze out beyond the tree line to that church spire in the distance. It was a long, long time since she had spoken to God, but she found herself offering up a silent prayer for Jack, nonetheless.

Dinner that evening was no better than teatime, and Audrey maintained such a hectic flow of chatter that Gabby stopped trying to keep up with it. When she was called upon to give her opinion, she said, "Ah, I am sorry. I did not quite understand . . ."

Jack's fair hair seemed to have darkened to bronze since Paris. His face was lined but somehow even more handsome than she remembered. Men were lucky that way.

She noticed Jack didn't reach for a cigar or even a cigarette after dinner, but he remained where he was while Gabby and Audrey left for the drawing room.

After only a few moments, however, he appeared in the doorway and almost hesitantly came into the room. He moved reluctantly, as if his feet were stuck in cement, and Gabby flushed. Could he make it any clearer he did not want her here?

Audrey rang the bell. After another few minutes' stilted conversation, there was a thumping on the stairs and a boy and a girl appeared, good-naturedly pushing and shoving each other to get through the doorway first.

"Uncle Jack!" The smaller child, the boy, clambered onto Jack's lap. "What are you doing here? I was looking for you all over."

The softening of Jack's grim expression as he ruffled his nephew's hair made Gabby's heart break in two. He was capable of looking the way he used to, then. It was just that she could not be the one to make him do it.

She watched, fascinated, as the small boy twisted Jack around his finger until his sister, the elder and twice his size, gave him a friendly punch on the thigh. "Francis, do give over. It's my turn now."

"Good gracious, the two of you are such hooligans," sighed Audrey. "Whatever will our guest think?"

The pair turned to look at Gabby.

"Are you the French lady?" The girl abandoned her uncle to approach. With an impeccable accent, she added, "*Bonsoir, mademoiselle.*"

A little light seemed to switch on in Gabby's chest and a warmth settled there. She smiled at the girl and asked her in French for her name.

"I am Isabelle and this is Francis," said the girl, again in French. Her long blond hair was thick and lustrous, but her freckled face was a little pinched and peaky looking, as if she'd been ill.

"I'm Frank, not Francis," said the little boy, puffing out his chest. "And I've lost a button."

"Oh, no, have you?" said Audrey. "Come here and let me see."

While Audrey inspected the damage to his striped pajamas, Gabby patted the space beside her on the sofa and smiled at Isabelle. "Come, sit by me and tell me all about yourself."

"I haven't been well," confided the girl, inching her bottom deeper into the sofa. "But Mama is taking me to the Riviera to re . . . *recuperate*. Isn't that right, Mama?"

"What?" Audrey looked up from Frank's shirt. "Oh, er, yes. Well, that's the plan, anyway." Her attention returned to the shirt and her voice rose half an octave. "I wish you would consider joining us, Jack. Mr. Pargeter could run things here."

"Oh, yes!" said Isabelle, her eyes shining. "That would be utterly brilliant. Do say you'll come, Uncle Jack."

Jack's gaze flickered, for an instant, to Gabby. Then he said, "Perhaps some other time. I'm busy here at the moment."

"But it's winter!" cried Isabelle. "There is literally nothing to do here until May, at the least."

"That shows how much you know about it," said Frank.

"Now, now, children," said Audrey as their voices rose in disagreement. "Don't squabble. If that is your uncle's decision, so be it. Not that I think it wouldn't do you a power of good—"

"Thank you, Audrey," said Jack, cutting her off. Then, with a marked change of tone, he added, "Come, you young brigands, say good night and I'll take you up to bed."

Frank lit up at the promised treat. "Can we read *Treasure Island?*" he said eagerly.

"I don't see why not."

Isabelle, clearly torn between the desire to stay with the adults and the fear of missing out on the story, reluctantly left Gabby's side. She kissed and hugged her mother, then suddenly came back to Gabby and threw her skinny arms around her neck. "Good night, madame."

Gabby breathed in Isabelle's soap-and-water scent and squeezed her eyes shut. "*Bonne nuit, ma fille,*" she whispered back, a catch in her throat. Somehow, the little girl's spontaneous affection made Jack's coldness even harder to bear.

"No, I'll take them," said Audrey briskly, putting a hand on her brother's shoulder before he'd even attempted to rise. "You've hardly spoken two words to our guest." She sent an unreadable glance to Gabby. "And I imagine there is much to say."

The children protested loudly at the last-minute substitute, but Jack was too well-mannered to echo their sentiments. Gabby caught the dark look he threw his sister, however, and abruptly stood. "I'll go up, too, I think. It has been a tiring day."

She sensed his relief as she left the drawing room. But as soon as she stepped out into the hall, Audrey caught her by the elbow and told the children to go on ahead.

"You're giving up? Just like that?"

It was futile to pretend she didn't know what Audrey meant. "He doesn't want me here. He has made that clear."

"That's not it at all." Audrey bit her lip and glanced back toward the drawing room. "Look, it's not my place to interfere, but just try again, can't you? He . . . he's not himself. But I think . . ." She gripped Gabby's hands tightly and shook them a little. "I feel you would be good for him, if only you will be brave."

"Mama!" Frank yelled from the landing above.

"Coming!" Audrey's eyes pleaded with her. "Please, Gabby. *Please.*" Then she hurried off to put her children to bed.

Gabby looked after her helplessly. She hadn't felt so confused and at sea since Jack had first come to the apartments at rue Royale. *He's not himself.* Audrey's words echoed through her mind. So it wasn't her imagination, then. But what was making him behave this way?

Slowly, she turned and went back to the drawing room to find out.

⤞⤞

"I HAVE DECIDED to return to London tomorrow if your sister is free to drive me to the station." Gabby stated it baldly, without preamble, as she walked back into the drawing room.

Jack's expression lightened. He was relieved. *Relieved* that she was going.

As if the words were forced out of him, he said, "So soon? Please don't go on my account."

And what was she to make of that? "You don't want me here." She blurted it out and saw him wince at her gaucheness. "But I don't understand why." Anger boiled up within her. "Common courtesy, at least—"

"*Courtesy*," he muttered. "Dear God."

She slapped her hand on a nearby chair. "Was I not kind to you? Did I not nurse you and care for you and hide you at great risk to my own life and the lives of everyone around me?"

She was becoming shrill. She hated herself for speaking aloud things that she would never in a million years have thought to say to him had he behaved like a normal human instead of this block of ice.

His eyebrow raised, but he wasn't meeting her eye. "Well, you got your medal, didn't you? What do you want from me?"

She gasped. Threatening tears clogged her throat. She had been determined not to reproach him, but his cruelty was so disproportionate, so undeserved, that her sense of justice could not let it stand. "Your sister invited me. Naturally, I assumed you wanted me here."

"Audrey has a habit of meddling in things that don't concern her." In a controlled, even tone, he added, "Don't you think that if I'd wanted you I would have come to Paris long ago? It's not as if I didn't know where you lived."

Gabby's entire body froze. She wanted desperately to run from the room, but her legs wouldn't cooperate. As she stared at him, he seemed to sag back in his chair, defeated, bitter, and dismissive.

Yet still she could not go. She had faced down the French Gestapo during the war, and yet she had never been so afraid. "I don't know what has happened to you. I don't know why you are being like this. But I . . . I want you to know that . . ." She swallowed, then lifted her chin. "I came here against my better judgment because . . . I love you. And . . . and life is short. And it is probably the case that I will not be able to say it to you again. So, there. I have said it and now I'll go."

She tried to gauge his expression but his head was bent, his face in shadow. This was not the man she had known in Paris, so gentle and loving and whimsical. He was angry, not indifferent. If he didn't care, he would be smooth and polite. She knew very well the code of men like him. Audrey was right. This was something else. She wanted to shake him, to slap his face, anything to get to the truth.

But she'd spent the full sum of her courage with that declaration of love. She could not bring herself to beg or rant. She was done.

"I will leave as soon as possible," she whispered. It hurt to breathe through the pain in her chest. "But if you ever do come to your senses, you will know where to find me."

She waited for a painful few seconds, yearning for him to reply, to say he'd made a mistake and that he still loved her, too. But he didn't. He simply sat there. So she turned on her heel and left.

YVETTE

When Yvette reached the front entrance to the club, Vidar was waiting, her coat slung over his arm, her hat in his hand, a cigarette between his lips.

How dearly she wished him to take charge at that moment. He could pull her into his arms and kiss her, tell her she was the only woman he wanted, whether she testified at this trial or not. Something told her he would scorn to use such tactics, however, and she was right.

Wordlessly, she let him help her into the heavy wool coat. She turned in the direction of the boardinghouse where she was staying and set off at a brisk pace.

He kept up with her easily, and it started to feel foolish to rush. She slowed a little. "There is nothing more to talk about."

He smiled. "I wasn't thinking about talking."

His graveled tone shot a spear of longing through her. She was grateful that the night protected her from scrutiny, because that one raw moment of desire would have betrayed her, exposed a weakness he would be all too eager to exploit.

"You have quite a nerve," she said. "Why I didn't simply inform on you to the Paris authorities is beyond me."

"I could take a guess."

She shrugged. "You need not sound so smug about it. I'm sure your powers of seduction are legendary. It's what makes you such a good spy, I think."

"I still have no idea why you think I betrayed you, Yvette. You must know that everything I did, getting you out of Paris like that, was for your own safety."

He had wanted to keep her safe, that was true. He had never betrayed her in that way. But she was terrified that he had somehow betrayed Catherine, that she, Yvette, had led him to her. But she couldn't allow herself to voice that concern. She could scarcely acknowledge it to herself. Instead, she shifted to firmer ground. "It is a pity Louise Dulac did not have a similar care. Or do you agree with what she did?"

He shrugged. "It's not what I would have done. But then, I recruited her to do much, much worse, so who am I to throw stones?"

"You recruited her?" She let that sink in. "You sent her to seduce Gruber, then."

"No. No, she was already with him when I made the approach. I simply . . . helped her to fulfill her patriotic duty. She was uniquely placed to observe Gruber and his associates, their growing dissatisfaction with Hitler."

So Dulac was a collaborator at heart. "In fact, she would not have become any sort of spy if you had not turned her into one."

"That's not how it happened. Look, she made it known to me that she was open to the approach. Getting close to Gruber was probably her plan all along."

Yvette was not so sure. "Did you ever think she might be working both sides to see who won?"

"Her information was good. Whatever her motives, she was an excellent asset." He turned to face Yvette, gripped her upper arms. "I hate what Louise did to you, but not because she was wrong to do it. It was a foul, dirty business, the occupation. I would be a hypocrite to condemn her when so often I persuaded good people to risk their lives in the same cause." He hesitated. "Sometimes, I had to do bad things to convince bad people to work with me."

"You were one of them, weren't you?" He'd confirmed a suspicion she'd held since the night Jean-Luc and his resistance cell were taken.

He sighed. "I keep telling you. I'm no Nazi."

"No, but you were involved with Berger's gang. The same ones who took Catherine and . . ." She couldn't bring herself to finish that sentence but blurted out, "I saw you, remember? I saw you talk to those men outside our apartment building on the night of the raid."

"Raid?" He seemed genuinely puzzled. "What raid?"

Yvette snorted. "Were there so many you can't recall? The raid on number ten rue Royale, of course. My sister was nearly caught harboring a fugitive."

"Oh, that." He shrugged. "I got there a little late to put a stop to it, I'm afraid. Busy night." He eyed her. "For you, also. Laying your life on the line for your boyfriend like that."

She stared at him. Was that jealousy she detected in his tone? Really? She didn't trouble to correct him about Jean-Luc. He could think what he liked.

"What happened to him, I wonder," mused Vidar, twisting the knife. "Did you ever learn?"

Shame washed over her. She didn't answer. Couldn't. Finding out would have been too painful. Maybe if she'd read the many letters Gabby had sent her in New York, she would know what had happened to Jean-Luc. Maybe, if she'd been able to bear the thought of him, she could have discovered for herself.

Walking in Christian Dior's fashion show seemed such a triviality now. She felt ashamed and fretful. Part of her wanted to escape from this man who insisted on touching all her wounded places. Yet he was the one person in the world who might actually understand.

They had arrived at the boardinghouse. She stopped and gazed up at him with a specific need burning inside her. He cupped her cheek in his palm, and the gesture felt like acceptance. "Yvette, listen to me. We can't change the past—"

"No more talking," she whispered. By the dim light from a streetlamp a few feet away, she saw a man who was still young, yet whose eyes betrayed the pain and experience of a seasoned veteran. She wanted to trust the instincts that had always told her he was good. "Heinrich Jäger-Hoffmann, Baron von Leitfeld."

"I told you the truth about that, Yvette," he said, but she put a fingertip to his lips, silencing him.

"You want me to call you Rick?" She shook her head. "I prefer Vidar." She wanted him to sweep her into his arms, sweep away her doubts. She was so tired of struggling against this need.

As if he had heard her secret longing, he gave a sharp exhale. Pulling her to him, he kissed her. She let the world, Louise Dulac, the war—everything—fall away, and lost herself in him.

Against her landlady's rules, Yvette smuggled Vidar up to her room. "It's a good thing we are spies," she whispered as they eased inside.

Her back was to the wall as he kissed her, hot, silent, and hungry, deliciously wrong. She put her fingertips to his jaw, felt the prickle of his five o'clock shadow, slid her hand to stroke the skin at his nape, pulling him closer. He was a mystery she needed to solve, but that could wait until morning.

Tonight, she suspended hostilities. She didn't care why he wanted her, only that he did.

GABBY

But you can't leave us already." Audrey dropped her toast and marmalade and regarded Gabby with dismay. "You've only just arrived! And your return packet is booked and paid for and you'll have to pay another fare . . . Oh, do be a trouper and stay." She leaned forward and gripped Gabby's hand in a strong clasp. "Just . . . walk to the village with me after breakfast and we'll talk."

All night, Gabby had lain awake, wondering how she had so misjudged what had occurred between her and Jack during his short stay in Madame LaRoq's apartment. That confrontation with him had been like a bad dream, a nightmare in which the solid ground shifts underfoot and everything you know as absolute truth down to the marrow in your bones becomes a lie.

The snow had melted overnight, and the walk to the village was a muddy one. Luckily, Audrey had made Gabby don an ancient but serviceable pair of rainproof boots, so she didn't have to worry about ruining her shoes.

At any other time, she would have reveled in the crisp, freezing country air, but now the weather, which Audrey described as "bracing," seemed threatening and grim. Gabby was beyond tired. It was hard to keep up with Audrey's quick, long-legged stride.

A mist rose from the ground, reaching out curling tendrils. The lake was like a sheet of glass, reflecting the lowering sky. They came to a bridge where the ornamental lake narrowed to a burbling stream. It was like a painting, this place, with its weeping willows and its arching stone bridge. No wonder Jack loved it here. She sighed, and as they came to the bridge's hump, Audrey stopped and leaned on the parapet, her hands clasped together. "I shouldn't be telling you this, so please, don't let on to Jack that you know."

Gabby's heart gave a quick, hard pound. "What is it?"

"I thought perhaps you might guess. I hoped you would, or that you would worm the truth out of him, but now I see that you are not a woman who uses wiles or trickery to get what she wants." She smiled. "I'm happy about that, of course, but I wish you would fight harder for him."

Something burned in Gabby's chest. "I fought as hard as I knew how. And besides, why should I be the one fighting? I came all this way, after all."

"Men." Audrey sighed. "They can be the bloodiest creatures on earth."

Gabby frowned. "*Comment?*"

"I mean stubborn, dear," Audrey explained. "Jack is too proud to tell you that he came off somewhat the worse after the war." She made a face, gripped the lichened balustrade. "Thinks he is not the man you fell in love with, I suppose. I don't know."

"'Somewhat the worse,'" Gabby repeated slowly. "What does that mean?"

"It's his lungs," said Audrey. "After he left you, he did not go back to England."

"What?"

Audrey shrugged. "Crazy, wasn't it? You nursed him too well." She made a face. "No, of course I don't mean that. But he felt fit enough to go on missions with the resistance, sabotaging German tanks and blowing up bridges and whatnot. By the time the Allies marched on Paris, he was in a state of collapse. They shipped him home, but then he came down with pneumonia. It affected his heart. Time after time, I thought we were going to lose him, but somehow, he pulled through."

Gabby felt as if a glass wall had slid into place between her and the world. She heard what Audrey was saying, but the words didn't quite touch her. She was cold and numb.

"Gabby?" Audrey put an arm around her and rubbed her hand up and down her bicep as if to thaw her. She felt the pressure of it but no warmth. She tried to speak, but only a strangled sound came out.

She tried again. "And this is why he was so cruel to me. He doesn't want to tie me to an invalid. Is that it?"

The sympathy in Audrey's eyes was more than she could bear. "He hasn't said as much, but I believe that is the case." She hesitated. "The doctor says a warmer climate would be the very thing for Jack's health, but he won't go. It's as if he can't bear to try, only to be disappointed." Her smile had a bitter edge. "But there I go, attributing motives where there might be none. I cannot tell what he's thinking and he never confides in me. When I heard him on the telephone recommending you for that medal, though . . ." Her eyes misted and she closed them. "The way he talked about you, the note in his voice—oh, it was as if the Jack I knew and loved had come back to me. I had never heard him talk about a woman like that before. I knew I had to come and find you, to bring you back to him."

"But he does not want me," said Gabby. "Even when I told him . . ." She swallowed hard. "Doesn't he know I would take care of him? I love him. I spend all my waking hours caring for people who will never love me back. Does he think that I would begrudge looking after someone who loves me?"

"I think he would prefer to be the one to look after you," said Audrey. "Men are funny that way."

"What garbage!" said Gabby. "If the war taught us anything, it's that we women can look after ourselves." She turned and ran down the bridge, ungainly in her rain boots but determined.

Audrey hurried to catch up with her. "Wait! What are you going to do?"

But Gabby didn't answer. She trudged and hobbled and ran all the way back to the house, only stopping to yank off her muddy boots.

She burst into the library and found Jack reading a book by the fire. There was a pause as she stood there in her stockinged feet, panting from her run. Then he rose with a pained, resigned expression, as if he were about to face a firing squad. "Can I take your coat?"

She blinked at this non sequitur. "No, thank you." The heat in this room made her acutely conscious that she was dressed for the wintry countryside. She tugged at the scarf she'd wrapped around her neck and cleared her throat. "Please. Sit down. I want to talk with you properly."

She realized she had been speaking in French. She had meant to stick to English but instinct had taken over.

"Ah." He seemed to comprehend. "You've been talking to Audrey."

"Don't blame Audrey. This is about you and me." She took the chair opposite him, sitting on the edge and leaning toward him. She wished they weren't so far apart, but this would have to do.

"I am insulted," she said. "You love me. And yet you think so little of me that you believe I would love you less if I knew of your health problems." She shook her head. "After all that we went through together, how could you believe that?"

"That's simple. I *don't* believe that, and you know it." He sent her a searing glance. "Do you think I don't know you, Gabby? You take care of people. It's what you always do."

"Oh, so you wanted to save me from this terrible sacrifice. Is that it? You made that decision for me, did you?"

"You wouldn't make it yourself." He threw out a hand and his eyes were infinitely weary. "I want you to be free. My darling, I know it's painful now. Believe me, I know. But you'll find someone else."

Gabby felt like a volcano, long dormant, ready to erupt. "What if I don't want anyone else? I haven't found anyone in the past three years, have I? I will live out my days taking care of the tenants at number ten rue Royale if you won't have me!" Even as she said the words, she realized how pathetic they sounded. How pathetic she must seem to him, sitting here, begging. She had abased herself last night and he had rejected her. Why was she doing it again?

And then, suddenly, fire was shooting through her veins, steam rising, her chest expanding, all the suppressed rage that had hardened like rock inside her turned molten with the pressure and the heat. He was right! She *was* tired of looking after people, tired of accepting that her only value to another human being lay in what she could do for them. Her mother, Yvette, Jack—everyone had told her and told her she needed to stop, but she hadn't listened. She'd needed to think of herself as that person. That kind, compassionate helper, the one they all could count on through thick and thin.

She was done. No more. No more cleaning up other people's messes. No more doing her mother's work for her, no more reliable, dependable, doormat Gabby.

She yanked off the scarf that seemed now to be strangling her and shot to her feet. "You know, Jack, you were wrong about me. I was wrong about me, too. I *don't* want to take care of you. I don't want you in this state. This pathetic, bitter weakling who won't even try to do what it takes to make himself better so he can live as my husband and as my equal. That is not the Jack I fell in love with. It's not the man I deserve. I don't know who you are now, but I know that you were right. You're *not* good enough for me. Not because you have this illness. But because you won't even try to get better. Until you are prepared to do what it takes to deserve me, I don't want you."

She'd leave today if she had to walk to the station. There was nothing for her here.

Chapter Twenty-Two

England, February 1947

YVETTE

Morning sunlight limned the tattered blinds when Yvette woke, still tangled with Vidar, on the narrow bed. The room was icy, but he was solid and warm, and she trailed her fingertips over him, marveling at the places where his skin was unexpectedly soft. His arm lay across her torso, his head pressed into the crook of her neck. She breathed in the subtle scent of expensive cologne and the earthier smell of man. A fierce longing swept over her, and in its wake, a tenderness that could only spell disaster if she didn't stamp it out.

Suddenly, she was angry. At herself, more than at him. Vidar had never pretended she meant anything to him. Last night, she had followed her impulse, ignored the warnings of her brain, and headed straight for trouble, as she had always done in the past.

Biting her lip, she tried to ease herself free. His eyes snapped open and he sat bolt upright, instantly alert for trouble. After a couple of beats, his shoulders relaxed. "Sorry." He looked down at her, his dark fringe shadowing his eyes, a rueful smile playing on his lips. Then he sobered. "Having regrets?"

Leaning down, he kissed her forehead, then the vulnerable space behind her ear. "Let me make you forget all about them." Sliding back beneath the covers, he pulled her against him. She yielded because she didn't know when she might see him again, and besides, she wasn't strong enough to deny herself the pleasure of his touch.

Afterward, he seemed in a somber mood. He lay on his back, his feet sticking out beyond the edge of the small bed in an endearingly comical fashion. He lit a cigarette, offered her one, but she waved him away. "You know I don't smoke."

"One doesn't like to assume," he said, "that things are the same with you as they were during the war."

Was that a probe about her level of experience with men? Inwardly, she smiled. "The truth is that we don't know each other very well."

"We know the important things." His chest expanded, held still, then he breathed out. "I think we should get married, don't you?"

She froze. She wanted to make jokes about honest women and such but she couldn't speak.

"Yvette? What do you think?" She heard the faint crackle of the cigarette as he drew on it. Her heart beat fast.

After some time, she said, "I think that is a terrible idea. I don't even know what you do for a living."

"Well, I'm a banker." The last thing she would ever have imagined he would say. "In Berlin. But there might be a diplomatic posting at some stage."

"I thought you were still a spy."

When he didn't answer, she looked up at him. "You are working right now, aren't you? I should have known."

"At this very moment, no. But I have been in Germany, hunting the gang from the rue de la Pompe."

That was dangerous work. Those men would be like cornered rats, vicious and fighting to survive.

He turned onto his side to face her and propped his head on his hand. "Don't you see, Yvette? It makes sense. As my wife, you could do real intelligence work, the kind you dreamed of during the war."

Now she realized. He only meant to marry her as a means to an end, a kind of business partnership. "How do I know you wouldn't treat me the way Louise did? Don't diplomats' wives have affairs and pass on pillow talk?"

He regarded her steadily. "I think you know the answer to that."

His proposal had nothing to do with love. She sat up and reached for her robe, pulled it on. "I'm afraid I must decline your flattering offer," she said, yanking the belt tight. "My life is in Paris with Dior. I could not go with you to Berlin, or to whatever foreign posting there might be in the future—if in fact you do become a diplomat."

She heard movement below. The landlady rattling pots and pans, starting breakfast. "You'd better go."

Vidar observed her for a long moment. She had to steel herself to return his gaze without expression. As if disappointed, he stubbed out his cigarette and began putting on his clothes.

"Think about it," he said. "If you change your mind . . ." He propped his card against the clock on her bedside table, then stooped to kiss her.

"I won't change my mind, Vidar," she said as he eased open the door.

He left without looking back, silent as a ghost.

Yvette stayed in bed like a slattern, pleading illness when the landlady tapped on her door to tell her breakfast was ready. It wasn't a complete lie. The thought of a greasy English meal turned her stomach. She wished she was back home again. She hated England, and she hated this boardinghouse in particular.

Why was she so miserable? Yvette rejected the most obvious answer. She hardly knew Vidar. She could not possibly be in love.

She wondered how Gabby was finding her visit to Burnley. She hoped it was going better than her own time in London. It could hardly be worse, could it?

This maudlin feeling could not be allowed to continue. She got up and dressed warmly and packed her bag, more than ready to leave.

She was putting on lipstick and feeling a little more like herself again when the door handle rattled. She was about to call out to ask what the landlady wanted when Gabby walked in.

The look on her face made Yvette's heart give a single, hard ache.

"Let's go home," she said, opening her arms to her sister.

Gabby nodded and walked into her embrace.

Paris, July 1944

GABBY

When Rafael and his henchmen had finally gone, Gabby rushed up to Madame LaRoq's apartment. She found Catherine Dior there with a dustpan and brush, sweeping up the debris.

Gabby scarcely acknowledged her but went straight to the cabinet, broken crockery crunching underfoot. She felt a shard of glass spear through her shoe and pierce her big toe but she didn't hesitate. With a heave, she rolled aside the cabinet to reveal Jack's hiding place.

No one was there.

"Gabby," Catherine said softly from behind her.

"What?" Gabby whirled around. "What have you done with him?"

"Gabby, let us sit and talk."

"Where is he?" She didn't wait for Catherine's answer. She flew about the apartment, checking behind curtains, under beds, any place he could be hiding. Jack wasn't there.

Tears gathered in Gabby's eyes. She stood in the spare bedroom, bewildered, lost, shaking her head as the implications of the empty apartment came home to her.

"My dear." Catherine's touch was light on her shoulder. "This whole business has been a horrible shock, I know."

Gabby let herself be guided to sit on the spare bed, the place where she and Jack had spent so much precious time together. "Where is he?"

"My dear. He is gone." Catherine put her hand on Gabby's. "It was time."

"No." Gabby snatched her hand away and glared at Catherine. "He is not well enough yet. He—"

"Nevertheless, you must accept it. Every day he spent here endangered us all. You more than anyone."

Gabby gave a choking laugh at that. "You might have considered this before you forced me to take care of him."

Catherine made no answer and Gabby knew her accusation had been unjust. Liliane Dietlin had urged her to be rid of the Englishman as soon as possible. It was Gabby who had felt compassion for her patient. Compassion, and later, love.

After a moment, Catherine handed her a wadded-up piece of paper. "He left this."

With clumsy fingers, Gabby smoothed out the torn page of foolscap. A little metal object dropped to the floor but she ignored it. The message was brief, written hastily. It said, *All my love, J.*

Catherine bent to pick something up from the floor and held it out to Gabby. Through a haze of grief, Gabby looked down. A small bird, stippled with diamonds, a tiny sapphire for an eye. She closed her hand over it, held it tightly, felt the pin pierce the fleshy part of her palm.

A soft knock at the door made Gabby want to wail. What now? Couldn't they all just leave her in peace? She shoved the note and the pin into her pocket.

"Good God, what did those pigs do to this place?" Yvette appeared in the doorway.

"Oh, go away!" Gabby snapped at her. "I can't deal with you on top of everything else." But she knew she would have to deal with Yvette's crisis even while her own world was falling apart.

"Actually, it is Mademoiselle Dior I have come to see." Yvette spoke quietly. "It is important."

More important than what had happened in this apartment tonight. More important than the love of Gabby's life vanishing without a proper goodbye.

But how foolish of her. How utterly selfish. If Jack had stayed to say goodbye, she would have done everything in her power to make him go. He had taken the only logical course of action under the circumstances. Rafael's men could have returned and found his hiding place.

She regarded her sister dully. "You'd better talk, then." To Catherine, she added, "Don't worry about me. I'll be fine."

Catherine moved to the door. "Perhaps it is best if we all sit down in the drawing room. There is much to discuss."

Catherine made them a tisane from the scant leaves madame had left in the pantry. Gabby accepted her cup and sipped with automatic politeness. It was faintly bitter, as if made partly from nettles, but she detected a calming note of chamomile, too. All she could think was how inadequate such gestures were on an occasion like this, and yet it was all they could do.

She wanted to hurl her teacup across the room. She wanted to sob and pull at her hair like grieving women in ancient times. Instead, she simply sat there on Madame LaRoq's wrecked sofa, staring into her teacup, wishing with all her heart that she could be alone. But her sister was in trouble, real trouble, and she had to rouse herself to help deal with it.

As Yvette related the story of Jean-Luc, Gabby's brow furrowed.

"Do you mean to tell me that you actually went to this gathering because you thought you could stop a bunch of men—*grown men*—from going on a suicide mission?"

Her voice had risen and Catherine halted her with an upraised finger. "Softly. Softly now," she said. "We have had enough disturbances tonight."

"I was trying to stop a friend from being killed," Yvette retorted in a low voice vibrating with passion. "I was sticking my neck out for someone else. Not that you'd know anything about that."

Gabby felt her face drain of blood. She had never been so furious with anyone in her life. "Some of us don't go parading our heroism for everyone to see. Some of us are cautious, and careful, and . . ." Now the tears came. Now, at the worst moment.

She dashed the heel of her hand across her eyes and let out a shuddering sigh.

"Gabby?" Yvette turned to Catherine. "What has been going on here?" She looked about her. "Where is madame?" Her eyes widened. She looked at the maid's room, exposed now, showing evidence of recent habitation. "Were you hiding someone here?"

"That is a discussion for another day," said Catherine calmly. "Now we must consider what to do with you."

"What do you mean, 'do' with me?"

"Yvette, my dear." Catherine's thin eyebrows raised. "You cannot remain in Paris now that Jean-Luc has been taken. You do see that, don't you?"

Yvette shot to her feet. "Jean-Luc would never, *ever* betray me."

"You little fool," said Gabby. "Don't you know what they do to the ones they capture? I've been to that place, heard the screams of grown men. They *all* talk in the end, just to make the pain stop." She swallowed. "You'd better pray that Jean-Luc is dead."

"Gabby!" Yvette stared at her, as if she didn't recognize her sister in this hard-hearted person.

"We cannot take the chance," said Catherine, leaning forward and fixing her gaze on Yvette. "Those men in the alley. Did they see your face?"

Yvette paled. "They had flashlights. But I was dressed as a boy—"

Catherine interrupted her. "Did anyone see you return tonight?"

Yvette frowned. "No. No one."

"None of the tenants? Everyone was stirred up by the disturbance tonight."

"It was pitch-black in the courtyard by the time I came up here."

"All right," said Catherine. "Then, Gabby, I think we need to say this: Yvette went out tonight without your knowledge and never returned. You don't know what became of her but you suspect a lover is involved. She is a headstrong girl and she was seeing a much older man."

"Vidar Lind, you mean?" said Gabby.

"No. You don't mention anyone by name. But you might say that you are a good Catholic, and if your sister is in that kind of trouble, then you wash your hands of her."

Gabby knew what this meant. She would lose the two people she loved most in the world in one night. Her chest cramped with the knowledge, but she could not afford to crumble now. Not when her sister needed her. She nodded curtly. "I can do it."

"Now, little one." Catherine turned and drew Yvette to sit down beside her. "I know this comes as a shock and it is all too sudden and you aren't prepared. But you need to get out of Paris before they come looking for you."

"But . . . but I can't leave Paris!" Yvette cried. "You need me. What about tomorrow?"

"There is no question of your making the drop tomorrow," said Catherine with a touch of impatience. "Surely you must see that."

"Drop?" Gabby stared at Catherine. "What are you talking about?" Did that mean Yvette had been working for Catherine, too?

But neither woman answered her. Yvette begged and pleaded, but though Catherine was kind and full of understanding, she remained firm. Finally, Yvette's arguments faded away. She hung her head and whispered, "I'll go."

"You will have to stay here until we can smuggle you out," said Gabby. "I'll get the maid's room ready for you." Setting aside her teacup, she got up stiffly, with a sense of unreality, as if she was acting in a play, not taking part in real life. She felt like an old woman. It was an effort simply to construct a complete sentence. Moving was almost beyond her, but for her sister, she made herself do it.

Yvette seemed subdued after her argument with Catherine. Gabby led her to the cell-like room where Jack had so recently hidden. It still smelled faintly of him—or was that her imagination? Gabby squeezed her eyes shut. What must he have endured while trapped during the raid?

"Gabby," Yvette whispered as she helped her make up the bed. "I don't want to go. I can't go. There's a mission. Something I have to do for Catherine tomorrow."

Gabby ignored her.

Yvette grabbed her arm. "Catherine's at risk. I can't let her do it on her own."

Anger boiled up. "You should have thought of that before you went out tonight! You risked us all, not just your precious mission. You heard what she said; you need to leave Paris."

"*Please*, Gabby. I can't leave. I won't do it! I . . ." Yvette looked about her wildly. "Maybe I could stay here in the maid's room until it is over. Until the Allies come. It won't be long now, will it? And you could bring me food just like you did for whoever was here. Oh, please, Gabby. *Please.*"

Gabby shook her off. "And you would get yourself into more danger, sneaking out of here, wouldn't you? I don't suppose you thought about the rest of us when you went on your mission of mercy tonight."

A look came into Yvette's face that Gabby had never seen before. A mature, weary defiance. "I went out of loyalty and friendship, Gabby. It was hopeless, but for Jean-Luc I had to try." Bitterly, she shook her head. "You would not understand."

The words sliced through Gabby's heart. "Then let this be your final heroic gesture, Yvette. Now that you have put me, Maman, Catherine, and everyone else here in danger, do us all a favor and go. If they can't find you, they might leave the rest of us alone."

"You don't understand what's at stake!" Yvette stormed back to the drawing room and grabbed Catherine's hands. "Just let me make that rendezvous for you, Catherine. At least let me do that."

Catherine seemed unfazed by Yvette's vehemence. "No, I'm sorry, little one. I cannot. Much as I admire your courage and your heart, your association with Jean-Luc, your actions tonight, have put the network at risk. If the *gestapistes* catch you, we are all as good as dead. No one withstands interrogation at rue de la Pompe."

There was a quiet authority about Catherine that made Yvette lower her gaze and subside. She did not argue anymore and meekly did as Catherine bade her, drinking up the rest of her tea. She went to the little bed in the maid's room with an air of submission. There was no protest when Gabby came to say her final goodbye.

Gabby sighed. "I am sorry, Yvette. I did not mean those things I said." Awkwardly, for the space around the bed was not large, she perched on the edge of the little cot, beside Yvette's curled-up form. After a hesitation, she reached out and stroked her sister's hair. "You are a brave girl, Yvette. Sometimes turning away from a fight is the bravest thing to do."

Yvette gazed at her with a new sorrow filling her eyes. "Gabby? Where is Madame LaRoq?"

YVETTE

Yvette woke in unfamiliar darkness, heart pounding with a nameless fear. She scrambled up, only to sink back again as her head throbbed with pain. Sluggishly, her brain caught up with her circumstances. She was in the maid's room at Madame La-Roq's apartment.

The news of madame's death broke over her once more in a great wash of sadness. How could Gabby have kept it from her all that time? And she . . . she had been too busy playing spies even to re-alize madame was gone. Not that she hadn't made the occasional attempt to visit, only to be headed off at the pass by Gabby, keeper of the key. But Yvette had been so self-absorbed, she hadn't even suspected all this intrigue going on right under her nose. They could have told her! Catherine, at least, knew that she could keep a secret.

The noise that had woken her came again. The heavy rolling of casters across the floorboards. A crack of light appeared around the door frame. Then the door opened and Liliane Dietlin was there, an enormous laundry bag at her feet.

Her smile warm and sympathetic, Liliane beckoned to Yvette with one of her cheerful, birdlike movements. "Come. You must be on your way."

"But it's broad daylight. How can I leave now?"

"In this, of course." Liliane nudged the laundry bag with her pointed toe, then held up a hand to forestall Yvette's protests. "No arguments, please. We need to get you out without anyone seeing. It worked for Madame LaRoq."

"You did this to madame?" Yvette's voice cracked.

"There's no time for this, little one," said Liliane. "You must get in and stay there, no matter what. Don't make a sound or come out until you are given the word, all right?" She kissed Yvette's cheeks. "Go with God, my dear. May He protect you."

Hearing the unwonted quaver in Liliane's voice, Yvette obeyed. She stepped into the center of the puddle of canvas and pulled up the drawstring edges until she stood, fully covered by the laundry bag. The strings were drawn tight above her head, then heavy footsteps sounded across the floorboards.

The light was orange inside the bag, and the air smelled faintly of musk and sweat. She saw a large shadow moving toward her, heard her own breaths, quick and shallow, then a masculine grunt as she was lifted, none too gently, and slung over what she guessed to be a large, meaty shoulder.

The light dimmed, there was a descent, then brightness again as they left the building. She was deposited on a hard floor and heard the double *thunk* of doors shutting behind her. A van? They were moving and she had no choice but to allow herself to slide this way and that as they turned corners. Thankfully, it was a short drive to their destination. The van stopped again, the doors opened, and she was lifted out, carried upstairs this time, and dumped on what she assumed was a bed, springs creaking under her.

The drawstring was untied, allowing Yvette to inhale fresh, pure air. Then she saw who had freed her. Vidar Lind.

"*You!* What?" She scrabbled backward, kicking away the laundry bag. "What's going on?" Surely, Liliane's contact hadn't delivered her into the enemy's hands.

Wildly, she looked around her. A tiny attic apartment, with just a bed and a washbasin. One exit, and Vidar was blocking it.

"Liliane Dietlin sent me." When she just stared at him, he added, "I'm here to help you."

"Just as you did last night?" she demanded.

His expression remained impassive. "You seem to be accusing me of something."

"I saw you," she hissed. "I saw you with the gang outside my apartment building. You looked very friendly with them."

"Is that all?" He relaxed. "You know, for an intelligent girl, you jump to a lot of silly conclusions." He got out a cigarette and tapped it on his silver case. Then he bent his head to light it, blew out smoke. "One must associate with many kinds of people in my line of work."

"And what is that line of work, precisely?"

He shrugged. "Look, I don't have time to waste bickering. I have to arrange your papers, tickets, everything. You will catch the train to Marseille tonight and then a guide will take you from there over the Pyrenees and into Spain."

"Spain?" She'd known she was to leave Paris, but . . .

His hand came over hers. "You've had a shock. It is all happening too fast. I understand, but you need to get hold of yourself now, Yvette. Everyone is depending on you."

Finally, it hit her. She was leaving not only Paris but France. And she would not return until the end of the war, whenever that might be.

"I wanted to see it," she said when at last she could command her voice enough to speak. "I wanted to be here to see it when we won." Liberation. They had all suffered so much and worked so hard.

How could a man be so duplicitous yet have such warm sympathy in his eyes? "You have played your part and played it well, Yvette. Now you must think of others and do what is right for them."

A sense of fatalism overtook her then. The future had been ripped from her grasp. Far too much had happened last night for her to come to grips with it all or face it with her usual determination.

She still felt groggy and a little sick, and her headache had returned in full force. She put a hand to her temple. "I don't feel well." Then something clicked. The tisane. Her eyes widened. "Catherine drugged me!"

She said it with such indignation that Vidar smiled. "I expect you would not be here if she hadn't."

He was right. She remembered now. Last night, she'd been full of rebellion. Now she felt numb.

Vidar said, "Stay here. Don't show yourself to anyone. I'll be back when I've made the arrangements."

He gazed down at her, a strange intensity in his expression. She thought for a moment that he might touch her, try to pull her into his arms. However, he must have read her mood, because he kept his hands by his sides. "If you want to leave, I can't stop you, Yvette.

But please do as I say. They are not looking for you yet, but it might only be a matter of time."

GABBY

The day Yvette left was so sultry and stifling, the heat seemed to throb inside Gabby like a living thing, compounding her misery. As she worked, beads of sweat formed, slid down her face, mingling with the occasional tear.

Jack was gone. Yvette was gone. And she was left to carry on just as before. Maman had accepted the news about Yvette far more stoically than Gabby had expected. Despite the efforts of both her daughters, Danique Foucher seemed to have guessed their secrets.

Gabby herself could hardly function for worrying about both fugitives. Were they safe? Had there been an escape route already planned for Jack, or had the network been obliged to improvise? By now, he could have been arrested, subjected to all kinds of brutality. And she was here, sweeping floors and sorting mail, powerless to help him. And what about Yvette, holing up somewhere in Paris, waiting for the night train? Any number of things could go wrong . . .

Gabby was polishing the bannister in the stairwell when Catherine came down, looking smart, as always, a clutch under her arm, a jaunty hat on her head. Despite the blazing heat, she appeared cool and poised in her navy suit.

"Good morning, Gabby." Catherine's smile was friendly but distant, as if they had not committed all manner of crimes together the night before.

But of course. Her mission. The one Yvette was supposed to be carrying out today.

Gabby glanced around, but no one was there to hear. A deadly fatalism swept over her. She felt oddly calm, at peace. "Don't do it. Let me go."

Catherine's eyes widened. "No. Out of the question."

"They don't know me. No one will watch what I do." She grabbed Catherine's arm as the other woman made to brush by her, an impertinence she would never have committed even the day before.

Instead of reprimanding her, Catherine leaned in close and spoke low, under her breath. "Go back to your work, Gabby, do you hear? This is *my* work. I will handle it."

A door opened above them. Clicking heels and the scamper of dog paws told them who had come out. Catherine slipped from Gabby's grasp and went swiftly on her way.

Dully, Gabby watched her go.

"You missed a spot," said a dry, crotchety voice. "And get that pail out of the way. Someone might trip."

Gabby turned to look up at Madame Vasseur. "One can only hope," she muttered. But she obeyed madame's commands, and even mopped up the paw prints the poodle left after they'd gone. He would only leave more upon his return. She would clean them up, too.

"I'm going out," Gabby told her mother when she returned to the *loge*. She needed a walk. Perhaps she'd go to the gardens, where the trees would provide a little shade from the sun. Or maybe to the river in hopes of catching a breeze?

She wandered without a purpose, her mind still numb with shock and grief. She'd experienced loss before. Her father. Her fiancé. This was different. Both those deaths had been sad but expected. To have the two people closest to her in the world ripped from her with no warning . . . She didn't know how to go on after that.

"Ah, good day, Gabby! How are you today?" The smiling, always cheerful Liliane Dietlin hurried toward her and kissed her on both cheeks. Then she gripped Gabby's arm and gave it a warning squeeze. "Come. Have a little coffee with me. My treat."

Bemused, Gabby went with Liliane to a café full of German soldiers. Catching Gabby's expression, Liliane laughed. "The safest place is in the thick of them, you know." She chose a table where she could put her back to a wall and observe the rest of the clientele. "Let us sit and discuss."

When they'd ordered, Liliane reached across the little table and took Gabby's hand in hers. She seemed to know that any expression of sympathy would set Gabby off, so she said, "Horrible weather, isn't it? But I am pleased to tell you that both packages are safe."

The relief made Gabby choke back a sob. It wasn't over, but at least there was no bad news yet.

Liliane's eyes sparkled with sympathy. "But no, do not cry, my dear. Women like us, we must be strong."

Gabby nodded, inhaling deeply to try to calm herself. "I know. I know I must." And suddenly, she knew that the humdrum existence that now stretched before her would send her mad if she didn't do something. After last night, she felt reckless, as if her own life did not matter too much anymore. For someone who had protected her own safety like a miser hoarded coins, there was a kind of liberation that went hand in hand with despair.

"I want to do more." She heard herself saying the words and could hardly believe they were coming out of her own mouth.

"There are at least four vacant apartments in the building. Other places, too . . ." She trailed off. "Or is it too little too late?"

"Not at all," said Liliane, her eyes shining. "There are still so many of us being rounded up. The Boches are on the run, and like rats they turn most vicious when cornered. It is a good thing, Gabby. A very good thing." Her gaze softened. "Jack would be proud."

Liliane didn't know Gabby's motivation was the opposite of bravery, but Gabby didn't intend to enlighten her. Someone so very courageous would never understand what drove Gabby now.

She drank the horrible fake coffee in one gulp. She took a deep breath and let it out again. "When do I start?"

Chapter Twenty-Three

Paris, July 1944

YVETTE

When Vidar returned hours later with her false papers and train ticket, Yvette said, "I must go out." It was six in the evening. Catherine would have completed her mission by now, be safe home. Yvette prayed it was so, but she had a sick feeling about it. She was stuck in this airless apartment, waiting, and that seemed to multiply her unease. All was set for her departure tonight on the train to Marseille, but she could not leave without knowing Catherine was safe.

Vidar sighed. "Yvette—"

"I must know one thing. I will find out, and then I will go."

"What is this thing you must find out? Let me help." He moved closer. "After all this, you still don't trust me?"

His gaze, intent and sincere, would have melted most hearts, but Yvette kept picturing him with those black-market thugs the night before. Just because Vidar Lind was involved with Liliane's escape network, it didn't mean she trusted him with information about her resistance cell.

She said, "It's not a matter of trust but a matter of protocol. You don't need to know. Therefore I do not tell you. Simple." With an effort, she broke eye contact. "After all, I am sure there are any number of things you don't tell me."

"That's different."

"Why?" She glared up at him. "Because I'm just a silly girl?" The knowledge that she had behaved foolishly enough to get herself into this mess sharpened her tone.

When he didn't answer, she said quietly, "I have a little pill. Liliane gave it to me. So don't be afraid I'll betray you. If they take me, I bite down on it. The end."

"That is hardly a comfort to me, sweetheart." Vidar reached for her, and she could almost believe he cared. But she knew that no matter how much he liked her, he did not have time to babysit her all evening.

She stepped back, evading his touch. "You have important things to do that cannot wait. I understand. So, unless you're going to tie me up or drug me again, you will have to leave me alone in here. And I will go. You can't stop me."

Vidar shook his head. "It does no one any good for you to be caught, Yvette. What can you possibly seek to gain? You've done your part. Leave the fight to others now."

He made sense, but she was beyond logic. She had a feeling in her bones that luck had run out for all of them last night, that

Catherine was no exception. That this should happen when the Allies were so close, when winning the war seemed almost inevitable, made it all the more heartbreaking.

Yvette could not return to the rue Royale, and publicly accosting Liliane at the museum where she worked would put Liliane in danger. She would try Monsieur Arnaud, then. If anyone knew anything, he would.

When she entered the bookshop through the alley behind it, the place was deserted but a suitcase stood by the door. The stillness was ominous somehow, as if the shop were a living thing holding its breath. Until a faint shuffle alerted her to another's presence.

"It's all right," she said softly. "It's me. Yvette."

Monsieur Arnaud emerged from the shadows behind a stack of boxes. "Oh, it *is* you." He took out a handkerchief to mop his brow. "When did I ever give you permission to use the office door?"

"I thought it best." She wasn't going to alarm him further by explaining why she couldn't be seen. "We don't have much time. Tell me. Catherine. Is she safe?"

It was the look on his face. He seemed to age before her eyes. He gave the slightest shake of his head. The answer hit Yvette in the stomach like a fist. She doubled over, retching, but she hadn't eaten anything that day, and all that came up was the sour taste of bile.

"Get out of here. Go! You need to go now." Monsieur Arnaud tried to shepherd her back the way she'd come.

"But how? What happened? Where did they take her?"

"I don't know. All I know is they took our leader to rue de la Pompe and they've rounded up several others. We have all been compromised. If you're smart, you'll get out while you can."

Rue de la Pompe. Berger's torture chamber. If they had taken Catherine there . . .

Only one person could help now. Yvette fled back down the alley and headed for the Ritz.

She longed for her bicycle, and she was hot and disheveled by the time she reached the hotel on foot. However, the doorman recognized her, even if he couldn't remember her name. She greeted him and headed, with a smile, toward the guards.

These were not the same young men who had taunted her on that first day she had visited mademoiselle. These were older, career soldiers by the looks of them. Perhaps those younger ones had been called to the Russian front, like Sabine's boyfriend and like so many others who had spent their leave sampling the delights of Paris. At any other time, she might have felt something about this, perhaps a twinge of sympathy, but now there was no room for anything but the need to save Catherine.

As one of the soldiers scrutinized her new identity papers, she held her breath through her smile. Would there be some telltale sign that they were forged? The soldier walked over to the other guard and showed him the identity card. They both stared at her hard for a few moments.

It's not you, she told herself. *They stare at everyone this way.* Though her heart banged in her chest, the thought of Catherine and all that she must be suffering now made Yvette keep her nerve. "Please let me pass," she said, attempting a flirtatious simper that felt more like a grimace. "Mademoiselle Dulac doesn't like to be kept waiting."

There was no answering smile from either of the men. Finally, with a curt nod, the guard returned her papers and waved her through. Light-headed with relief, Yvette hurried up to Louise Dulac's suite.

Yes, it was a risk, for all kinds of reasons. She and Louise had parted on bad terms. However, Yvette banked on the fact that Louise would not want Yvette captured in case she pointed the finger at her. Whatever Louise had been doing with coded messages and the like, clearly it was not in Werner's best interests.

That Gruber himself might be in the suite made Yvette hesitate outside. She'd have to make some excuse about being sent from Lelong. If only she'd thought to bring a package with her . . . How long ago it seemed that she was a delivery girl for the famous designer. Couture, its artistry and delicious frivolity, belonged to another lifetime.

She knocked and the door opened. The German maid narrowed her eyes at Yvette but gave no sign that she knew her rival was now wanted by the authorities. No reason why she should know, of course. Men like Gruber had little to do with the dirty work of rounding up and torturing spies.

Yvette stared stonily back. "Mademoiselle Dulac, if you please. I have an important message for her from Monsieur Dior."

"Who is it?" called Louise. She appeared in the doorway of her boudoir looking every inch the screen goddess in high-waisted wide-legged camel trousers and a cream blouse, gold jewelry at her wrists and throat. It reminded Yvette of the outfit she'd taken from Louise's wardrobe, the one she'd ruined with a resistance worker's blood.

The memory lent steel to her tone. "I have a message from Monsieur Dior, mademoiselle."

Dulac inclined her head, and Yvette followed her to her boudoir. She shut the door but they both knew the German maid would be listening.

"How have you been, Yvette?" she said, taking a glass-framed picture from the wall and placing it on her desk. "It is so long since we spoke. I must thank you for the return of my pearls."

Yvette had forgotten all about the pearls. "I haven't come here to talk about old times."

Louise took a sheet of letter paper, then laid it flat on the glass surface of the picture, so as not to leave any impressions of their writing that could later be read. Handing Yvette a thin gold pencil, she gestured for her to write her message down.

"Work has been busier than ever," Yvette said in a clear, loud voice. "It is as if the women of Paris seek refuge from the war in beauty." At the same time, she wrote: "Catherine Dior arrested. Please help."

Louise used a gold lighter to set a flame to the end of a cigarette, drew on it heavily, then blew smoke into the air. A quick shake of the head was her only response. "It is the same with film, I believe. Anything to escape."

"But why not?" Yvette wrote. Then, when Louise simply blinked and stared at her, unresponsive, she added, "You owe me."

The movie star's beautiful face hardened when she read that. She bent and plucked the pencil from Yvette's grasp, knocking her hand clear of the page. "G suspects me. I can't."

As they talked about social gatherings and the parties Dulac had been to, the furious written exchange carried on.

"But it's Dior. Christian's sister. You could say the appeal came from him."

"My credit is not high. Nor is Gruber's. Not worth the risk."

"You could do it if you wanted."

A shrug. "I don't want." Then she added, "Does Vidar know?"

"He might, but I didn't tell him."

They came to the end of the page. Dulac whipped it from beneath Yvette's hand, flicked her gold lighter, and set the paper on fire. They both watched as the flame rose higher, then Louise dropped it into an ashtray before it singed her fingertips. She grabbed Yvette's arm and hustled her into her en suite, turned on the tap so the rush of water covered her speech.

"You gave Vidar my message. The one I meant for the jeweler. That was clever of you. But how did you know about the two of us? I can't believe he's a man who would kiss and tell."

Something inside Yvette shattered. Until that moment, she had not even guessed. Though she should have. She should have known. She tried to keep her face blank, but the pain and anger must have shown.

Louise gave a soft gasp. "You *did* not know. Oh, dear, and now I have been indiscreet. But Gruber was becoming suspicious. It's why he set the maid on me as a watchdog."

This was all spoken in a breathy undertone. Then she turned off the tap and added more loudly, "There. I've burned his letter. Tell him to stop pestering me, will you? He was only ever a flirtation and now he has become a bore."

It took Yvette a few seconds to realize she had talked about burning a letter to explain the slightly chemical smell of burnt paper that now pervaded the boudoir. The woman thought of everything, didn't she? And Yvette was always a step behind.

Again, Dulac's voice came low and hard, a whisper in her ear. "Would you like to know Vidar's real name, Yvette? It is Heinrich Jäger-Hoffmann, Baron von Leitfeld. An Austrian. And an officer of the Third Reich."

"No!" The denial came automatically. "You are making that up."

Louise put her finger to her lips. She was enjoying this, her eyes sparking with malice.

Yvette's brain was starting to piece it together. Heinrich. *Rick.* He'd told her Rick was his real name, though not about the rest.

But then . . . whose side had Yvette been working for when she had taken that message to him? Who was he working for now? There was the raid, the bicycle, his association with the Berger gang . . .

She reached across to snatch up another piece of paper to continue their silent argument, but Louise caught her wrist in a surprisingly strong grip. The film star's eyes were cold and hard. "Goodbye, Yvette. I doubt we'll meet again."

Yvette couldn't go back to the apartment. She didn't want to see Vidar's lying, traitorous face. Under a black cloud of betrayal and lost hope, she wandered the city, hardly knowing where she went.

Perhaps no one had betrayed her. Perhaps no one would. Only Jean-Luc, Catherine, and Liliane knew her name. But it was a very slim chance. She had to admit it. Catherine had been right. There was no choice but to leave Paris, scurry away like a whipped cur while Jean-Luc and Catherine and countless others suffered unendurable pain.

She had thought that nothing could be worse than knowing Catherine's capture was all her fault. But Louise Dulac's revelations about Vidar had ground her spirit into dust. She could only wander the streets like a homeless waif until it was time to leave Paris. The dreams she'd had of making a difference in this fight faded to nothing. She had helped in some small way for a short period of time. That ought to count for something, but right now, it didn't seem anything like enough. Not compared with the sacrifice Catherine Dior was making at this very moment. All because of Yvette and her impulsive, stupid wish to save a friend who was even more stupid and impulsive than she was.

She walked until thunderclouds rolled overhead and rain came down in fat, punitive drops. The downpour intensified and lightning blitzed the sky. She stood on the Pont Neuf and watched the rain pummel the Seine like an enemy. At least there would be no bombings tonight.

People all around her scattered to find shelter, but she kept walking, her hair plastered to her head, trying to make herself believe what Louise Dulac had said was true. Vidar Lind was in fact a Nazi officer. Why, then, did he never wear a uniform?

First, he had told her he was a Swedish diplomat. Then, he'd claimed he worked for the resistance . . .

A horrible suspicion dawned on her. Maybe he was working undercover among the French to dig out resistance cells? If so, why on earth would he help Yvette escape?

As if some homing instinct had led her there, she found herself in the avenue Matignon, near the House of Lelong. She couldn't approach her old workplace in case the Gestapo had been there looking for her, so she walked on, finding the deeply recessed doorway of an abandoned atelier, where she and Jean-Luc used to spend their break sometimes when it rained. They would sit on the old stone stoop that was worn with age, and Jean-Luc would smoke, and they would gossip and make each other laugh. Poor Jean-Luc! And Catherine . . . Yvette squeezed her eyes shut and tried to block out the pain.

There is a numbness that comes from sheer emotional and physical exhaustion. Yvette had reached the limit of her capacity to resolve this mess. She could not think of one more thing she could do to help those she loved, except to remove herself from their vicinity. She was doing no good at all here in Paris.

When it was finally time to catch her train, Yvette dashed through the rain to the station. Would Vidar be there, too, or would he have given up on her when she ran off?

The platform was crowded, noisy and bustling and full of the stench of unwashed, damp human. But she saw him, head and shoulders above the stooped, undernourished Parisian crowd. Who was he, really? *What* was he? And it struck her that she would never know.

Whatever side he might be on, he had genuinely tried to help her. In time, perhaps she would forget the rest and forgive him, but at that moment, the wound Louise Dulac had inflicted was too raw.

Yvette saw Vidar looking for her, his gaze raking the crowded platform. But before he could turn her way, she bent her head to hide her face and quickly boarded the train.

Chapter Twenty-Four

Paris, February 1947

GABBY

Gabby had never felt so utterly hopeless. For the journey home, she had held her head high, even though her world was shattered beyond repair. But despite her enormous effort to appear normal, Yvette treated her as if she were one of Monsieur Dior's most delicate creations, only to be handled with gloves.

When they finally reached the Ritz and Yvette surrendered her suitcase to the porter, Gabby moved to kiss her sister goodbye. But with a mischievous lift of her eyebrows, Yvette said, "No you don't! You are coming with me."

Before Gabby could reply, Yvette had asked the porter to take Gabby's luggage also, grabbed her hand, and pulled her inside the hotel.

"Oh, no, I can't!" said Gabby, digging her heels in.

"If you want me to drag you up the grand staircase of the Ritz, I will do it," said Yvette. Gabby had no choice but to follow her up if she did not want to make a scene.

When the porter had deposited their suitcases in the suite and Yvette had paid him a tip, she said, "You are home early. Maman does not expect you until the end of the week. Why not have a little holiday with me here before you go back?"

Gabby drank in the sheer luxury around her; the very air tasted like champagne bubbles. "I couldn't." This was the kind of existence she would never, ever have. Like watching the show at Dior, it gave her both pleasure and pain.

"Of course you could!" Yvette reached up to whip Gabby's beret from her head. She tossed it onto one of the many occasional tables scattered around the suite. "A reward for being an honest Parisian while women like Louise Dulac lived like queens."

Yvette kicked off her shoes and padded over to the drinks tray. "Cocktail? Me, I plan to get *very* drunk tonight."

Too tired to argue, Gabby sank down onto the sofa and removed her shoes, one by one. She pointed her toe, eyed a large and ugly ladder in her precious wool stocking, and thought it was entirely typical.

Yvette handed her a drink and curled up beside her, cradling her own. "I'll ring for food in a moment. What would you like?"

Gabby shuddered. She couldn't eat. Not with this squirmy, black feeling in the pit of her stomach. She sipped her martini and nearly choked. "This is very strong." But already, a pleasant warmth was spreading through her chest. She drained the glass and held it out for more.

Yvette took the glass, but she didn't move immediately. "What happened to you at that place?" And the understanding in Yvette's eyes, perhaps an answering pain there, was like yanking on a bow. The tight bindings Gabby had wrapped around herself came undone all at once and she gave a great gasping sob.

"Oh, Gabby." Yvette put down their glasses and wrapped her arms around her. It felt so good to be held after the coldness of Jack's reception. Gabby could not seem to weep, but she stayed in Yvette's arms and let herself be miserable. She had always been the sensible older sister. It felt strange and rather lovely to be comforted by Yvette.

"My poor Gabby," said Yvette, rocking her like a child. "So strong for such a long time. I'm sorry he hurt you."

And then it all came out. About Burnley, and the dogs and the children, but most of all, about Jack's coldness. Gabby had laid her heart on the line and he had rejected her, treated her worse than if she had been some beggar off the street.

"I can't understand it," she said into Yvette's shoulder. "He used to be courteous and kind. And yet it was as if he was so angry he couldn't bear to look at me."

"He is a man and therefore very stupid when it comes to his emotions," said Yvette.

Gabby caught the bitter note in her tone but let it pass. "Could I have another drink?"

"Indeed you may," said Yvette, swiping both glasses from the table and crossing to the liquor cabinet. "If we don't eat something, we will soon be drunk. And very sick in the morning."

"I don't suppose that matters," said Gabby, feeling reckless. "They don't need you at Dulac's trial until later in the week. You don't even have to be at Dior until the afternoon. And I don't have to be anywhere." She hesitated. "I am sorry I did not tell you about Madame LaRoq."

Yvette gave a long sigh and rubbed her face. "You were trying to protect me." She stared into the past, memories playing over her face like firelight dancing. "I think it's how she would have wanted to go, don't you? Doing her bit for France."

They drank a toast to Madame LaRoq and then, after a small hesitation, Gabby broke the news gently about Jean-Luc. "He died at the café, Yvette. Caught in the cross fire."

Yvette tilted her head back, closed her eyes. "Thank God. Thank God it was quick." Her hand trembled as she raised her glass to her lips and drank deeply. "And Monsieur Arnaud?"

"He escaped through Spain, same as you, but Liliane lost touch with him after the war. He never came back."

They talked deep into the night. At some point, they ordered food and someone came in to lay a fire. The sisters ate, and drank wine, and kept talking, and being with her sister like this almost made up for everything that had happened in England. Had it taken the loss of Jack to bring Yvette back to her?

Gabby was lying full-length on the sofa with her feet in Yvette's lap when she broached the question that had been playing on her mind. "What did you do in London while I was gone?"

Yvette was silent for such a long time, Gabby had to lift her head to make sure her sister hadn't passed out or fallen asleep. There was an expression on Yvette's face that was very hard to interpret. Gabby nudged her with her foot. "What?"

Slowly, Yvette said, "I saw Vidar."

"Vidar Lind? What was he doing there?"

"He had followed me."

"Really?" Yvette didn't seem flattered or happy about it. "I always thought he liked you."

"Oh, it was not that," said Yvette. "He is anxious for me to testify."

"Ah." Gabby thought she understood. "Is he in love with Louise Dulac, then?"

"I don't think so." Yvette started massaging Gabby's foot with her thumbs. "It is more complicated than that."

Yvette told her the story, though Gabby sensed she omitted certain elements of it. "He is Austrian by birth, Gabby. A Nazi officer, according to Louise." Yvette sighed. "I thought he might have been using me to get information, collaborating with the rue de la Pompe gang. But he says he was working for the Allies all along. I don't know what to believe." She stared, glassy-eyed, into the fire. "My head told me all these things about him simply didn't add up, and yet . . . And yet whenever I was with him, I felt it *could* not be true! How could I have fallen in love with the enemy?"

Gabby sat up, her foot slipping from Yvette's grasp. "Is that what you have been thinking all this time?"

Yvette turned her head. "What? Why? What do you know about it?"

Gabby shook her head in wonder. How could Yvette have gone on believing this? But then, of course, she had left Paris before the fighting began. And clearly, she had not read one word of Gabby's letters. That stung, but Gabby was too fired up to dwell on petty concerns now.

"Oh, my dear Yvette, Vidar is a war hero! Did you not know that? He is one of the men who saved Paris."

YVETTE

W hat?" Yvette rubbed her face, as if that would wipe away her confusion. Certainly, she'd had too much to drink, but she doubted this would make sense if she were sober. "Are you mad, Gabby? What do you mean?"

"He did not tell you?" Gabby said. "That is taking modesty to extremes."

"Tell me what?"

Gabby reached for her wine. "In August, after you'd gone, the Third Reich brought in General von Choltitz to take command in Paris. Hitler himself ordered the general to raze the city to the ground, blow up the bridges, the Eiffel Tower, all of our beautiful monuments."

"I read about it," Yvette said slowly. "The resistance saved Paris—"

Gabby held up a hand. "Yes, that is de Gaulle's story, but there's more to it than that. The Nazis were going to do to Paris what they did to Warsaw. Obliterate it, leave only rubble behind. It was the Swedish consul who persuaded the general to delay following Hitler's orders. Not only that, he gave the general a way to honorably surrender to the Allies without burning Paris to the ground. And do you know who arranged it all? The introductions, the diplomatic negotiations? Vidar, of course!"

Something was clamoring in Yvette's head like a church bell. She couldn't take it all in. "Why 'of course'? There is no 'of course' about it."

"No, but *listen!*" Gabby was a different person from the lachrymose woman who had poured her heart out to Yvette at the beginning of the night. She was bright-eyed and passionate, ready to beat her sister over the head with this knowledge. "It was all very thrilling and utterly mad," she continued. "I only heard this from Monsieur Dior, who heard it from the consul himself, if you can believe it. Vidar came to see me after the liberation and never said a word."

"I can believe that," Yvette said dryly. His stubborn reticence exacerbated all their disagreements.

Gabby held up a finger to silence her. "*Anyway*, the general couldn't simply order his troops to stand down because Hitler was holding his family hostage in Berlin. But he agreed not to blow up Paris if the Allies marched on the capital within the next forty-eight hours. There was no way to get this message to General Patton except to drive to the battlefront, so that is what Vidar did."

"This is crazy," said Yvette. She could almost laugh to think Vidar had once told her his job involved mostly paperwork!

Gabby nodded. "Vidar and some other men piled into the embassy car and set off, first for Versailles, to persuade the Germans at the checkpoint that they were authorized to cross enemy lines. After that, they had to drive through no-man's-land with mines all around them. They only avoided getting blown up because a German soldier threw himself onto the hood of the car to warn them and then guided them through."

Here, Yvette interrupted. "Wait. Before you continue, I think I need something stronger." She set down her empty wineglass and went to the drinks cabinet to pour herself a cognac from a crystal decanter. Cool, debonair Vidar Lind—or Rick, or whoever he was—behaving like some hero from the movies? When she thought of the accusations she'd flung at him, it made her sick. She sat on the sofa beside Gabby and curled her legs under her, then drank deeply, let the fiery warmth spread through her body. "Go on."

"Well, eventually, they got through to General Patton with the message that Paris would be saved only if the Allies changed their plans and marched on the city before General Choltitz had to give the order to blow it to smithereens."

So, Gabby had not exaggerated. Vidar really had helped to save Paris. "Oh, God," Yvette whispered. Her chest felt hollow. How could she have misjudged him so badly?

"And when the Allies marched into Paris, Vidar marched with them, in British uniform," Gabby ended triumphantly, seemingly oblivious to Yvette's distress. "But that's not all, Yvette. He did everything he could to help us try to save Catherine. No man could have done more."

Tears of remorse were pouring down Yvette's face by this time. She wanted to curl up and die. Not only because she had wronged this man so greatly, but because now she had to face the facts: It was she who had failed Catherine Dior, and she alone. Had Catherine not gone to that meeting at the Place du Trocadéro instead of Yvette, Berger's gang would not have arrested her.

"But that is not at all true," Gabby protested when Yvette managed to explain the source of her grief. "Is that what you have been thinking all this time? Oh, poor, poor Yvette."

Gabby hugged her tightly, then drew back to wipe away her tears, but Yvette couldn't allow herself to be comforted. She didn't deserve it.

"Your circuit was betrayed, Yvette," Gabby said. "The leader, Jean Desbordes, was taken, and many others were rounded up, too, all falling like dominoes one day after the next." She gripped Yvette's shoulders as if she would shake the truth into her. "My dear, if Catherine had not been taken at the Place du Trocadéro, she would have been arrested the next day, or the one after that. Someone within the network named names. It was nothing to do with you."

The logic was irrefutable, but it did not lessen Yvette's guilt. Perhaps Gabby could not understand this. Yvette didn't understand it herself. Catherine, so loyal and brave, had not given up Yvette or Liliane or any of her contacts to those monsters at the rue de la Pompe, not even under torture. That only made Yvette feel worse.

"Please, Yvette," said Gabby. "No one blames you. You cannot blame yourself."

Yvette took Gabby's face between her hands and kissed her on each cheek. "You are such a good sister to say that. But I think I cannot talk anymore. I must . . . I must lie down and not think."

She felt old and tattered, worn out with regret. But one thing she didn't regret: refusing Vidar's proposal. Clearly, he was far and away too good a man for her. And besides, he had never said he loved her. But oh, she burned to beg his forgiveness for the mistakes she'd made, the things she'd said. And he'd tried to help Catherine . . . She couldn't bear it.

"You are kind to me," she murmured as Gabby's strong, gentle hands pulled the covers up to her chin. "And I have been so selfish, ignoring your letters, and—"

"Sleep now," Gabby said. After a few minutes, Yvette felt the mattress tip as Gabby curled up in bed beside her.

ↄↄ←

THE FOLLOWING DAY, Yvette refused to let Gabby draw the curtains until noon. Occasionally, she squinted open an eye to see that her sister was dozing beside her. How nice to be together again, for once not arguing. Supporting each other in the bad times, together against the world.

There was not an awful lot Yvette could do about her own problems, but perhaps there was a way she might help Gabby. While she was still sleeping, Yvette searched through Gabby's things and found Audrey's card with her address and telephone number printed on it. She noted down the details and returned the card to Gabby's purse. She was going to try to fix things for her with Jack. She wasn't sure how, but she'd try.

Eventually, she rang for breakfast and got ready for her three o'clock fittings at Dior. Work would get her through. "What will you do today?" she asked Gabby.

"I want to take a long, long bath, then walk down to the river." Gabby's expression was grim.

"You are not going to throw yourself in, are you? That would rather defeat the purpose of the bath."

"Of course not. I am a good Catholic, I'll have you know." But Gabby's somber expression had lightened a little at the awful joke.

Before she left, Yvette checked her makeup in the mirror above the mantelpiece and caught Gabby rubbing her cheek on the softness of her hotel robe in a rare gesture of sensual pleasure.

"Don't go back," Yvette said. "Stay here with me until the trial is over."

"No, I can't do that." Gabby raised an eyebrow. "You are going to testify, then?"

"Yes." Of course she would testify, and not only that, she would support Louise's story as far as she could. If Vidar was on the side of the Allies, it meant that Louise Dulac had been working for them, too. It was a relief, knowing her instincts had not failed her when it came to these two complicated people. Now she could defend Louise, certain that she was innocent. Not only innocent, but a daring and coolheaded agent for the Allies, however badly she might have treated Yvette.

She picked up her gloves and purse. "I need to get back to work." Then she bent to Gabby and kissed her cheek warmly. "I hope you change your mind. It has been good to have you here."

Paris, August 1944

GABBY

Gabby had been afraid and on edge for so many days at a time, so many weeks, in fact, that this heightened state of anxiety had begun to seem almost normal.

Even at the peak of her preoccupation with looking after Jack, Gabby had never neglected her duties as much as she did that July. The news of Jean-Luc's death reached her some days after her sister's departure, and no one came knocking on the door demanding Yvette. What did that mean? That Catherine hadn't been tortured at the hands of the Berger gang? That she was dead already?

Gabby could do no more for her own sister, but all through those weeks of worry and strain, she worked closely with Christian Dior, helping him try every avenue they could think of to rescue Catherine.

She longed to go to Berger's lair, to confront him and demand Catherine's return, but it was too dangerous. She would only invite more raids on rue Royale, perhaps get herself arrested as well. And now that she had three men squirrelled away in empty apartments, she couldn't afford to draw that kind of attention. Besides, a man like Berger would hardly listen to her. She didn't even dare waylay Rafael and demand to know how Catherine was being treated. It was all so hopeless . . .

"She's alive!" Christian Dior found Gabby in the courtyard to the apartments one August morning and gripped her hands tightly, his eyes moist. "I just had word she has been moved from rue de la Pompe to Fresnes."

"Oh, monsieur!" said Gabby, almost faint with relief. The absolute certainty and horror of Catherine's suffering, the fear that she would die at the hands of those monsters at rue de la Pompe, lifted for the first time. Fresnes was a fortress, and a grim, awful place to be, but at least it was a proper prison, not a torture chamber run by criminals. If Catherine was in Fresnes, perhaps they could use official channels to get her out.

Gabby tried every possible contact she possessed, even going so far as to ask Madame Vasseur if she knew anyone who might intercede on Catherine's behalf. For once, madame was not her usual waspish self. She looked grave and shook her head.

Gabby had even thought of Vidar Lind, the Swedish diplomat, and tried in vain to contact him. The secretary who answered his phone told her he was away on business and she did not know when he'd return. It seemed an odd time to leave Paris, but no other information was forthcoming, despite Gabby's throwing all pretense of politeness aside and interrogating the girl.

She had even asked to be put through to someone "higher up," though she had no clear notion who that might be, nor why they would possibly wish to deal with her. The secretary was not intimidated, however, and politely expressed her regret that she could not comply with Gabby's demand.

"Please, please, give him my message as soon as you can," said Gabby. "We need his help."

HAD ANY AUGUST ever been as hot as this? Gabby couldn't remember, and as she sat with Monsieur Dior in the waiting room outside the Swedish consul's office, she felt as if her buttoned-up collar might strangle her. The blades of an electric fan simply shifted hot air from one place to the next.

Poor Monsieur Dior, so precise and perfect in his light, summer-weight suit, looked as if he might expire.

Gabby offered him a weak smile. "It is better hope than we have had yet."

He nodded and blinked. He looked very tired. It had been more than a month since Catherine was taken, and in that time Christian had worn himself to the bone, begging everyone he knew who might possibly have influence to try to free his beloved sister. But there was nothing anyone could do.

One day, Vidar Lind had stopped by the *loge* with news of Yvette's safe arrival in Spain. Gabby threw her arms around him with gratitude. Laughing a little, he set his hands on her shoulders and said, "But did you doubt the little termagant would get through? She is tough, that one."

Gabby shook her head, smiling through her tears. Despite not hearing a word from Yvette, she had known in her bones that her sister lived. She could still feel Yvette's fury reaching out across mountains to her. "She did not write?"

"No, but you must not take that to heart," said Vidar. "All is chaos at the moment. And it is more than anyone's life is worth to be found smuggling papers across the border."

They talked a little more about the unrest in Paris. As Catherine had warned, certain elements of the resistance had not waited for the Allied invasion. Fighting had broken out in the Paris streets. No one felt safe.

"God willing, it will be over soon," she murmured.

Vidar rose to his feet. "Well, it has been a pleasure, mademoiselle, but I must be getting back." Throughout their brief conversation, Vidar had been his usual charming self, but there was a weary expression in his eyes, as if he had not slept for weeks. She wondered what he had been doing all this time. Secret work? She hardly liked to add to his burden, but for Catherine, she'd discovered she had no compunction.

Gabby smoothed her skirt. "Monsieur, I wonder if you could help me with another matter . . ."

It turned out that Vidar could. In fact, he was precisely the man to help her, because he was going to see the Swedish consul that very day. Monsieur Nordling had been negotiating with the Nazis for the release of certain prisoners. He would be the man to get Catherine back if anyone could. "I will set up a meeting," Vidar promised.

He refused to listen to her heartfelt expressions of thanks but disappeared as suddenly as he had arrived.

The relief of hearing that help would come at last made Gabby burst into tears.

"What's the matter?" Maman came in with her mop and bucket. Since the night of the raid, she had begun to take back more of her old duties as concierge. Gabby could only be grateful. Her time was fully occupied with tending to her fugitives and helping Monsieur Dior in his quest to free Catherine.

"Oh, it is good news!" Gabby had managed, when she could speak at all. "Two pieces of very good news, Maman."

And now, just as Vidar had promised, she waited with Monsieur Dior to see the Swedish consul.

Finally, the door to Monsieur Nordling's sanctum opened and the two of them shot to their feet. Gabby could feel Monsieur Dior's tension as he exchanged polite greetings with the consul's assistant. They were brought to an office quite grand in its appointment, though its furniture was unexpectedly utilitarian. The consul's desk was no mere ornament, and the large battered filing cabinet that stood against the wall behind him suggested frequent use. The man himself was portly and distinguished looking, with hooded blue eyes and a pencil mustache. It seemed to Gabby that Monsieur Nordling carried the weight of the world upon his shoulders. How kind of him to make time to see them.

"Please sit down," said the consul as he finished writing something and capped his pen. "I sent for you because it seems we are in luck. I've managed to get the Germans to agree to release political prisoners who are still on French soil into Swedish hands."

Gabby and Monsieur Dior looked at each other and simultaneously let out breaths of relief and elation.

The consul added, "However, I am sorry to say that after a lot of to and fro this morning I discovered that Mademoiselle Dior is already on a train to Germany."

"Ah, no!" exclaimed Gabby.

Monsieur Dior turned so pale, Gabby thought he might faint. "Can we not get to her?"

The consul held up a hand. "Right now, they are at Bar-le-Duc. I've been assured that if I call the station master before two forty-five P.M., we can get her off the train. I have someone else phoning through the authority to them. The timing will be tight and we all know how rigid the Germans are about schedules. We must pray we are not too late."

He raised his head and called to his secretary through the doorway, "Olsson! Did you get through yet?"

"Not yet, sir," Olsson replied. "I can't get a line. The resistance might have cut the wires. It's pandemonium out there."

"Try again!" said Monsieur Nordling. "And again and again until you get through."

The distant crack of gunfire punctuated the tense silence. Gabby could not stay still. She jumped up and paced, hardly caring that she might be going against protocol. The men stared at the shiny black telephone on the consul's desk.

With a muted, metallic clang, the clock, which like every other clock in France was set on German time, chimed the quarter hour: two forty-five P.M.

"Olsson!" snapped the consul. "Have we a line?"

"No, sir. I'm trying!"

There was no single moment when Gabby felt the breaking of her heart. Hope simply waned, wasting away until there was none left. The clock's hands moved slowly, inexorably toward the hour and still, they could not get through to stop the train. She wanted to scream at this Olsson fellow to do his job properly. Silently, she begged God to turn back the hands of time, to give them a second chance . . .

"Sir! We're through."

The consul snatched up his telephone receiver and spoke German into it. Gabby's attention was so focused on him that she caught every expression, every movement, and tried to interpret what each might mean for Catherine. But at last, Nordling hung up, met her gaze, and gave a curt shake of his head.

Catherine was lost. The train had left France, crossing the border into Germany. There would be no retrieving any prisoners after that. Monsieur Dior sat very still.

They'd been so close. And now, for the sake of a few minutes, they might never see Catherine again. Fury exploded inside her. "Damn them!" Damn the Nazis and their ruthless efficiency, their inflexible adherence to rules.

Gunfire, closer now, broke the heavy silence that followed her outburst.

Monsieur Nordling's telephone began to ring once more. Gabby touched Monsieur Dior's arm. "Shall we go, monsieur? The consul is a very busy man."

She had to repeat the request. Monsieur Dior sat there unmoving, stunned at their failure, at his loss. Catherine was gone. The Allies would march into Paris any day now, but they would not be in time to save her.

Chapter Twenty-Five

Paris, February 1947

GABBY

Yvette left for work while Gabby was running her bath. "Enjoy yourself," she said, grinning. "Order anything you like."

But there was nothing like having your heart broken to make you realize how little luxury truly mattered. Gabby bathed and dressed and repacked her suitcase. Then she went to the pretty little desk by the window and wrote Yvette a note.

Dear sister,

My heart is heavy. You know this. I would give anything for things to have turned out better for both of us on our journey to

England. But for one thing, I will be forever grateful. I have my sister back. I love you, Yvette. Never forget.

                                        Gabby

Refusing the doorman's offer of a taxi, Gabby set off for the rue Royale, but instead of going straight home, she turned toward the river.

Jack did not want her and never would. Her suitcase weighed heavily upon her, and the very air around her seemed oppressive, cloying, as if she were suffocating, even in the bitter cold. Why did people find this city so romantic? To her, it was a very large prison, and the *loge* at number 10 was her cell.

She trudged through the Tuileries and along the quay, all the way to the Pont des Arts. The Seine looked dark and ominous under the frozen sky. The beautiful palaces and museums that lined the river seemed grim and unwelcoming. She walked halfway across the bridge and stared up at the Eiffel Tower, and her life felt as stripped back and stark as the famous monument. "There is nothing left for me now." She wished she had never allowed Yvette to answer that telephone call from London. It had been far, far better thinking he'd died than to know Jack was still alive and so woefully imperfect.

She dug into the pocket of her coat and brought out the velvet case with its medal inside. Then she took aim for the point at which the very tip of the Eiffel Tower met the sky and hurled the medal, case and all, as far as she could. She didn't even hear the splash when it hit the rippling waters of the river.

When Gabby arrived back at the *loge*, she found her mother sitting on the floor among stacks of mail. She was humming—

actually humming—a jaunty tune as she sorted, holding first one envelope, then another, up to the light. The kettle boiled and chirruped. Had she been using steam to open some of those letters? Forget Yvette; their mother was the family's most accomplished spy.

At one time, Gabby would have hastened to snatch back her self-appointed task, but she took her suitcase to the bedroom, then went to rescue the boiling kettle and make herself a tisane.

"Back, are you?" Danique kept going with the day's post.

"Yes, we cut the trip short." Gabby didn't even feel inclined to protest her mother's investigations into the private lives of the tenants. She felt divorced from everything, separate from this narrow existence. She sat down in Danique's favorite chair and watched her work.

Her mother eyed her as if she might say something, then seemed to think better of it. After a few minutes, she held up a letter. "For you, Gabby. From Miss Dior."

Gabby's heart gave one hard thump. "From Catherine?" She took the letter and retreated to her room, ripping open the flimsy envelope as she went.

Trembling, she scanned the lines. She gasped and put her hand to her mouth, reading the letter over and over, unable to believe what it contained.

Dear Gabby,

I hope this finds you well. In Callian, we are preparing for the spring, when the May rose carpets our fields and we spend our days picking blossoms in the sunshine. It is a joy to me to grow the flowers that gave such pleasure to my mother in her garden in Granville, and to supply great houses such as Dior with the essences for their perfumes.

The business is expanding rapidly and I find I need an office manager—someone I can trust—to keep the accounts and do various other administrative tasks. There is a small cottage that goes along with the position and I would like to offer both the position and the cottage to you.

I realize it is not an easy thing to leave Paris, and I wondered if you would like to spend the summer down here with me. We would love you and Yvette to join us. You can tell her I've made all right with my brother for her to take a leave of absence if she chooses to accompany you. Then you can see how the business runs and decide whether you would like to accept . . .

This was it. Her chance to leave Paris, to have a fresh start. Gabby went to her mother and handed over the letter for her to read.

Danique scanned the note. "Dior, Dior! Those people, always meddling in our lives." But she smiled a little as she said it. She drew in a breath, then gave a decisive nod as she handed back the letter. "I think you should go. Take the job, too."

"What?" Gabby couldn't believe it. "But what about my duties? You would let me go?"

Maman touched Gabby's cheek. "You're a grown woman. You can make your own decisions. If not for the war, I would have lost you to marriage years ago."

Gabby stared around her, stunned. "But what about this place?"

Her mother chuckled. "I ran number ten long before you took over. I can do it again." She sighed. "When your papa passed away . . . Well, I worked because it was easier than dealing with the pain—yours, Yvette's, mine—and I'm sorry for that." She spread her hands. "Then war came, and more duties fell onto my shoulders, and I worked myself into a state of collapse. And you were so capable, Gabby, and after losing Didier, you needed something, just as I did when Papa died. It became a habit to let you take over." Danique shrugged. "But that's a long time ago now. These past days it's been just me here on my own and I have to say, I've enjoyed it. Makes me feel young again." She cleared her throat, as if embarrassed to have revealed so much.

Gabby was about to protest, then shut her mouth. Her mother really wanted this. She was happy to let Gabby go. She exhaled a delighted breath and said, "Thank you, Maman. Thank you." She hugged Danique tightly and kissed her, then hurried away to write Catherine back.

As she opened her leather satchel, her gaze fell upon the story she'd written and illustrated after the Dior show. She slid it out and leafed through the pages, smiling a little at some of the sketches. Then she took out her notepaper and began a reply.

YVETTE

At Dior the next afternoon, Yvette had clients to see and fittings to attend, but her mind was not on fashion.

She needed to write to Audrey about Gabby and Jack. Then there was Vidar. She felt an overwhelming need to see him, if only to apologize for having wronged him so badly, and to thank him for his efforts on Catherine's behalf. But after that horrible morning in London, she would probably never set eyes on him again.

And now, Louise Dulac's trial had begun, and Yvette's testimony would be required tomorrow or the next day. According to Monsieur LeBrun, one never knew quite how long it would take.

Wintry afternoon sun was streaming through the enormous garret windows of the atelier as Marie stood on a chair to throw the Chérie gown over Yvette's head, allowing it to swirl around her in an inky cascade of taffeta petticoats and narrowly pleated silk. Yvette felt like a princess in a fairy tale as the seamstress buttoned her up, then gradually less enchanted, as it was freezing in the atelier despite the sunshine and the fitting seemed to take forever.

"You are too thin, Yvette," complained Marie, who was pinning a seam on the bodice for alteration.

The seamstress was probably right; Yvette had eaten less and less since she'd arrived in Paris. Were the habits of wartime coming back to her, along with the memories? She'd order a banquet tonight and savor every last bite. Yvette smiled to herself. Wouldn't Marie be mad if she had to let out the seams again?

A commotion at the staircase caught her attention. Everyone was craning their head to look. Was it Monsieur Dior? Yvette stood straighter, hoping he would like how she looked in this gown.

But the man who burst in upon the busy scene was not le patron but the lawyer's clerk.

"Monsieur LeBrun!" Yvette caught Marie's hands and put them away from her and moved forward to intercept him. "You must not be here."

The clerk was panting so hard from running up all those stairs that he could scarcely get a word out. His face was red all over. There was even red showing between the precise lines of hair on his scalp.

"Is it the trial?" she asked him.

Gasping for air, he bent over, his palms resting on his knees. "You must come immediately," he panted. "*Now*, Mademoiselle Foucher. There is not a moment to lose. The court is waiting for you."

He grabbed her wrist and dragged her out of the workroom. She was halfway down the stairs before she recalled she still wore the Dior gown.

"Wait! No, monsieur, no!" Yvette tried to pull away but he was stronger than he looked, and he half-pushed, half-pulled her the rest of the way down and out into his awaiting car, stuffing the gown and all its petticoats in after her and slamming the door.

As they sped away, Yvette turned to him, wide-eyed. "What did you just do, monsieur?" She looked down at herself in her Dior gown and didn't know whether to laugh or cry.

She would likely be fired for setting foot beyond the door of the atelier with one of monsieur's beautiful creations on her back. Pins dug into her side as she shifted around, smoothing her skirt beneath her, trying to make sure the dress wasn't completely crushed. "Monsieur, I will be in huge trouble. Would you turn the car around, please, and take me back to Dior so I can change?"

"We don't have time," said the clerk. "No more games, mademoiselle. You *will* come with me to the Palais de Justice, mademoiselle, and you *will* tell the court the truth about what Louise Dulac did for France during the war."

She blinked at his vehemence. She'd made up her mind to support Louise Dulac's version of events when Gabby had told her the truth about Vidar. But of course LeBrun didn't know that. "But I was going to—"

"Listen to me," he said, his voice low, as if he didn't want his driver to overhear. "Dulac has threatened to expose our mutual friend if you do not testify."

She recalled Louise threatening Vidar when they'd visited her in Fresnes. "She wouldn't do that."

"You know her," said LeBrun, fixing Yvette with his earnest brown eyes. "Do you think she would stop at anything to save her own skin?"

The clerk was right. Yvette did know Louise Dulac. "Well, I'm here now," she said as they pulled up at the courts. "Please, will you help me get out?"

As they crossed the square in front of the court building, the chill bit into her bare arms and she began to shiver. For the first time, LeBrun looked her up and down. "What *are* you wearing?"

She stared at him. Had he not just dragged her out of a fitting at a fashion house? But now that she was here, she couldn't worry about the trouble she'd be in at Dior. She had to prepare for the interrogation ahead.

Monsieur LeBrun began to struggle out of his overcoat. "Here. You'd better take this."

"No, thank you." Yvette drew herself up and lifted her head high. She would prefer to freeze than to look ridiculous. "Lead on, monsieur."

As they hurried across the courtyard and up the steps to the Palais de Justice, the clerk muttered instructions. "Confine yourself to 'yes' or 'no' as much as possible. Be brief, to the point, and only talk about things you actually saw or heard. Do not speculate or give an opinion on anything. Do you understand?"

Yvette nodded. And she would not, under any circumstances, mention Vidar.

Then the heavy door to the courtroom opened and she walked in.

⚶

AT THE ENTRANCE to the court, the enormity of the occasion hit Yvette with full force. The room was a sea of men in suits. Seated up high at the far end of the massive chamber were the judges— three of them, she thought, though it was difficult to tell. There seemed to be several judicial-looking men up there dressed in black gowns and white lappets.

The atmosphere was one of ferocious anticipation; the crowd was out for blood. They all wanted to be in at the kill, to see the glamorous actress brought down, to feed off her remains like jackals when the lions of the law were done. But it was not only men who were there. Yes, now that she paid closer attention, she saw women dotted among the crowd. She was reminded of the *tricoteuses*, knitting at the foot of the guillotine.

The aisle down the center of the court seemed to stretch forever. Yvette would have to walk down it with everyone's eyes upon her, like a bride in a cathedral, like a queen processing to her coronation.

Her manner of dress might have made her look ridiculous, but she forced herself to lift her chin and proceed without hurrying, imagined herself back at Dior, promenading through his elegant salons in this exquisite gown.

There were comments, vile insults about her virtue, speculation on what she'd done to get about in a dress like that, but she pretended not to hear. They were talking about someone else. And anyway, when they heard what she had to say, they would no longer look at her as if she were something they'd found on the soles of their shoes.

Louise Dulac sat in the dock, thin but immaculate in a well-tailored suit and a hat. Her blond hair had not lost its shine and was well cut, her makeup skillfully applied. Yvette wondered if she had been advised to dress down for this occasion. After all, part of the reason Dulac was so hated was that she had lived the high life while the rest of France starved. If she had received that advice, she had ignored it. Yvette was glad. If people were here to see a victim, they would be sadly disappointed. All the same, it was not sound strategy on Dulac's part.

Wearing a Dior gown to court was hardly likely to win Yvette any favor in the public eye, either. It was too late to do anything about it now. She stepped up behind the curved wooden railing that made up the witness stand at the side of the courtroom and faced the judges. She was glad that her back was to the audience, but she felt alone and exposed, standing there, waiting to be grilled about her association with an accused traitor by these godlike figures from on high.

However, she reminded herself that she wore haute couture of the very finest, that in Dior, a woman can accomplish anything. In a clear, carrying voice, she stated her name, took the oath, and waited for the questions to begin.

Yes, she knew Louise Dulac during the war. How did she know her? She delivered clothing to her from the House of Lelong.

Was she more to Louise Dulac than just a delivery girl? No. At least, she did not know what that question meant. Would his honor please explain? A slight flutter of the eyelashes with that one. Silly, silly girl.

Yes, she accompanied Louise Dulac to the Château de Saint Firmin. Why did she do that? Mademoiselle had taken a liking to her, she thought. She was French and Dulac was surrounded by Germans. But Yvette had to leave the château one night. Mademoiselle Dulac had broken some pearls and Yvette had to take them back to Paris to be restrung.

Then the question she had been waiting for. Slowly and clearly, she answered. "Mademoiselle Dulac was spying for the resistance."

The room fell still. After a long pause came the question, "How did you know this?"

"The night she broke her pearls, she asked me to do something." Yvette hesitated, then lowered her gaze, her embarrassment not entirely a pretense. "I was to distract a German SS officer, Obersturmbannführer Werner, while she searched his room."

Sniggers rippled through the courtroom.

"And what form did this distraction take?"

She bit her lip and hesitated, then mumbled a response.

"Speak up!" the judge growled. "And look at me when I'm talking to you."

Bracing her shoulders, Yvette spoke out. "I stalled and stalled, but the Obersturmbannführer tried to kiss me. It was horrible. And then I did something awful. Oh, too awful to tell."

"Nevertheless, mademoiselle, you must tell."

She could feel the audience, the judges, everyone hold their breath, waiting for the lurid details. "I threw up on him," she said.

The room held silent, then erupted into laughter. This, they had not expected.

"You did what?" One of the judges glared at her beneath beetled brows.

Yvette spread her hands. "He was like a pig and he was a Nazi and he made me sick." She spoke in a loud, clear voice. "Oh, but very sick, all over him. And he went away then, but by that time Mademoiselle Dulac had found what she needed and she came back. She wrote out a message in code and I was to deliver it to a jeweler in Paris, along with the broken string of pearls. But then when I got there, someone told me the jeweler had been taken by the *gestapistes,* so I gave the message to a man I knew who was also working for the resistance. And I do not know what happened after that."

"You cycled all the way back to Paris from Chantilly?"

"Mademoiselle Dulac had obtained a pass for me from Ambassador Abetz to get me through the checkpoints." Yvette drew herself up proudly. "Oh, but I was *very* sore afterward."

A few more sniggers greeted that statement.

"You don't know what the message contained, or who it was for," said another judge. He rubbed at his spectacles with the sleeve of his black gown, then set them carefully back on, as if to peer at her more closely.

"I only know what Mademoiselle Dulac told me. She said it was a report on a local munitions store. Her message was in code."

And that was all that needed to be said. Yvette glanced at Dulac, sitting straight backed and proud in the dock, and wondered if she detected a faint air of relief about her. No, Yvette decided. Louise did not betray any weakness whatsoever. A risky move, that. Yvette's ingénue act was far more palatable to those old chauvinists, and to the crowd, as well.

"And did you have further dealings with mademoiselle after that?" inquired the bespectacled judge.

"I saw her one more time." The fury and despair of the day she tried to save Catherine rose up, into her chest and throat. She took a moment to force it down, deep inside to the pit of her stomach. "A friend of mine was taken by the *gestapistes,* the rue de la Pompe gang. I begged for Mademoiselle Dulac's help in trying to free her."

She swallowed hard and threw her shoulders back. "There was nothing she could do."

There were more questions to test Yvette's evidence but she stuck by the facts, as Monsieur LeBrun had told her to do, and thus she gave no indication of the doubts she had entertained about Louise, nor of the resentment she felt toward her. The bald facts were not quite enough to prove Louise was working for the resistance—after all, what had that message actually contained?—but Yvette hoped it was enough to tip the balance against a conviction.

Then, suddenly, one question took her by surprise. "The accused claims a man recruited her. A fellow who used an alias, the name of Étienne Planche. Did you ever hear of him or come across this man?"

The breath caught in her throat. It was Vidar. It had to be. But wait. Louise had given them an alias, not Vidar's real name, which she well knew. She had not betrayed Vidar's true identity, despite her threats. "I do not know anyone by this name." Wide-eyed stare. In a literal sense, that was true. Yvette had never heard him use that particular cover.

She prayed they wouldn't probe further. If they did, she would have to tell the truth and expose Vidar. Her heart was beating hard, her hands shaking. Thank goodness for Monsieur Dior's long skirts, for no one could see how her knees trembled.

Mercifully, the questioning ceased. Yvette tried not to rush as she escaped the witness stand, but her stomach was heaving. On her way out, she caught Monsieur LeBrun's eye. He gave her a brief nod, then sagged back into his chair and mopped his brow.

Yvette returned to the atelier and finished the workday, receiving only a mild scolding from Madame Raymonde for her outrageous behavior—far less punishment than she deserved. However, since the gown had been returned without incident or damage, there was no real harm done.

It would be too much to expect that no one would tell *le patron* what had gone on, however. Even if they hadn't, Yvette's picture was plastered all over the evening newspapers, and the morning ones as well. She saw them all spread out on Monsieur Dior's desk when he called her to see him the next day.

"Dior Girl Leaps to Movie Star's Defense" ran one headline. Yvette smiled a little sourly. It was better than the cartoon that showed her vomiting all over Hitler.

Monsieur Dior waited for her to speak. She hung her head. "I am sorry, monsieur."

He made a funny little purse of his lips and shook his head. "The gown . . . It is not that, Yvette." He shrugged. "Already I am besieged with orders for the Chérie, so I suppose your little stunt has only done me good. *Not* that I want you ever to repeat it," he added with a severity belied by the amusement in his eyes.

"No, monsieur. But never."

"It is this," he said, indicating the most detailed report of the court proceedings. "They say you went to Louise Dulac to plead with her to try to get a friend released. Was it . . . ?"

Her insides twisted as if he had wrung them out like a sponge. "Yes, monsieur. But it didn't work."

"Even so, I wanted to thank you, Yvette." His light voice wavered on the words. "You and your sister have been true friends to Catherine and me. We will never forget."

She couldn't speak. She just closed her eyes tightly and took a deep breath. After a long struggle with her guilt, she managed, "May I go now, monsieur? La Baronne has given me time off to see the final day of the trial."

However, by the time she reached the Palais de Justice, it was all over, and she had to fight her way through the crowds spilling down the courthouse steps and out into the square. The atmosphere was uncertain, volatile. Louise Dulac had been cast as the villain for so long, inspiring such hatred in the French people, and then overnight, the tide had turned. Before, there had been placards vilifying the movie star. Now the strength of that fervor seemed to have swung in the opposite direction. People yelled that Dulac was a heroine of France.

Suddenly, Louise appeared at the top of the steps, triumphantly free. Despite her ordeal, she glowed with that same confidence and feminine power Yvette had felt when she'd first met her at the Ritz.

The movie star raised her hand to acknowledge her adoring fans, camera bulbs strobed all over, then the gendarmes cleared the way for her, linking arms to hold back the surging crowd as she moved down the steps.

Yvette would never get through all those people. She looked around behind her in the direction Louise was headed and saw Monsieur LeBrun waiting in a car. Yvette would intercept her there.

Louise swept along as if she were walking the red carpet at a movie premiere, not escaping a charge of treason. She didn't even glance at Yvette as the car door opened and she stooped to climb inside.

"Louise Dulac!" The words came out more sharply than Yvette had intended.

Louise paused, then straightened and turned to look at Yvette. A slow smile curved her lips, but her eyes were watchful. "So you testified after all." She raised one shoulder in a half shrug. "You should have known I wouldn't betray him. You never understood me, did you?"

"But no, mademoiselle," Yvette replied. "You should have known there was no need to blackmail me into giving evidence. But then, you never even tried to understand me."

Louise stilled, and for the most fleeting instant, Yvette saw an odd expression cross her face, a slight spasm of those beautiful features. Then she got into Monsieur LeBrun's car and was driven away.

Yvette thought about that look, the brief air of vulnerability it had given the former agent before her shining veneer slid back into place. She considered the lonely and frightening life Louise had lived, working undercover for all that time, with no one to turn to except an inexperienced, idealistic young Parisienne who occasionally helped her dress.

Dulac's masters—whoever they had been—had expected her to risk everything in a way that they would never be called upon to do, only to leave her dangling out on a limb for the entire country to hate when she had served her purpose.

Louise had used Yvette and lied to her, and Yvette had hated her for it. But for once, Yvette had not let her emotions overrule her judgment. She had done what was right and just.

And now, she must honor her other obligation. She must face Catherine Dior.

Chapter Twenty-Six

Callian, May 1947

GABBY

Gabby was glad of Yvette's company on the train journey south to stay with Catherine Dior. She glanced at her sister, who was reading a novel, her body swaying with the movement of the carriage. There had been something subdued about Yvette since she had testified at the trial of Louise Dulac. She'd made a sensation in the newspapers, turning up to the courthouse in a Dior gown. Gabby shook her head. Trust Yvette to do something outrageous.

She had looked so exquisite in the photographs, Monsieur Dior had forgiven her and joked that it was good publicity, though not quite of the expected variety.

For Gabby, things were looking up. Recently, Gabby had come into a little money. Having survived the deprivations and harsh conditions of the war without a hitch in her step, Madame Vasseur had died quietly in her bed. She left everything she owned to Gabby, provided that Gabby looked after Chou-Chou in the manner to which he was accustomed. Gabby was happy to do so. Even now, the poodle was curled up at their feet, better behaved than many of the humans on board.

"What are you thinking about?" said Yvette, closing her book with a yawn. "You have a little smile on your face."

Gabby leaned down to bury her fingers in the poodle's wool and felt the reassuring warmth of his body. "I was thinking of Madame Vasseur."

"Not much to smile about there," said Yvette. "Or were you contemplating your inheritance?"

"I was thinking that people can surprise you," Gabby said. "How are you feeling about this trip?"

Yvette pulled a face. "Truthfully, I am sick to my stomach. I was hoping Monsieur Dior would forbid me to go."

Gabby smiled. "He would never disoblige his favorite sister."

Yvette rested her head back against the seat. "I just . . . I don't know how to face her. I don't know how to make amends, what to say."

Gabby realized what she meant. "Oh, Yvette! You must not talk to her about the war." After the horrors of rue de la Pompe and Fresnes and the harrowing train journey to Germany, Catherine spent eight long months in labor camps, being worked to the bone, moved from place to place. When she returned, she was like a skeleton with the skin still on. She could not manage solid food for months.

Poor Monsieur Dior had been beside himself when he heard Catherine was coming home and had instructed his cook to scrape together all the rations she could to make his dear sister a soufflé. But when it came to it, Catherine couldn't manage to eat even that. Monsieur was utterly distraught.

"She does not want your apologies or your pity, Yvette." Gabby tried to put it gently to take out the sting. "In her shoes, you would feel the same."

"Yes, you're right. I understand." Yvette turned her face to the window and didn't speak again.

They had nearly reached their destination when Gabby said, "You know it wasn't your fault. I told you how it happened. If it had not been that day, they would have arrested her the next."

But sometimes guilt has no relationship to logic. Yvette shook her head and continued to stare out of the window at the passing countryside. Forgiving herself would take time, thought Gabby. It would take everyone in France a long, long time to make peace with their regrets.

Catherine sent a car to pick them up from the station, and as they drove further north, the mountains gave way to stunning fields of flowers, blankets of purple, white, and pink. The scent wafting through the open windows of the car was dizzying. "It's the May rose," said Gabby as they drove through seas of blowsy pink blossoms. "Look! You can see the workers out picking them."

As they pulled up outside the farmhouse, Catherine appeared at the doorway, opening her arms wide.

"Welcome!" she said, embracing Gabby and kissing her cheeks. "Go in, my dear. How wonderful to see you both. And Chou-Chou, too!" She bent down to pat the poodle, who frisked about them briefly, then scampered off to hunt for interesting smells.

Yvette was still hovering by the car. Gabby hesitated, then

obeyed Catherine and headed into the house. Better to leave them to it.

As she passed into the comparative dimness of the entry, she heard Catherine say, with a wealth of understanding and affection in her soft voice, "Yvette, my dear."

YVETTE

By the time they pulled up outside Catherine's house, Yvette's stomach churned and her heart raced. Working as a courier for the resistance seemed child's play compared with meeting Catherine Dior again. According to Gabby, Yvette must act as if everything was normal, as if the war had never happened. Of course, she was right about that.

She got out of the car and hung back as Gabby moved forward to return Catherine's delicate embrace.

Catherine still looked far too thin, and Yvette mulled over what Gabby had said about the starvation rations the Germans had kept her on during that horrible time she'd spent in the camps. It was a miracle she'd survived, a testament to her mental toughness, to her ingenuity and grit.

When she had completed her hellos with Gabby, Catherine turned to look at Yvette. Shading her eyes against the sun, Catherine called something to her. Though Catherine's face was in shadow, somehow Yvette could tell she smiled, and also that the smile would not reach her eyes. She dreaded looking into Catherine's eyes more than anything else, to see them haunted by suffering and loss.

Yvette wanted to cry. She wanted to throw herself at Catherine's feet and beg for absolution.

She took one step, then another.

"Ah, Yvette! Why so shy?" It was motherly and chiding, that tone. Yvette forced herself to take those final steps, to put her arms around Catherine gingerly as they kissed cheeks.

"*Ma belle*," Catherine said, looking Yvette up and down. "I am not surprised Christian is wild for you."

"Not at all, mademoiselle," said Yvette, following Catherine into the house. "To your brother I am still that scrubby little delivery girl, I think."

"I know for a fact that is not so," said Catherine. "You are clearly one of his favorites! Go on through to the terrace. I'll fetch something for you to drink."

The weather was warm but a light, cool breeze blew as Catherine brought out lemonade to the terrace. "You will want to freshen up, of course," she said, "but first, I wish to hear all about New York."

"There is not much to tell." It had been hard at first in a new city, knowing no one at all. But how could Yvette complain of such a thing, considering all that Catherine had been suffering at the time? "I picked up some catalog work there," Yvette added, "but I was not a very successful mannequin. Over there, the magazines all want the sporty look, you know, tanned and athletic. To them, I seemed . . ." She flushed. She had been about to say "undernourished," but that would be grotesque. ". . . Not quite right."

Ah, this was so hard! She had expected to feel guilty, not that she would spend the entire time avoiding conversational land mines. By the time they'd finished the lemonade and retired to wash and change, she was exhausted and emotional.

"It's hard at first," agreed Gabby. "But you don't need to walk on eggshells with her. After all, she's been through the worst experience any of us can imagine. A few tactless words are not going to bother her too much. It's not as if she could possibly forget."

At dinner, Catherine's friend the Baron des Charbonneries joined them, and his gentle good humor made them all relax. Yvette was buoyed to see the two of them so in love. It seemed that life was good down here in Callian. Catherine's flower business was thriving.

"I'm afraid I will be fully occupied tomorrow morning with the picking," murmured Catherine as they said good night, "but I want you to wear something special for an alfresco party in the afternoon. We are going to a small gathering at a villa near Cannes. Liliane Dietlin will be there."

Finally, Yvette fell into bed, exhausted, next to Gabby. Then she laughed. "Look at us, sharing a bed again. I suppose it will be for the last time."

She envied Gabby the solid future ahead of her. Although Yvette had only been reliving her wartime experiences in her mind, talking with Catherine today had made her feel even more unsettled. Since that night she'd spent with Vidar in London, she couldn't stop thinking about the proposal he'd made. If he repeated the offer, now that she knew all about his heroism during the war, would she take him up on it? Oh, not the marriage part, of course, but the rest?

Maybe she would. Maybe she just might, at that.

But her testimony at the Palais de Justice had freed him to pursue whatever it was that he was pursuing these days. Capturing war criminals. Spying for the British, perhaps. Having rejected him with such finality, she was unlikely ever to find out.

GABBY

The party was already under way by the time they arrived at the villa in Cannes the next afternoon. Gabby felt she looked her best in a pale blue dress, cut on the bias with a frill at the bosom, and Yvette dazzled in a lemon sundress. Gabby's heart lifted as Liliane came out to greet them.

"Aha! There you are, my lovely ones!" Liliane kissed each of them warmly and shepherded them through the house and out to the terrace to meet their hosts. "I can't quite see . . ." She stood on tiptoe, scanning the crowd. "Well, never mind. They are here somewhere. No doubt you'll bump into them soon enough."

The terrace was perched dizzyingly high on the side of a sheer cliff. The sea below was a stunning, sparkling blue and the terra cotta–tiled roofs of the houses clinging to the hillside had faded to the color of a ripe peach. A marina stretched out to the sea, flanked by the yachts of the rich Americans and Europeans who were now swarming to the Riviera. The air seemed faintly misted, as if someone had pulled a veil over the prospect before them, making it seem even more magical.

"Paradise," Gabby breathed. Yes, she could definitely make a home down here. Oh, not in a magnificent villa like this one, but still . . .

Glasses were filled, happy toasts drunk, and they enjoyed a sprightly conversation during which Liliane seemed to have wiped the war from her mind completely. "But where has Jean-Paul gone? You must meet my husband." She flitted off to find her spouse.

"Liliane is married now?" said Yvette. "I have missed a lot."

Catherine raised her eyebrows and looked amused. "I should have known this 'intimate gathering' would not be so intimate if Liliane had anything to do with it. I hope you don't mind."

"Of course not." Gabby felt young and full of *esprit* with these cheerful people around her, jazz playing in the background, and the sweet waft of sea air ruffling her hair.

Catherine knew many of the guests and introduced them around. They were talking with a retired professor of archaeology when Catherine broke off midsentence. "Will you excuse us?" She smiled at the professor and took Gabby's hand. "My dear, there is someone I absolutely must have you meet."

Gabby nodded to the professor and turned to follow Catherine. A tall, slim man with dark blond hair was standing in the doorway, scanning the crowd. *Jack.* Gabby nearly dropped her glass. What was he doing here?

"Yvette made sure to keep in touch," murmured Catherine.

"Yvette? How . . . ?" Fear gripped her. There was time to get away. Jack hadn't seen her yet. Gabby dug her heels in, tugging her hand free of Catherine's grip. "No. You don't understand. I can't."

"But, my dear, you must," said Catherine, smiling. "He is our host. It would be rude not to greet him."

Host? Gabby's glass slipped from her fingers and smashed on the tiled floor, making several guests jump out of the way. The crash attracted Jack's attention, along with everyone else's, and as he stood head and shoulders above the other guests, he saw Gabby instantly. His expression lightening, he started toward her.

Her cheeks burned. She wished the ground would swallow her. "Sorry! So sorry," she said to the people around her. She was only prevented from stooping to pick up the pieces of her broken glass by Catherine's hand gripping her wrist. "Forget about that. Someone else will clean it up. Go to him. Go now."

Legs trembling, Gabby picked her way through the shards of glass. Jack. Here in France. She did not dare to assume he was here for her. But then there was this party and this house. Had he really decided to live in Cannes? Audrey had said something about it, hadn't she? About bringing Isabelle here to convalesce . . .

She reached him and he held out his hands to her, a tilt to his head and a rueful smile on his lips. "Gabby. My Gabby. I've been such a fool." He glanced at the rest of the guests, who had all turned to stare at them both now. "Will you come with me? I have something to say to you in private."

She nodded and he indicated a flight of steps leading down. She moved toward it, her heart beating fast. He had done as she'd ordered him back in England. He had done something about his health. And . . . what? She did not dare to hope.

Careful in her new high heels, she picked her way down the curving staircase and found herself on a smaller terrace than the one above, with a wrought iron balustrade and stone vases spilling pink geraniums.

She stopped and stared out to the infinite blue of the sea, gripping the railing with clammy palms. After what he'd put her through, she ought not to forgive so easily, but life was short, and . . .

"Gabby." All he had to do was to say her name in that deep voice of his and her knees turned to blancmange. She had thought that money and independence would be enough. She'd thought she could be content without him. But that had been a lie.

She turned to face him. He looked much better than when she'd seen him in grey old England. Lines of suffering still bracketed his mouth, but there was less strain in his face and his color was good.

In fact, he had a golden tan that made his eyes seem lighter. Highlights of blond streaked his hair. He'd put on a little weight. Just enough.

"Gabby," he said softly, taking her hand. "Can you forgive me for being such a boor when you came to Burnley? My behavior was . . . appalling."

The warmth of his hand made her feel things she was not sure she wanted to feel, but she ached for him so badly that she could not seem to make herself draw away. "You are forgiven, if that's what you want."

"That is the least of what I want." He looked down at their joined hands. "Gabby, after I left you in Paris, I went on another mission. It was too much. I suffered a relapse and nearly died."

She knew this, but she let him speak anyway. "Go on."

He smiled a little. "I know you would dearly love to berate me for my foolhardiness, but believe me, there's nothing Audrey hasn't said a hundred times."

"When Audrey told me, I was furious," she admitted. "After all that I went through to make you well again! But I realized that you would not be the man I—I had grown to admire if you had gone tamely home." It had been a desperate time, and in his shoes, she probably would have done the same. They had all risked their necks in the name of liberation. Even Gabby.

His face lit up with hope. He'd caught her slip. She'd almost said she'd loved him. He lowered his gaze and cleared his throat, as if he was telling himself not to overstep. "I was too ill to leave my bed for months. As I got better, I was given the news that I would never fully recover, that I would never be able to exert myself beyond a certain point without putting a severe strain on my heart."

His jaw tightened. "I am ashamed to say that I reacted . . . badly. I was very angry about it, in fact, and hated the world."

He stared out to sea but he didn't seem to take in the spectacular view. "Audrey will tell you I can be very stubborn at times. This was one of them. I didn't try to get better. My doctor suggested moving to a warmer climate, but my home—my life—was in England. I inherited Burnley from my father and he from his, down the centuries. I refused to leave it in someone else's hands."

He turned her hand palm upward and began to trace the lines there. "But then you came to us and wrecked this uneasy truce I'd made with my condition. I hated you for doing that, for making me want what I'd thought I could never have."

Her fingers closed around his hand and held it tightly.

He squeezed his eyes shut and returned the pressure. Then he opened them and held her gaze. "But it turned out that a slap in the face from you was just what I needed, because once I'd finished flaying myself for the way I'd treated you, it made me want to try everything and anything I could to get better, to prove myself to you. I've been living here in Cannes for the past three months and my health has improved tenfold. My lungs have cleared and I feel I'm getting stronger every day." He gave a smile that went awry. "I can even carry my bride across the threshold. If she'll have me."

Gabby could not breathe. She hadn't let herself hope . . .

"Marry me?" Jack said, raising her hand to his lips. "I don't deserve it, but I love you so very dearly, my Gabby. Let someone take care of you for a change."

"But I do not need someone to take care of me," she said, smiling up at him. "I am a woman of independent means, I'll have you know."

"Is that so?" He looked intrigued but not at all cast down by this news.

"*And* I'm going to write and illustrate children's books," she said with the certainty of one who had come to this decision years ago instead of that very minute on that very terrace. "So, I am afraid I will no longer have the time for things like housework and nursing people."

"Well, that's simply marvelous," said Jack. "I remember your talent well. But don't keep me in suspense, Gabby. Will you have me? Because I think that I'll probably throw myself off this terrace if you turn me down."

"So dramatic," said Gabby, leaning out a little to peer over the edge. "You might not die if you fell down there. Then you really would need a nurse to care for you."

"We'll take care of each other." He caught her hand and pulled her back, roughly, into his arms. So, he *had* regained his strength. She laughed up at him, and as his arms wound around her tightly and his head bent toward hers, her heart seemed to ignite with happiness. There was a rush in her ears as he kissed her, but it might have been the distant roar of the sea.

Chapter Twenty-Seven

Cannes, two years later

YVETTE

Ordinarily, Gabby and Jack would have left their villa in Cannes to spend the summer with Audrey at Burnley, but this time, Gabby was too big with her second child to contemplate leaving home.

Yvette dined with the family early one sultry August evening, and afterward, while Jack enjoyed a brandy on the terrace, Gabby fed the baby while Yvette read to her from the social pages. When Gabby had settled little Tom in his cot, Yvette put her sister to bed in turn, tucking her in as if she were a child and Yvette the tender *maman*.

Gabby smiled up at her sleepily. "We have everything we ever wanted. At least, are *you* happy, Yvette? I hope so."

"Yes," Yvette said. And it was true. She had become one of

Christian Dior's mannequins, traveling the world, showing his collections, and meeting many interesting people. If she had regrets, she didn't let them stop her taking pleasure in life.

"I am happy, too," murmured Gabby, her eyelids heavy. "And do you know? It would never have happened without Catherine Dior."

The name no longer carried pain in its wake. Guilt is mere self-indulgence if you cannot do anything to fix the past that created it. Yvette realized that while spending time with Catherine at Callian. So much had been taken from Catherine that summer in 1944, and in the months after that. She'd lived through it, and had the courage to keep on living, to work and love and find beauty in life after experiencing the depths of its ugliness and despair.

That was courage. Not the kind that people talked about or awarded medals for, but courage all the same.

"Isn't there a party tonight?" said Gabby, breaking in on her thoughts. Gabby always seemed to sense when her sister was reliving the past. "Why don't you go out? Have some fun."

She was right, as usual. "Yes, I believe I will." Yvette kissed Gabby's forehead. "Sweet dreams, sister."

As Yvette stepped onto the marina where all the millionaires' boats were docked, the hairs rose on the back of her neck. She turned, but no one was following her. Attempting to shrug off a feeling of unease, she quickened her pace, with the stiff sea breeze ruffling her hair and the sound of flags from all different nations snapping in the wind. Why, on this occasion, did she feel that breathless excitement, that stirring, that she had not felt since the war? But no, that was not entirely accurate. She had felt this at other times, whenever she thought she might meet Vidar.

She hadn't come across him again, however, and it wasn't likely that she would do so now. He was a banker or a diplomat, and a spy. He was probably married to some society lady by now and had forgotten all about her and their time during the war. She wished it were so easy to forget him.

Strings of lights twinkled in the distance. The chink of glasses, rumbles of laughter, shrieks, and hoots floated toward her, in counterpoint to the muted jazz melody from a lone trumpet. She guessed that might be her destination and headed toward it, wishing now that she had agreed to meet her friend Sylvie beforehand rather than turning up alone.

The name lettered on the side of the boat told Yvette she had guessed correctly. She stepped up the gangway and gingerly climbed aboard, the tight skirt of her cocktail dress making elegance difficult but not impossible for a mannequin from Dior. She scanned her surroundings, the tension in her chest at odds with the careless good cheer of the crowd.

"There you are!" Sylvie kissed her on both cheeks, then drew her hands wide so as to look her up and down. "That dress! Is it a Dior?"

Yvette nodded. She could not afford Dior, of course, but his established mannequins were allowed to keep one sample garment per year. The fitted, knee-length black dress she wore was from Monsieur Dior's new "scissors" line, strapless and low-cut across the bosom, but with a panel that went around her shoulders like a stole, then crossed in front.

Sylvie took Yvette's hand and dragged her toward a waiter, then scooped two glasses of champagne from his tray and offered one to her. "Have a drink. Gervase will be here soon."

Her friend appeared to have indulged already. The champagne spilled over and Yvette stepped back neatly to save her shoes. "He is missing his own party?"

Sylvie waved her hand. "He had a business meeting that ran late. But he is most eager to meet you."

It didn't seem so to Yvette. Looking around, she wondered why she had come. There was a distinctly raffish edge to the people aboard this yacht. Yvette could not imagine Vidar in such a milieu. "I'm leaving." She drained her glass and put it back on a passing tray. "This was a bad idea."

Sylvie's hand clamped her wrist. "No, no! There he is. Look."

With a jolt, Yvette saw that she was right. There he was. She recognized this man, though she did not know him as Gervase. It was the black-market villain who had smashed up Monsieur Arnaud's shop. "*Rafael.*"

"No, no, his name is Gervase Marron, remember? See? He is handsome, no?" whispered Sylvie in her ear.

Yvette couldn't answer. The blood had drained from her brain. Her tongue felt thick and dry and she gripped the rail beside her for support. She had hoped that the man who claimed to want to meet her was using an alias. But never in her wildest dreams had she imagined he would turn out to be Rafael.

"Yvette? Yvette! What is the matter with you?" Sylvie was like a gnat buzzing in her ear, but she didn't answer.

The nerve of him! Yvette watched the glint of a gold signet ring as Rafael lifted a champagne glass to his lips, the crinkle of his eyes as he drew on a fat cigar, then puffed a perfect ring of smoke that hovered briefly in the air like a dirty halo, before dissolving into the breeze. He slapped backs and shook hands with the men and kissed the women, moving through the crowd slowly, inexorably, in Yvette's direction.

All too soon, he was there, standing in front of her, close enough to touch. And with a wink and a wave of his hand, he made Sylvie vanish. Suddenly, it was as if the two of them were alone together on the foredeck of this crowded yacht. He looked Yvette up and down, an appreciative grin on his face. As if he thought she'd dressed this way for him.

"How can you show your face in France?" she demanded, her voice hoarse and low. Why she should be concerned about their conversation being overheard, she didn't know.

He glanced around. "What can you mean, beautiful lady? This is my yacht."

"You wanted me to be here. Why? I could expose you to all these people. Tell the truth about you."

He contemplated the ash on his cigar. "Half these people are on my payroll. The other half . . ." He shrugged. "They are nothing. Hangers-on. Besides, they won't believe you. Why should they want to? They don't like to think too much about the war. Everyone has moved on." His jabbed an index finger at her. "You should, too."

"There are enough patriots left in France to be disgusted by your profiteering," she said. "Not to mention the rest." She thought of Catherine Dior's circuit, of the countless others who had suffered at the rue de la Pompe.

"Still not married, Mademoiselle Foucher. Why is that?" Again, his gaze traveled up and down her until she wanted to punch him in his tender place. Just a quick, short jab and he'd be at her feet, rolling around on the ground. Then he would not be grinning at her in such a way. It was very, very tempting . . .

But no, that was not the way to deal with him. She couldn't do it on her own, but if she could find help, she might bring this war criminal to justice. Would Catherine have the contacts? Yvette didn't know.

"It's too crowded at this party," she said. "I'm leaving." She turned to go but he caught her arm in a strong grip.

"Not so fast. I have a message for you, little one."

Their faces were very close. She looked him dead in the eye, refusing to show her fear. "Let go of me or I shall scream." His hold loosened but he didn't release her.

He leaned in, his hot breath stirring the hair behind her ear. "Take care, little one. You don't know everything. Some of us were not all we seemed in the war. And some of us are on the side of the great and the good now, after all."

She reared back, her eyes widening as she stared into his face. Was he trying to tell her he worked for the Allies now? What next? Had Hitler himself been a double agent?

"I have a message for you from a friend." Rafael spoke softly, his graveled voice barely discernible above the noise of the party. "There is another yacht at this marina. The *Mistral*. Berth one-oh-three. Find it and you'll see."

Then he let go of her and sauntered away.

Yvette's feet were moving in the direction of the gangway, even though her mind had not yet caught up with this turn of events.

Rafael. Vidar had known about the raid on her home. He was there. They had been associates of a sort during the war. Were they associates still? Was Rafael now working for Britain, as Yvette assumed Vidar must be? Had Vidar used him as a go-between?

The world seemed to be revolving in reverse. She nearly stumbled as she stepped off the gangplank and cursed under her breath. Scarcely hampered by the high heels she had chosen to wear, she ran along the marina in the gathering dusk, squinting to make out the numbers of the berths, the names of the sleek vessels moored there. Had Rafael sent her on a wild-goose chase? It seemed like there were hundreds of yachts, thousands. They multiplied the longer she searched.

And then she saw him. A lone figure in a dark suit, silhouetted against the deepening sapphire of the sky. She stopped, the leap in her chest answering the question she had been asking herself over and over since the end of the war.

With a burst of exhilaration, she started toward the *Mistral*.

At the top of the gangway, she stood before him, not unsure of her welcome, precisely, but aware that they had not parted on the best terms.

He held himself still, watching her. There was a lantern swinging gently in the breeze; it cast light, then shadow, then light again over that young, handsome face with its world-weary eyes.

Yvette thought of his heroism in those final, tense days of the occupation, of the daring feats he had accomplished—many still unknown to her, she was sure—and she wondered what he saw in her at all.

He said, "You came through for her in the end. Thank you."

It took her a second or two to register what he meant. The trial. She could have said she'd done it for him. "You don't need to thank me. I was always going to support her story."

He inclined his head. "Then you lied to LeBrun. To me as well."

She shrugged, hardened by her wartime experiences, just as Louise had intended she should be. "Louise Dulac sent me to be raped by a Nazi. I caused her a little anxiety over the course of . . . what? A week or two? I think we are probably even."

His tension seemed to ease. "Well, I am grateful to you, whatever your motive. I would have been obliged to give evidence if you had not. That would have been . . ."

"Awkward?"

"Disastrous." He removed his cigarette case from the inside pocket of his dinner jacket.

Yvette didn't know why she felt compelled to defend the movie star. "She wouldn't have named you, you know. Even she has a code."

His gaze lowered, then lifted to hold hers. "Why do you think I recruited her?" He shrugged. "My recruit, my responsibility. But it didn't come to that in the end. Because of you."

Yvette said nothing for a while. The moon was rising over the sea, a great golden disk that floodlit the water, and it was like a scene at the end of a movie, not the beginning of one. It made her strangely melancholy. She drew a breath. "Well, she is free. And more in demand than ever, it seems."

He nodded, but absently, as if he did not care very much about Louise Dulac and her burgeoning film career. "It occurred to me," he said, selecting a cigarette and returning the case to his pocket, "that I got it all wrong with that proposal I made."

That struck Yvette dumb. She stared at him, wanting him to continue, but afraid that once he said it, she would have to respond. And she didn't quite know how she would do that.

He cleared his throat and kept turning the cigarette end over end between his fingers, as if it were a new invention and he was trying to figure out what it was for.

"Vidar, I—"

"No. Please let me finish. I do have feelings for you, Yvette. They are . . . complicated."

She had to stop this. She wasn't sure of much, but suddenly she was positive it was the wrong time for such declarations. "Do you know what I would like?"

His gaze snapped up, relief and disappointment mingled almost comically in his expression. Then he smiled, a smile of recognition and acceptance that warmed her all over. He glanced away, then back at her, and tilted his head. "No. Do tell me. What *would* you like, Yvette?"

There was a tingle in her fingertips and in her toes. "I would like to work with you, I think. I want to learn how to be a proper spy, not one who carries out missions she doesn't understand and blunders around in the dark."

He said nothing for a few moments, and she wondered whether she had hurt his pride by sidestepping his declaration. But one of the things she liked about him was his utter lack of arrogance. His smile turned rueful. "Of course. I'm sure something of the sort can be arranged." He eyed her speculatively. "Working for Dior could be the perfect cover."

"Eventually, I might even become a diplomat's wife."

"Really?" he said, tossing his cigarette away and stealing an arm around her waist. "I'll have the captain marry us tomorrow."

She put her hands to his chest to hold him off. "But no! I said *eventually*. If we find that we are suited."

They needed to get to know each other properly, without the shadow of war hanging over their heads. How could she marry a man before she had even grown accustomed to using his real name? "Besides," she added, "when—*if*—I get married, I want a big, fancy wedding with a gown made by Monsieur Dior."

"Ah, it's the *gown* she wants." He touched a fingertip to her chin. "But what about the vows, my little *résistante*? Do you think you can convincingly promise to love, honor, and obey?"

"Of course I can," she said.

"Oh, really?"

"But yes! I was a spy during the war, you know. I am *very* good at pretending."

He laughed at that but sobered almost immediately and drew her closer. "Are you sure it's what you want, this life? It's not for everyone. And you must understand that you cannot simply do as you think fit at all times. Not everything is black-and-white in this world, Yvette. It never was, but at least during the war we knew who our enemies were. Now we move in the shadows."

"Yes," she said. "I am sure. But for me, you understand, some things can never be grey." Rafael was one of those things, but of course, Vidar knew that. No doubt they would have a reckoning about this very soon. "I will never stop having a conscience," she told him. "I will never stop trying to do what is right. Even if that doesn't make me the smooth, professional spy." Half-apologetically, she added, "Even if that makes things harder for you. You understand?"

He searched her face, then nodded. "Do you know something? That's exactly why we need you." His voice grew thick as he pulled her to him. "Why I need you."

"Then we will get Rafael. Together, we will bring him to justice."

"Yes. We will get Rafael. After he leads us to the others."

He sighed as if she had lifted a burden from his shoulders rather than complicating his life even further, and buried his face in her neck, kissing the tender skin there. She put her arms around him, and it was the strangest feeling to be held by this man again at last, a scintillating and dangerous feeling, yet utterly, perfectly right.

It was like an exciting new adventure. And it was like coming home.

ACKNOWLEDGMENTS

I am tremendously grateful to my agent, Kevan Lyon, for the hard work she has invested in this book at all levels and for her staunch support and excellent advice. Thank you to my clever editor at William Morrow, Lucia Macro, for her insight and expertise and for being such a delight to work with, unfailingly positive in the face of these "interesting times."

I spend so long inside the story world that it is a surprise and a miracle to me when that world manifests in the form of a book, and that book finds its way to readers. It is no miracle, however, but all due to the hard work and dedication of the talented people at Harper-Collins. Many thanks to Asanté Simons and the rest of the team.

On a personal note, I'm grateful for the support and advice of writers Anna Campbell and Denise Rossetti and for the fellowship of the talented and fierce Lyonesses. To my friends and family, much love and gratitude for putting up with my writerly ways and for always cheering me on: Allister and Adrian, Cheryl, Ian and Michael, Robin and George, Lucy and Jason, Yasmin, Vikki and Ben.

About the author

About the book

Insights,
Interviews
& More...

Meet Christine Wells

Bill Tsiknaris

CHRISTINE WELLS writes historical fiction featuring strong, fascinating women. From early childhood, she drank in her father's tales about the true stories behind popular nursery rhymes, and she has been a keen student of history ever since. She began her first novel while working as a corporate lawyer and has gone on to write about periods ranging from Georgian England to post–World War II France. Christine is passionate about helping other writers learn the craft and business of writing

fiction and enjoys mentoring and
teaching workshops whenever her
schedule permits. She loves dogs,
running, holidays at the beach,
and window-shopping for antiques,
and she lives with her family in
Brisbane, Australia. ❧

Behind the Book

When I stumbled across an article about Catherine Dior's amazing courage during World War II on the Jezebel website in 2017, I knew I had to write about this heroine of the resistance who seemed to have gone largely unrecognized. Perhaps this was due to Catherine's own reticence about her experiences during the war.

Documented details of Catherine's activities as a courier for the Massif Central Franco-Polish intelligence service are scant, but in this novel I have stuck to the facts as much as I could: Catherine's periodic visits to Christian's apartment and the comings and goings of various contacts were recorded by contemporaries; her friendship with Liliane Dietlin, another heroine of the resistance, endured throughout their lives; Catherine's eventual capture and the heartbreaking near-rescue by the Swedish consul is outlined in Prosper Keating's article "The Courageous Life of Catherine Dior" and in the chilling *Tortionnaires, truands et collabos: La bande de la rue de la Pompe* by Marie-Josèphe Bonnet.

The latter gives an account of how the Berger gang rounded up Catherine's circuit and their monstrous treatment of the prisoners they kept in the basement at rue de la Pompe. While Berger was

captured in Milan in 1948, he escaped
and lived out his life in hiding in
Germany. Fourteen members of the
gang, including two women, were
brought to trial in 1952 and Catherine
Dior gave evidence against them.
The newspapers of the time were
particularly aghast at the involvement
of two women in the torture of resistance
agents; witnesses claimed Denise Delfau
sat on the edge of the bath making
notes of confessions while victims were
treated to the torture of the *baignoire*.
In addition to rounding up Jews and
resistance workers and interrogating
prisoners, the gang is infamous for
arresting thirty-five resistance members
who had planned a raid on a German
armory and gunning them down by a
waterfall in the Bois de Boulogne.

The French citizens who worked
for the Nazis, such as the rue de la
Pompe and Bonny-Lafont gangs,
were technically recruited as auxiliaries
to the German Sicherheitsdienst.
Sometimes known as the "Carlingue,"
they were also called "*gestapistes*,"
a contemptuous diminutive of
"Gestapo," by French patriots.
I have used the term "Gestapo"
to refer to the Sicherheitsdienst
and the Sicherheitspolizei, both
for the sake of simplicity and because
that is how the French tended to
refer to the German secret police. ▶

While Yvette's inclusion in Dior's first fashion show is fictional, in *Dior by Dior: The Autobiography of Christian Dior,* the couturier does mention that the mannequin Marie-Thérèse stumbled on her first walk and was so upset, she could not finish the show that day. Someone must have worn the garments designated for Marie-Thérèse, and indeed there were usually stand-ins for the principal mannequins at the ready, but I thought it would be fun to have Yvette walk in that parade, so I made her the substitute.

There has been much discussion about Parisian couturiers collaborating during the war by designing gowns for Nazi wives. In his article "The Courageous Life of Catherine Dior," Prosper Keating maintains that in fact this occurred rarely, and usually only where the Nazi wife had long been a customer of the Parisian couturiers anyway. It is easy to sit in judgment of French collaborators from a comfortable distance in space and time, but it is due to the pragmatism and courage of designers like Lucien Lelong that Paris remained the fashion capital of the world, contributing significantly to the national economy. Lelong resisted all German attempts to move the entire industry to Berlin. In occupied Paris, sometimes it was a matter of choosing your battles.

Keating also makes the point that it is unlikely Catherine Dior would have used Christian's apartment for clandestine meetings as the designer does not seem to have been involved in the network and was not suspected by the Nazis. However, Dior was a close friend of writer and filmmaker Jean Cocteau, whose former lover Jean Desbordes (code name: Duroc) was a key figure in the resistance. Moreover, there are reports from other associates of the Diors that there were all sorts of strange comings and goings at the apartment at number 10 rue Royale while Catherine was in residence. For the purposes of this novel, I have adopted the latter theory, and as there is no real evidence (despite Keating's well-reasoned argument) to contradict it, I feel justified in bringing Catherine's associates into the apartment building itself.

It was certainly the case that many Parisian concierges were either informing on their tenants to the Nazis or working against the occupiers, hiding Jews and dissidents wherever they could. However, I am not aware that the concierge of number 10 rue Royale did either. Danique and Gabby Foucher are purely fictional, and I have adapted their living and working arrangements to my own purposes here.

The character of Vidar Lind is ▶

Behind the Book *(continued)*

heavily based on a real Austrian aristocrat, Erich Posch-Pastor, Baron von Camperfeld, a dashing, courageous, and handsome young man with whom I fell utterly in love during my research. He was only in his twenties when Austria was annexed to the Third Reich. His regiment in the Austrian army was one of the few that resisted the Germans, after which Posch-Pastor was interned at Dachau for a year. Perhaps because of his family's standing—his grandfather had been the last Austro-Hungarian ambassador to the Vatican—he was later released and given officer status in the German army.

After being wounded in Russia, Posch-Pastor was transferred to Paris, and there, he joined the Goélette-Frégate resistance network in 1943. When he was awarded the Médaille de la Résistance, part of the citation read: "For eight months without letup, he passed economic and military information of the highest importance to the Allies, including some of the first designs of the V-1 rocket."

Is Paris Burning? by Larry Collins has been an invaluable source in understanding the role Posch-Pastor played in those final days of the occupation. Acting as a go-between for the Swedish consul and the Nazis in Paris while also spying for the British, Posch-Pastor was instrumental in saving the city's monuments and bridges from being razed by the Germans, a thrilling account of which is contained in *Sauver Paris: Mémoires du consul de Suède* by Raoul Nordling. However, Erich "Riki" Posch-Pastor refused to speak about his wartime exploits. His silence led me to imagine a new life for him after the liberation as a Cold War spy.

Unfortunately for my purposes, the real Posch-Pastor married a beautiful Spanish noblewoman, Silvia Rodríguez de Rivas, toward the end of the war, so I had to fictionalize him just a little to keep him as Yvette's romantic lead. Vidar's connection to the rue de la Pompe gang is not based on fact; however, during negotiations with General von Choltitz, Posch-Pastor did work closely with Émil "Bobby" Bender, a shadowy businessman who turned out to be a senior German counterintelligence agent with anti-Nazi sympathies.

The character of Louise Dulac is inspired by Corinne Luchaire, a young movie star who became the mistress of the Third Reich's ambassador to France, Otto Abetz. After the war, Corinne was put on trial for collaboration and stripped of her citizenship, then died of tuberculosis shortly afterward. Corinne Luchaire certainly did not spy for the Allies, however. That was all Louise.

Jack is a purely fictional character. ▶

Behind the Book *(continued)*

I am not aware that Catherine Dior was involved in either hiding fugitives or smuggling them out of France, but her friend Liliane Dietlin certainly was part of an escape network, so I used this circumstance to create a story line for Gabby.

Liliane Dietlin worked as a courier for Stan Lasocki, the chief of the Massif Central section of Polish intelligence in France. Yvette's escape from Paris is based on the escape of Gitta Sereny, described in Sereny's *The German Trauma: Experiences and Reflections, 1938–2001,* which Liliane Dietlin and a Swedish diplomat arranged for her. Coincidentally, the Thomas Cook travel agency where Gitta obtained her travel documents was situated on the rue Royale. ~

Reading Group Guide

1. Wartime Paris is described as different for wealthy collaborators than for ordinary citizens: "It was as if to these people [people like Louise Dulac], the war did not exist. They went to horse races and receptions and drank champagne in the company of high-ranking Nazis, while their countrymen suffered and starved." Does this confirm your thoughts of what Paris during the Second World War was like? Is life, in the book, more or less normal than you've imagined?

2. Yvette and Gabby, like many sisters, have similarities and differences. What do you see as their strongest difference and similarity? If you are comfortable with it, describe how you and your siblings are alike or not alike.

3. Why do you think the New Look caused such an uproar? Surely it was a bit overboard to have riots over fashion—or was it?

4. Were you surprised to hear about Catherine Dior and her role in the resistance? ▶

5. Given what you have read, do you feel Catherine's brother, Christian Dior, approved or disapproved of her position? And given how his gowns were worn to balls and political events, was Dior neutral and practical— or a collaborator of sorts?

6. Would it have been truly possible to be French and remain neutral during the occupation? Is it possible there were Germans who also tried to remain as "neutral" or sympathetic to the French?

7. The role of French criminals like the rue de la Pompe gang in rounding up resistance workers in occupied Paris is not widely known. Were you surprised that it was this gang who arrested and tortured Catherine Dior, not the Gestapo? Why do you think the Germans gave vicious criminals these policing powers toward the end of the war?

8. Was Jack right or wrong for avoiding Gabby after the war? Was Gabby right to accept him back in her life, given his actions? Do you think Gabby would have been fulfilled if Jack had returned immediately?

9. Yvette is eager to put herself in more danger, to use her brain and make a "real" difference, but do you think she has any true sense of the danger she will be in? Or is she acting in a state of willful denial about what would happen to her if she were caught?

10. Which sister has the more realistic viewpoint of the dangers they face?

11. Do you feel Louise Dulac would have abandoned Yvette to her fate if she were caught? Is she the kind of woman who would lie to save herself, or to save her country?

12. Is Yvette's guilt over Catherine's capture justified? Do you think if she had been captured instead of Catherine that she would have survived all that Catherine endured?

13. Yvette and Gabby choose very different paths after the war. Were you surprised by their actions? Why or why not? ◖